Advance Praise for

THE
EMPTY
CHAIR

Not even the sultry Caribbean sun can burn off the dark clouds that seem to follow Olivia Benning. Returning to an island home to settle affairs, she has no information about her mother's sudden and suspicious death, no resources and little money, she's alone and unsure who to trust.

Penny Goetjen uses the idyllic setting and island culture so effectively, the reader is tempted to savor ocean views from *The Empty Chair*, but don't pause too long—danger is never far away.

—Kathryn Orzech,
Author of *Premonition of Terror*, a paranormal thriller,
and *Asylum*, a dark suspense saga.

THE EMPTY CHAIR

Julianne:

Paradise

isn't always

what it

seems......

November 17, 2016

PENNY GOETJEN

THE EMPTY CHAIR

MURDER IN THE CARIBBEAN

SECRET
HARBOR
PRESS

For information about this title or to order other books and/or electronic media, contact the publisher:
Secret Harbor Press, LLC
www.SecretHarborPress.com
SecretHarborPress@gmail.com

Library of Congress Control Number: 2016908748

ISBN: 978-0-9976235-0-5

Printed in the United States of America

Goetjen, Penny, author.
    The empty chair : murder in the Caribbean / Penny
Goetjen.
    pages cm
    LCCN 2016908748
    ISBN 978-0-9976235-0-5 (pbk.)
    ISBN 978-0-9976235-1-2 (e-book)
    ISBN 978-0-9976235-2-9 (audio bk.)

    1. Murder--United States Virgin Islands--Saint Thomas
(Island)--Fiction. 2. Saint Thomas (United States
Virgin Islands : Island)--Fiction. 3. Detective and
mystery fiction.   I. Title.

PS3607.O3355E47 2016   813'.6
                    QBI16-1116

To Kurt, Austin & Kelsey,
I feel so blessed to be your mother.
Thank you for all the precious memories we
created during our family trips to St. Thomas.
Love you always.

CHAPTER ONE

Her father had purchased her airline ticket so she could make the trip to St. Thomas one last time. Olivia surmised he was relieved she had volunteered to go, to take care of settling her mother's affairs. She imagined that meant putting the property up for sale, paying off the outstanding bills, and gathering any personal effects she couldn't part with that reminded her of happier times she had spent on the island with her mother.

It was a long, sad flight from Boston's Logan Airport to Puerto Rico. She had just enough time to change planes for the short twenty-minute jaunt from San Juan to St. Thomas in a small, regional jet with a narrow aisle between sixteen rows—two seats on one side and one on the other. There was barely enough room to stand up. It made her a bit nervous as she watched the flight attendants shifting some of the passengers from one side of the plane to the other to distribute the weight evenly. The flight didn't last long enough for them to push a beverage trolley down the aisle. They were there for safety reasons only.

On final approach to Cyril E. King Airport on the southwest end of the island, the plane came in low over the water. It seemed as though they were skimming the surface, which turned gradually from a deep blue to a beautiful, serene turquoise. Olivia breathed in deeply. She could imagine the warmth of the salty sea air.

Before long, the plane taxied to the gate of the tiny airport. After waiting patiently for her fellow passengers to gather their belongings from the overhead bins, Olivia found herself lingering at the top of the stairs in the doorway of the small jet to let the tropical breeze caress her face, her camera bag slung across her body and resting on her hip. It was late afternoon, but the August sun was still surprisingly strong. The hot, humid air was beyond steamy. It was sultry. Looking out across the only runway at the airport to the University of the Virgin Islands sitting up on the hill, it was all pleasantly familiar to her.

Sensing movement behind her, Olivia realized other passengers, anxious to start their vacations, had a greater sense of urgency than her own. Reluctantly she descended the metal rollaway stairs and followed the line of passengers that had already deplaned, heading across the hot cement tarmac toward the modest terminal. She felt her feet dragging as she tried to delay the inevitable.

It had been several days since they received the devastating news, and Olivia still struggled to grasp the concept. Liv Benning had only been in her early forties, infinitely energetic and larger than life itself. Olivia loved being with her, visiting her on the island. They shared a special bond, one she sensed her father was jealous of. Her mother made her feel as though she could accomplish anything. Following in her mother's footsteps, she discovered her love of photography during visits to St. Thomas.

An open doorway lay ahead of her. She could see a plump, middle-aged woman with beautiful dark skin standing just inside the entrance holding a tray with small, white plastic cups. A representative from the local rum distillery with welcome shots. Olivia smiled.

"Afternoon, thank you, no," she said and continued to make her way to baggage claim.

Olivia walked past a small group of people standing on the right side of the corridor open to the outside holding signs with last names on them. Quickly glancing through the signs, she didn't see "Benning" so she kept going. She thought her father had given her flight logistics to an acquaintance on the island. Hopefully she would meet up with him.

She passed a duty-free liquor store, restrooms, and a small bar on the left on her way to retrieve her suitcase. The baggage claim area had the feel of a warehouse with its high ceiling and rudimentary furnishings. It was hot and noisy with all the passengers milling about, waiting for the conveyor belt to start moving. Open slats at the top of the walls on the runway side made it sound like the planes were tearing through the terminal when they took off. Since there were only two carousels, it wasn't hard to figure out which one she needed to stand near. A painted wooden sign hanging from the ceiling listed which carousel each airline used. Olivia stood a few feet away from the second one, about midway on the loop.

Across from baggage claim were booths for a couple of rental car agencies, a time share company, an island tour company, a couple of empty spaces, and an office for those unfortunate passengers whose luggage hadn't caught up to them.

Taxi drivers passed through the crowd calling out to secure their next passengers, competing with each other while trying to fill their vehicles. Skycaps pushed empty carts, offering assistance to anyone who would listen, silently condemning all the rollaway bags that took business away from them.

Bursts of laughter from the open side of the terminal where pickups and drop-offs occurred caught Olivia's attention. In the Caribbean, nearly everything was open to the outside. It was hot and humid. Olivia breathed it in. She loved the vibe. She loved the island.

Furtively, Olivia glanced around as she waited for her suitcase, looking for someone she had never met, wondering if she would be able to connect with him. Although she knew there were other transportation options, they would eat into the paltry amount of cash she had scraped together to make the trip. Her father had sprung for the plane ticket, and she didn't want to reveal to him her financial status was anything other than secure. She would make do with what she had. There was no choice.

A loud screech announced the conveyor belt's movement, stirring the bystanders to life. One by one, suitcases of varying sizes traveled along the predetermined path. Randomly along the way, hands reached out to grab handles and yank the attached bags off the belt. Olivia was nearly hypnotized by a sea of black bags bobbing along in front of her but was amused by the occasional suitcase that expressed more personality.

A small pink rollaway with large white polka dots brought a smile to her face. After it passed, she heard a small voice squeal and she turned to watch a man, who she imagined was a father, retrieve it and hand it to a young girl with tight blonde curls on her head. As the child grasped the handle with two small hands, she seemed tickled the bag had made the journey successfully. Her tiny feet were barely able to stay planted on the floor, dancing on tiptoes around her pink and white polka dots.

Olivia continued to survey the passing bags. Colorful ribbons tied to handles distinguished some bags from others. Tattered boxes contained unknown contents. Long rectangular hard-sided containers suggested golf clubs were inside. A lone child car seat passed in front of her, lying on its back. It was eerily empty as it crossed her line of sight.

CHAPTER ONE

Several minutes ticked by before a familiar tattered rolling suitcase could be seen making its way along the dusty and faded black snake. The crowd standing around waiting for baggage had thinned to a small handful of tired travelers. As the bag got closer, she managed a chuckle. Too exhausted from a long day of traveling to be embarrassed, she reached down and grabbed it by the broken handle held together with duct tape. It certainly had seen its fair share of travel and had been tossed around by less-than-careful baggage handlers.

With her pitifully well-worn bag at her side, Olivia tried to stand taller than her five-foot-two slender frame and look more confident than she felt. Considering her options for transportation, she nervously grabbed a piece of wavy blonde hair that fell just past her shoulders and pushed it behind one ear. She was startled momentarily by the engine roar of a plane taking off. Then, from behind her, came a voice.

"You need a lift somewhere?"

Drawing in a short breath, she turned to look up into the gentle eyes of a man who looked to be in his late twenties, perhaps early thirties, slightly older and several inches taller than her. She quickly became lost in a sea of blue. Once she pulled back from her narrow focus, she noticed he had subtle laugh lines framing his eyes and dark blond, shoulder length hair with blonder highlights she imagined had been tousled from a ride in some sort of an open-air vehicle that was a common mode of transportation on the island. Yet he looked as though he had stepped off one of the planes that just arrived. He was dressed casually, a loose fitting, light cotton, long-sleeved shirt buttoned down the front with rolled-up sleeves and a squared-off tail that was not tucked in, long dark shorts, and brown leather flip-flops. He was holding a small duffle to one side, a guitar case on the other.

Her first impression was he was harmless and had good intentions. She was pleased by his sweet gesture.

Her father's voice interrupted her thoughts. It was as if he had abruptly stepped in front of Olivia to protect her from this stranger who undoubtedly meant her harm. One corner of her mouth turned up slightly at how protective he was. Certainly one to take risks, although they were more or less calculated, he had different standards for his daughter taking them. It was more a matter of control for him. Olivia, to her father's dismay, was a lot like her mother, particularly with respect to listening to him. And the older Olivia got, the less influence her father had over her.

Olivia broadened her smile toward the kind gentleman. Her knight in shining armor. She didn't seem to have any other options.

He smiled back.

"I'm Colton."

Switching the duffle to his left hand that was already holding the guitar, he extended his right hand. They shook briefly. His grip was firm but gentle. His hand was soft and warm. A strange but pleasant sensation coursed through her. She may have held on longer than necessary.

"A friend of mine is picking me up. I'm sure he won't mind giving you a ride, too. The island's not that big. Here, let me get that for you." He reached down to grab her bag, but she protested, putting her hand out.

"Oh, no. That's okay. I've got it." She spoke firmly, uncomfortable with him trying to pick up her personal possessions. Quickly reaching down and snatching the handle of her tattered suitcase, she took a step back, pulling her bag closer to her. She pushed away her sweet smile, replacing it with a stern expression.

He recoiled, examining her face for a moment. "No problem . . . no worries." He looked slightly embarrassed. "Can I at least help you get where you need to go?" he tried again.

Olivia looked deeply into his eyes while searching inside herself for the right answer. She was tired and needed a ride but desperately didn't want to make the wrong move. Though alone on a tropical island, albeit a territory of the United States, without any friends or contacts to rely on, she chose to go with her first instinct and accept a ride with him, or at least his friend, whom she hadn't yet met. Taking one last look around, she concluded no one else was there to meet her.

"You're very kind. Thank you for going out of your way for a stranger."

The tanned, ruggedly handsome man with broad shoulders chuckled to himself. "Well, if you tell me your name, we won't be such strangers." There was a twinkle in his eye.

Olivia wanted to think she was usually pretty good at reading people, sensing their character. But she was getting mixed signals. With few other options, she had made a quick decision, one she hoped she wasn't going to regret.

"It's Olivia."

"Well, Olivia, good to meet you."

He used his free hand to push back loose strands of hair on both sides of his face. Intrigued by him, she sensed he was unlike anyone she had ever met before. There was a quiet confidence about him. Olivia found that quality rather attractive.

"Likewise," was all she could come up with in response.

"Let's head out front to see if we can track down my buddy."

The roadway in front of the airport was congested with passenger cars and open-air safari taxis as well as more traditional cabs in the form of commercial vans, similar to what one would see in the States.

They were inching through the loop from the airport entrance, past the rental car lot, around to the passenger pick-up area, to the taxi stand and then back out to the airport exit.

Olivia and Colton made their way through the crowd, down the sidewalk with their luggage in tow until they passed the taxi stand. Leaning against a pillar along the edge of the roadway, a dark-skinned man played steel pan music on his shiny silver drums. Breathing in the vibe of the island, she closed her eyes and inhaled deeply. Something about the rhythmic island sounds resonated within her.

Working his way over to the curb, Colton found a spot to stand. Olivia navigated around a couple who had stopped in the middle of the walkway and slipped into the space next to him, sneaking a glance to study his features. His face seemed kind, yet strong and determined. She wondered what he was really like.

Colton scanned up and down the vehicles alongside the curb and those moving slowly through the airport drive until finally his hand shot up to signal. An older, white pickup truck pulled over quickly and squeezed into a small opening along the curb, one that seemed too small to fit the tiniest of vehicles, yet the driver managed to fit his. Rusted dents punctuated the door and the side panel toward the rear of the truck. Colton stepped close to the driver's window and they exchanged exuberant hellos. Their hands clasped with great energy. Leaning into the cab he had a few private words with his friend. The driver shook his head, nodded, and then looked directly at Olivia as if assessing what Colton was asking of him.

Becoming less optimistic she'd be getting a free ride, she again reviewed the options. She pushed away her father's cautions echoing in her head.

Colton turned back to her and yelled over the din of the crowd, "Throw your bag in the back." He put his duffle and guitar case gently in the bed of the pickup as if to guide her to do the same. He didn't seem to want to offend her again by offering to put hers in for her. Olivia was grateful his friend was willing to give her a ride, but she didn't like the idea of putting her suitcase in the back of a beat-up pickup truck. Then she realized it looked so pitiful it didn't matter where she "threw it." Following his lead, she picked up the tattered bag and tossed it over the side. Too tired to care, she and her suitcase needed a ride.

Looking toward Colton, she was struck by how his spontaneous warm smile penetrated within her unexpectedly. They walked around the back of the truck, and he opened the passenger side door and motioned for her to get in. Hesitating for a moment as she considered what she had gotten herself wrapped up in, she figured she was in it that far and decided to keep going. Olivia climbed onto the bench seat, next to Colton's friend, and then Colton slid in next to her. Her nostrils flared as she detected a pungent odor that permeated the cab, a mixture of stale cigarettes and wet dog. Instantly she felt trapped. Had she made a terrible mistake accepting a ride from these guys? She turned to Colton and he looked into her eyes. Feeling a rush of emotions she wasn't sure she understood, she fought to control them. Colton spoke unexpectedly.

"Hey, David, this is Olivia."

He grunted his reply.

In turn, Olivia uttered a guttural response that sounded something like a "Hey." Glancing quickly toward David, she gave him a once over. Clearly he hadn't placed a high priority on combing his hair or putting on fresh clothes that morning. Looking rather disheveled, he was sporting short, reddish brown hair sticking up all over his head that made him look like he had just rolled out of bed. Olivia mused that perhaps he had.

The trio inched through traffic in silence until they reached the airport exit. A couple speed bumps later, they were driving along the solar panels lining one side of the runway.

Sounding as if he would be glad to get rid of her, David asked where she needed to be dropped off. She explained she was going over to the north side of the island, just over the mountain on the way to Magens Bay. She detected a bit of discontent on his part but shrugged it off. He would have to get over that. His friend had already committed him.

The pickup turned right out of Airport Road onto Route 30, a busy, four-lane road that ran along the south side of the island, known more familiarly as Veterans Drive. Farther east, it became Waterfront Highway and then narrowed to a two-lane road and became Frenchman Bay Road and then Bovoni Road as it meandered its way toward Red Hook. Of course, none of the locals used street names or route numbers. The island was small enough they didn't bother.

Olivia and the guys were heading toward Charlotte-Amalie, the largest town on St. Thomas and the capital of the U.S. Virgin Islands. Traveling on the left side of the road was a dramatic change from Boston, one Olivia found exciting. It usually took a couple days to get used to driving on the "wrong" side no matter how many times she visited but, nonetheless, she enjoyed the challenge. Some roads on the island didn't have any lines painted on them, or they had worn away over time. Drivers had to use their best guess of where the center line should be and where their half of the road was, adding to the challenge she embraced wholeheartedly.

With the windows down and the tropical breeze streaming in, they passed a section of small local businesses—gas stations, a lumber yard, empty store fronts, and a grocery store.

Colton seemed anxious to get a conversation going. "So, Olivia, what brings you to St. Thomas?"

She was expecting that question. It was a logical ice breaker.

"I have some business to take care of." Olivia tried to answer his question while being as vague as possible. She didn't want to share too much information, at least not before she got to know him a little better, if she would even have the chance. He pressed further.

"What kind of work do you do?"

She patted her camera bag, still hung on one shoulder and resting on the opposite hip. "I'm a photographer." She paused, anticipating his questioning to continue.

Large cranes off to the right at a commercial port loaded shipping containers the size of semi-trailers onto a huge cargo ship. A junior high school that looked a bit neglected with overgrown grass was just beyond the port.

"Oh, are you here for a photo shoot?"

"Not exactly. I have some other business to wrap up. What do you do?" She tried to take the focus off herself and switch it to him.

"Well . . ." He paused as if trying to create suspense. "I'm a boat captain by day and musician by night."

His answer surprised her. She looked to him for more details.

"I take people out on a boat for day excursions, mostly tourists, and then evenings my band plays different bars on the island and over on St. John, and we practice a lot in between."

"Sounds like you've got your hands full."

"Yeah, I'm pretty busy. But I love what I do." He ran his fingers through his hair and then rested his elbow on the open window.

"Are you guys any good?" She couldn't keep from smiling as she teased.

Colton laughed, looking forward through the windshield. "Yeah, we're not too bad. You should come hear us while you're here." He turned toward her to see her reaction.

"I just might have to find the time to do that." She maintained a straight face and didn't let on she was more than marginally curious.

A red light brought them to a stop next to a cemetery on the left where, due to the fact the island was essentially a big rock, the deceased were entombed above ground in rectangular cement boxes painted bright white. There was nowhere to dig down. Some were stacked two or three high with colorful plastic flowers resting on top. On each of her visits, Olivia couldn't pass the cemetery without having strange images flash through her mind as she tried to reconcile the custom with what she was used to in the States.

Across lanes of traffic on the right, a neatly painted sign announced the entrance to Frenchtown on the corner of Rue de Saint Barthelemy. The Frenchtown post office stood proudly on the opposite corner.

After the light turned green, the old white pickup lurched into the intersection and Olivia caught a familiar sight. From the south, a seaplane was coming in for a landing in the harbor. It reminded her of a trip she and her mother took to St. Croix on a photo shoot for a promotional brochure.

Since Olivia was visiting at the time, her mother didn't hesitate to take her along as a photographer's assistant. She was excited to ride inside the small plane with an aisle splitting three seats—one on the left, two on the right, for a total of eleven rows. Sitting close to the front, Olivia was fascinated by the pilots manipulating all the complicated instruments. It was a relatively short trip, similar in length to her flight from San Juan but noisier inside the fuselage. The concept of taking off and landing on the water was thrilling to young Olivia. Once the photo shoot was complete, she and her mother took advantage of some down time, rescheduling their return trip to a later flight. Heading to Christiansted, they poked through the quaint shops and strolled on the boardwalk, taking in the Danish architecture and picturesque bay before grabbing a bite to eat in a restaurant along the waterfront. Great memories for Olivia.

"Now David, here, is a pretty talented guy." Colton seemed to be deflecting the focus from himself. "He plays bass in our band and can fix just about anything. Cars, boats, plumbing problems, you name it. If you have something that's broken, except maybe a broken heart, he can fix it. Right, David?" Colton smiled broadly at his poke.

Olivia glanced over and noticed David had a wry smirk on his face. He remained silent but clearly enjoyed the unexpected endorsement in spite of the jab.

An assortment of shops located in renovated old warehouses dominated the downtown shopping area they passed on the left. Deep open water on the right allowed ferries and private yachts to dock next to the road. Fort Christian loomed ahead of them, looking out over the harbor.

Just past Vendors' Plaza where the outdoor market was held, they took a left onto Route 35 that traveled up over Crown Mountain, the beginning of which was called Hospital Gade. The word "Gade," pronounced "gah dah," was a holdover from the days when the Danish ruled the island. On the corner was the criminal justice building painted in an orange yellow that housed the Virgin Islands Police Department, the Territorial Court and related offices. Partway up the road was the sign for Blackbeard's Castle on the left. Farther up the mountain, Route 35 changed names a couple of times but no one really kept track. It was a narrow, winding rough road with potholes, hairpin turns, and a yellow line that faded in and out along the way. Earthen walls lined the mountain side, and dramatic drop-offs defined the side open to the harbor. A couple stretches were unexpectedly steep, and good brakes were requisite, particularly on the way down. When encountering an oncoming car, they occasionally had to slow down and pull to the side to allow room for both vehicles to pass.

Houses randomly punctuated the sides of the road. Some were meticulously cared for with gates at the end of the driveway while others needed maintenance. A few had suffered such extensive damage from the last hurricane they had been abandoned by homeowners who had no insurance. Olivia was intrigued by the handful of small residences perched precariously on the side of the mountain on stilts with barely enough space to pull a car off the road to park next to them.

"Where exactly are we heading? Do you have a house?"

David remained strangely quiet, not engaging in the small talk.

"Yeah, it's my mother's. . . . A small place off of Crown Mountain Road."

"Sounds great. I'm not too far from there, over on Skyline Road. It's not much, but the view is incredible. Never get tired of it."

Olivia understood that sentiment. She believed she could stare at the view of Magens Bay from her mother's place forever and it would never get old. The thought of having to put it on the market broke her heart. Guess David wouldn't be able to help her with that.

The old pickup struggled to reach the top of the hill from the south side of the island where 35 met Skyline Drive from the east. Just beyond the intersection, 35 curved sharply to the right and plummeted downhill on the way to Magens Bay. It was a challenging spot where four roads met with steep inclines and a couple of blind curves thrown in. Those coming up from Magens Bay on the north side did not have a stop sign. The hill was steep, and the final sharp curve made it nearly impossible to do anything other than roll right through.

As if trying to recover from the steep climb, the aging truck coughed and sputtered as David steered it through the busy intersection and then left onto Route 40, which became Skyline Drive heading west. Another turn put them onto Crown Mountain Road. Olivia instructed David to slow down when they were close to her mother's driveway. It had been a while since she'd been there, and she didn't want to overshoot it and then have to turn around and go back. It was harder to find from the other direction.

Before long, the trio was heading down a steep and narrow, partially paved driveway. The asphalt was cracked from baking in the Caribbean sun and loosely resembled cobblestones. Olivia was excited to see the house again. David negotiated a couple turns on the way down to the house perched at the top of a hill overlooking Magens Bay and out to the Atlantic Ocean. When the bay came into view, Olivia gasped.

Colton appeared pleased with her reaction. David stopped the truck just before the end of the driveway, to the right of the house.

Sitting on approximately half an acre of land, the cute little bungalow was painted in bright, colorful colors just as she had remembered. Her mother loved it that way. Sunny yellow, vivid coral, and vibrant turquoise. The Caribbean was one of the few places you could paint your house like that and get away with it. It looked like such a happy place. At least it used to be. A small hand-painted wooden sign on the front of the house read, "Serenity Villa."

Opening the passenger side door, Colton stepped out of the truck allowing Olivia to slide across. Apparently assuming the drop-off wouldn't take long, David left the engine running. Colton shut the door, leaned in, and exchanged a few words. His friend turned off the motor in response. Reaching into the back, Colton grabbed her suitcase and turned toward the house, clearly hanging behind to observe her walking slowly to the front door.

Enamored by the sight of the familiar bungalow, she stopped several feet from the bottom of the front steps, taking it all in, mesmerized.

Colton caught up quickly. "Nice place." He sounded sincere.

His words popped her daydream bubble. "Yeah," Olivia giggled nervously, "it's everything you could want in a Caribbean hideaway."

Turning back, she scanned the driveway where her mother's Jeep should have been parked. A light blue Jeep Wrangler. Olivia delighted in driving it when she came to visit. It was a wind in your hair, barrel roll down a grassy hill on a hot summer day kind of fun. "It's gone." She spoke softly, to herself. Why was it missing? What was she going to do for transportation? An unsettled feeling crept into her bones at the unexpected turn of events.

Returning her gaze toward the house, she realized something there didn't look right either. Something was missing. Her mother's kayak. A bright orange one-person kayak she loved to take out to explore the coastline of the island. When Olivia visited they rented a second one for her to use. Her mother stored hers on the side wall along the gallery. The hooks were there but were strikingly empty.

"Do you think your mom's home?"

"Uh, well, I don't . . . she . . ." Olivia struggled to say the words. "No, she's not here." She fought the emotions pushing to the surface. "Her car's not here," she spoke softly, straining to maintain a steady voice, intent on keeping the conversation on the obvious.

Colton looked puzzled. "Well then let me at least make sure you can get into the house."

"Oh, that won't be necessary." She reached down to take the suitcase handle from him, but her thoughts diverted quickly elsewhere. Remembering her manners, she turned, took a couple steps, and yelled over to the truck, "Thanks, David. I appreciate the ride."

Colton's friend waved once, appearing to be anxious to get going. The truck engine stirred to life.

Turning back toward the house, Olivia could see Colton had already closed the distance to the steps of the bungalow, her suitcase in hand. She was through protesting and just followed behind. Holding the screen door, he stepped back to allow her to open the inside door. At some point over the years, the key to the front door had disappeared, but her mother never seemed too concerned about it. She simply stopped locking up when she left. With her eyes closed and her fingers mentally crossed, Olivia turned the knob. Much to her relief, it turned easily.

Leveraging her body weight against the door, she coaxed it open as the wood groaned against the pressure. Pushing it inward, she entered the small shadow-filled living room of the house with Colton on her heels. The air smelled a bit stale as if the house had been closed up for a while, yet she noticed a couple windows were cracked on the far side in the kitchen. Perhaps her mother had intended to be gone for only a short time.

An uneasiness stirred within her, and she no longer felt comfortable with Colton inside her mother's house. Wanting to be alone, she tried to dismiss him as quickly as possible.

"Colton, it was nice to meet you. Thanks for the ride. I really appreciate it."

"No problem at all. Like I said, I'm just down the road from you. Not too far away. If you need anything . . . well, actually, you must be hungry. How about grabbing a bite to eat? That is, if you don't already have plans. Looks like you are without transportation at the moment, and who knows what your mother has left for you in the fridge. I'm sure mine is questionable after being away." He laughed as if recalling a particularly disgusting fridge situation. "I'll have David drop me off at my place. I'll grab my car, and I can swing back here in a little while. Say half an hour? Does that give you enough time? We'll grab something downtown. I know I'm starving. You must be, too."

When he began his pitch, she was ready to turn him down, thinking of several reasons she couldn't join him, but by the time he got to the part about grabbing dinner downtown, he had her. She was too tired to think about cooking. Who knew if there was anything edible in the kitchen anyway, and she certainly had no way to go pick up food. The nearest little neighborhood store was not within walking distance and walking on the winding, curvy roads was dangerous at best. She would have to be careful how much money she spent on dinner.

"Thanks, that sounds nice." Even she could hear the fatigue and relief in her voice.

"All right. See you then." He sounded pleased.

They quickly exchanged phone numbers and Olivia followed Colton back outside. David had already turned the truck around and was waiting with the front of it pointing up the driveway. Colton barely had his door shut when the vehicle started back up the steep hill.

As Olivia returned to the solace inside her mother's house, the screen door closed with a loud click. Memories came rushing back to her, yet it felt different than she remembered. An emptiness filled the space. It was hard to believe her mother was gone. Olivia felt painfully alone. "Oh, Mom . . ." As she closed her eyes, her heart ached like it never had before.

Standing in the small living area just inside the front door, she peered through the house and out to the unforgettable view of Magens Bay on the north side of the island. It was a horseshoe-shaped bay that ran northwest to southeast with a beautiful mile-long, heart-shaped white sand beach along the bottom of the horseshoe on the southeastern side. Peterborg Peninsula separated the bay from the Atlantic Ocean. Hans Lollik Island lay to the north of the peninsula with Little Hans Lollik tucked behind it, out of sight. Magens Bay

Beach was a favorite of locals and tourists alike and was touted as one of the best beaches in the world by travel magazines. When cruise ships were in dock, many passengers found their way to Magens Bay. Although it tended to attract a crowd, the length of the beach enabled everyone to stake out a claim for a spot to spread a beach towel. It was a full-service beach with a snack bar, showers, changing rooms, and water sport rentals.

Returning her attention to the inside of the little bungalow, Olivia surveyed the small sitting area with a pull out couch and a couple of worn but comfortable chairs. Nothing fancy. An old cargo trunk with a flat top served as a coffee table. Only a small loosely woven basket with a small handle on either side occupied the surface, a catch-all with loose change lining the bottom.

A few feet toward the back of the house was a small kitchen with the sink under the windows looking out to the bay. A couple stools at a counter, separating the kitchen space from the living area, made it an eat-in kitchen. The appliances didn't match and appeared to be on their last legs but were sufficient for a photographer who was in and out and probably didn't entertain much. Off to the right of the living area was a door to a small gallery that wrapped around to the back of the house, also with incredible views. There were a couple of small rooms to the left of the living space, one toward the back of the house her mother used as a bedroom and one in the front she used for a studio, and a small full bath in between that served the entire house. She poked her head into the bedroom and laughed out loud when she saw the Mahogany wood, four-poster bed was not made. The covers were thrown to the side as if someone had just rolled out of it. Her mother's priorities never had included housekeeping.

Moving next door to her mother's studio, Olivia leaned against the door frame and let out an extended breath. There was a worktable in the middle of the room with several prints scattered on top as if she had been in the midst of reviewing her work and had stepped away unexpectedly. A handful of her mother's favorite photos had been enlarged and now hung proudly on the walls in frameless glass. Most were from a photo shoot she had done a few years earlier for a coffee table book about St. Thomas. She had been thrilled to do the shoot because it gave her the opportunity to go up in a helicopter to take pictures from a markedly different perspective than on land or by boat. It was that photo shoot that brought her down to the tropics, away from the frigid New England winters she despised, and she never left.

Olivia's father's career in finance kept him rooted in the Boston area although he traveled extensively. Being a true New Englander, he made it clear he had no intention of following his wife to the stifling hot climate of the tropics. During several years living apart, they often talked about making their separation official, but Olivia held out hope they would reconcile one day. The devastating news that the divorce was finalized came a few weeks before they received word of Liv's death.

After her parents' separation, Olivia stayed in Boston with her father upon his insistence and attended Rhode Island School of Design, much to her father's disappointment. He thought she should go to a more traditional college and major in a more practical field of study than photography. After becoming frustrated by the structure of classroom education, however, Olivia eventually dropped out. She longed to learn photography from her mother, but her father refused to let her go. In the time since she walked away from RISD, she often asked herself if she should have stuck it out and finished with a degree. Every prestigious studio looking to hire a new photographer wanted a degree or experience, usually both. On her own, she'd had to work hard to drum up photography assignments so a large portion of her meager income was derived from selling framed prints of iconic Boston locations in local shops. During the summer months, she set up a table outside Faneuil Hall at Quincy Market and sold her work to tourists. She was able to make decent money as long as the weather was good, but she knew there was much more out there, if she could just get a chance to prove herself.

The silent emptiness that permeated the tiny bungalow took on a sound she had never heard before. She ached for her mother to walk in the door and light up the room. How could she really be gone? She missed her generous hugs, compassionate smile and animated conversation. Her companionship. A tear found its way to the corner of her eye and rolled down her cheek.

"Miss you, Mom." Her words sounded odd in the empty house. They nearly echoed.

Olivia's feet trod noiselessly on her way to the kitchen where she grabbed the handle of the refrigerator. But then she stopped herself. Considering how long the contents could have been sitting there, there was no point in opening it. It might be filled with smelly, moldy food. Releasing the handle, she looked above to the rudimentary wine rack. There were a couple bottles in a rack that could hold a dozen. Her mother wasn't a big wine connoisseur, but Olivia pulled out each bottle to see what her options were. One red, one white. She opted for the red. A Merlot. After rummaging around in the drawers, she located an old corkscrew and fumbled for a while before finally opening the bottle. There were no wine glasses to be found so she used a juice glass. It felt good as the liquid made its way down her throat. Although it warmed her inside, she shivered unexpectedly.

Crossing the room back toward the lumpy couch under the front windows, Olivia flopped down into the well-worn cushions and slowly sipped her wine. It was early evening, but the length of the day was taking its toll. She felt overwhelmed sitting in her mother's house, the responsibility of handling her affairs sitting firmly in her lap. Her mother's missing Jeep weighed heavily on her mind as well. Why was it gone? How was she going to get around the island? She had counted on that car and admonished herself for assuming it would be there. Unfortunately she was not close to downtown Charlotte Amalie with its sidewalks and shops.

Olivia took another sip, holding the rich red wine in her mouth for a while before she swallowed. She loved the sensation as it trickled down her throat.

From behind her, Olivia heard the sound of a car making its way down the steep driveway. It took her by surprise at first. Then she remembered she had committed to going to dinner with the guy she had just met. She hated that she didn't have a lot of options and, in particular, no transportation. Olivia stood up from the couch, drank the last sip of wine, dropped her empty glass on the counter and walked to the door. Colton was already out of his car, an older model, dark metallic blue open Jeep Wrangler with a roll bar. She looked it over. It was eerily similar to her mother's car, just a different color. As she recalled, her mother usually kept the soft top on her Jeep, but apparently Colton preferred his with it off.

Watching him walk confidently toward the house, she couldn't help but feel giddy inside. There was something about him she liked. She hoped she wasn't completely misreading him and getting blindly sucked in. Before he got to the door, he looked up, and noticing her in the doorway, stopped short of the steps, smiling broadly.

She opened the screen door and stepped out, returning his smile. "You came back."

Flinching in response, he looked surprised at her comment. "Of course I did. I said I would." His arms were outstretched with palms facing up.

Feeling herself blushing, she turned her face away from him ever so slightly.

"You know, I was actually thinking that—and you can tell me no. . . ." He gestured with one hand while the other shoved deep into the pocket of his shorts. ". . . instead of going downtown and spending money on going out to eat, we could stay in . . . at my place." He paused, examining her face and then continued. "I ran over and picked up a few things at the little market. I didn't have much in my fridge so I needed to stop anyway. It wouldn't be anything fancy, but we could have a nice dinner. What do you say?"

Olivia tried to keep herself from blushing further. This was not what she was expecting at all. At the same time, she didn't want to spend money going out for dinner either. She could feel her feet taking little steps but going nowhere.

She opened her mouth to respond but couldn't find the words.

"Seriously. It's no big deal. Just two people having dinner at the same place. No commitment. No worries. You *should* have a 'welcome to the island' dinner when you first arrive, you know. What do you say?" He stepped closer and looked deep into her eyes.

Olivia beamed at the offer. What could she say? He made it sound like a reasonable proposition. She cocked her head sideways with a grin, pulled the inside door shut behind her and followed him out to his car. The screen door shut on its own with a click.

It was a short ride over to the small house on Skyline Drive. Partway there she wished she had grabbed the other bottle of her mother's wine. She hated showing up on someone's doorstep empty-handed.

Colton easily navigated the intersection at the top of the hill from Magens Bay as she imagined he had done many times before. There was less traffic than earlier, making it a smoother transition from one road to the other.

As they pulled into his driveway, he announced, "Welcome to Riptide." He looked pleased to be able to share it with her.

Colton's view was remarkably different from hers. While her mother's house looked north out to Magens Bay, his house faced south, down to Charlotte Amalie and the harbor beyond. It was a breathtaking view. From their vantage point, they could see a cruise ship tied up at the West Indian Company Dock at Havensight. During high season WICO could handle three ships at one time, lined up end to end. Two to three more could dock at nearby Crown Bay, also located on the south end of the island, just to the west. On particularly busy days, there might be a cruise ship anchored in the middle of Charlotte Amalie Harbor, in which case, passengers would be tendered to shore by smaller boats.

Colton turned off the engine and they both scrambled out. Immediately after they shut the car doors, she heard a dog bark twice. It sounded like it was coming from inside his house. A furry face appeared at the door of the modest abode that looked like stucco and had been painted a creamy ivory a long time ago. Even in the waning daylight, she could tell it could use a fresh coat of paint. There was a hand-painted wooden sign to the right of the door proclaiming the name of the villa as Radical Riptide, an apparent nod to a love of surfing.

Colton reacted to his canine friend. "Hey, Jake! We're back! Good to see you, old boy!"

The Australian shepherd was excited at Colton's return. Olivia could tell he was trying hard to behave himself and not jump on the inside of the screen door, practically wiggling out of his skin waiting for Colton to open it. As soon as he entered, Jake sat down obediently, waiting to be petted. Definitely well-trained. Olivia stepped into the doorway behind Colton, but the dog did not react to her presence. It crossed her mind to be offended, yet instead, she was impressed with his behavior. Colton bent over and stroked his face with both hands and then moved one hand to the dog's side and stroked him over and over. His free hand came to rest on his own upper thigh. Jake was enjoying the attention.

"Nice dog, Colton." She wondered if he could sense a hint of surprise in her voice.

"Thanks. He's a great guy. We've been together for quite a while, ever since I rescued him from the local shelter." He kept one hand resting on Jake's back while he spoke. "My next door neighbor loves him, too, and takes him when I have to go off island."

"That's great. You're lucky. . . . He's lucky." Olivia thought Jake looked to be purebred. "And such a handsome dog."

"Yeah, it works out well for both of us." He stood up but Jake didn't move, keeping his eyes on Colton. "Come on in."

Moving in from the front entryway, she could see his house was set up similarly to her mother's. There was a small living area immediately to the right with a small cut out in the wall that opened to the kitchen in the back. Following Colton, she walked past an open space on the left with comfortable furniture and an open door on the far left wall she assumed led to a bedroom. Drawn in by the view, Olivia kept walking toward sliding glass doors to the gallery that ran along the back of the house while Colton veered right into the small kitchen. Jake was close at his heels.

"Like the view?"

Standing in the open doorway, she turned toward his voice. "It's stunning."

Opening the fridge, he pulled out a couple of beers, lacing his fingers between the tops of the two bottles.

"Wanna brew?" He winced slightly. "Sorry, I didn't think to get wine, in case you prefer wine. I guess I had my heart set on beers tonight."

"Oh, no problem. I'd love a beer." She surveyed the space inside the doorway she had ignored on her way to the view and deduced it was his music room with an electric keyboard and two amps set up in one corner. Next to them were the guitar case she had seen him carrying in the airport and a couple different guitars resting against the walls in random places. There was also a futon, two mismatched stools and a distressed wooden coffee table with handwritten sheet music and pencils scattered across the surface as if there was a composition in progress. A small tarnished and bent brass chandelier with four spindly arms was tied up to the center of the ceiling to prevent anyone from bumping into it. She was amused that his music space was much more important than a formal sit-down dining area. The focal point of the room was the brightly painted surfboard leaned up against the remaining corner, as if it was there to drip dry.

"Ya sure? I could see if my neighbor has any wine, if you'd like."

"Heavens, no. I would love a beer. Thank you." She was not about to get picky when he was being more than generous.

"Oh, and of course I always have rum on hand. Some coconut rum on ice? I may have some pineapple juice I could mix with it." He rummaged through the small cupboard above the stove, pushing the bottles in front aside and peering farther inside. "No, sorry. Guess we're all out of rum. That's odd."

"A beer is fine. Really. Thank you." In passing, she was curious who he had meant by "we."

He examined her face as if to see if she was just trying to be a good sport. Finally he opened each top with his hands and held out a bottle. She took it willingly and their eyes met. They clinked the tops of the bottles in a toast.

"To being back on the rock. Cheers."

"Cheers." The beer tasted crisp and felt refreshingly cold in her mouth and throat on its way down.

"So, I've got some mahi-mahi I'm going to grill and make into fish tacos, if that's okay with you. They're all seasoned and ready to go."

"That sounds delicious." Was he kidding? She could have eaten the packaging the fish had been wrapped in, she was beyond hungry. Hopefully she would be able to eat with some discernible table manners.

"I've already chopped veggies, cilantro, and mango. The rice shouldn't take long either. Let's head outside and I can grill while we enjoy the view with our beers."

Sounded like heaven to Olivia. She wondered how she had gotten so lucky to meet him and hoped he turned out to be a good guy. He was off to a great start.

Before long, they were eating a deliriously scrumptious meal while being gently caressed by the evening breezes. Jake settled into a corner at one end of the gallery under a hammock hanging limp in the shadows. Lights came on down below in Charlotte Amalie as evening crept into the harbor. They wove their way through polite conversation that just scratched the surface of safe topics. Olivia was careful not to get too detailed about herself or why she was back on St. Thomas. Did anyone need a reason to come back to the island?

They paused their conversation long enough to watch the cruise ship back out and steam out of the harbor, leaving a gentle wake behind it before turning east, disappearing behind Muhlenfels Point. Colton only left her side long enough to throw dishes in the sink and grab a couple more beers. Jake jumped up and trotted along right behind him, intent on not letting him out of his sight. Even though Olivia insisted on helping with the dishes, Colton refused and said he would take care of them in the morning. The night was for relaxing.

He returned to the gallery, leaning against the railing next to her, gazing out to the harbor. Jake settled back down not far away with a gentle thud and a soft groan. The twinkling lights from Charlotte Amalie below seemed magical to Olivia. They shared the stillness of the moment, both lost in private thoughts.

A voice from inside the house startled them.

"Should have known!" Her voice was loud and grating.

They turned simultaneously to see a beautiful young, dark-skinned woman in the doorway, dressed as though she was heading out on the town—skinny black jeans; heels; a low-cut, black-and-red-geometric-patterned loose shirt, and enough makeup to last the evening without reapplying.

Olivia could sense tension in the air as Colton groaned, and his posture became rigid. Jake sat upright, on guard, keeping an eye on the intruder. He growled half-heartedly as if afraid of being heard.

"You don't waste any time, do you?" Her voice escalated as she walked toward him, her thin index finger wagging at him accusatorily. "I thought you might be back by now, and I came to pick up the rest of my stuff."

"Alana—"

"Oh, don't let me interrupt." She lunged closer and raised the rest of her fingers on her right hand to expose her palm to him and glared into his face. Long, deep red nails curved beyond the ends of her fingertips.

Thankful to be just the spectator, Olivia prayed it was going to stay that way. She didn't know Colton and certainly didn't want to get to know his acquaintance.

"I'll just grab what I need and leave you two alone." She glanced at Olivia, holding her glare for a moment then running her eyes down the front of her and back up again.

Olivia felt a chill rip through her body and she shifted her feet, securing her stance against the railing and folding her arms, shielding herself from any ancillary aggression.

Alana then turned and stormed back into the house. "Lord knows I wish I'd done this a long time ago." Her voice trailed off.

Olivia didn't dare look at Colton, but she watched out of the corner of her eye as his shoulders fell.

He loped toward the door, turning on the threshold to speak to Olivia. "I'm sorry. I'll just be a minute." The stress lines on his forehead and his pursed lips revealed his embarrassment. Jake trotted into the house behind him to assist. After a few minutes of subdued conversation she couldn't discern, the tense atmosphere abruptly deteriorated. It sounded as though pots and pans were being tossed onto the kitchen floor.

"Lana, please." His voice was firm.

The clanging sounds quieted, and Olivia could only hear murmuring coming from the kitchen. She turned her back to the turmoil, returning to her spot, looking out to the harbor, trying to act as inconspicuous as she could. More loud words were exchanged from what sounded like the bedroom, mostly from the female intruder. Olivia wondered exactly who Colton was and whether she had been smart to take him up on his invitation for dinner. Again she reminded herself she hadn't had any other options. She suddenly felt stranded.

After an excruciatingly uncomfortable wait, the noise behind her subsided and the sound of the front door slamming shut announced the altercation's conclusion. Colton returned and slipped next to her on the railing. Jake followed on his heels and curled up in his spot at the end of the gallery. No words were spoken. The silence became awkward until finally Olivia laughed softly and, not knowing what came over her, decided to poke fun.

"Colton, what *have* you gotten yourself tangled up in?" she teased, feeling a bit mischievous.

He grimaced and turned to her, visibly relieved she was showing her sense of humor. His eyes shifted to the floor. "You have no idea. . . . Wish I did before all this started. But now I think it's finally over. I'm sorry about the intrusion. Let's try to salvage the evening." He gently touched the small of her back and motioned toward the chaise lounges facing out toward the harbor that was now quiet, except for a small boat traversing silently in the distance. His touch sent a tingle throughout her body.

The setting sun had brought dusk and eventual darkness as nightfall snuck in. Colton and Olivia settled into the two comfortable chairs, struggling to keep the conversation going. The length of the day and the effect of the beers had drained her energy. Before long, her body was so relaxed she was fighting to stay awake. Her head bobbed forward. Losing her fight, she forced herself to sit up.

"It's probably late. I don't want to keep you. This has been so pleasant. Thank you, Colton. I'm glad I met you. . . . Thank you for giving me a ride from the airport and an amazing dinner." She hated to leave, but if she couldn't keep her eyes open, she wasn't going to be much of a companion.

Colton turned toward her, looking deep into her eyes. She held her gaze, waiting for a response.

"I'm glad we met, too. Thanks for coming to dinner." He reached over and laid a strong hand on her forearm resting on the arm of the chaise.

"It was entirely my pleasure." Olivia was trying to keep her emotions in check, maintain a safe distance. He was making it hard for her.

"So you've had enough of my view?" There was a twinkle in his eye. "Let me find my car keys, and I'll give you a ride back." They both stood up and Colton turned to head back into the house, pausing on the threshold. "Do you think your mother will be home by now? Did she know you were coming?"

Though they seemed liked casual questions, Olivia fought to maintain her composure.

Lingering in the doorway, Colton looked expectantly toward her. "She'll probably be getting worried by—"

Olivia turned away from him and reached for the deck railing, uncomfortable with his intrusion into her mother's situation. Her energy draining, but unable to avoid answering his question any longer, she finally spoke. "No, I know she's not there." Then she turned back and looked into his eyes.

The expression on his face made it clear he was looking for more of an explanation. Her eyes brimmed, but he stood silent, waiting for her to continue.

A tear rolled down her cheek. He stepped closer, reached out, and took hold of her right shoulder gently but firmly. "What's going on?" His touch was warm. She was feeling mixed emotions, not sure which to fight off and which to embrace.

Another tear escaped and followed the first. "She's gone. She's . . . she passed away several days ago." Her words hung in the air. She felt keenly alone, even with him standing next to her.

Colton looked stunned. "What happened? . . . So that's why you're here," he deduced, putting the pieces together, speaking slowly and gently. His face showed concern for her. He removed his hand from her shoulder but remained close to her, waiting for her to answer.

Olivia took a deep breath and then tried to continue. "We . . . my father and I got a phone call telling us my mother had passed away unexpectedly. Some sort of an accident." She turned her head and closed her eyes. The pain was still excruciatingly raw.

"Someone called you from here?"

She opened her eyes and nodded.

He pushed for more information. "Do you know who?"

"I thought I would remember his name. He said he was calling from the police station. . . . I can't believe this is happening. And I don't know why my mother's car wasn't in the driveway at the house." Her head was spinning.

Looking pensive, Colton seemed to be considering her answers. "I am sorry, Olivia." He paused, clearly thinking about what to do next. "Let me give you a ride back so you can crash and try to get some sleep tonight. Are you comfortable there alone?"

"Yeah." She choked on the word.

"I'm going to see what I can find out in the morning. What's your mother's name?"

"Benning. Liv Benning. I was named after her."

"And what kind of car did she have?"

"It's a light blue Jeep Wrangler. Very similar to yours."

"All right, Olivia. I'll get you back to your place, and I will see what I can come up with tomorrow. Okay? . . . Hey, I'm sorry you're going through this."

"Thanks, I appreciate your help." Feeling a little lightheaded, she was grateful when they opened the door to the cool night air.

They walked slowly without a sense of urgency to Colton's car, his arm loosely around her. Jake trotted out alongside them. Colton guided Olivia to the passenger side and opened the door, giving her a hand into the Jeep. Shutting the door, he glanced down and saw his buddy looking up at him. Jake appeared puzzled he hadn't been allowed to sit in the passenger seat as he usually did. Colton grinned and tugged on his collar, directing him around to the other side of the car. Then he opened the driver's side door, pulled back the seat, and gestured for him to hop up into the back. Jake hesitated, took another look into Colton's eyes, and then jumped in.

"Good boy, Jake. Good boy." He brushed the top of his head.

They drove the short distance to her mother's place in silence, weighed down by the gravity of the circumstances. In spite of it all, Olivia became quite drowsy. She was looking forward to putting her head on a pillow and dealing with the overwhelming situation in the morning.

As the Jeep came to a stop in front of the little bungalow, Olivia let out a long sigh in a feeble attempt to release some of the pent-up anxiety. Colton walked around and opened her door. No sooner had she exited, than Jake hopped into the front seat to take his usual spot, poking his head through the open window and wagging his tail exuberantly. He looked entirely pleased with himself.

Returning his arm loosely around her, Colton walked her to the door and saw to it she got in safely. He assured her he would be in touch the next day. Reaching out, he stroked her hair on one side and then slipped a kiss onto the top of her head.

The front door clicked as she closed it behind him. Although the inside of the house was unlit, moonlight streaming in through windows provided enough light for her to slowly make her way to her mother's bedroom. Flipping the switch to the right of the door as she walked in illuminated a small lamp next to the bed on the far wall. The bed covers were still tossed to the side as they were earlier. It seemed strange she would be sleeping in her mother's bed without her there.

"Mom, I wish you were with me, but I'm going to sleep here tonight. . . . Hope that's okay." Olivia was at a loss for what else to say. She fiercely wanted her mother to be home, at Serenity Villa.

After freshening up in the small bath, she returned to the cozy bedroom and opened the two windows that framed the headboard. A salty sea breeze spilled into the room. The night air was invigorating, yet comforting, to her soul.

Yanking the covers down to the bottom of the bed, Olivia ran her hands across the sheet and pillows, checking for centipedes, millipedes, scorpions, and any other creepy crawlers that might be hiding there. She didn't mind the critters when they were outside, but she had no intention of sharing a bed with them at night. After satisfying herself she would be sleeping alone, she replaced the bedding, pulled the mosquito netting around the four posts, and slipped under the light covers. Before long she was dozing lightly, the events of the day still swirling in her head.

A noise from the next room startled her awake.

CHAPTER TWO

O*livia froze in the bed.* The sound was coming from her mother's studio. An intruder? Should she lie still and pray they found nothing worth taking and moved on to another house? Should she get up and investigate, confronting the intruder? Beyond scared, her body stiffened. She didn't know if she could move if she had to. As she lay there listening, some semblance of a defense mechanism locked in. This was her mother's home, and she wasn't going to let someone steal from her. Throwing the covers off, she pulled back the mosquito netting and bolted out of bed, into the office. Hoping to surprise the burglar, she flipped the light switch on the wall by the door. No one was there, yet the noise continued in the far right corner where the combination printer/copier/fax machine sat on the counter. A sheet of paper that hadn't been there earlier dropped silently into the output tray. Slowly she crept toward it, scanning the room and tiptoeing as she went, fully expecting someone to pop out from under her mother's worktable or any of the lower cupboards with doors.

Nearing the printer, she slowly reached for the paper. Just as she touched it, something hit the window next to her with a thump. She jumped back, knocking the paper from the tray. Landing hard against the edge of the worktable, Olivia tried to maintain eye contact with the window. Nothing was visible but she tried hard to convince herself it had just been a large moth attracted to the light inside the room. Were there Luna Moths in the Caribbean? There were certainly no birds out at night, and she simply couldn't entertain the idea of it being anything human. Taking a deep breath, she let it out slowly, her heart beating wildly. Finally she remembered the paper and bent down to recover it.

It appeared to be a handwritten note faxed to her mother.

> *Liv*
> *I've been unable to reach you on your cell.*
> *It's been a while since we've connected.*
> *Just wanted to be sure you're ok.*
> *Have some info for you. Please call my cell.*
> *—CK*

Staring at the sharp contrast of the black words on the white piece of paper, she wasn't sure what to make of the note. Obviously someone was concerned about her mother. She wondered who CK was. There was no other information to go on. Not even a fax number from the originating machine. Staring at it was not going to change a thing, particularly not at such a late hour. Laying it back on the output tray, she decided she would revisit it in the morning.

CHAPTER THREE

Morning sunlight poked in through the windows and woke Olivia
from a sound sleep. She was surprised at how well she had
slept and how late the hour was. Swinging her legs over the side of
the mattress, she endeavored to haul her achy body out of bed. The
surprisingly squishy mattress was not exactly what she was used to,
and she couldn't fathom how her mother could sleep on it on a regular
basis. Shuffling to the kitchen, she craved a cup of tea. Perhaps some
plain toast. When the bay came into view off to her left she stopped
in her tracks. Stunning. The sun was bright, not a cloud in the deep
blue sky. She looked beyond Magens Bay, out to Hans Lollik Island,
an uninhabited island she found intriguing. If only she could afford
to buy such an island and have it all to herself. Delightful to dream
about. Complete privacy. Yet at a huge cost. To resemble any sort
of civilization, water and electricity would have to be run out to it.
Certainly not in her budget.

A grumbling stomach brought her back from the horizon. Then the
reality sank in she had no clue what was in the cupboards. Bracing herself
for the unexpected, she pulled open two light blue wooden doors at a
time, rummaging through her mother's kitchen, still not brave enough

to open the refrigerator door. Her mother's inventory consisted of a couple cans of tuna, open packages of crackers and whole wheat wraps Olivia assumed were stale, cans of tomato sauce, dry elbow macaroni, a British-label instant hazelnut coffee, and powdered milk. The last two items puzzled her. She wasn't sure why her mother would have those on hand but let it go to move on to more important matters. Wrinkling her nose, she decided her late breakfast was going to consist of tuna and some stale crackers. Unfortunately she was not a big fan of tuna, but she was desperate. She was also not a big coffee drinker, especially instant. Instead, she settled for a glass of water but longed for a cup of tea.

After struggling with a handheld can opener, she carried her meager breakfast out to an old bistro table on the gallery, reasoning her food might taste better if she ate it outside. Sitting down before she realized the chairs might need wiping off, she guessed her backside had just taken care of one of them. Slowly she tried to make her way through the tuna, forcing herself to chew and swallow. Before long, it became unbearable to ingest anymore and chewing came to a grinding halt. Staring at the crackers, she decided they weren't doing anything for her either. Breakfast was over but she was still hungry. Pushing back her chair, she gazed out to the bay. The beautiful turquoise water had a way of distracting her.

The sound of a car engine brought her back from the view. Colton appeared on the side of the house and made his way around to the back gallery. Trying to restrain the grin bursting from inside, she was tickled to see him.

"Hey, Olivia, good morning."

He looked a little sleepy, as if he hadn't been awake any longer than she had. His hair was pulled back into a ponytail.

"Good morning, Colton." She glanced at his hands, which carried a to-go cup in one and a small bakery bag in the other.

Smiling as he noticed what her eyes had discovered, he held out the breakfast goodies. "Thought you might need something to start your day. I didn't know how you take your coffee. It's black but there should be stuff in the bag."

Struggling to contain even a hint of excitement on her face, she thanked him as she took the coffee and small white paper bag from him, touched by his thoughtfulness. The coffee wasn't her first choice, but she decided to drink it anyway after stirring in all available creamers and sugars. Longing to see what was in the bag, she took a quick peek. He had brought a light yet buttery croissant and a large muffin loaded with blueberries. It took tremendous willpower to restrain herself from diving head first into the bag of baked delights.

"Mind if I sit?" He pointed toward the empty chair at the bistro table.

"Oh, of course! Please have a seat and . . . and enjoy *my* view." Her face blushed with embarrassment that she hadn't offered him a chair and he had to ask. She had been too focused on the food.

He nodded, turning toward the bay, seeming to appreciate the boundless views of the island from the little bungalow.

"Another gorgeous morning in the Caribbean." He leaned back in the chair and stretched his tan, muscular legs.

"Absolutely perfect."

"It's nice to see this side of island for a change . . . not that I'm tired of my view, but change is good." They sat in silence for a while as they both drank in the beauty of the island. She polished off the croissant and moved on to the muffin, taking sips of sugary sweet, watered-down coffee in between bites.

With a glance over to the side yard, Olivia admired the beautiful Adirondack-style chair painted in a bright turquoise blue and situated off to the side by itself but with a great view of Magens Bay. She had fond memories of her mother sitting in that chair for extended periods of time, garnering inspiration. Olivia wondered how long it had been since she had enjoyed it.

Finally she felt the need to break the silence. "So, how long did you say you've lived here, Colton?" With a little food in her stomach, she could finally focus on conversation.

"Almost ten years." He scanned the horizon and appeared to be recalling the details. "I came here on a whim with a friend."

Olivia was interested in hearing more but he had another idea in mind, changing the subject.

He turned back toward her, looking contemplative. "I didn't get up this morning as early as I had planned. I haven't been downtown yet. I'm sorry. I know I said I would—"

"No problem." She couldn't very well fault someone who had volunteered to help her.

"I did take a few minutes last night and did a search on my iPad to see if I could find anything about your mother's disappearance or a boating accident or anything related to that in the area. Unfortunately I came up empty. There was nothing at all that popped up."

As Olivia listened intently to his words, her eyes grew wide. She didn't recall saying anything about a boating accident to him the night before. She kept her eyes locked on his face, trying to read him.

"I did learn a little bit about your mother, though, on a professional basis. Very impressive."

Looking across the top of her Styrofoam coffee cup at him, she grew uncomfortable as he smiled broadly. A corner of her mouth turned up in response, yet she was unsure how she felt about him doing a search on her mother.

"She's quite a lady. Obviously very talented."

"Yeah. She's *is* quite a lady. An amazing talent. I learned everything I know about photography from her. . . . You know what, Colton, if you could drop me at the police station. I think it makes sense for me to start there." She stood up, leaving half of a muffin on the table. Taking control of the conversation, she was determined to make it clear she had a sense of urgency and was going to take charge. "Thanks again for breakfast. That was sweet of you."

"Sure. No worries."

Olivia quickly wrapped the muffin and took the last sip of coffee, wincing uncontrollably, and then retreated into the house. Coffee really wasn't her thing.

Colton waited for her to come back out and then the two set off for Charlotte Amalie.

The blazing sun beat down on them in his open-air vehicle and she embraced the warmth, but the breeze was surprisingly strong as they descended the hill. It quickly became obvious why Colton had pulled his hair back, and she wished she had done the same. And while Olivia tried to catch glimpses of the breathtaking view down to the harbor, she also kept her eye on the winding road and oncoming cars. Giving her shoulder strap a tug, she wondered how much good it was going to do her if they went over the edge. The backseat driver in her decided to put her faith in Colton's ability to get them down the mountain safely.

Before long, they were near the end of the road looking across the harbor. Colton deftly slipped his Jeep into a parking spot along the curb, just up the block from the three-story Farrelly Justice Center. An uneasy twinge rippled through her stomach as they entered the open wrought iron gates and ascended a few steps, pausing in the center of the complex. She turned toward Colton.

"Look, I'm sure you've got better things to do than play taxi driver for me. Thanks for the ride down. I'll take it from here."

"Don't be silly. I don't mind. Let's get some answers for you." He walked like he had a purpose over to the double doors with the V.I. Police Department shields displayed on them, pulled open the door to the left, and stood back waiting for her to enter.

Although Olivia wasn't sure she wanted him to be involved in such a personal matter, she chose not to argue. She would find another logical point where she would dismiss his involvement once and for all.

Stopping at the front counter, Olivia resolved she was going to be the one to do the talking. The policewoman behind the counter spoke with a young man in front of them. She was short, yet stocky, with very dark skin and wore a name tag that read "Ofc. Gladys Barnes." The medium blue shirt of her uniform was pressed to perfection, with creases running along the sides of the short sleeves. A shiny gold V.I. Police Department badge was pinned prominently on her left chest pocket. She spoke with a thick island accent that Olivia strained to understand, and she sounded quick tempered and impatient with the matter she was discussing. Olivia's stomach clenched tighter than it already was. Finally the boy was sent away and the policewoman turned her attention to Olivia. Obviously sizing her up and down, she asked what she could help with.

Olivia gave her name and then told the story of how she had received a phone call breaking the news of her mother's death. When she had finished with the pertinent details, Olivia asked the officer if she could give her more information.

The policewoman turned her head to the side, still looking at Olivia, and then turned to look at Colton, clearly drawing some conclusions of her own, and then back to her again. "You're not from around here, are you?"

"No, I'm from Boston, but my mother lived here. I got a—"

"And someone called you and told you your mother passed away?" Her tone gathered attitude with each sentence. "Someone from here?" The overbearing woman leaned forward, closer to Olivia's face than she cared for.

Stepping back to create more space between them, Olivia answered in as even a tone as she could manage. "Yes, I think so."

"So you don't know for sure?" A hand found its way to one hip.

Olivia felt herself squirming from the questioning. "No, but I thought—"

"Well, I don't know why it would have been someone from here."

Olivia's mouth dropped open slightly. Feeling as though she was losing control of the conversation, she held her gaze firmly and waited.

Finally the policewoman broke the awkward silence. "Well, hold on. Let me see what I can find out." She turned to walk away and then turned back. "What did you say her name was?"

"Liv Benning. It was less than two weeks ago. They said it was a boating accident."

Walking away from them with a commanding strut, the officer mumbled something about the fact she would have been the first to hear about something like that. The bright yellow stripe on her navy blue pants bent oddly at her knees as she walked. It crossed Olivia's mind to wonder why they didn't wear Bermuda shorts. After all, the daytime temps were in the eighties year round.

Turning to look at Colton for support, she realized he wasn't standing next to her anymore. He had wandered over to a bulletin board and was scanning wanted posters. Shaking her head in amusement, Olivia turned back to the deserted counter. She could see the policewoman talking with someone seated at a desk a few yards away in a grouping of half a dozen desks, each one a banged up standard-issue grey metal with an uncomfortable looking, ergonomically incorrect, wooden ladder-back chair pushed up underneath. Papers and files were stacked on top of the desks in varying states of disarray.

Finally Officer Barnes returned to the front counter. "We have no record of anyone from here calling you about a boating accident within the last couple of weeks. I'm sorry." Her tone of voice didn't sound like she was sorry. She was just stating the facts.

Olivia's eyes widened. She opened her mouth to speak and nothing came out. It didn't make sense. Finally she found her voice, quietly pleading, "How can that be?"

"Well, I don't know what else to tell you." The officer's tone turned defensive. "How do we even know that call was made?"

Stunned, she couldn't find the words to convince the woman to investigate further. Tilting her head and squinting slightly, she fluttered her eyelashes in rapid succession, a trademark Olivia response in a particularly annoying or stressful situation. A voice from behind came to her rescue. It was Colton.

"Can you at least tell us if there was a coroner's report?"

Shifting her eyes to Colton and back again, Officer Barnes seemed annoyed at his intrusion and made it obvious she didn't want to discuss the matter with him. "How long have you been on island?"

Olivia wasn't sure where this question was leading but answered anyway. "I got here yesterday afternoon."

"And your mother wasn't at her house?"

Infuriated with the ridiculous line of questioning, Olivia glared at the officer but tried to humor her.

"Well, the best advice I can give you is to come back tomorrow afternoon, when you've been here forty-eight hours, and file a missing persons report."

Olivia looked deep into her eyes. "Why would I need to do that?" She was losing her patience but trying to keep her cool on the outside.

"Because until the person has been missing for a full forty-eight hours, you cannot file that report. Until you arrived yesterday, you had no way of knowing she was missing."

"What? I got a phone call—"

"But you can't tell me who it came from," she demanded, smacking her right hand on the edge of the counter. "I have nothing to go on." The officer was not backing down.

Colton stepped in again and gently put his arm around Olivia's shoulder while looking at the policewoman. "All right, no problem. We'll come back tomorrow. Thank you very much for your time." His strong hands slowly turned Olivia's stubborn shoulders, and he guided her back out the front door.

Neither one noticed the male officer standing in the doorway of a side office who watched them walk away, and then approached Officer Barnes to inquire about their discussion. Once they were back out onto the sidewalk, Olivia pulled away from Colton and demanded answers.

"What the hell was that all about?" Her voice felt louder than she had intended, but she needed to make a point.

A couple of uniformed officers exited the building and walked past them.

Grimacing, Colton put an index finger to his lips. He kept his voice discreet. "Look, you were not going to get anywhere with her. There was no point in escalating the situation when you'll probably have to face her tomorrow."

"But she wasn't making any sense!" Her arms flailed to exaggerate her point. "Why would I have to file a—"

"I know, I know. But there wasn't anything either one of us was going to say to convince her otherwise. You're going to get a lot further if you can refrain from screaming and stomping your feet. Trust me on this one."

"I didn't scream or stomp or—"

Olivia turned away, exasperated the encounter turned out differently than she had envisioned and annoyed with Colton's condescending tone. However, reluctantly, she began to see his point.

They walked in silence down the steps leading out of the complex onto the sidewalk in front.

"All right, but I haven't gotten anywhere yet and this is my second day here. Now what am I going to do?" This was her dilemma to solve. She just didn't expect it to be so difficult to get information about what happened to her mother. This island was part of the United States, not a foreign country. But at that moment, she felt a long way from home.

Colton seemed intent on keeping her moving, or at least busy. "Listen, I have to run over to Red Hook to talk to a guy about some dates my band is going to perform. You want to take a ride with me?"

She turned back to face him. "Colton, ordinarily I would love to take a ride over to Red Hook. But not right now, not today. I think I'm going to go walk around the shops and try to clear my head."

"You sure? It's a beautiful day for a ride to the east end."

"I know and it's kind of you to ask, but I think I'll stay downtown and see what trouble I can get into." She winked, turned, and dashed across the street before he could think of another angle to try and persuade her. "Thanks anyway!" She waved over her head.

"You'll need a ride back," he yelled from across the street.

Olivia stopped on the other side and turned around with a somewhat mischievous smirk on her face. "I'll figure something out." She turned back and resumed walking away, feeling uncomfortable having Colton so involved. It was time to take the matter into her hands. After all, she had met him less than twenty-four hours earlier. She really didn't know him and wasn't ready to trust him entirely. Not yet anyway.

CHAPTER FOUR

The main shopping district in downtown *Charlotte Amalie* was pre-dominantly located within three parallel streets—Waterfront Highway which, as its name implied, ran along the harbor, Dronningen's Gade also known as Main Street and Back Street. Several smaller perpendicular streets and even smaller pedestrian alleyways connected these three streets to each other. Old, historic warehouses used to store goods like sugar and molasses during the commercial shipping era hundreds of years earlier now housed a large assortment of shops. Built from the ballast used to weigh down ships on their journeys from Europe so long ago, the present-day alleyway walls still displayed a beautiful patchwork of muted colors that were rough to the touch. Constructed so well, they had stood the test of time and endured an untold number of hurricanes. Tall, brightly painted wooden shutters framed many of the shop doors and were closed at night, each secured with a dark metal chain and an old-fashioned padlock.

Out on Waterfront Highway, Olivia passed a t-shirt shop, a sunglasses boutique, and a handful of jewelry stores. As she moseyed along, she was amused by people who passed by. Some were clearly tourists with their pale, or worse yet, sunburned skin, who brushed past her without making eye contact. Others were locals trying to get to and from their places of work or taking care of errands. Most looked her in the eye and greeted her with "morning." She surmised they regarded her as a tourist even though she didn't feel that way at all. But she forgave them, understanding their assumption.

Turning down one of the narrow alleyways, Olivia planned to get lost in some of the smaller, boutique-style shops she found intriguing. Meandering through the small passage, she admired the bricks and stones beneath her feet that added to the allure and historic charm of the area. Stopping in front of a small art gallery tucked between a diamond shop and a clothing store, Olivia felt herself drawn in. Artfully displayed in the window were striking watercolors and acrylics of local flora in addition to beautiful photographs that captured the island in all its splendor. Stepping inside, she noticed an attractive, light-skinned woman who looked to be about her mother's age seated behind a small carved wooden desk toward the back. The woman rose and approached Olivia as she entered. Her ivory-colored, gauze-like top was trimmed with small abalone buttons down the front and an open weave lace along the bottom that undulated as she walked. Her short brown hair was styled in a perky bob that framed her face. As the woman got closer, Olivia could see she had beautiful hazel eyes that exuded warmth.

"Afternoon." She extended her hand. "I'm Stacie."

"Afternoon." They shook and Olivia felt a subtle, yet very real, connection with her.

"Is there anything in particular you are looking for?"

Olivia chuckled to herself. "No, I just love to look at beautiful things, and your gallery drew me in."

Stacie was visibly pleased by her response. "Well, take your time. Let me know if you have any questions. I would be happy to tell you about any of our local artists."

Her last comment struck a chord. "Thank you. I appreciate that." She grew curious about the shop owner. "So how long have you been on the island? Did you grow up here?"

Stacie laughed and shook her head. "Oh, no. I only figured out four or five years ago what a beautiful place this is. My brother had been here for several years before that, and I finally got a chance to visit him and absolutely fell in love with the rock. I wished I had visited sooner. But I'm sure you know how that all works out sometimes. We get so busy with our lives we don't always make the time to do what we were meant to do all along."

As Olivia listened to her words, they sounded a bit too familiar. She could only nod in response.

"Well, I'm glad I finally got around to it. Once I realized this would be an ideal place for an art gallery, I left my business partner to run our Phoenix gallery and opened this one here."

Olivia grinned in acknowledgement. "I see. Good for you."

"I'll let you enjoy the art. Let me know if I can assist you in any way."

Olivia turned away to peruse the vivid art on display. From pottery to jewelry, watercolors to oils, she took her time to examine each original piece, wanting to appreciate the effort and talent of every artist. She felt herself connecting with the art and with her surroundings. Then she turned a corner and laid eyes on framed photography. She gasped when she recognized the artist's work. It was her mother's, without a doubt. The photos were vibrant and captured what made the island an unforgettable place to visit—the serene turquoise water at sunrise, midday and sunset, bays and inlets only frequented by locals, the twinkling lights of Charlotte Amalie at night, parrots, iguanas, pelicans, and the ever elusive mongoose. Olivia stepped closer to get a better look. The photos had her trademark "LB" scrawled in the lower right corners, along with the year. Olivia felt goose bumps emerge all over her body. She was immensely proud she was looking at her mother's work. She was proud of *her*.

"Beautiful works of art, aren't they?" The gallery owner startled her.

Olivia turned toward her. "Yes, absolutely gorgeous. Probably out of my price range, though."

"Oh well, I'm sure we could find something that would fit."

"That's okay. I'm just looking around at this point."

"I'm happy to answer any questions you may have. Here, let me give you my card." She reached into the pocket of her shirt and pulled out a stack of cards, peeled off the top one, and handed it to her.

Olivia took it, glanced at it superficially, and then looked up into the woman's hopeful face.

"Can you tell me anything about the photographer?"

"Absolutely. Ms. Benning is a relatively new artist for this gallery. I think she has been on the island for several years, but we've only been fortunate to be able to represent her over the last couple. She is from the States—New England, I believe. She's worked on several promotional brochures for the islands and contributed to tourism websites as well. I've heard major companies have consulted with her before doing photo shoots for magazine spreads and entire catalogs to determine the best locations to bring their models and the best time of day for light."

"Wow, she's been busy." Olivia pretended it was all news to her because she enjoyed hearing her mother's accolades.

"Yes, she is very good at what she does, and from what I understand, she is persistent and will stop at nothing to get what she's after. The perfect photo, that is."

Olivia knew all too well about her mother's determination. Sometimes she was persistent to a fault. "Good for her. She's certainly talented."

"And in high demand. I haven't been able to get her to update any of the work she has here for quite a while. I think I heard something about another big project that was going to take her away from her photography pursuits for a while."

"Oh, what is she doing?" She was counting on Stacie to give her more info.

"I'm not exactly sure. I honestly haven't spoken to her in over a month, and I don't think she was able to give me many details at the time. I keep hoping she's going to pop in the gallery at any moment."

Olivia did her best to keep the expression on her face steady. She knew exactly how the woman felt.

Thanking Stacie, she made her way to the door, biting her lip and fighting the conflicting emotions within her—pride and pain. After she got back onto the sidewalk, it hit her she had been talking as if her mother were still alive. If only it were true. A feral mother hen with a brood of chicks scattered at Olivia's feet.

The gallery owner watched her go, shaking her head, stunned by how much the young girl looked like the photographer Liv Benning.

CHAPTER FIVE

F*eeling drained from the hot sun* and lack of a sea breeze, by early
afternoon Olivia had had her fill of downtown. It was time to
head back. But, of course, she had no car. With a not-so-subtle moan
she envisioned the long and dangerous walk back up the hill. That
didn't seem to be a good option, but she hated to spend money on
a cab. Then it came to her. The open-air safari taxis the locals used
were reasonable. Passengers shared the ride and hopped on and off as
they traveled all over the island, much like the public transportation
buses in the States. Patience was a virtue, though, as the safaris often
ran on "island time."

Heading back out to the waterfront, she located a taxi stand. After
asking people standing around her and each driver that stopped by,
she finally got onto what she prayed was the right taxi to get her up
the mountain. She crossed her fingers and hoped for the best. After
a couple of stops, the taxi pulled up in front of a grocery store. It was
a good-sized building made of turquoise corrugated metal, long since
faded from the sun.

Recognizing her opportunity to stock up on essentials, Olivia
hopped off onto the sidewalk, realizing too late she would have to

pay for another safari taxi to take her up the mountain. But it was a small price to pay. She needed to pick up a few things to sustain her until she could get her mother's affairs straightened out.

Crossing the weathered and cracked asphalt parking lot of the grocery store, she stepped carefully to avoid landing in a pothole. The lines for the parking spaces were barely visible, originally painted many years earlier. A handful of small, older model cars occupied a few of the spaces. Some appeared as though they had been in a fender bender or two. Others looked like they would be difficult to start.

Glancing at the doorway as she approached, Olivia noticed there were people standing around nearby. Three teenagers were convers- ing in a lively conversation but looked like they had nothing better to do. An older, gray-haired gentleman was seated on an overturned milk crate staring off into the distance, his arms resting on his legs with hands clasped in front of him. An elderly woman standing next to him, clutching a plastic grocery bag on either side of her body, appeared to be waiting for someone to pick her up.

Olivia passed through the people gathered out front and entered the store, picking up a small carryall basket as she passed the stack. She couldn't afford the contents of an entire cart. She had to keep it simple. Quickly surveying the aisles, she decided it had the feel of an inner city discount store. The linoleum floor, cracked and miss- ing in places, looked dated and didn't seem all that clean. There was an interesting smell she couldn't place and probably didn't want to know, but it was a little too similar to the pungent odor of something decaying. Directly in front of her was the produce section. Force of habit sent her down that aisle, but she was immediately disappointed. She had forgotten that, despite the year-round balmy temperatures, St. Thomas was not much of an agricultural island. With the excep- tion of rum, almost everything else had to be imported, which made groceries rather costly. The robust fruits and vegetables she was used to enjoying in the summer months in the States were not only more expensive on the islands, but they also tended to look a bit anemic. Olivia wrinkled her nose. On her modest budget, she would have to make do with predominantly non-perishables during her visit.

Making her way up and down a few more aisles, Olivia could feel eyes on her at every turn, every aisle. She imagined the locals assumed she was a tourist and a few made their curiosity obvious. She tried to shrug it off and focused on picking up enough of the essentials to get her through the next few days. She grabbed bread, cereal, peanut butter, pasta, sauce, cheese, crackers, hummus, and the ever important morning beverage, tea. She grabbed a couple bottles of cheap wine, a Chardonnay off the shelf and a chilled Pinot Grigio from the small refrigerated section. A small carton of milk rounded out the basket and she could check out.

Fumbling as she removed her groceries from the basket and placed them on the stationary counter, she was anxious to wrap up and exit the store. Sensing still curious eyes, her fingers failed her as she tried to count out the correct number of bills after the cashier announced her total.

Finally the uncomfortable transaction was over. Grabbing her two plastic, environmentally unfriendly bags, Olivia exited the door, leaving the oglers behind, and made a beeline across the parking lot to where the safari taxi had dropped her off earlier. Once there, she willed the next taxi to arrive as quickly as possible. Feeling hot and drained, she was anxious to get back to her mother's house. A few other people also waited—a young mother with two restless children in tow who tugged at her arms, and an older, nicely dressed gentleman with three small cloth bags that probably held a week's worth of food for him. The heat of the day was peaking, and she felt lightheaded.

Then she realized she hadn't bought any drinks. Tap water back at the house would have to do. She kept taking deep breaths, in and out, hoping the dizziness would dissipate. It wasn't working. Panic rose inside of her.

A firm hand grasped her upper arm just as her knees buckled, and she landed in a heap on the hot pavement.

Olivia opened her eyes to see the same blue eyes that had rescued her at the airport. Attempting a smirk, she asked meekly, "What happened?"

Colton beamed back at her and brushed an errant strand of hair from her forehead. "It seems you shopped 'til you dropped," he teased, clearly amused by his wit.

"All right, I'm fine. Really, I'm fine." Olivia waved off the other bystanders who stood over her and struggled to get to her feet. When she wobbled, Colton put his arm around her and steadied her.

She stood still for a moment, trying to gather herself.

"I'd be happy to give you a ride back up the mountain. Here, let me get those bags."

Olivia didn't argue. Feeling drained and weak, she was happy to have the help of someone she knew. Well, someone she was beginning to know. At least a familiar face.

Colton helped her to his Jeep while carrying her bags. Once she was seated securely in the passenger seat, he tossed her groceries in the back seat, rounded the car, jumped into the driver's seat and fired it up. He glanced over to her with a concerned look.

Hating the fact he had to rescue her for the second time, she flushed with embarrassment. Although she tried to be resiliently tough and independent, at the moment she felt frail and totally dependent on him.

Appearing far too entertained by her predicament, he handed her a water bottle. "Here, drink this."

She took it obediently with a sheepish grin on her face.

"You were lucky I was on my way back from Red Hook. I saw you standing at the taxi stand so I pulled in." He seemed rather pleased with himself for coming to her rescue again.

They rode up the mountain in silence. Neither one attempted conversation. Again she wished she had taken the time to pull her hair back. She could only imagine what it would look like by the time she got to her mother's house. But that was probably the least of her worries at the moment. She sipped from the water bottle until she had drained the last drop, making a mental note to stay hydrated in the future.

After skillfully negotiating the mountain and the tricky intersection at the top, Colton turned down the street to her mother's house and then steered the Jeep down the winding driveway and slowly brought it to a stop prematurely before the bottom.

"Company?"

Olivia looked up. There was another Jeep at the end of the driveway. A light blue Jeep Wrangler with a soft top. Olivia gasped.

Her eyes were wide as she jumped out of Colton's Jeep and strode toward the new arrival, walking slowly as she tried to take it all in. Colton was right behind her. His eyes were almost as wide.

Olivia turned and looked at him. "What the hell? Is it really hers?"

Colton shrugged and spoke hesitantly. "I don't know."

She bit her lip and walked closer, stroking the vehicle as she walked alongside. She didn't speak. Her mind raced.

Finally Colton broke the silence. "Is it your mother's?"

Avoiding his question momentarily, Olivia devoted her attention to the light blue Jeep. Finally she turned to him and looked deep into his eyes, incredulous. "Yes, I think it is . . . but how could it suddenly show up like this?" It just didn't seem plausible.

Colton closed his eyes, pausing for a moment, apparently trying to tread cautiously. Finally he looked directly at her. "I don't know. I wish I had some answers for you."

Suddenly her face lit up as if a light bulb had been turned on, her expression animated with expectations. She bolted toward the house.

"*Mom!*" she shrieked, grabbing the screen door handle, practically pulling the door off the hinges. The door slammed behind her as she continued to call for her mother from within the tiny bungalow, running from room to room.

Colton stayed put and waited for her on the driveway.

Finally Olivia slowly re-emerged from the house deeply disappointed and saddened. She looked at Colton and shook her head in response to the obvious question hanging in the air. Then, turning away, she walked solemnly back toward what she thought was her mother's car. Colton reached out to console her with the touch of his hand, but she brushed it off, making it clear she needed space.

Olivia contemplated if she should call the police and have them come and check it for fingerprints. Was it worth the trouble? She wasn't sure. Fearing she would regret not calling, she pulled her cell out of her pocket and pressed the buttons for the Virgin Islands Police Department.

After several rings, a male voice with a thick island accent answered. It took her a few minutes to make him understand who she was, that she had stopped in earlier to report her mother missing, and that her mother's car showed up unexpectedly while she had been away from her mother's house. The gentleman at the other end of the phone didn't seem to have a real sense of urgency. Olivia guessed he wouldn't have been in a hurry even if his wife was in labor with their first child. At times, she found it challenging to be on the islands. Everyone was on island time. Things didn't get done as quickly as they did in the States, certainly not as quickly as she would like.

Olivia finally convinced the officer someone should come out and check for fingerprints and then ended the call. She had a feeling it was going to take a while but vowed to make the best of it.

"Look, would you like to come in?" she offered to Colton.

"Sure." He didn't seem to have anywhere to get to anytime soon.

They grabbed her grocery bags out of the back of Colton's Jeep and headed to the bungalow. Olivia stole another look at her mother's car as she walked by with Colton close behind her. She longed to get under the hood and check it out, see what condition it was in.

"Make yourself at home, Colton." Her words sounded odd as soon as they left her mouth. She wished she hadn't spoken them but tried to let it go.

Without wasting any time, she uncorked the bottle of Pinot Grigio since it was already chilled and offered him a glass. His face lit up, apparently glad to see happy hour was starting early and readily accepted the wine.

Realizing she had perishables, Olivia considered the refrigerator for a moment. She hadn't been brave enough to open the door yet.

"Colton, go ahead outside. I'll just put these things away and be right out." After the screen door latched behind him, she hesitated for a moment, deciding what to do. She wasn't going to tackle cleaning the entire fridge. That would surely require a block of time she wasn't willing to devote yet. Only the cheese, hummus, and milk needed to be kept cool so she improvised and put the three items in one plastic bag. Opening the freezer, which was barren with the exception of a couple of ice trays, she tossed the bag in for the time being. With a grin on her face she carried her glass out to the gallery. She had bought herself some time.

Olivia joined Colton at the railing where they enjoyed the wine and lazily admired the view out to Magens Bay.

"God, I never tire of this." She was avoiding the issue sitting in the driveway.

"I know what you mean. I feel the same way."

"It's such a shame I'll have to sell it," she lamented.

He turned to her, clearly surprised at the revelation. "I'm sorry to hear that."

"Yeah, there's no way I can hang onto it. I'm going to have to put it on the market. I certainly can't afford to keep it, and I know my father has no intention of paying to keep it going." She choked on the words.

Colton let her last statement hang in the air for a while, probably connecting the fact her parents lived a long way apart from each other. They stood in silence, leaning on the railing and taking in the view. A couple of small boats bobbed in the bay below, perhaps fishing away the afternoon, not seeming to have a care in the world.

As expected, the police didn't arrive right away, so Olivia retraced her steps back inside to refill their glasses, returning to the gallery with a small plate of crackers and hummus. They settled into the chairs at the bistro table, nibbled busily, made small talk and silently wondered if the police were ever going to show up. Half an hour turned into an hour. The hour turned into two. Mid-afternoon turned into late afternoon. They had long since polished off the first bottle of wine, but she didn't dare pull out the second. Happy hour needed to be over, and the police needed to show up and do their job.

Olivia also acknowledged she was perfectly capable of waiting for the police on her own. "Colton, this is silly for both of us to have our afternoons completely wasted. I appreciate what you're trying to do for me, but who knows if they will ever show up. I'm sure you have plenty of other priorities." Again she found herself trying to get rid of him, but he didn't seem to want to leave.

"Don't be silly. Of course I'll wait with you. It's not a problem at all. Besides, the view is amazing." He turned his body away from the table to face toward the bay and put his feet up on the railing as if to settle in, his brown leather flip-flops dangling from his toes.

Olivia noticed for the first time the pinkie toe on his left foot was missing. She found that slightly amusing. There was undoubtedly a story behind it.

"And the company is . . . well, just as amazing." He turned his head back toward her with a twinkle in his eye, appearing too elated for her comfort level.

She blushed in response, unable to think of a comeback that would convey to him she needed her space and wanted him to move on. A noise in the driveway caused them to turn their heads in unison. A late model dark blue SUV with bright yellow stripes and "V. I. Police" along the sides made its way down the steep, sinuous drive. As the cruiser got closer, Olivia could read the department's motto emblazoned on the side. "WORKING WITH YOU 24/7." Very comforting. Olivia sprang from her seat and bolted around to the front of the house, sensing Colton wasn't far behind. A young, small framed, dark-skinned policeman exited the patrol car, trying to stand tall and look important on his walk over to take care of the less-than-important task he'd been assigned.

"Miss Benning?"

"Yes."

He glanced down to a small spiral notebook as if double-checking what he had been sent to do. "You reported a missing car?" His island accent revealed his roots.

Olivia fluttered her eyelashes and cringed, trying to keep her cool and maintain her patience. "It *was* missing but suddenly showed up." She glanced over to the light blue Jeep in question.

A puzzled look crossed the rookie officer's face. Obviously, he did not see where there was a problem. "So maybe a friend borrowed it without asking and then returned it?"

Olivia frowned, pursing her lips. "No." Her voice was firm.

All eyes were on her. She let the silence speak for her for a moment.

Finally she began to fill in the blanks for the young man. "Look, I am here on the island because I got a phone call from someone telling me my mother had passed away unexpectedly. This is her house." She gestured with one hand toward the bungalow behind her. "When I got here yesterday, her car was not in the driveway. This morning I stopped into the police station to find out what happened to her, and no one knew anything about it. And they told me to come back tomorrow to report her as a missing person. When I got back here this afternoon, the car was sitting in the driveway. Something is not right about all of this. You need to see if there are any fingerprints on the car you could use to identify someone with."

The officer stood still, listening to her story, blinking more frequently than was normal. His unchanging expression gave the appearance he was uninterested in the details. "So . . . what happened to your mother?"

"The person I talked to on the phone said it was some sort of a boating accident."

"Oh, then if it was a maritime accident, I'm not sure I should be getting involved. That's not my jurisdiction."

"Look, I know that's what it sounds like, but all the pieces are not adding up. Could we just do the prints so we have them if we need them?" Wincing at her lame attempt to persuade him, she needed to find a way to be more convincing. He looked like he was ready to turn around and climb back into his department-issued SUV.

Colton stepped closer and took charge. He extended his hand and shook firmly. "Officer . . . Colton."

Olivia found it odd he never introduced himself with a last name.

"I'm sure you have a busy afternoon and undoubtedly a lot more important things to be taking care of. But if you wouldn't mind indulging us for the couple of minutes it would take to get a few prints and be on your way, we would appreciate it. Who knows, it may end up being totally unnecessary. But then again, if this thing turns into something totally unexpected and we lost the opportunity to get vital evidence, then that would be a crime. And I know you would rather be a hero who took the time to help a young woman."

Olivia squirmed with his last comment but it seemed to have worked.

"Let me see what I can do." He returned to the squad car, walked around to the back and opened the hatch. After rustling around for a couple minutes, he closed it and walked back to rejoin them. He was empty-handed.

"I'm going to have to go back to the station to get a fingerprinting kit. I thought I had one in my car, but I don't."

Olivia clenched her jaw and repressed a reaction to his announcement.

Colton continued in his role. "All right, but we can expect you to come right back. Correct?"

The young officer nodded, looking indignant at the question.

"Fine, we'll wait right here for you." He held his gaze for effect.

Biting her lip as the rookie cop retreated to his car and headed back up the hill, Olivia hated being the damsel in distress. She wished Colton would stop playing that card.

Without a word or a look between them, they returned to the gallery overlooking the bay. It was understood they would wait there until the young cop returned to do his job. Neither one shared if they expected him or any other police officer to return.

Time passed in silence. Colton settled into one of the chairs at the bistro table and Olivia was not far away, leaning with her elbows against the corner of the deck railing gazing toward the view without actually noticing it. The late afternoon Caribbean sun was strong, but the breezes off the water were quite soothing. Green parrots in the trees overhead squawked as if trying to alert them to their presence. It was remarkably peaceful, yet neither was tuned into their surroundings.

Finally Olivia broke the silence. "I just don't understand what's going on. Why doesn't anyone know what happened to my mother? I don't even know where to start." Considering possibilities for a moment, she turned toward him with her eyes wide. "What if the officer is right and someone just borrowed her Jeep? Maybe she's on some extended assignment and hasn't been around for a while. I could see her loaning her car to a friend. That's just the type of person she is."

Colton looked into her eyes, showing her he was listening, allowing her to think out loud.

"But, of course, that begs the question, who called me to say my mother had died and why?"

"Is your mother comfortable around the water?"

Olivia was taken aback by his question. "Of course. She loved to go kayaking. Had her own kayak. It seems to be missing, though, just like her car was."

Pausing to consider his question further, she refused to believe her mother's fate had anything to do with her ability to swim or how comfortable she felt around the water.

"The assignment that brought her down to the islands involved going out on a boat and up in a helicopter. She was pretty excited about it. Her job was to capture the essence of St. Thomas from the land, sea, and air. The end result was a beautiful hardcover book that depicted St. Thomas in all its glory." She stopped abruptly, realizing she was going off on a tangent, promoting her mother again.

"So she was comfortable swimming?"

Olivia found the question odd but continued. "She swam in college. Her events were the longer races, like the 500, the 1,000. I think even the 1,650, which is the mile. She's a pretty tough lady. Self-sufficient. Independent. Resourceful. Probably too much so, for my father's liking." She stopped again when she realized she had shared too much and he didn't need to know what her father did or didn't like with respect to her mother. "I really admire her. She followed her dreams and I know she loves being here. The islands have become a huge part of her. She is good at what she does and apparently is in high demand."

Colton nodded, recognizing Olivia was proud of her mother. "When was the last time you had contact with her?"

Olivia shifted her stance and leaned with her backside against the railing, her arms crossed. His question was excruciatingly uncomfortable for her. "Uh . . . it was probably, uh, I think it was about a month ago." She was embarrassed to admit it.

"A month ago." His tone was even, not seeming to be passing judgment. He was just reiterating.

"Yeah. That was probably the longest time we had gone without being in touch but, yes, it was about a month ago."

"Okay." His questioning subsided for a moment, which gave her a chance to think.

"If my mother wanted to go out on a boat, if it wasn't for a specific assignment, how or where would she do that?"

"It's simple, really. She could hire a boat with a captain through the company I work for or any of the other companies on the island that hire out boats. It's quite common. Tourists very often charter boats for the day, but locals enjoy a day out on the water, too."

"And where would they take the boat out of? Where would the boats be docked?"

"Any number of marinas. There's one on the right just before Red Hook where our boats are docked. A lot of private boats are docked there."

Nodding, Olivia filed away the information he shared.

Colton waited to see if she had more questions.

"Okay, thanks."

His eyebrows raised in response, as if he was surprised at the abrupt end to the discussion but used the cue to change the subject.

"So, let's move on to tonight. If you don't have any plans, but then again maybe you do, my band is going to be playing at Izzies from eight to eleven. I would love to see you in the audience. You know, a friendly face? It should be a lot of fun. This is one of our favorite places to perform. It's right on the beach and we usually get a great crowd." He looked eagerly toward her. "I know you have a lot on your mind, but it would be good for you to get out and have a little fun."

Olivia's thoughts were stuck at the marina at Red Hook. Finally she turned and acknowledged him. "Sure, that sounds like fun. What time?"

"Eight . . . at Izzies."

"Okay, I'll try to head over there tonight."

"That would be awesome." He sounded pleased.

A noise behind them made them turn away from the view. They were relieved to see it was a police car making its way back down the driveway.

The rookie cop had returned with a fingerprinting kit. They made their way back out to the driveway to meet him. He quickly got out of his vehicle and strutted over to the light blue Jeep.

"No one has touched it, have you?"

Colton and Olivia shook their heads in unison. Olivia spoke on their behalf. "No, of course, not."

The young officer went straight to his task, making short work of it. Before long, he had finished and began to pack up. "There weren't a lot of prints. Actually rather clean. But I took what I could." He couldn't resist asking the question on his mind, though. "Do you have a key to the Jeep? There doesn't seem to be one in it."

Olivia's body stiffened at the thought. The car was sitting in the driveway, but she still couldn't use it. She kept her cool. "Oh, I'll see if there's an extra set in the house. Shouldn't be a problem." She sounded much more confident than she felt.

As the officer returned to his vehicle and then retreated back up the driveway, she diverted her thoughts to the key, earnestly hoping to find it. Otherwise she was still stranded with no way to get around.

Colton seemed anxious to head out behind the officer. "I'll see you later at Izzies?"

Amused by his persistence, Olivia was relieved she would soon have some time to herself. "I'll see what I can do." Then the photographer in her stepped in. "Maybe I'll bring my camera and get some photos of you and your band performing."

Colton's face lit up. "That would be great. We've never had a professional photographer taking pictures. Usually it's just friends with their phones. It would be awesome to get some decent pics for promotional purposes. The guys will be stoked."

Not wanting to commit, she smiled coyly. "I'll see if I can get there."

With a wink, he walked around to the driver's side of his car, jumped in and started it up. He quickly backed up, poked his hand through the opening where the roof would have been to wave, and roared back up the steep driveway.

Drawn to the Jeep sitting in front of her, Olivia was curious to see what condition it was in. A far cry from an expert auto mechanic, her mother at least knew the basics of car maintenance and usually kept her vehicle in pristine condition. Back when they lived under the same roof, Olivia made a point of hanging around to learn as much as she could from her.

Opening the driver's side door, she reached in and pulled the release lever with a thud. Letting the door shut, she walked around to the front and lifted up hood, securing it in place. At first glance it looked surprisingly clean. She reached for the oil dipstick and pulled it out. After wiping it clean with a broad leaf from a nearby bush, she re-inserted it and pulled it out again. The oil level was where it should be. Glancing underneath, near the bottom of the engine, she could see the oil filter looked brand new, apparently changed recently. Olivia continued her assessment by checking the rest of the fluid levels, the coolant, windshield washer, and brake and power steering fluids. Puzzled, she stepped back for a moment. The vehicle looked as though it had been thoroughly serviced. She wasn't sure if that provided her with any more information other than the Jeep was probably in good working condition, which was certainly a pleasant surprise. Now, if only she could find a key.

Olivia returned to the somber solace inside her mother's Caribbean bungalow, ambling to her mother's studio. She stopped on the threshold out of respect for her mother's workspace.

Shaking her head, she let out a sigh. "Mom, I could use your help here," she pleaded, speaking as if her mother were sitting at her worktable positioned in the middle of the room. "I have *no* idea what to do . . . where to go, who to talk to," she continued, stepping inside the studio, gesturing with her arms as she spoke. "God, I hope you're alive. . . . I just wish I knew." Discouraged, her voice trailed off. She stood there for a moment, then turned and slipped back out through the doorway.

After throwing together a simple pasta dinner, she carried it outside to enjoy while taking in the view of the bay. She pictured Colton doing the same thing on his deck but gazing out to Charlotte Amalie Harbor instead. Trying to appreciate every detail around her and commit it all to memory, she didn't want to forget any of it, especially after the place was sold. Realizing she could do better than that, she promptly retrieved her camera from the house, returning with it strapped around her neck, and went straight to work, capturing the stunning views. Then she turned her attention to the outside of the brightly painted bungalow.

Olivia painstakingly documented every angle, capturing the charm of the colorful little house. Moving on to the vegetation, she photographed the flowering bushes growing naturally around the small yard, at times focusing on single blooms. She was in her element. Time stood still when she had her camera in her hand. After a lengthy stint behind the lens, she came around the side of the house where the Jeep came into view. Deciding to include her mother's car in the photo shoot, she started with the driver's side and worked her way around it. Then she opened the driver's door and climbed in, getting interesting perspectives from both seats in the front and back. Pleased with her work and uncomfortably hot from the oppressive summer heat, she declared her photo shoot complete and scrambled out of the car.

Olivia was looking forward to getting out for the evening but then it dawned on her she still didn't have a key for the vehicle. It didn't look like she was going anywhere unless she found it or called a cab. Her eyes widened as she recalled her mother used to keep an extra key under the mat on the passenger side of the front seat. Tickled at the possibility, she dashed around to the opposite side of the car.

Rustling in the brush on the far side of the house caused her to pause. A couple of birds? A mongoose? She had the uncomfortable feeling she was being watched. As casually as she could muster, she glanced around the perimeter of the yard, not noticing anything out of the ordinary but concerned why she had sensed something. Noticing the shadows were getting longer, she could tell the sun was on its way down.

Quickly she climbed back into the car and her fingers groped for the floor mat. She pulled up one corner. Nothing. She tried another corner. Nothing. Two more corners. Still nothing. Her heart sank. She gave the entire mat a good yank, and then flinched as both eyes were accosted with dirt and sand from an untold number of visits to the beach. Falling back against the seat, she dropped the filthy mat in her lap. Each blink was painful as she tried to flush the grit from her eyes. She coughed and brushed dirt from her face and lap. Once she regained her composure, she turned her eyes back to the floor, expecting to see something shimmering. She was disappointed but carefully ran her hand across the entire floor space in front of her seat to be sure. Feeling defeated, she threw the mat down, leaving it off-kilter where it landed.

Getting out and walking around the car, she checked the other three floor mats to no avail. Her body slumped in frustration. Hot and tired from the heat of the day, she took a few steps back toward the house but then stopped in her tracks. She retraced her steps to the driver's door and got back in. Leaning over to the passenger side, she opened the glove compartment and pulled out the driver's manual, the registration, a couple of brochures from local attractions, and several takeout menus. No key. Bending over to look deeper inside, she swept the dark cavity with her hand but it was empty. Disappointed, she fell back into the seat but believed it had been worth the effort. She couldn't get a break. Her frustration escalating, she shoved the contents of the compartment back into the small space and slammed the door shut, catching a corner of a brochure sticking out. The small plastic door popped back open. She shoved the papers in farther and then slammed it shut again. This time the door stuck. Relieved, she exited the stifling hot vehicle.

A set of eyes peeking out of the brush along the edge of the yard followed her as she moved across the yard and up the steps.

Olivia slammed the screen door shut and staggered slightly toward the kitchen, but something on the coffee table caught her eye on the way by. She took a step back and glanced down into the small catch-all basket. At first she couldn't make sense of what she saw. It looked like the key to her mother's Jeep, complete with the light blue-and-green-striped ribbon tied to it as it had been for as long as Olivia could remember. But how did the key get there, and why didn't she notice it before? She wondered how long it had been sitting there. Was the heat getting to her again? Olivia looked closely at the key with its ribbon to be sure of what she was seeing, concerned her brain was creating the image because she wanted it to be true. She reached down and picked it up. It felt good in her fingers. A tingling sensation rippled through her stomach in anticipation of driving the Jeep. She wanted to run back outside and fire it up.

Restraining herself from hastily departing, she headed to the kitchen to drink a couple glasses of water in an effort to keep herself hydrated. She hated the idea of someone having to come to her rescue (again) simply because she had neglected to drink enough. The tap wasn't particularly refreshing, though, as the water didn't get cold no matter how long it ran. Just another aspect of island living. Although there was a desalination plant on St. Thomas that used reverse osmosis to transform sea water into drinking water, only a minority of homes on the island benefited from it directly.

At her mother's bungalow, like most other homes on the island, the corrugated metal roof funneled rainwater through a downspout into a cistern below the dwelling. Most people used the cistern water for taking showers, washing clothes, and cleaning dishes but purchased jugs of purified water for drinking. Olivia's mother had installed a water purifier next to the kitchen sink so she could also drink the collected rain water. Living on an island meant every drop was precious. If the cistern got low, during extended periods of particularly dry weather, homeowners had to pay to have water delivered by truck.

Olivia freshened up with a quick shower and clean clothes. A sheer, feminine, off-white sleeveless top with the same color camisole underneath and slim-fitting black denim capris with strappy black sandals accented with a little bit of sparkly bling near the toes. After all, she was going out on the town. She was glad she had tossed them in when she packed, just in case. On her way out the door, she grabbed her camera as she had promised Colton. The screen door clicked behind her as she made her way out, a real spring in her step in anticipation.

Jumping into her mother's Jeep, she laid her camera carefully on the passenger seat. The key slid easily into the ignition. Slowly she pressed her eyes closed and turned the key, willing the engine to turn over but instead it groaned. Her eyes popped open. It wasn't happening! Olivia was not giving up that easily. She gritted her teeth, stared straight ahead, and turned the key again. This time the engine grumbled initially and then roared to life. Her eyes widened and she pumped her fist into the air. Finally something was going her way.

An overwhelming wave of excitement combined with a healthy dose of apprehension coursed through her veins. Tightly grasping the steering wheel, her hands felt sweaty and tingly. She put the Jeep in reverse, turned it around, and ascended the steep, curvy driveway, pausing at the top.

"Stay to the left. Stay to the left." She hoped she would remember. Some habits were hard to break.

CHAPTER SIX

After negotiating the tricky intersection just up from Magens Bay, Olivia reached the crest of the mountain with Charlotte Amalie sprawled out below and the harbor beyond. The view took her breath away. Trade winds were strong and, once again, she hadn't remembered to pull her hair back before climbing into the Jeep. Fortunately her mother's had the soft top on it. She would deal with her hair when she got there. As she drove down the mountain, she was tempted to steal a peek at the view out to the harbor along the way but didn't dare. Keeping the car on the left side of the road, and not off the edge, was much more of a priority. Her hands were clamped tightly onto the east and west sides of the steering wheel. Slowing down every time an oncoming car passed her, she did her best to ignore an impatient driver who remained close behind her all the way down the mountain.

Replaying the conversation with Colton, she was curious about the marina on the way to Red Hook and felt drawn there to at least take a look around. Perhaps she would find someone to talk to. She wasn't entirely familiar with the area, but she vaguely recalled the marina was on the way to the bar. She would figure it out.

Before long, she was sitting at the traffic light at the bottom of the mountain looking out to the water. "Stay to the left. Stay to the left," she whispered, pleading with herself. Instead of turning right toward the downtown shops, she turned left onto Route 30 to head east toward Red Hook. The road followed along the curve of the harbor and became more congested as she approached Havensight where the cruise ships docked. Shops and restaurants lined both sides of the street and orange Jersey barriers filled the center due to road work still going on from her previous couple of visits. She chuckled to herself as she inched through traffic. Even the construction was on island time.

Emerging from there, the narrow road snaked up the hill and into a more residential area curving back and forth, up and down. Her right foot darted from the gas pedal to tap the brakes and back again as she endeavored to hug the curves in the road and willed the oncoming cars to stay on their side. The line in the middle faded in and out as if it weren't brave enough to commit to the road completely. "Stay Left" signs, meant for tourists, outnumbered speed limit signs but most local drivers ignored them anyway. Olivia mused they should just post signs that read, "Drive at your own risk."

Some turns were so sharp and inclines were so steep, the tips of her fingers tingled and her knuckles turned white on the steering wheel. When she reached the top of one hill, in particular, she hesitated because she couldn't see below to the other side. She said a quick prayer and eased the car back down the hill, feeling like the car would slip off the surface of the road and fall straight down. It reminded her of cartoons where the car zipped to the top of a ridiculously steep incline and came to a halt on the pointed top where it teetered until its momentum landed it onto the other side. Then it zipped straight down again. The experience was similar to being on a roller coaster. Her stomach certainly couldn't tell the difference.

Along the way, the landscape was peppered with an interesting array of abodes, from tiny cinder block or wooden shacks near the road to palatial multi-room villas perched high up on the hillsides, which afforded the occupants magnificent ocean views. Olivia's eyes were drawn to both extremes, all the while continuously pulling her focus back to the left side of the road. Before long she came upon the driveway on the right for Izzies. It surprised her it was before the marina area she was heading toward but shrugged it off. It had been a while since her last trip to the island. Her memory was not completely accurate.

Olivia continued to make her way along the winding, island road. On the way up another hill, her phone vibrated in her pocket. Deep down she knew she shouldn't take her eyes off the road. She did her best to pull it out of her pocket, press "answer," and switch it to speaker before dropping it in her lap. It was her good friend, Laurie, back in Boston. She was pleased to hear from her.

"Hey, girlfriend!"

"Hey, girlie! How's it going?" Laurie's demeanor was always upbeat and her voice lilting.

"It's going okay," she lied. "How are things with you?"

"Great. Things are great. But everything is going okay with you?" Laurie asked again to confirm. Her friend knew her well. It was going to be difficult to convince her.

"Yeah, Laurie. I'm okay. Just trying to get things squared away. A lot of loose ends."

"I'm sure. But I know you can handle it. I wish I could have come with you. I wish you didn't have to handle this by yourself. You know that, don't you?"

It was great to hear her voice. Laurie's sweet and uplifting spirit was energizing to everyone around her. Olivia could use an injection of positive.

"Of course, absolutely. But you *are* helping me and I appreciate it."

"Oh, heavens! I'm not doing much at all," Laurie scoffed.

"Yes, you are," Olivia insisted. "How is little Chloe doing?" She tried to redirect her friend in a positive way.

"Oh, she's great. A perfect angel. I think she and I are actually bonding. Imagine that!"

Olivia sensed Laurie was being overly positive, perhaps even stretching the truth a bit. She wasn't a huge fan of felines but tolerated Chloe only because she and Olivia were such close friends.

"Good to hear. Next thing you know she'll be sitting in your lap," Olivia teased, knowing her friend was allergic to cats.

"Oh, I hope not! Anyway, I also wanted to give you a quick call and let you know there was something in the mail I brought in that I thought you might be interested in. It's a package. You know . . . kind of a flat, padded envelope. Not real big."

Olivia listened intently, waiting for a reason to be interested.

"It's addressed to your father."

That wasn't it. Olivia frowned slightly. She knew she had no business looking at her father's mail and was confused as to why Laurie would even ask.

"Laurie, if it's his then I don't see—"

"It looks like it might be postmarked the U.S. Virgin Islands. It's not real clear, but it looks like it could be. There's no return address though."

Olivia took a moment to think, still keeping her eyes on the road, and then concluded she shouldn't be opening her father's mail. She'd be foolish to entertain the idea.

"You know what, Laurie, I appreciate you asking but if it's addressed to him, I can't very well . . . he has business practically all over the world." She knew it was a slight exaggeration, but she was trying to make a point. "I'm sure it has nothing to do with me and what I'm doing down here. Especially if it's addressed to him. I'll let him open it when he gets back. But thank you for thinking of me. I appreciate it."

"Okay. No problem. Let me know if there is anything else I can do. . . . Livvie?"

"Yeah?" Olivia stared off into the distance, somewhat leery of what was coming next.

"If you don't mind me asking, what does your father do? We've never talked about it. I always had the sense you'd rather not. But he's always gone. Always traveling. I'm sorry if I'm prying but we've been friends forever, and it just seems odd I don't know."

Uncomfortable she didn't know the specifics of what her father did either, Olivia stalled, not wanting to admit it. He wasn't around much to talk about his work or anything else for that matter. Her father traveled extensively for his job, leaving her alone much of the time, forcing her to fend for herself. Olivia never cared enough to ask when he did blow through town. She had grown uncomfortably distant from him, having been essentially on her own since her parents separated when she was twelve. It's just the way it had always been. She didn't know anything different. But she also didn't know how to answer her best friend's question. Squinting her eyes, she struggled to come up with something.

"Oh, Laurie, I don't know exactly. . . . It has to do with finance. Investments of some sort. I'm not sure. It's all so . . . I don't know. Confusing to me. He travels a lot. We don't talk about it." Anxious to change the subject, she added, "Anyway, I appreciate what you're doing for me."

"There's something else for you. It's a hand-addressed envelope to you, and the return address is Abigail Adams Studios."

Olivia's eyes widened. She hoped it was good news, but she pulled back her expectations in case it wasn't.

"Yeah, why don't you open that. Let's see what it's all about." She knew what it was and crossed her fingers in anticipation.

Listening to rustling on the other end of the line, Olivia tried to wait patiently, keeping an eye out for the marina as she drove.

"Oh! Do you want me to read this to you?"

Sounded like it was good news. She gave her the go-ahead.

As her friend read the letter, Olivia learned she had apparently made it into the top ten finalists out of thousands of applicants for an apprenticeship she had applied for with none other than Boston's renowned Abigail Adams Photography Studio. She shook her head in disbelief, never dreaming she would make it that far. She had applied on a whim.

"Wow, that's great. I never expected that."

"Olivia, that's amazing! Good for you." Laurie's enthusiasm was contagious.

"Yeah, now what? I have to wait and see?"

Olivia had reached the end of Route 30 where it intersected with Route 32. She carefully navigated a right turn, crossing the oncoming lane to get to the left side.

"It says they will be in touch over the next couple of days."

"Okay, great. I don't have time to worry about that right now, but it's great news. I'll just have to see what happens."

"Olivia! Oh my gosh, this is amazing! Are you familiar with the Abigail Adams Studio?"

"Seriously, Laurie? I applied for the apprenticeship. Of course, I'm familiar with the studio. And just because I get a letter saying I'm in the top ten doesn't mean there is anything to get excited about yet. We all know how these things work. Even though it looks like the application process is legitimate, it doesn't mean it is. So much in life is about who you know."

"It's still fantastic news. I'm proud of you."

The sign for the marina came into view ahead of her on the right.

"Oh, Laurie, I have to go. I'm coming up on my turn for my next appointment." Again, a slight exaggeration.

"Okay. No problem, Livvie. You take it easy, okay?"

"Absolutely. And thanks again for taking care of things in Boston for me. I really appreciate it."

Slowing the vehicle as she approached the entrance, Olivia surveyed the marina quickly and pulled in. The tattered sign read "Blue Water Marina" in blue block lettering with black outlines on a white background. Paint was peeling from the sign, but Olivia interpreted that as a repercussion of the island's weather and relaxed island attitude, not an indication it was a less than viable enterprise.

"Any time, girlfriend. Call me if you need anything."

"Thanks. Gotta go," Olivia blurted out, cutting Laurie off abruptly, but she needed to focus as she entered the dry dock section of the marina and meandered through rows of boats perched high up on wooden platforms in the dirt lot. Pulling the car into the first spot large enough for it to fit, she shifted the Jeep into park and turned off the engine.

"Bye, Liv. Miss you!"

"Miss you too. See you soon." Olivia pressed the button to end the call. Grabbing her camera from the passenger seat, she climbed out of the vehicle and slammed the door shut, anxiously anticipating what might be in store for her, hoping to find someone to talk to.

Scanning the boats perched up high all around her, in the process of getting renovated or repaired, she found some so large and towering they were daunting. There was no one in sight working on any of them. It was eerily quiet and looked more like a boat graveyard where the unwanted and neglected were dumped.

Quickly snapping photos, not stopping to look around or assess her surroundings, she was fascinated by the contrast in size of the boats and the extreme conditions some were left in. Black and white photographs would do a better job of telling each boat's story. Reaching the end of the dry dock section, she arrived at the edge of the marina where the docked boats were, passing a small outdoor restaurant to the left. It sounded like a couple of regulars were engrossed in animated conversation at the bar.

Olivia stopped for a moment to survey the vast number of boats bobbing in the water. Veritable poetry in motion. The water was relatively calm, yet subtle disturbances caused the boats to bob from time to time. Olivia was mesmerized by the naturally choreographed ballet. These vessels had a different feel than the boats suspended on wooden frames, barred from heading out onto the water anytime in the near future. Instead, the docked boats were only temporarily tethered, just a couple tugs on the ropes away from heading out to the open sea.

Slipping stealthily onto the dock, she snapped pictures in rapid succession as she ambled. The metal dock under her feet felt alive as it responded to the ebb and flow of the water beneath it. Slowly she inched along, glancing down from time to time to be sure she didn't misstep and end up in the water. A dog barked in the distance.

Olivia stopped next to a sleek white boat with two large black engines on the back of it tilted out of the water. She didn't have a working knowledge of boats, but it looked fast. It appeared to have seating for at least eight passengers, four at the stern, four more toward the bow, with a Hunter green canopy over the captain's wheel. Her mother came to mind for a moment, and Olivia wondered if she had been out on a boat like this.

"*Hey!*" a gruff voice bellowed from behind her.

Nearly dropping her camera, she turned to look into the approaching face of aggression.

"Who are you and what the hell are you doing?" A large muscular man with rounded shoulders and rough features charged toward her. His white t-shirt with its sleeves ripped from the seams and grease smudges across the front suggested a hardworking yardman. Anger radiated from his unshaven and sunburned face. His short white hair stuck out at odd angles.

Olivia recoiled as it crossed her mind it could be a private marina. Her stomach tightened into a knot. She forced what she hoped was a calm face to avoid divulging how nervous he was making her. "Evening . . ."

He advanced toward her, lunging his face uncomfortably close to hers with eyes wide and nostrils flaring, demanding answers to his questions.

A strong whiff of sweat accosted her nose. Olivia took a step backward to put more space between them and fought to control her facial expression as her body grew rigid with fear.

"Well? What are you doing here?" His anger seemed to be escalating.

"I'm—uh—I'm just—" She stammered in her attempt to find the right words to calm him while trying not to panic. "Look, I'm sorry. I didn't mean to offend anyone." Glancing furtively across the marina, she drew in a quick breath while searching for someone, anyone, to assure her she was not alone with the irate man. Not a soul was around.

"Offend anyone! Lady, you're trespassing on private property." His temper was not subsiding.

"I'm sorry. Really. The marina is so beautiful I got pulled in off the street. I just thought this would be a great place to snap some photos. I didn't mean any harm." She cringed at her attempt to pacify him. Sounded too obvious.

His face seemed to soften. She prayed she wasn't just imagining it.

Olivia instincts yelled at her to run but the man, in all of his rage, stood between her and the way off the dock.

"Lady, you can't just waltz in here because you think it's 'pretty'." His voice lilted on the last word. "These boats are privately owned, and I don't think the owners would appreciate what you're doing."

"I should have known better. I'm sorry." She hoped her groveling was working. "Sometimes this camera gets the better of me, and I get carried away." She chuckled a nervous laugh, trying to lighten his mood.

"You need to get on out of here before trouble arrives."

Olivia shuddered at the thought of more trouble than him. She was more than happy to leave before the situation got any worse, but he stood firm in his stance on the dock.

"All right!" She threw up her hands as if to surrender. "I'm out of here. No worries. I'm gone. Thanks for . . ."

She wasn't sure what to thank him for. For not grabbing her by the arm and throwing her head first into the water with her camera still strapped to her neck? For not snatching her camera and throwing *it* into the water?

"Just thanks."

That was the best she could come up with. It would have to do. She left it at that and then strode toward the imposing figure who could easily prevent her from leaving. To her surprise and relief, he stepped back enough to allow her room to walk past him. Her feet tread a bit too close to the edge of the dock for her comfort, sending a chill through her body, but she pushed her way through her anxiety. Walking as quickly as her legs would carry her without actually running, she reached the end of the dock, stepping off onto the edge of the dirt lot. Solid ground. That made her feel a little more comfortable.

She hesitated for a moment but didn't want to waste an opportunity. Turning back toward the docks, she could see the man still stood next to the sleek white boat. His arms were folded firmly across his wide girth, feet spread in an authoritative stance, still wearing an ornery glare as he watched her leave.

Did she dare? She didn't feel she had a choice. "Excuse me." She took a step closer to him but remained at a relatively safe distance. "Could I ask you something?" She stood tall, trying to maintain a confident posture.

His eyebrows arched above his eyes as if in disbelief she was so bold.

She continued without waiting for a response. "Would you know anything about a boating accident recently? Like within the past couple of weeks or so?" Knowing she was taking a risk, she hoped she hadn't pushed him too far.

The yardman stared straight through her. Finally he shifted his body weight and then walked down the dock toward her. He kept walking until he stopped uncomfortably close to her again. Having a sizable one-step vertical advantage standing on the dock, the angry, smelly man towered over her.

She retreated a couple of steps but maintained eye contact with him.

"I don't know what you're referring to." His voice was firm and unwavering.

Olivia waited for more, but it was clear he had nothing else to say to her. She wondered if what he hadn't said spoke volumes more than what he had. She held eye contact with him but then reluctantly turned and walked slowly back to her car. She climbed in and laid her camera on the passenger seat. Disappointed and unsure where to turn to next, she inserted the key in the ignition and fired up the engine. As she backed slowly out of the parking spot, the sunburned face of the white-haired man suddenly appeared in the rearview mirror. Gasping, she jammed on the brakes, jerking the vehicle to a halt, stirring up gravel and dust in the unpaved lot. Shifting back into park, Olivia nervously waited for him to walk around to the open driver's side window.

Slamming a hand on the roof of her car, the intimidating man leaned in toward her. "Look, shit happens all the time." A pale pudgy finger on his other hand wagged in her face. His breath was hot and sour.

Olivia pushed her back into the seat, trying to put as much distance as she could between them. She could hear a dog barking like before, but louder.

Leaning in closer, he continued. "People do stupid things out on the water. People think they know how to handle a boat, but they really don't. They go out farther than they should or find themselves in places where they shouldn't be. When weather turns or if there is alcohol involved, things go wrong. Accidents happen." He looked as though he wasn't finished. "But you might want to be careful where you're sticking your nose and asking questions like that." He turned and walked away, leaving her to wonder if there was something specific he was referring to and what else he might know.

Olivia sat for a moment as his words hung in the air. Finally she shifted the Jeep into drive. Glancing into her rearview mirror again, she was relieved to see the man with the wild white hair had disappeared.

Weaving through the silent nautical giants looming above her, she retraced her route through the dry dock toward the entrance to the marina, disappointed her visit hadn't been more productive. A nondescript white van pulled into the marina parking lot as she pulled out. The driver sized her up on his way by.

"Stay to the left. Stay to the left," she reminded herself and turned left to head back toward Izzies.

CHAPTER SEVEN

Olivia maneuvered the Jeep along Route 32, back the way she had come, navigating the narrow winding road for the short distance before it met Route 30 and then turned left. Relieved to leave the marina behind, she cringed, thinking about the mess she could have gotten tangled in, and reprimanded herself for being careless. Before long she came upon the sign for Izzies and turned left into the bumpy entrance leading to the dirt parking lot. There were quite a few cars already there. Colton would be pleased with the turnout. She drove up one row and down another, finally deciding on a spot at the end, next to a Humvee. She imagined it belonged to a tourist who had splurged on a fun set of wheels to explore the island. Grabbing the camera from the seat beside her, she returned it to its natural position around her neck and headed down the walkway toward the bar. An annoying nervous twinge returned to her stomach, in anticipation of the unexpected, and a bit of guilt that she was heading out for an evening of fun. Olivia did her best to look confident.

Rounding the curve in the path, Olivia's eyes caught sight of the beach and beyond to the beautiful blue water that made her pause for a moment. Small waves crashed onto the beach, more turbulent than the calm waters of Magens Bay, yet she was drawn to it. There was a gentle murmur as the waves rolled toward the beach, cresting in white foam, before spilling onto the sand. The sights and sounds were soothing.

The din from Izzies quickly called her away from the ocean, and she redirected her steps toward the bar, passing a water sports rental shop on the way. Izzies was a restaurant and bar "en plein air," like most other eating establishments on the islands, with only a roof for protection from the elements.

Members of the band were running through mic tests and making minor adjustments to their setup. Their backs were to the beach and the beautiful aqua ocean beyond. Olivia quickly looked around to see what her options were for seating. Besides the stools at the bar, there were raised round tables on large barrels that fit four to six patrons and several were taken by couples who were finishing their meals and probably had no intention of budging since live music would be starting soon. Many of them may have walked over from the hotel just down the beach.

Smaller, square tables were situated around pillars, with two to three chairs pushed up next to them. Older-model, tarnished-wire oscillating fans lending a retro touch were mounted at the ceiling along the outside walls at each support post and ran full blast. A string of white lights sprung to life under the banister along the perimeter. Two lengths of thick nautical ropes, fashioned into a railing of sorts, ran parallel underneath.

The bar had a quaint island feel to it. Fashioned into three sides of a rectangle, bamboo lined the base of it like tin solders, and a thatched roof overhang looked like it was made from hula skirts. A smaller, matching roof hung on the inside of the bar over a pass-through window. The door to the kitchen was located to the left of the bar and rich Caribbean spices caught Olivia's nose, making her mouth salivate. She found an unoccupied stool on the corner of the bar nearest the band next to a middle-aged woman with shoulder length, brown hair on her right and a balding guy with an unnaturally dark tan on the other side. He had his back to her and was engrossed in a conversation with a young woman next to him.

Olivia shifted the seat out and turned it to the right to give her a better view of the band. Climbing up onto it, she glanced over and caught Colton's eye. His face lit up and he gave her a nod, visibly pleased she had arrived. Feeling herself blushing, she turned away and focused on getting the bartender's attention. It didn't take long before a large man with cornrows down to his shoulders and a dark scruff of hair on his chin stopped to see what he could get for her. He wore no name tag but sported a vibrantly colored t-shirt tie-dyed in a spiral pattern with the Izzies logo on the back. In keeping with the spirit of the islands, Olivia ordered a piña colada with a glass of water. Stealing another glance over to the band, she could tell Colton was clearly the one in charge, giving some last-minute instructions to the rest of the guys. Olivia was amused to see he was wearing the same brown flip-flops.

The drinks arrived quickly along with a bowl of popcorn placed between her and the woman sitting next to her, who looked up from her cell and reached for the fluffy, white kernels. In doing so, she knocked a few pieces out of the bowl, and as they tumbled onto the bar, she noticed Olivia.

"I just can't resist the popcorn," she confessed and chuckled at herself, her friendly eyes smiling as much as her mouth. She didn't seem to be with the young couple sitting next to her. Olivia guessed they might be on their honeymoon, in their own little world and very attentive to each other. Bright gold wedding bands stood out on their left hands.

Olivia smiled. "It's one of my weaknesses, too." As she grabbed a generous handful, a few kernels escaped her grasp and danced across the surface of the bar. She left them where they came to rest.

"You plan on taking some photographs?" The woman glanced at the camera around Olivia's neck.

". . . Oh, yeah." She had almost forgotten it was still hanging there. "I promised one of the guys in the band I would try to get some publicity shots for them."

"Oh, you know the band?"

"Well, not exactly. I just met—" They were interrupted by Colton's voice through the microphone.

"Good evening, everyone. Good to see all of you here tonight! Thank you for coming. We have a great show planned, so sit back, relax, and enjoy the music. If you feel like dancing, feel free to get up and move around. The place is yours to enjoy. We're The Rum Runners." With that, the band led off with an eighties hit with a reggae twist to it. The crowd responded with heads bobbing.

Olivia listened to the familiar melody for a while but was eager to engage the woman next to her in conversation. "So where are you from?"

"From right here on the island, at least now I am. I used to live in New England, but the winters got longer every year to the point where I'd had enough of the cold and headed south. Don't miss it for a minute. The pace of life is incredibly different down here. I love it."

"Yeah, I know about those winters. I'm from Boston."

The woman acknowledged her comment with a nod as she sipped from her tall brown beer bottle. "Ah, yes. So you are familiar. Yeah, I'm originally from Connecticut."

"How did you pick St. Thomas?" Olivia had to speak loudly to be heard over the band.

"I had vacationed here a few times and got to know the Virgin Islands including the BVI but felt at home here. Besides, I knew since it's a U.S. territory, I could continue to sell real estate fairly easily. It made sense."

"Oh, you're a Realtor." Olivia hated what was about to come out of her mouth. "I actually could use your help."

They were fighting the volume of the music behind them but pushed on.

"Really? Are you looking to buy something? Step into my office." She grinned broadly, gesturing her outstretched arm over the bar with a flourish.

"Actually, I need to sell my mother's place." Olivia choked on her words, suddenly grateful for the background noise.

"Okay, sure. Do you mind my asking why you're selling?"

It was a legitimate question, but Olivia hesitated because she wanted to steer clear of specifics. "It's a long story." The setting wasn't exactly conducive to a heart-to-heart conversation. "We can no longer afford to keep the place. It's a shame, but there isn't much of a choice in it." It was hard to grasp she was uttering the words. "We've had it for a while, but it doesn't make sense to hang onto it."

The Realtor examined her face and seemed to be able to tell Olivia was holding back and pained by the situation. Pulling out her card, she quickly assumed the role of real estate agent and placed it on the bar in front of Olivia.

Glancing down to pick it up, her eyes brimmed and a lone tear escaped and rolled down her cheek. Olivia wiped it away and blinked hard a couple of times, struggling to regain her composure.

"If you'd like, and it's convenient, I can stop by tomorrow afternoon to take a look at the property. We can talk about your options. We'll figure it out together. Okay? It will be all right." She reached over and squeezed Olivia's shoulder. "I'm Sarah." She extended her other hand and they shook.

"Olivia."

"Nice to meet you."

Olivia appreciated her kindness. She liked her and had a feeling she could work with her on her unbearable task. "Thanks, Sarah. Tomorrow afternoon is great. I should be around."

Charmed by the fact no specific time was mentioned, Olivia gave her the address and then the two became silent, listening to the sounds of Colton's band. The eighties remake was followed by a couple of Bob Marley songs, one by Tribal Seeds, and an original piece by The Rum Runners. The audience was enjoying the music and the members of the band seemed to love entertaining. The dance floor was full of sun-kissed bodies moving to the music. Breaks were few and brief.

The bartender returned to see if Olivia wanted to order anything to eat. Even though she had grabbed a bite before she left, she glanced up at the handwritten menu on the chalkboard behind the bar and quickly decided on the grilled fish sandwich with pineapple salsa and pasta salad for her side. Sarah piped up she'd have the same but changed the side to sweet potato fries. The two engaged in more small talk while they waited for their dinners. In a lull in the conversation, Olivia pivoted in her chair to survey the crowd that had filled in since she had arrived. She was always looking for interesting characters to photograph, and there was rarely a shortage in tourist areas. As she inspected the crowd, Olivia strained to keep a straight face and refrain from chuckling out loud.

The table closest to her was occupied by a family of four with parents and two teenagers. The father was wearing a bright turquoise-and-white, horizontally-striped polo shirt stretched over his protruding belly and tucked neatly into his belted khaki shorts.

His wife was wearing a solid light blue polo shirt untucked over her white Bermuda shorts. The teens looked fairly close in age and were completely engrossed with their phones, using both thumbs to type frantically. The parents, whose fair skin looked painfully sunburned, appeared uninterested and distant, as if they had given up long ago on trying to get through to their kids. Sadly, there was not even a resemblance of conversation between the adults. Perhaps they were nearing the end of their vacation and ready to return home, back to their lives that were physically close, yet emotionally removed from one another.

The table next to the dysfunctional family was filled to capacity with three animated couples in their fifties who probably had arrived for happy hour and were staying right through for the entertainment. The men, with their brown beer bottles in front of them, were dominating the conversation and seemed to be competing with each other for air time. They were all wearing Tommy Bahama-style island shirts they probably picked up in the gift shop of their hotel for their night out. The largest of the three waved a fat, unlit cigar as he gestured during his narration, his voice bellowing over the other two men. The wives appeared unengaged, looking almost bored with their husbands. Two of the ladies were dressed in white sun dresses in different styles. The third had on a royal blue, black-and-white-paisley-print, halter-style maxi dress. The white dress ladies exchanged a few words from time to time, leaving the third out of the loop. In the awkwardness of the moment, she feigned interest in the music.

Arriving behind Olivia, the bartender delivered her sandwich. She spun around on her stool to the most tantalizing aroma. If she had ever been able to taste a smell, that was it. Surprisingly hungry, she couldn't wait to dig in. Sarah had already taken a bite and was enjoying it. Olivia jumped in as well. The unusual combination of ingredients was a contrast of sweet and spicy. Her taste buds wished it didn't have to end.

Without turning to look, Olivia could sense the man to her left was no longer conversing with the young girl. Perhaps she was no longer there. The man became quiet, but he seemed the type to need to hear his own voice. She knew he would be looking for another victim. To her relief, she could hear him engage the bartender. He tried to sound like he was more than somewhat knowledgeable about a sports figure who had just flashed on the big screen TV.

Chancing a glance down his end of the bar, she observed a few men seated and standing nearby who appeared to be locals. Izzies was definitely in full swing. All of the tall tables were full. Everyone was clearly enjoying the infectious music of The Rum Runners. Her body was moving to the beat. She continued to scan the venue, people watching while she finished her meal.

Remembering she had brought her camera for a reason, Olivia spoke to her new acquaintance, excusing herself before sliding off her stool. Grasping her camera with both hands, she quickly went to work taking multiple shots of the band at different angles, close-ups and wide angles, the camera clicking quickly. She made several adjustments as she worked, trying to adapt to the waning natural light and the artificial lighting in the bar. She thoroughly enjoyed using her camera. Behind the lens, her focus was only on her subject, an escape for her. She had left the sad scenario she brought with her to the island back at the bar with Sarah. Even though it would be there when she returned, she was fully immersed in her task and enjoying it thoroughly.

Olivia circled the perimeter of Izzies and then backed up to the bar, taking photos in rapid succession. A commotion stirred behind her. Impassioned voices could be heard over the music and what sounded like breaking glass. A beer bottle? Just as Olivia turned toward the disturbance, someone's elbow or fist found its way to her cheek. A flash of light and the left side of her face exploded in pain. The blow was enough to shift her balance and knock her off her feet. Letting go of her camera, she got her hands out in front of her in time to brace her fall. As she lay dazed on the ground, she could sense feet shuffling around her and more voices yelling. Her throat felt constricted and she realized someone was pulling at her camera. Defense mode kicked in. Grabbing the straps with one hand, she swung at anything within reach with the other. The shouting suddenly grew more pronounced because the band had stopped playing. Someone pulled her attacker away from her, but he disappeared in the crowd. As strong hands from behind pulled her upright, she struggled to stay on her feet. Her head was spinning. Grabbing for a stool that was no longer there, her hand made contact with the edge of the bar. An arm slipped around her. Sarah's voice boomed in her ear.

"Let's get out of here. This isn't over yet. It could get even uglier."

Olivia wasn't going to argue. The crowd of people was animated and in a nasty mood. One man was restrained by another but wiggled vigorously to break free. Sarah quickly led her out with an arm wrapped tightly around her, dashing down the path to the parking lot. They got as far as the dive shop when Olivia heard a familiar voice.

"Olivia!" Colton jogged to catch up to them. He touched her upper arm and looked into her face. "Are you all right? I'm sorry you got hurt. You—"

"I'll be fine. I'd just like to get out of here." Her hands grasped for the camera straps, confirming it was still hanging around her neck.

He examined the red swollen splotch on her face. "You need some ice. Let me get you some before you leave."

"No, I'll be fine. I'll get some back at my place." Did she call it hers? No matter. She was eager to leave Izzies behind.

"Hang on a second. I'll grab some from the bar." He turned and jogged back.

"We're going to head out to the parking lot." Sarah called after him.

The two women kept walking. Sarah's arm had slid down and found a place around Olivia's waist. Since her Jeep was closer to the walkway than Sarah's car, they made a beeline there. Olivia eased behind the wheel and allowed her body to melt into the seat. The evening had not turned out the way she had expected.

Sarah established her position as protector, next to the open driver's side door, one hand resting loosely on the top of the frame.

"Are you going to be all right?" She looked closer at Olivia's cheek in the glare from the parking lot flood lights. "That could be a nice bruise by morning."

Olivia laughed. "Yeah, just what I came to the island for."

Colton came jogging back with a clear plastic bag filled with ice. Pushing past the Realtor, he pressed it to Olivia's cheek.

Flinching, she reached up to take hold of the bag of chilly cubes with one hand and pushed his hand off with the other. "Easy." The three maintained silence as if reflecting on what had just transpired. Olivia spoke first, manners intact. "Sarah, this is Colton. Colton, Sarah."

They exchanged pleasantries, mentioned something about meeting a time or two before, and turned back to Olivia.

The two stood alongside Olivia like two doting parents. The solemnity of the evening's events was not lost on any of them.

"All right, look. I'm fine. Really. I'll be fine. I'd like to get out of here." Olivia tossed the dripping bag on the seat beside her, shoved the key in the ignition and fired up the engine, then closed the driver's side door and lowered the window. "Sarah, I'll see you tomorrow afternoon. Colton, thanks for the ice. It's been . . . well, your band sounded great. I enjoyed listening. I think I got some good shots, as long as my camera didn't get damaged. Thanks for the invite tonight. I'll see you again soon."

Putting the car in reverse, she eased it out of the parking spot, waving to her acquaintances in her rearview mirror. Turning back out onto Route 30, she reminded herself to stay to the left. She grabbed the bag of ice and blinked as she reapplied it to her face. Recognizing the winding, twisting roads were more challenging at night, she repressed the urgency to get back to familiar surroundings. Carefully she retraced her steps to Serenity Villa, her camera still hanging from her neck.

The thirty-minute drive from Izzies seemed to take forever. Olivia was worn out from the long day, and the throbbing lump on her cheek made her feel as though her whole head was swollen and was going to split open. After negotiating the hairpin turns back up the mountain and making her way through the tricky intersection, she was finally heading down the narrow road to her mother's house. Slowing the Jeep as she got close, she carefully turned into the driveway and zigzagged down the hill. The dark shape of the little bungalow lay quietly at the bottom. She wished she had put on a light or two before she left earlier in the evening. At least she wouldn't have to worry about guiding the key into the lock in the dark.

Leaving the Jeep at the end of the driveway, she plodded toward the front door, the dripping ice bag in one hand. Even though it was a beautiful summer evening and the stars were shining brightly, shadows predominated the yard around her mother's house. Across the bay, only a few lights were on in homes scattered along Peterborg Peninsula. A breeze off the bay caressed her face.

The front door knob turned easily, and she gave the door a shove with her body as she had done many times before. This time, however, the door didn't open all the way. It got stuck on something just inside the door.

CHAPTER EIGHT

Peering inside the shadowy little house, it was hard for her to see anything beyond the window in the door. She pushed the door harder, anxious to get inside. A strange foreboding came over her. Giving the door another push, more firmly than before, she created just enough room to poke her face inside, but she still couldn't see in the dark. Using her body to push the door enough to squeeze through, she flipped the switch on the table lamp by the door then tossed the ice bag toward the coffee table. There was an odd sound when it hit the floor instead of the table. Pulling her camera up over her head, she gently laid it on the couch under the window.

At first it was difficult to make sense of what she was looking at. The small throw rug usually lying by the front door was bunched up and wedged partway under it. The coffee table was overturned and things were strewn across the floor from the living area to her mother's studio. Papers. Photographs. Immediately she was concerned for the studio and broke into a run, straight for it.

Pausing in the doorway, she flipped on the switch and gasped. It took her a moment to survey the scene. Cupboard doors hung open, exposing bare shelves. Drawers stripped from their rollers lay haphazardly on the floor, their contents spilled and scattered. The framed photos had been ripped from the walls and shattered across the worktable. Shards of glass, sparkling in the overhead light, littered every surface in her mother's studio. Olivia reached down and collected photographs, picked up pens and pencils in an unrealistic attempt to return the room to its former condition. Before long, she stopped, completely overwhelmed by the extent of the mess.

"Mom, I'm so sorry." As her knees gave way, she grabbed onto the edge of the worktable while her back slid along the lower cupboard behind her, ending in a folded heap on the floor. "How could someone do this?" she whispered under her breath. "Why would . . . I don't get it." She was at a loss. Her mother's beautiful work, destroyed by someone. A thug. This was not a careless, random act.

Her melancholy turning to anger, she sprang to her feet. Her hand slowly curled into a fist, and she swung at an open cupboard door. It slammed shut with a loud bang and then popped back open again. Olivia let out a scream. She pounded the door again. This time a stabbing pain shot through her hand. She didn't care. Someone had awakened anger inside her she had never felt before.

Unable to stomach the mess any longer, she headed for the bedroom and continued to vent her feelings. "What the hell were you looking for?" Her voice was loud and resounding, yelling at someone who was invisible, yet becoming very real to her. She grabbed onto one of the posts of the bed for support. "Stay out of our house! You don't belong here. If you found what you were looking for, then stay away!"

Pausing her rant, she sensed someone behind her. Her heart was racing, her adrenalin pumping. She spun around, feeling like her back was against a wall and there was no way out, but she was ready to take on anyone to defend her mother's house.

Colton was standing just inside the front door. Slowly she stepped out into the living area.

"What the hell do you want?" she shrieked.

He looked as if he was unsure how to approach her and kept his distance. "Someone broke in?"

"No! They didn't have to break in because the door was not locked, but they sure made one hell of a mess." Her voice was still loud and full of anger. Her arms flailed. "I have no idea if they took anything. I don't know if they were looking for something in particular, but they've ruined my mother's studio. All of her beautiful photos. All of her work. They've destroyed it! Who does that?" Her heart pounded inside her chest and her mind raced.

"Want me to call the police?"

"Are you serious?" she yelled at him. "What good would that do? They can't even figure out my mother is missing. Forget it! They're not going to be any help." Pausing, she examined his face, her tone of voice turning accusatory. "But maybe you know something about all this." Something in her gut suddenly warned her not to trust him. He seemed to show up at just the right moment.

He tilted his head and searched her face with a puzzled look on his. It appeared the tides had turned and the waters had come crashing in on him unexpectedly, even for a seasoned boat captain.

"Oh yeah. Play innocent. I think you know more about what's going on around here than you're letting on. I don't know what your deal is, but I don't want you here anymore. Just get out!"

Colton leaned backward with his hand raised in defeat. "Olivia, you're obviously upset right now, and you have every right to be. I'd like to help."

"Help! I don't think so. You've done enough. Get out!" She walked closer and pointed an accusatory finger at him, the volume of her voice escalating.

He took a step back. She held her glare.

"All right. I'm out of here. I really do want to help you, Olivia. If you can get this figured out on your own, fine. But when you calm down, give me a call. I'll be happy to give you a hand. And I don't feel comfortable with you staying here by yourself tonight." His eyes were pleading with her.

"Just go!" Her voice was firm and unequivocal, her teeth clenched. He looked hurt, but she didn't care. She didn't trust anyone at the moment . . . especially him.

He stared into her eyes long and hard as if searching for something he hoped was still there and then turned to leave. Olivia was right behind him. As soon as he was through the doorway, she closed the front door and turned the latch on the deadbolt, for the first time, ever.

Flopping down onto the sofa under the front window, Olivia listened as Colton started his Jeep, turned it around, and sped back up the driveway, churning up gravel as he went. The silence that spilled into the little bungalow rang in her ears. She had never felt so alone. There was no one she could trust. Unsure where to turn, she got up and walked over and locked the door that led out to the gallery and then stood there scanning the perimeter of the house through her mind to see if there were any other locks that needed turning. A sinking feeling crept into her gut when she remembered there was no key to lock the door from the outside. At least Olivia could feel safer while she was inside.

Her phone vibrated in her pocket, jolting her body. It was her father, the last person she wanted to talk to at the moment. Rubbing the tension out of her forehead, she decided there wasn't much of a choice.

"Hey, Dad." Olivia tried to keep her voice calm and as upbeat as she could muster.

"Hey, Ollie, how's it going down there?"

She knew she had to be careful what she revealed to him. If it had been a usual evening for him then he undoubtedly had been drinking. It wouldn't take much for him to go over the edge. Determined to handle the situation on her own, she maintained a calm, positive tone. "It's going okay."

"Why, what's going on?"

"Oh, it's not a big deal. There's some paperwork I need to take care of at the police station. It wasn't ready when I stopped in today. I'm going back in the morning. It will be all right. I'll take care of everything," she assured him, sounding too matter-of-fact and casual. She was uncomfortable lying to her father but needed to keep the conversation straightforward, with few details he could latch onto.

"All right, Ol. I know you can handle it. I'm sorry you have to go through this. I'm at O'Hare waiting to get on my next plane to L.A. I'll be away longer than expected. Is your friend, Laurie, bringing in the mail and looking in on Chloe?"

"Yeah, I talked to her earlier today and she's taking care of everything—"

"Okay, great. I appreciate that. Look, I've got to go. I think they're calling my flight now. Keep in touch. Love you." He seemed anxious to break away.

"Love you, too, Dad. I'll call you soon." There was a click on his end before she had finished her sentence.

Olivia wished she could feel as optimistic as she sounded. Unsure what she was in the middle of, her heart was heavy and she felt incredibly alone. She had just blown off the only person she had made a real connection with since she arrived on the island. But as often as Colton appeared, it seemed like more than a coincidence. She could go it alone. She had to.

Stumbling into her mother's bedroom to crash for the night, Olivia flopped onto the edge of the bed, and taking a deep breath, let it out again. Her hands brushed back and forth on the smooth cool surface of the bedding as she contemplated what the next day might bring. Her toes tapped the wood floor while she reviewed recent events. The break-in moved to the forefront. Was it a random robbery? If not, what could they have been looking for? Did they find it? The damage was almost exclusively contained within her mother's studio. Did she interrupt them when she returned from Izzies? Would they return to continue their search? Where else might they want to look in the house? Then she glanced down to where she was sitting.

The bed had been untouched. Had her mother hidden something there? Intrigued by the possibility, Olivia felt compelled to take a look. Leaping off the bed, she spun around toward it, immediately shoving her hand deep between the mattress and box spring. Nothing. Running her hand down to the end of the bed, she frowned. Nothing. Not willing to give up, she continued along the bottom and then around to the other side, running her hand the length of it. Nothing. Had she reached all the way to the middle? Pushing her arm as far into the mattress as she could, the tips of her fingers hit something hard. A tingling sensation ripped through her body. She leaned deeper into the mattress and pushed her arm toward her target. Her fingers wrapped around something cold to the touch and slowly she pulled it out.

CHAPTER NINE

For a moment, *Olivia sat there staring* at the heap of black metal in the palm of her hand. A small pistol. Apparently, her mother's pistol. It didn't make any sense to her. Why would she feel the need to own one? It was all new to her. The tingling sensation in her stomach returned, nervous to be holding a gun for the first time. What did this mean? It was more than Olivia could comprehend so late in the evening. She shoved it back under the mattress and turned to the task of getting ready for bed.

Tomorrow would be another day.

Olivia was up early. Rest hadn't come easily. Too many unsettling, at times frightening, thoughts. She tried to wipe the sleep from her eyes, being careful not to touch her cheek, still sore from her brush with violence the night before. Her head still harbored a dull ache. And even though intuition cautioned her not to take a look, her curiosity got the best of her. Stepping into the small bathroom next to her mother's bedroom, she flipped the switch on the wall. Turning to the right to get a better look, she leaned closer and examined her face carefully. It didn't look as bad as she had expected. Some moderate bruising under her left eye, although she knew it would look worse as the healing progressed.

Her walk from the bedroom to the kitchen reminded her that her mother's little house had been violated. Papers strewn about. Furniture askew. Olivia veered toward the living area to set the coffee table upright. The night before seemed like a distant nightmare. She needed to make a fresh start, find a new direction, preferably without putting herself in danger. Then it hit her she had unceremoniously dismissed Colton in the heat of the moment, suddenly feeling unable to trust him. Why did he seem to walk in at the wrong time?

Pulling together a small breakfast of toast and tea, Olivia remembered the carton of milk she would need for her tea was still in the freezer. Laughing to herself, she pulled it out and reached for a spoon. She chiseled out enough of the icy milk to add to her tea and then tossed the carton back in the freezer, vowing to get around to cleaning out the refrigerated section.

Out on the gallery, it was a bright, pleasant, summer day in the Caribbean with a light breeze. The water on the bay sparkled in the sunlight and the long sandy beach called to her. It had been a while since she'd touched the white sand. Anxious to leave behind the mess in her mother's house, she decided Magens would be where she would start the day.

After making a peanut butter sandwich for later, she filled a thermos bottle with tap water and ice. Looking forward to seeing where the day would take her, she let the screen door shut behind her. First stop, Magens Bay. A five-minute drive away.

The resident sticker on her mother's car got her waved through the gate. She easily found a parking spot since it was early enough in the day that the tourists hadn't arrived yet. Only a few locals.

Practically skipping on her way to the beach, Olivia felt like she was miles away from all the turmoil she had found herself in, and it couldn't catch up to her there. Kicking off her sandals, she snatched them up with a couple of fingers and kept walking toward the water. Soft white sand yielded under her feet and wedged between her toes, not yet scorching from the sun as it would be by midday. The sparkling water was a gradation of beautiful shades of turquoise and aqua. Stunning.

Shaking her head, she realized the camera was still on the little couch by the front door where she had dropped it the night before. Disappointing. The incomparable beauty of the bay would have to wait to be captured another day. Scanning the mountainside, looking for her mother's little cottage up on the hill, she thought it was aptly named. Serenity Villa. The view out to Magens Bay was certainly a source of serenity, and she yearned to become part of what she was gazing at.

A couple walked leisurely along the water. A few swimmers swam along the shore, and a young boy threw something into the water for what looked like a black lab mix. It was early enough for the dog to be on the beach before the lifeguards showed up and the rules kicked in. The dog tore after the toy and retrieved it with such exuberance Olivia stood and watched them for a moment. The boy and his furry companion seemed to have a special relationship. Something not always seen on the islands. Not everyone viewed dogs as companions, but instead as possessions and, on occasion, were discarded at will. When times were tough, it was the dogs that suffered, often abandoned on the streets, referred to as throwaway dogs. Olivia was pleased to see this happy dog. He was one of the lucky ones. She pictured the local shelter brimming with not-so-happy animals rescued from deplorable conditions, waiting to be adopted and loved.

Olivia squirmed from an uncomfortable pang in her gut. She had wanted a dog as long as she could recall. Her father detested the idea of having a pet. After enduring much cajoling, he finally agreed to a kitten years earlier, figuring a cat would be easier to care for than a dog. Olivia had to agree to take full responsibility for the four-legged critter and, while she had embraced the responsibility and loved her beautiful Siamese with all her heart, she held a deep yearning for the companionship of a dog.

A passing thought intrigued her. With the situation she was in, it could be useful to have a dog. For comfort and companionship but potentially for protection, too. In a fleeting moment she considered visiting the St. Thomas animal shelter. At least it was fun trying on the idea for size.

Taking a seat on the sand with her knees pulled close to her and her arms wrapped around them, she continued to watch the boy and his dog. Appearing to be around ten years old, the young child had light skin and straight brown, neatly trimmed hair that flopped loosely as he jumped and ran. He clapped his hands with excitement as the dog retrieved the toy and galloped back toward him, splashing water in his wake.

Noticing some snorkelers off to the right side of the bay, Olivia flashed back to a day trip she and her mother had taken several years earlier to St. John. They drove her Jeep to Red Hook, put it on the ferry, and took the twenty-minute ride to the U.S. Virgin Island that was two-thirds national park. Once the ferry docked at Enighed Pond outside of Cruz Bay, they headed over to Trunk Bay, a popular place for snorkeling with an underwater trail marked with points of interest. As in the rest of the Caribbean, the water was crystal clear. The placards could be read easily. After an unforgettable experience snorkeling together, the afternoon was topped off by a ride around the island on the meandering, circuitous roads, past several other picturesque bays until they eventually found their way back to the ferry. They enjoyed an early dinner at one of the small family-run yet highly-acclaimed restaurants in town and then returned to St. Thomas. For Olivia, the day had come to an end far too soon but was etched in her memory forever.

Sensing someone approaching from her left, Olivia noticed the couple had returned from their walk down the beach. The way they had their eyes on the boy suggested a connection between them. Parents? They called to him and he waved but quickly returned to playing with his dog. They didn't appear to be in a hurry and let the pair continue to frolic in the blue water of the bay.

Olivia spoke from behind the parents. "They look like they're best friends."

The couple turned in unison. The father seemed eager to engage her. "Yes, they really are."

Standing up, Olivia brushed the sand from her backside and walked the few yards that separated them to allow a conversation without raising their voices. "Are you guys from around here?"

The woman glanced sideways at the man, looking for him to respond.

"Yes, actually, we are. Not originally, of course. We moved here a couple years ago. My work brought us here."

It seemed as though he didn't want to elaborate, as if it was a bone of contention between the couple. But then he continued. "This dog has been a lifesaver for us. Our Jeremy," he motioned toward the water, "didn't handle the move well. He is mildly autistic, and the dramatic change was almost too much for him to handle."

"Almost?" the wife piped in, sounding cynical. She looked tired with dark circles under her eyes.

The man grimaced but continued. "He had made such progress with his therapy back in the States, to the point where he could be mainstreamed into the classroom with all the other kids. You could tell he was proud of himself and happy. Then we made this move and his world caved in. He regressed and didn't want to go to school at all. Someone suggested getting a dog for him and, honestly, we didn't know if we could handle caring for a dog on top of our challenges with Jeremy. We'd never had one before so we were resistant to the idea. Finally, we stopped into the humane society to find out more about it. Turns out we could foster a dog on a trial basis to see if it could work for us. With no commitment to keep the dog, we took the next step and looked at what they had available. We were stunned by the sheer number of eyes staring into ours, begging us to save them. It was heartbreaking."

As he took a moment to reflect, his wife took over the dialogue. "What I found amazing was the number of black dogs there were. Apparently black dogs are less likely to get adopted than lighter-colored dogs. They told us it's called 'Black Dog Syndrome.' I think that's terrible. It's like racism for dogs."

Her husband chuckled at her comment. "That's one way of looking at it." Resuming his story, he shifted his feet in the sand.

"We brought our son back to see a few dogs we had identified as a possible match. He didn't seem interested at first. In fact, he was overwhelmed by the noise of all the animals in unison. A lot were barking for attention and pawing at the front of their cages. We thought we had made a huge mistake. But when Jeremy met this sweet pup, he was sitting there not making a sound. Seemed very timid. Jeremy walked right up to the cage and the dog leaned toward him. Sniffed his hand. Jeremy started talking to him and the two quickly bonded. We knew he was the one we were going to bring home. We've had our fingers crossed, but that day was a year and a half ago."

Olivia couldn't help but feel delighted at the conclusion of Jeremy's story. She loved happy endings. "That's awesome. Good to hear."

The father appeared to blush. "Wow, I'm sure that was much more information than you wanted to hear. Sorry, I get ecstatic when we have successes like this with him. This was huge for us."

"Of course it was. No worries. Thanks for sharing with me."

"Look, we've talked your ear off. We'll let you get back to enjoying the beach." With that dismissal, they exchanged farewells and the couple continued their walk toward the other end of the beach.

Olivia sat back down and breathed in the salty sea air, listening to the stillness of the bay. There were no waves to speak of, only the gentle sound of water lapping on the beach as it crept up toward the high water mark and then quickly retreated. Wanting to listen to what she needed to hear from within, she tried to clear her head. She sat completely still, becoming one with her surroundings. Listening.

Unaware of the time that had passed, her focus was broken by a jogger crossing her line of sight. She blinked a few times and looked around, noticing the beach was filling up. It looked like there must be a couple cruise ships docked in town.

Olivia started off on a walk to the quieter south end of the beach, turning back from time to time to check on Jeremy and his canine buddy. She returned to the couple's experience at the shelter. Perhaps she would stop in and check out all of the black dogs.

As she walked along the edge of the bay, subtle waves gently grabbed at her feet, tempting her to walk deeper into the clear turquoise water. Before long she found herself at the end of the beach. Movement to her left caught her eye. A typically elusive mongoose scampered for shelter under the mangroves. Not an unusual sighting, but certainly not common.

Turning back to retrace her steps, she noticed the couple she had spoken with earlier was standing ankle deep, talking to their son and motioning for him to come out of the water. Time was up for dogs on the beach. A lifeguard with red swim trunks, a whistle, and some sort of flotation device tucked under his arm stood nearby, his stance projecting a position of authority. She continued her walk as the threesome and their furry black companion meandered up the beach toward the parking lot with no particular sense of urgency, the young boy scattering sand with his bare feet and slipping farther behind with each step.

Olivia returned to the point where she had entered the beach, but she kept going toward the north end to complete the loop. Her thoughts were scattered as she tried to sort out what had transpired since she arrived on the island.

It was a mystery to her why the police had no knowledge of what had happened to her mother. How could she have disappeared on such a small island, and no one seemed to know about it? And why did someone break into her home? Was it just a random break-in? If not, what were they looking for and did they find it? Who was CK and would he or she know what was going on? The more time she spent thinking about the situation, the more uncomfortable she felt. She had no idea who she was dealing with. Having a dog as a companion didn't seem like such a stretch of the imagination, but from a practical standpoint, she wondered if she would be able to transport it back to Boston with her.

Reaching the end of the beach, Olivia turned to head back toward the car. Several more beachgoers had trickled in and were spread out along the mile-long beach but still had plenty of room in between. Locating the nearest foot shower, she washed off as much of the beach as she could before putting the sandals back on, her wet feet slipping on the soles.

A few yards away, leaning casually against one of the grand palm trees along the beach, a man who appeared to be from the islands watched her as she prepared to leave.

CHAPTER TEN

Leaving beautiful *Magens Bay behind*, with every intention of returning again with her camera, she urged the Jeep up over the mountain on her way back downtown. On a whim and for curiosity's sake, Olivia took a slight detour and stopped into The Humane Society of St. Thomas. Successfully locating their new location on Weymouth Rhymer Highway, she pulled into the parking lot. Unexpectedly, Olivia's stomach twisted into knots at the prospect of a furry friend she might find there. She was torn. Although she longed for a loyal four-legged companion that could be at her side and help to protect her, the responsibility was a bit overwhelming. What if she couldn't spend the time necessary to care for a dog? She had only cared for a cat in the past. And while she had done a good job with her beautiful Siamese, a dog required much more effort. Yet the possibilities pulled her inside. As she was drawn in by the sound of incessant barking, a grin crossed her face. The anticipation was exciting.

Pulling open the glass door with the humane society's logo on the top panel, she wrinkled her nose as a sour odor hit her in the face. The air was somewhat cooler than outside, circulating from fans sitting at either end of the counter. Dogs barked loudly out of sight.

A young dark-skinned girl greeted her sweetly. After Olivia asked about adoption, the girl excused herself, slipping through a door to the left of the counter, most likely the way to the kennel. Moments later an older woman, who looked like she could be the young girl's mother, stepped through the door with the girl right behind her. She introduced herself as the person standing in for the director and asked how she could help. Upon learning Olivia was interested in adopting a dog, she handed her an application and told her she would have to fill it out and submit it for approval.

Olivia flipped though the multi-page form with a furrowed brow. Seemed overly complicated. All she wanted to do was to rescue an unfortunate creature from dismal circumstances, and they were looking for her life history and references. Sorely disappointed, Olivia thanked her and asked if she could at least take a look at the dogs available. The woman apologized and said it wasn't a good time. They were doing a thorough cleaning and encouraged her to stop back again.

Feeling as though she was being shooed away, Olivia frowned and walked slowly toward the door, a sinking feeling in her stomach. The hot, humid outside air hit her in the face but smelled a lot better than the shelter. On the short walk back to the Jeep, she confessed she had been naïve thinking she could simply walk in and pick out a dog to take home, but it didn't make her feel any better. Climbing back into the car, she tossed the form onto the passenger seat.

Returning downtown, she remembered she still needed to stop into the police station to file a missing persons report. After pulling the Jeep into a lot around the corner from the waterfront, Olivia marched toward the front door of the police station, determined to have a more productive visit than last time. As she reached for the handle, a young attractive male police officer pushed through the door from the other side and then held the door for her to pass. She hesitated for a moment and then walked through, grinning at the gesture. Chivalry wasn't dead, it just rarely made public appearances anymore.

Her feet stopped abruptly inside. Long line. Lunch hour. The air was hot. Many people were waiting patiently and she prayed the calm would last. Considering leaving and coming back later, she dismissed the reckless notion and dug down deep to find her patience.

After several uncomfortably sticky minutes inching along in line, watching an oscillating fan near the ceiling push the hot air around, Olivia finally reached the front and explained why she was there. She was told she would have to fill out a report and then get back in line to file it. With a wry smile she tried to take it all in stride. Had she really expected anything else? She took the form with her, vowing to fill it out once she got back to her mother's house. Returning to her mother's Jeep, she tossed it on the seat next to her, on top of the humane society form.

Heading back up the mountain, her stomach growled in protest. She glanced over to the soggy peanut butter sandwich lying lifeless on the passenger seat and the corners of her mouth turned down. It looked incredibly unappetizing. Although she didn't want to eat it, she didn't have much choice. Of course, eating it while navigating her way up the hill was not an option.

After ascending the mountainous road and sliding through the tricky intersection, Olivia steered the Jeep down Route 40 and then down the side street. As she pulled into her mother's driveway, she tapped the brakes. A car down below, parked next to the house, made her heart skip a beat. Easing the Jeep to the bottom of the hill, she surveyed the grounds and checked inside the car. No one was in sight. Olivia's stomach tightened. She slowly pulled in next to the unfamiliar vehicle, threw hers into park, and turned off the engine. Quietly she slipped out of her car, leaving the door ajar so as not to attract any more attention to her arrival than was necessary. As she walked past the faded navy blue Ford Explorer, she peered inside the vehicle and then scanned the yard back and forth and studied the windows of the bungalow for movement. Cautiously she inched toward the front door, glancing all around her. Feeling extremely vulnerable, she asked herself if she dared to enter the house. Were they lying in wait? Images of the previous night's break-in flashed through her mind. After climbing the front steps, she reached out and grabbed the door handle, hesitating to listen for a moment. She stood up straighter and stiffened her back, readying herself to confront whoever was in her mother's house. As she squeezed the handle, a voice came from the side yard.

"Oh, Olivia, there you are!" Her lilting, effervescent voice broke the tension.

Olivia turned toward Sarah, still hanging tightly onto the door handle. The Realtor she had met the night before made her way around the side of the house, running her hand along the green, healthy bushes as she meandered.

Relief flooded through Olivia as her shoulders relaxed and the rest of her body followed suit. "Sarah, good to see you." Embarrassed she had forgotten Sarah was stopping by, Olivia acknowledged she was partially in denial the house had to be sold. She descended the front steps and the two women walked toward each other.

Sarah stopped in her tracks a few feet from Olivia and raised her eyebrows. "Wow, you ended up with quite a black eye from last night, didn't you?"

Taking a step backward, Olivia turned away from her. "Oh, it's not as bad as I was expecting."

"Suppose it could always be worse. The good news is it will heal."

Olivia snickered to herself. "Yeah."

"Hope you don't mind. I was taking a look around outside until you got back."

"Oh, no problem at all. Make yourself at home." Olivia realized she said that far too often.

"Looks like a really cute bungalow. Can't wait to see the inside."

Sarah's enthusiasm bothered Olivia. It was happening too quickly. She couldn't bear the idea of letting go of her mother's house. The cold cruel reality of the matter was it had to be done. And the responsibility lay squarely on her young shoulders.

"Absolutely." She pretended to be enthusiastic.

"So tell me what your situation is. You mentioned last night this is your mother's house, but you couldn't keep it going any longer. What's going on?" Sarah looked to Olivia to fill in the blanks.

Olivia hesitated and the question hung in the air, pressing her for an answer. It wasn't an easy one to tackle, but she knew she needed to level with the agent. Her feelings were still raw, though, and it was difficult for her to talk about it. Finally, she found her voice.

"My mother passed away recently."

Sarah's face fell and the palm of her hand found its way to her heart.

"Yeah, it was a complete shock." Olivia explained how she and her father received a phone call informing them her mother had perished, how her parents were divorced and her father had no interest in keeping the property.

"And how do you feel about it?"

"Oh, God," she gushed. "I would love to be able to keep it. I adore my mother and I loved being here with her. I would love to move in and build a photography career like she did or at least be able to come once in a while. I just can't afford that right now. It's not possible." Blinking to fight back the tears, she searched for something in the trees to focus on.

"I am sorry, Olivia. . . . You know, maybe this is too soon for you." Sarah clearly was prepared to bow out and let her have the space and time she needed.

"No." Olivia paused for a moment. "No. Unfortunately I don't have much time on the island, and I need to get this taken care of." The harsh reality nudged her further than she really wanted to go.

"Okay. Let's take a look inside, and then we can talk about your options."

"Absolutely," Olivia said, trying to sound more convincing than she felt, turning to head back to the front door. As soon as she stepped inside with the Realtor at her heels, the sight of the vandalism from the night before made her stop short.

"Oh, no." Sarah's eyes quickly scanned the inside of the modest home, resting momentarily on upturned furniture and scattered personal items.

"Oh, yeah. Apparently I had a visitor last night while I was out."

"What?" Sarah looked genuinely concerned for her. She examined the room more closely.

"Yeah, I found this when I got in. They made such a mess."

"Did they take anything?"

"Oh . . ." Olivia pursed her lips in disgust. "I have no way of knowing. I don't know what my mother had." She reached down and picked up the soggy bag of water that used to be ice and tossed it across the room, landing it in the center of the kitchen sink.

Sarah nodded in silence, acknowledging she understood. "Did you call the police?"

Olivia didn't want to get into specifics about it. "Yeah, I've been in touch with them," she fibbed in an attempt to move along the conversation.

"I'm sorry, Olivia."

"Thanks." Her voice was barely audible.

The two scrutinized the mess in silence for a moment.

"I didn't take the time to pick it all up yet. I can't stand looking at it."

"I can imagine. Would you like some help?"

"Oh, that's sweet of you but I'll handle it myself."

The agent walked over and placed her hand on top of one of the upturned upholstered chairs. "How about if I help you with these, at least."

"Yeah, that would be good." Olivia chuckled as she pictured herself trying to lift the two bulky chairs without any help. "Thanks."

Once they righted the two mismatched, well-worn chairs, they wound their way through the little bungalow as Olivia embellished the guided tour with colorful anecdotes and pleasant memories, tidying the mess as they moved along. Sarah commented on all the positive features she noticed that would make the house desirable to buyers. She remarked on how well maintained the property appeared to be, inside and out, the surprising size of the lot, the incredible view and how tastefully, albeit simply, the home was decorated.

Olivia chortled inside. Her agent was being rather generous describing her mother's house as tastefully decorated.

Sarah elaborated that it was much better when the décor was simple. That way, buyers weren't distracted by the sellers' personal taste and could picture themselves living in the house.

"As you might expect, there are a lot of homes listed for sale, and in a dizzying range of conditions. Properties in such good shape like this one will sell much more quickly than those that are not, especially if they are priced right."

Olivia tried to push away the raw pain. The idea of her mother's bungalow selling quickly and suddenly no longer hers to enjoy was heartbreaking.

Sarah cut her spiel short when she noticed Olivia struggling. "I'm sorry, obviously this is hard for you."

"It *is* hard," she acknowledged. Her head swayed back and forth slowly.

"I can only imagine." Sarah's face was contemplative. She hesitated for a moment, seeming to examine Olivia's eyes and then continued. "On the positive side, what you have is a solid piece of property that would be very desirable to buyers. It could sell quickly. Of course, speed is relative in a market with listings that languish for months, sometimes years."

"Years?"

"Well, yes. Those are properties that are not priced properly, where the sellers have insisted on a particular listing price and aren't being realistic in their expectations and/or they're not in a hurry to sell so it doesn't matter to them if the property sits for a while. They think if they wait long enough, the right buyer will come along who is willing to pay their asking price, or at least close to it."

Fighting her emotions, Olivia listened patiently to her words.

"There is another option to selling you might be interested in."

Olivia perked up. She was listening.

"You could rent it out."

Her eyes grew wide.

"Olivia, there is such a strong rental market on the island, you could keep the house. It would be available when you wanted to come down and then rent it when you're not here."

A slight smile tugged at the edge of her mouth. Olivia saw the possibilities in what Sarah was saying. "Brilliant."

"And I could take care of the logistics for you. Renters could check in with my office to get a key. I could arrange for a housekeeper to go in after each renter has checked out. The rental income could offset your expenses. Do you know if your mother had a mortgage on the place or if she owned it outright?"

Olivia paused for a moment. She didn't know. She wasn't privy to her mother's finances.

Sarah continued. "Either way, you could probably cover your expenses with rent on a place like this."

Olivia liked the sound of the proposition. A whole new realm of possibilities opened up to her that she hadn't realized before. Then her father's predictable objections came to mind and her hopes were quickly dashed. He certainly wouldn't be interested in the possibility of hanging onto the place. Olivia would have to evaluate her options.

At least she had options. She loved the way Sarah's mind worked and how she conducted business.

"Sarah, would you like a glass of wine? We could have one out on the gallery. You could really appreciate the view out to Magens Bay." She couldn't keep from wrinkling her nose as her suggestion sounded a bit trite, like a pick-up line.

"I'd love to."

To Olivia's relief, Sarah sounded pleased at the offer.

"Awesome. Let me grab a bottle. Do you prefer red or white?"

"Oh, I'm not particular. Whatever you'd like . . . or whatever you have open."

It crossed Olivia's mind that their age difference made it feel almost like she was having a drink with her mother. She wished she *could* have a drink with her mother.

Olivia pulled out the bottle of red she had opened the night she first arrived. After apologizing for not having wine glasses, she led the way onto the gallery to relax at the small table and chairs. Sipping the Merlot, they watched the sun dip in the sky. The breezes off the bay were refreshing. Their eyes followed a solitary boat silently slicing through the water as it headed toward the beach.

Feeling the effects of wine on an empty stomach, Olivia's thoughts returned to the night before at Izzies and how grateful she was to have met Sarah at the bar. Shaking her head, she pictured Colton's face later in the evening when she dismissed him abruptly in the heat of the moment. Turning her focus back to her mother, she broke the silence to re-engage with Sarah.

"Sarah, can I ask you something?"

"Sure."

"Did you know my mother, by any chance? Liv Benning?"

"I've definitely heard of her. I don't know if I've met her, though. I understand she's a talented photographer."

Olivia beamed with pride.

"She has some beautiful work displayed in a gallery downtown. A friend of mine is the owner."

Recalling her recent visit to the art gallery, she smiled. "Yes, I stopped in there yesterday. There were so many talented artists represented. I would love to have my work displayed there some day."

"Olivia, what happened to your mother?" Sarah's voice softened. "That is, if you don't mind me asking."

Olivia's face fell. She was unsure how much she wanted to divulge. "It's a little complicated. Apparently there was a boating accident."

"I'm sorry."

"Yeah . . ." Olivia fell silent, holding her gaze on a remote spot out to sea, somewhere beyond the peninsula.

No words were spoken for a while.

Draining the last sip of wine from her glass, Sarah stood up slowly, taking in one last look at the panoramic view. The breeze tossed her hair about and she brushed it back with one hand. "Look, I'm going to get busy doing some digging. I'll look up some comps and work up some numbers for you. I'll put together what I would recommend for a list price but also what you could ask for rentals. You'll have options, okay?"

Olivia perked up and stood to see her agent out. "Sounds good. Thank you for your time."

"Oh, my pleasure. Your mother's place is such a gem. I could definitely get it sold. It's such an adorable bungalow in such a great location. But I certainly understand if you want to hang on to it."

Olivia cringed on the inside, knowing her father would be extremely upset if he knew she was considering holding onto Serenity Villa and renting it out. Figuring there was no harm in finding out what her options were, she was elated at the possibility as she walked Sarah to her car.

"Thanks again. I appreciate it."

Sarah reached out and hugged her. It felt good. Olivia might have held on longer than she should have, but Sarah didn't let go until she did. Finally they stepped back but Sarah held onto one shoulder.

"I'm so sorry for your loss, Olivia, but I'm glad we bumped into each other last night."

"Same," she whispered, forcing a contented look that took more effort than usual, sad to see Sarah go. Perhaps her Realtor would turn out to be a good friend, someone she could trust. She hoped so but wasn't ready to let down her guard completely. Not yet.

As Olivia watched the Explorer disappear through the robust greenery, her mother's mailbox caught her eye. Charging up the hill on foot, she wondered what it might hold. How long had mail been piling up inside? As she reached the crest of the steep hill, the muscles in her thighs began to burn.

The mailbox was a rounded rectangular box of battered metal that used to be white. It was mounted sideways on a four-by-four, wooden, unpainted post, parallel to the street. She tugged on the latch and the door did not give easily. She tugged harder and the stubborn door finally gave way. To her surprise, it was empty. She stared at it for a moment, bent over to look closely inside and ran a hand across the bottom of it all the way to the back wall to be sure. Nothing. She furrowed her brow and pushed out her bottom lip. Disappointed, she slammed the mailbox door shut and retreated back down the driveway. It didn't make sense. No bills. Did she pay them all electronically? Not even any junk mail or flyers.

Olivia felt a vibration in her pocket and pulled out her phone. It was a text from Colton. Though still feeling guilty for snapping at him the night before, she was annoyed by his intrusion and wanted him to stay out of her way and let her handle it.

|| Olivia don't forget to file the missing persons report. ||

She stared blankly at the words and then shoved her phone back in her pocket without responding.

Reaching her mother's Jeep, she remembered she had left some things in her car when she quickly exited earlier, so she walked around to the passenger side. As she reached for the door handle, her pocket vibrated again. Olivia closed her eyes briefly, trying to control her emotions. She pulled her phone out and wasn't surprised it was Colton again.

|| The police won't do anything to investigate your mother's disappearance unless you file it. They can't. ||

Breathing in deeply and exhaling slowly, she knew he was right. She hated to admit it, but she certainly wasn't about to let him know. Before she could put her phone away, it vibrated again.

"*What?*" she yelled in exasperation. Olivia wanted him to butt out.

|| I know you don't want to hear from me but please listen anyway. ☺ ||

Olivia did a double take. Was there really a smiley face at the end of his last text? Seriously? It put a smile on her face she tried to wipe off, but just couldn't.

"Damn it, Colton." She wanted to stay angry but felt herself give in. "I can handle this," she insisted out loud. But deep down she knew she wasn't, and perhaps she couldn't. She didn't even have her next steps planned out. The last thing she wanted to do was to go crawling back to him, but he could be someone who could help her. Her time was limited not only by the amount of money she had, but her father would be expecting her to get it all wrapped up and return home soon. She hated to concede, but she needed help. At a loss for where to turn next, she felt overwhelmed.

Olivia reached into the car and retrieved the forms from the humane society and the police station along with her lukewarm water bottle and the soggy peanut butter sandwich. The latter of which was certainly not edible after spending a good part of the day in the car. Even if it was, she wasn't interested in it.

Heading inside, she dropped the forms on the kitchen counter, the water bottle in the sink, and the soggy mess in the trash can. She considered the missing persons report and deemed it a priority. Rummaging through the kitchen drawers, she pulled out a pen. At first it was stubborn and wouldn't work, but she banged it against the counter a few times, scribbling on the back of the humane society application in between whacks. Finally it rolled out ink. Compartmentalizing her mother's narrative into a bunch of lines on a form seemed totally inadequate. She'd have to talk with someone when she dropped it off so she could fill in the rest of the story.

When she reached the bottom, she vowed to take it right back down the mountain. It crossed her mind that every time she took off in the Jeep, though, she was burning costly fuel that would have to be replaced at some point. She needed to make her trips more efficient. After this one.

Her stomach's grumbling signaled her body had already absorbed her light breakfast and was looking for more, but she ignored it and returned to the Jeep with a fresh water bottle in hand. Before long, she was sailing back down the mountain toward Charlotte Amalie Harbor. A sizable cruise ship was docked at Havensight in the distance. Black smoke billowed from a broad red column near its stern and wafted away, dissipating as if it had never existed.

At the bottom of the hill, Olivia found a spot for the Jeep on a side street and strode down the sidewalk to the police station, hoping to portray an air of confidence. Only a couple of people were in line in front of her this time. She waited patiently but felt anxious about making a third appearance. There was something about the place that made her nervous.

Finally she reached the counter and was relieved to see the person standing behind it in his crisp blue short-sleeved uniform shirt was not Officer Barnes. Yet he had a familiar face. Perhaps she had seen him on one of her previous two visits. He seemed pleasant enough but only wanted to take the form from her.

"Could I just talk with someone who could help me?"

"Ma'am, we have your form. It will be reviewed, and someone will get in touch with you."

Olivia's shoulders drooped and she let out a long, exasperated exhale. Why did such an urgent situation get turned into something so routine? How many missing persons did they have in a day . . . or even a week? A month, for that matter. Disappointed, she stormed back out to the street, teeth clenched and a frown on her face.

It wasn't long before she felt as though someone was following along behind her. She quickened her step, trying to get to her car as quickly as possible. She grabbed the door handle, jumped in, and started it right up. Before she could back out of the spot, a face appeared abruptly and leaned in at the driver's window.

"Hey, Miss Benning."

Her eyes grew wide and she turned to see the rookie cop who had stopped by the house twice and gathered fingerprints on her mother's car.

"Yes?"

"Look, I probably shouldn't be talking to you about this, but I know you're trying to find your mother . . . or at least find out what might have happened to her . . . and . . . well, I can sympathize with what you're going through right now." He shuffled his feet nervously. "I talked with my older brother, who is a doctor and fills in from time to time in the coroner's office when they need him."

Olivia listened intently, anxious to hear where this was going.

"He said there haven't been any—" He hesitated, apparently realizing he needed to choose his words carefully in such a delicate matter. "—victims of any type of boating accident brought in lately. It's been rather quiet."

"Really?" A wave of relief coursed through her and tingling reached the tips of her fingers. Deep down she could feel her mother was still alive. Of course, if she was, then where was she? "Thanks, I appreciate you making the effort to look into that for me." She pondered for a moment as to where that left her. "I hate to ask, but where do I go from here?" She looked into his eyes and estimated he was about her age. Probably just beginning his career in law enforcement, trying to do his best but lacking the experience necessary to help her. At least his heart was in the right place. She appreciated his effort, his good intentions.

He shifted his eyes toward the pavement. "I . . . I don't know. I wish I knew what to tell you. You filed a missing persons report, right?"

"Yeah." Not that she expected anything to come of it.

"If I hear anything I could let you know, but I have to be careful. This is my first job and I can't blow it."

"I understand completely, and I wouldn't want you to jeopardize your job to help me. I certainly appreciate where your heart is. You're a good man."

The rookie cop shifted his stance and blushed.

Olivia wiggled uncomfortably on the inside at her comment but pressed further. "Let me give you my number in case something does come up that would help me locate my mother." She wrote her number down on the corner of one of the takeout menus from the glove compartment and tore it off. She had no sooner handed it to him than he disappeared without a sound.

Sitting still for a moment, she contemplated her next move. Should she be encouraged there were no bodies at the local morgue that needed identifying? Perhaps nothing had washed up yet. Appalled she was thinking of her mother that way, she surmised she had to be realistic. Olivia was no further along than she had been before the rookie cop paid her an unexpected visit. She applauded his efforts, though.

As Olivia listened to the engine idling, she tried to listen to her gut. Deciding to take a walk back to the waterfront, she cut the engine. Something was pulling her there.

CHAPTER ELEVEN

Leaving her car parked along the curb, she took a walk down the block toward the harbor. On her way past the police station, she glanced at the lot across the street where all the police cars were parked. The lot was nearly full. Puzzled, she wondered why more cars weren't out and about on the island. Shouldn't they be "serving and protecting," or whatever their motto was?

Reaching the busy thoroughfare that ran along the waterfront, Olivia waited for the light to change so she could cross to the other side safely. A young boy on the sidewalk peddled water bottles from a basket on his bike. The large cruise ship docked across the harbor at Havensight dwarfed everything else around it.

Crossing the street and turning right, Olivia found it comforting to be near the water. There was something about the salty sea breeze on her face and the mesmerizing turquoise water as it lapped against the wall along the edge. Olivia imagined during tropical storms or, worse, hurricanes, waves crashed up over the sidewalk and covered the road, flooding the stores along the waterfront.

Pausing to gaze past Hassel Island out to the open ocean, her thoughts were with her mother. What had happened? What terrible fate had she met? Or was she still out there somewhere? Pain tugged at her gut, which ached from loneliness.

The low vibrating sound of a ferry grew louder as it crossed the harbor. It looked like it was going to dock not far down the waterfront from her. She resumed walking and picked up her pace with the intention of meeting it. The buzz of a seaplane taking off diverted her attention momentarily as it built up speed and took off up over the harbor, banking south as if it was heading to St. Croix.

The ferry pulled up alongside the sidewalk, demonstrating it was, indeed, a relatively deep port. As she approached, a dozen passengers disembarked, some with rolling luggage, others less encumbered. Olivia patiently waited until everyone was off before she walked up to a young crew member at his post alongside the boat. He was dressed in a white short-sleeved shirt and pants that hung on his small frame like they were a half size too large.

"Excuse me."

"Yes, ma'am." He turned his head toward her abruptly, looking slightly startled.

"Could I have a word with your captain?"

For a split second, his face fell. It didn't look like he was confident he could make that happen. He glanced at his watch as if they were on a tight schedule.

"It would just take a moment."

The young skipper considered her request. "All right, follow me."

He turned and led the way onto the boat, and Olivia followed him up to the bridge where the captain talked with another crew member. Quickly ending their conversation, they turned to their unexpected visitor. The two subordinate crew members excused themselves, leaving Olivia to talk with the captain, who was also dressed in a crisp white uniform, except his had more bars on the pocket of his short-sleeved shirt. His shiny gold name tag read "Capt. John Mason," and he certainly looked the part of a boat captain with his deeply suntanned skin and wire-rimmed sunglasses. He stepped away from the controls, removed his sunglasses, and laid his eyes upon her kindly like a proud father gazing upon his daughter. He looked to be in his mid to late forties.

"Afternoon." He extended his right hand and they shook. "Captain Mason."

She was close enough to smell a slight aroma of aftershave, which was unexpected.

"Afternoon, it's Olivia."

"To what do I owe the pleasure, Olivia?" He seemed overly pleased to greet her.

"Listen, I just need to ask you a question." She needed to get right down to business.

"Sure." He examined her face more closely.

Olivia hesitated, contemplating how to broach the subject. "I'm not exactly sure where to begin."

The captain squinted his eyes and cocked his head as if he were sizing her up.

"You see . . ." She pursed her lips and took a quick breath inward. Finally she blurted it out. "Are you aware of any boating accidents in the last couple of weeks or so?"

"Boating accidents?"

"Yeah. Either in the U.S. Virgin Islands or the BVI."

He considered her question. "What kind of a boat? Commercial? Private? Small craft?"

"I'm not exactly sure."

The captain looked intently at her. "I haven't heard of anything recently, but if it's a small craft, word of that might not necessarily get around quickly."

She listened to him closely. Every word. None of them helpful.

"What's going on? Why do you think there may have been an accident?"

Olivia could sense movement behind her and felt anxious that new passengers were boarding the ferry for the return trip to wherever it had come from. She decided to use that to cut the conversation short before it got too personal.

"Look, I don't want to hold you up. You have a schedule to stick to, and I know I am keeping you from your work." She gestured to the passengers filling the rows of hard white wooden benches behind her and turned to make her exit, but the captain had one final word.

"I'm sorry I couldn't be more help."

She turned back to thank him.

"You could try checking with the Coast Guard."

"The Coast Guard?" Her face brightened.

"Yeah." He pointed east. "They're right on the water, just past Vendors' Plaza on the right. Across from the fort. They might be able to help you."

Of course, the Coast Guard. She had forgotten they were stationed on St. Thomas. She thanked the captain for his help and slowly pushed her way off the boat, squeezing past oncoming passengers, feeling a bit like a salmon swimming upstream.

After thanking the young man who had returned to his post on the starboard side, she followed the sidewalk along the waterfront toward the Coast Guard station, which she had passed on many occasions but never had a reason to notice before. It was a white, nondescript one-story brick building with dark blue shutters and faded red metal roof that sat next to the harbor, nestled among a few hardy tees. It was secured by a plain wrought iron fence along the front and chain link fencing around the remaining sides that stood in sharp contrast with the decorative iron fence surrounding the stately legislative building next door. A sliding chain link gate closed off the entrance to a small parking area on the right side of the building.

Just before reaching the Coast Guard station, Olivia's pocket vibrated again. She pulled out her phone without slowing her gait. Another text from Colton.

"Yes, Colton?" She spoke out loud to no one in particular. A tone of exasperation in her voice.

|| Olivia, can we meet somewhere? ||

Olivia bit her lip. She didn't want to deal with him, but she had a nagging feeling he might have some information she could use. Whatever it was could wait.

Setting foot onto the USCG property, Olivia passed an official-looking sign out front that read UNITED STATES COAST GUARD, MARINE SAFETY DETACHMENT, ST THOMAS USVI. It gave her a notably different feeling from the police station. Slowing her step as she neared the wide metal gate, a small car approached from inside and the gate slowly slid to the right. After the car exited but before the gate closed again, Olivia slipped inside and darted toward the entrance.

Once inside the Coast Guard station, she welcomed the refreshing blast of cool air on her face. Her stomach tightened at the prospect that they might be able to help her. She approached a young, light-skinned man who sat erect behind a desk. Ensign Ryan, his nametag read.

"Oh!" Clearly she was an unexpected visitor, particularly one who had slipped in through the closing gate. "Afternoon, ma'am."

Ma'am? Did she look like a ma'am? She didn't feel like one. They appeared to be about the same age.

"Afternoon."

"What can I do for you?" His blond hair was trimmed close to his head, and his eyes were a deep brown. Darker than any she had ever seen before. His trim and fit body looked almost uncomfortable inside the crisp white shirt that had been pressed neatly with creases along the sides of the short sleeves. She imagined the pants had similar crisp creases plunging down the front of the legs.

Olivia hesitated. She didn't have much information to give him, but she had to at least try. "I'm looking for my mother."

He opened his mouth to speak but closed it again, and an inquisitive look crept onto his face.

"What I mean is . . . I think there was a boating accident and my mother was involved." She shifted her stance slightly as her shaky assertion hadn't come out quite right.

The ensign furrowed his brow. "I see."

Olivia introduced herself and continued to fill him in on the phone call she and her father had received, her discussions with the local police, and the missing persons report she had filed.

The ensign listened carefully and then creased his lips tightly. "Miss Benning, I'm not aware of any boating accident in the Virgin Islands within the last couple of weeks."

Olivia tilted her head and fluttered her eyelashes in rapid succession. She'd had her fill of hearing that response. Her demeanor turned abruptly.

"*Look!*" Her tone was loud and emphatic. Two other guardsmen, who had been talking discreetly at the back of the room, glanced toward the sound of her voice. "I don't care if you haven't heard anything about it." She was pleased she sounded firm and in control. "You need to help me find out what happened to my mother. It doesn't matter that I don't have any specific facts to give you. Clearly she is missing. The police have the report I filed and their jurisdiction is on the island. Yours is in the water around it. I expect the Coast Guard to investigate." She glared without blinking.

"Ma'am, we need to be able to justify sending manpower—"

"Don't you *dare* call it a wild goose chase!" She thrust her fist down onto the surface of his desk. The volume of her voice rose and her face grew redder with each word. "This is my mother we are talking about. Find out what happened. What else do you have going on?" She was being presumptuous but she didn't care.

Remaining calm, Ensign Ryan rose slowly from his desk as though he had every intention of regaining control of the conversation. His serious expression remained unwavering as he maintained eye contact with her.

A more senior officer approached and introduced himself as Lieutenant Woods. His short hair was light blond and he looked to be closer to thirty. Standing much taller and broader than the desk jockey, he had obviously spent more time in the sun than the younger officer.

Olivia trusted he had overheard enough of the conversation to understand why she was there, and she wasn't backing down. He seemed as though he was going to take her more seriously than his subordinate. She hoped he wasn't just patronizing her.

"Miss Benning, I will personally look into this. I certainly can't make any promises beyond that. I don't know if I will find out anything, but I will try."

Olivia wasn't ready to ease up yet. "All right, good. How do I reach you?" she pushed further, holding him accountable.

The lieutenant reached into his shirt pocket, pulled out a couple of business cards and handed them to her. "Here is my card. Use the second one to jot down your contact information."

Olivia glanced toward the ensign who seemed to be able to read her mind. He lunged toward her and handed her the pen in his hand. She leaned on his desk to fill out the back of the business card and then handed it to the lieutenant. As he took it she looked deep into his eyes, looking for a flicker of hope he was earnest. She had to believe he was.

He asked her indulgence in filling out some paperwork to officially document her request. Silently she wished she had made a copy of the missing persons report to save herself the trouble but honored the lieutenant's request on behalf of her mother.

Before long, she found herself back outside in the steamy tropical heat, asking herself if that stop had gotten her anywhere. It certainly hadn't hurt. He had assured her he would be in touch. But Olivia guessed she would be the one to contact him first.

Time to return to Serenity Villa.

As Olivia eased the Jeep back down her mother's driveway, she pressed her foot to the brake, anxious to steal a glance out to the bay. It never got old. She was going to miss that view. Parking in the usual spot, she retreated inside the quaint and colorful bungalow.

No sooner had she stepped inside than she heard a noise coming from the studio. Olivia froze. Another intruder? She listened. As the noise continued she crept toward the sound, eyes searching for movement within the room. Once she reached the doorway, it became a somewhat familiar sound. The fax machine. She stepped closer to it and cocked her head to read the message as it inched out of the machine.

Liv

I wish I knew if my previous message made it to you. I don't know how else to reach you. I trust this phone line is secure. The last thing I would want to do is blow your cover.

Her cover! What was that supposed to mean? Eyes peeled, she watched as the page inched out of the machine and the note continued.

My source tells me they're going to try again tomorrow night, possibly the next night, but they've moved. The location is in Bovoni. Down the road to the landfill. There's an abandoned shack tucked away in a clearing on the left side off the road. Study your satellite images ahead of time to get the lay of the land. I would expect them to get started around 10:00 PM or so. You should be able to see lights once you get in there and get close.

Please be careful and stay out of sight. If you feel like you're in danger, get out of there. I know you're hell bent on your "mission" but these pictures are not worth your life. Please let me know you got this. I'll be anxiously awaiting your call or text.

—CK

The paper settled into the output tray and Olivia stood there staring at the words on the page. Her body turned numb. What had her mother gotten herself mixed up in? A strange tingling sensation rippled through her body at the possibilities. She shivered to shake off a chill.

The first solid lead to find her mother, though. At least to find out what she was working on that may have cost her life.

"CK, could you give me a clue who you are?" She spoke aloud to the four walls in her mother's studio.

Fatigue washed over her. Her eyes welled up in anguish. It had been a long day and she hadn't eaten much.

Fighting the urge to have a glass a wine and head off to bed, she pulled together another simple dinner of plain pasta, this time with olive oil and dried herbs she had rummaged from the cupboard. As the pasta boiled, Olivia opened her last bottle of wine. The Chardonnay. Because she still wasn't brave enough to open the refrigerator, it was at room temperature from sitting on the counter, so she tossed in an ice cube from the tray in the freezer. As she sipped the oaky, dry wine, sea breezes gently tossed the tree branches outside the kitchen window. Daylight was waning. And so was her energy level.

Olivia enjoyed her dinner out on the gallery as night fell on the Caribbean. Shortly afterward, she cleaned up the dishes and turned in, turning the latch on the deadbolt as she passed the front door. A tall white pillar candle on the simple wooden bedside table beckoned to be lit. Olivia rummaged through the drawer beneath it and found some matches. Lighting the flame filled a small void inside her. The flickering light spread a soft glow in the room. Olivia slipped into some comfortable shorts and a t-shirt before closing the mosquito netting around her and slipping between the sheets. A warm breeze from the bedroom window tugged gently at the netting. A good night's sleep would help her face the unknown that awaited her the next day.

Olivia awoke with a start in the daylight to some sort of a tapping noise.

CHAPTER TWELVE

A *tapping noise. A woodpecker?* Her head was groggy from sleep. Did woodpeckers exist in the Caribbean? She rolled over and attempted to fall back asleep, yet a feeling of foreboding consumed her. With eyes opened wide, she listened intently. What had she heard? Silence. Olivia felt compelled to take a look around. Pulling back the mosquito netting, she threw her legs over the side of the bed, slipping her feet into her well-worn, casual flip-flops with thin black leather straps.

Creeping silently across the floor, she shuffled out into the living area and stopped a few feet away from the upholstered chairs to listen again. Silence. Movement in her peripheral vision caught her attention. Out in the yard a man peered into the driver's side window of her mother's car. Olivia studied him. He was a tall, well-built black man dressed in a light-pink collared polo shirt, light khaki shorts, and boat shoes. He wore aviator sunglasses. Not what she would have expected from an intruder, yet an uneasiness crept in that she couldn't shake. Who was he? What did he want? Her thoughts returned to the gun under her mother's mattress.

He walked all around the car, looking into the windows and then made his way back toward the front door. Olivia darted back away from the windows, finding refuge behind the kitchen counter. The man approached the windows along the front of the house, above the sofa. He cupped his hands on either side of his eyes and peered in. Olivia maintained her hiding place in the kitchen, peering out enough to get a glimpse of him. Holding her position until he turned and headed around the side of the house toward the gallery, she took advantage of the opportunity to run to her mother's bedroom.

On her way into the room her gaze fell on the unlit candle on the bedside table and for a fleeting moment wondered if she had blown it out the night before. Perhaps she did . . . or the breeze from the window had taken care of it.

Kneeling quickly down next to the bed, she shoved her hand under the mattress. Her hand made contact with the cold, hard surface of her mother's gun. She pulled it out and found it heavy and awkward in her hand. Pushing past these sensations, she vowed to confront the intruder.

Feeling trapped inside the house, Olivia figured she had a better chance of defending herself if she was outside. She took one quick look at the bedside table and jerked it away from the window, just catching the lamp before it toppled over. Dressed in the t-shirt and shorts she had slept in, Olivia pushed open the window and shimmied out with the gun in her right hand, trying not to drop it or catch it on something. The bushes snapped as they broke her landing, branches poking her hair and scratching her arms and legs. After getting to her feet, she circled around to the front of the house, slipping stealthily to the side gallery, the gun dangling awkwardly to her side. She tightened her grip to prevent it from slipping. Her hand was starting to perspire as much from nerves as from the tropical heat.

Parrots squawked in the trees above her as if they were aware of the tense situation. Creeping out into the side yard, she scanned the property as she moved, desperate to locate the man before he detected her. Olivia's heart throbbed hard within her ribcage, echoing loudly inside her head. For a fleeting moment she questioned her sanity.

What the hell was she doing? Never before had she held a gun, much less fired one, and now she was stalking someone outside her mother's house, defending it with everything she had. Would she be able to shoot if she needed to? Her mind raced. Aim for the legs so he can't run? His torso, to increase her chances of actually striking him? Her heart beat faster, her breathing was rapid and shallow.

A couple more steps and the black male came into view. Her feet froze. The man was on the gallery at the back of the house peering through a window into the living area, both hands pressed against the glass, cupped around his eyes.

Olivia took a couple of steps closer and raised the gun with both hands, pointing it toward him. "Hey!" she yelled in a loud gravelly voice even she didn't recognize.

The man spun around and looked stunned to see her standing there. "Uh . . ." he murmured.

Struggling to maintain even breathing, she adjusted the gun to aim at his chest. "Who are you and what do you want?" she demanded, glaring at him. Her hands wavered as she struggled to hold the heavy firearm steady in her sweaty fingers.

His hands slowly raised awkwardly into the air as if someone else was controlling them. His eyes were locked on the gun. "I'm . . . I'm Carson."

She imagined his eyes behind his sunglasses were nervously moving from the gun to her face and back again.

"Take off the shades." Her tone wasn't welcoming.

He pulled off his aviators, folded them against his chest with one hand and smoothly slipped them into the pocket of his polo shirt.

Olivia immediately connected with his penetrating hazel eyes. Not what she had been expecting behind the tinted lenses. Their connection became uncomfortable. She blinked and averted her eyes.

Olivia found him to be extremely attractive with handsome dark skin, upper arm muscles bulging out from underneath the short sleeves of his polo shirt and chest muscles hidden under the rest of his shirt.

His arms drooped. The tension in his face eased. "You look just like her." His voice was barely audible. A look of disbelief settled into the smooth skin of his face. "So familiar." Then he repeated, more loudly, "You look just like her."

Olivia kept the gun pointed in his direction, but the muscles in her upper arms were starting to burn.

"Is Liv your mother?" He had a lyrical island accent.

"Who are you?" She held her glare. She wasn't going to fall for his congenial chitchat. She wiggled the gun to remind him who was in charge.

"I'm Carson. I'm a friend of Liv's. A good friend," he added for emphasis. "You must be her daughter, Olivia?"

Unable to suppress a skeptical frown, Olivia knew he could have dug up the information online. Nothing was private anymore.

"She speaks of you often. You're as beautiful as she is." He gazed tenderly toward her. "I assume that's her gun." He motioned with one of his raised hands toward the obvious firearm in her hand. "Found it under the mattress, I bet?"

Olivia's eyes flared. Lucky guess? She grew increasingly uncomfortable with how much he knew.

"Look, you can put that down."

Olivia glared at him, not knowing if she should trust him. She had no idea who she was dealing with.

"Unless you found the ammo in the cookie jar next to the kitchen sink, it probably isn't loaded."

Olivia hadn't thought that through, but there was one way to find out. Deciding to give it a try, she pointed the gun toward the ground and pulled the trigger. The sound of the shot was deafening and the small handgun recoiled. Olivia's entire body jolted in response. Dirt displaced by the bullet sprayed out from the point of impact and a cloud of dust hovered momentarily before settling back down again. She glanced over to see her visitor straightening back up after apparently hitting the deck.

Olivia's eyes grew wide in disbelief. Carson's eyes were just as large as hers and his arms were back up in the air. She turned the gun to its side to examine it more closely, wondering momentarily why there hadn't been a safety on it for her to disengage. Was it not equipped with one or had it already been turned off?

Although she had believed it was loaded before she fired, somehow firing the gun to confirm the fact made it seem much more dangerous. Carson appeared to feel the same way. A prudent person would have pointed it back at the intruder, but she couldn't bring herself to do it. She pointed it, instead, in his general direction.

"What are you doing here?" She wasn't letting down her guard just yet.

"Look, Olivia. I've been trying to catch up with your mother. I haven't seen her in a while. I've been worried. She hasn't answered her phone calls or texts. I've stopped by a few times over the last few days and her car wasn't here." He examined her face as if to see that his words were sinking in. "I knew she was busy with work, but it's not like her to suddenly stop communicating. When I stopped by to check on her this morning, I saw her car and I thought she was back. Is she here?" He looked hopeful.

Olivia was reluctant to reveal much. Although, the fact he was speaking about her mother in the present tense was encouraging. Trust, however, was still an issue.

"She's not here. No." She held her expression steady and looked for a response from him.

"Is she okay?" He looked genuinely concerned.

Olivia softened toward her would-be intruder as she sensed perhaps he was harmless. It sounded as though he cared about her mother. Instinctively, she lowered the pistol and it dropped to her side.

Her mother's friend lowered his arms. He seemed to be feeling more comfortable she wasn't going to blow off his head.

Olivia started toward the gallery. It was time to meet Carson. Clumsily, she switched the gun to her left hand and extended her right hand to her visitor. He reached out over the railing and firmly grasped her hand, looking overly eager.

"Pleased to meet you."

"So how do you know my mother?" She backed up again to put more space between herself and her new acquaintance, not willing to trust him completely. Not yet anyway.

He closed his eyes as if recalling their time together. "We met on a photo shoot."

Olivia pictured him as a model on one of her mother's assignments.

"We just clicked." He appeared uncomfortable explaining the relationship to Liv's daughter and unsure of how far to go. "Olivia, we've had a lot of fun. Spent a lot of time together."

Olivia listened, taking it all in, realizing her mother's relationship with this guy was more than a friendship. A corner of her mouth curled up as she estimated she was looking at a man who was easily ten to fifteen years younger than her mother. Atta girl, Mom. Way to go.

"Olivia." He stepped closer. "We were . . . uh, very close."

146

Olivia's smile broadened. "You go, Mom," she said under her breath. Her words were meant for her mother, whom she wished were nearby. Although she was happy for her mother's personal life, she refocused on more pressing matters.

"What do you do here on the island? What do you do for work?" She gestured with the hand holding the gun. More information was necessary.

"I have a water sport rental shop on the east end of the island in Red H—"

A loud sound rang out that startled both Carson and Olivia. He fell back toward the house, hitting the side of it before sliding down and dropping onto the floor of the gallery with a thud.

Olivia's eyes grew wide. What had she done? Was she too wrapped up in their conversation to realize she had discharged her mother's gun? Had her sweaty hands pulled the trigger inadvertently?

"*Oh God!*" She ran to the gallery and knelt down next to Carson's body. It was lifeless. Blood was everywhere.

CHAPTER THIRTEEN

O*livia stared down at the motionless, bloody body before her.* Grabbing his shoulders, she rocked him gently. His eyes were shut. What had she done? *"Carson!* Oh my God." She grabbed onto his right arm, searched for a pulse at his wrist but couldn't find one. No! It couldn't be. She shook her head violently back and forth in denial. Tiny puffs of air inward were all she could manage. "Carson!" She tried desperately to think straight, struggling to grasp she had shot him and needed to get help. Her trembling hand was still clinging to her mother's gun. Carefully she laid it down on the floor as far away from her as she could, nudging it farther with a blood-covered hand. She had no business hanging onto it, being anywhere near it. She yanked her cell out of her pants pocket and frantically pressed buttons. Her blood soaked fingers slid across the face of the phone.

In her haste to call for help, her fingers struck random buttons until a calm voice within her broke through and urged her to press 9-1-1. When she finally connected with the right numbers, a dispatcher kept her on the line to determine where she was located and what her situation was. Olivia's head spun. It all seemed like a horrible dream.

In an attempt to curtail blood loss, she pressed her hand against his wound just below his right shoulder, oblivious to the blood oozing out and covering her hands. An irrational thought crossed her mind that he wouldn't be able to wear his shirt again. The colors . . . red . . . on pink . . . reminded her, in a twisted sort of way, of Valentine's Day. She wondered if they had celebrated it together. Had they known each other that long?

In the distance she heard sirens and didn't connect that the emergency vehicles were heading toward her mother's bungalow. She became dizzy and fought to stay conscious. Strong hands pulled her off the bloody mess she was hanging onto. People moved all around her. Talking. As they relocated her to a chair at the bistro table, the words that tumbled out of her mouth resembled a confession.

"I didn't mean to shoot him. I had just met him. My mother . . . oh, my mother will be angry. She never gets angry but . . . but she'll be angry. I'm sorry, I'm so sorry. Tell her I'm sorry." Olivia was rambling, somewhat unintelligibly. Shock had set in.

Voices. Words . . . were they speaking to her?

"There's a lot of blood on her. Is it his? Hers?"

The world around her became a blur. She was being led away from the house. Someone gripped her upper arms tightly. There was pain somewhere in her body. Her feet were tripping over each other. They couldn't move fast enough to keep up. She felt as though she was being dragged. Did someone pick her up? The door of some sort of vehicle opened, and she was guided into the back and someone fastened a restraint. She was being transported somewhere and couldn't resist. Feeling the vehicle moving and the straps constraining her, she looked at her hands. They didn't look quite right. She squinted in the dim light. They looked red. Was it blood? Was she hurt? Her head bobbed with the movement of the vehicle, swaying left or right with every turn. The vehicle stopped. The door next to her was yanked open. Someone pulled her out. Her legs were wobbly. Multiple hands reached out to steady her and escort her through the doors to the building. Lots of bright lights. An odd smell. Rubbing alcohol? Formaldehyde? She wrinkled her nose. It was an offensive odor. There were voices. Angry voices? Excited?

She felt herself being lifted. Onto a table? More restraints. The table was moving. Long narrow lights above her moved too fast. It made her dizzy. She closed her eyes and could still feel herself moving. The sound of double doors opening. She tried to squirm but the restraints were tight. The table stopped. Another bright light overhead. Then darkness.

CHAPTER FOURTEEN

O*livia's head felt fuzzy when she woke.* Blinking her eyes, she tried to get a clearer picture of where she was and what was going on. Since the curtain near her was open, she was able to look across the room. It was long and narrow with beds on both sides against the long walls. Ivory-colored curtains hung from the ceiling on tracks encircling each bed. Some were completely closed. Others were partially open or drawn back all the way. The two beds on either side of her were empty. She was disappointed no one was there. No one to interrogate to find out where she was.

Pain shot through her body. It originated from her left shoulder. She groaned quietly. This was something new.

Voices at the other end of the room.

Olivia tried to piece together what she could remember. Her mother's friend at the house. They were talking. But she was holding a gun. A shot was fired and Carson dropped. Bloody mess. Everything after that was a blur. How did she get hurt? Probably from the officers handling her roughly to take her away from the crime scene.

Olivia looked around her bed. There was an IV stand with a bag dripping into a tube. She followed the tube to the back of her left hand. That seemed extreme. Footsteps got closer.

"Miss Benning."

Her body jolted at the sound of her name. ". . . Yes?" She squinted slightly to scrutinize the man with dark skin and graying, short-cropped hair standing at the foot of her bed.

"How are you feeling?" The man was dressed in a white lab coat. He wore round, black, plastic-rimmed glasses that made him look almost childish. Perhaps his objective was to look younger than he felt. The shape of his eyes suggested an Asian background. She couldn't make out the name on his tag, but it looked like it had MD after it.

"I'm fine," she asserted, ignoring the stabbing pain in her shoulder.

The doctor chuckled to himself. "That's good to hear. Do you have any idea what just transpired . . . why you're here?"

Olivia didn't feel comfortable revealing anything just yet. She tried on a "deer in the headlights" look.

Again he chuckled.

Not appreciating his sense of humor, she served up one of her standard glares she dished out when she was particularly annoyed. Movement from the other side of the room distracted her attention away from the doctor.

A policeman strode confidently across and approached the doctor. Even though they spoke in hushed voices, she overheard him asking if he could have a word with her.

Olivia cringed. What she had done back at the house was, well, reprehensible. It was disgusting. How could she live with herself after that? She shuddered to think of the consequences. Even though she had no intention of it turning out the way it did, the fact of the matter was a man had been shot down in cold blood and she was responsible.

The doctor nodded once, clearing the officer to speak with Olivia, but lingered nearby, maintaining a position of authority.

The policeman stepped around to the left side of her bed and hovered over her. "Miss Benning, I'm Detective Benson. I need to ask you a few questions."

He was a big burly black man who could have been a linebacker for a professional football team. No one was going to get past him that he didn't want to let by. His rhythmic accent revealed he was probably native to the island, at least to the Caribbean. He towered over her, making her feel vulnerable, almost threatened. There was a slight odor of perspiration emanating from his body as if he had just come in from spending time outside in the hot sun.

She looked into his deep brown eyes under bushy graying eyebrows, fearful of what was in store for her. "Okay."

He proceeded to ask about Carson and why he was at her house.

She didn't like how the conversation was developing. "He said he was a friend of my mother's. Hadn't seen her in a while and was hoping to catch up with her." She was trying to sound as matter-of-fact as she could.

He wanted to know if her mother owned a gun.

Yeah, the one you undoubtedly found lying next to me.

"Apparently she does. Guess she feels she might need to protect herself." She deliberately kept references to her mother in the present tense. She didn't feel the need to do otherwise.

Then he asked about the caliber.

Who knows what caliber it is!

"I have no idea. I don't know much about guns," she answered, keeping a cool, calm demeanor.

"Except how to point and shoot them." The detective narrowed his eyes.

"Yeah, something like that."

He had her red-handed. There was no getting away with this. It was an accident and she'd had no intention of firing the gun. But she shouldn't have had it in her hands.

The detective turned to walk away and then stopped. He turned back toward her. "One more question. How many gunshots do you recall hearing?"

Olivia furrowed her brow. "I heard one shot."

One shot out of my gun!

He appeared to be considering her answer carefully and then turned away again, walking the rest of the way across the room and disappearing through a doorway with an illuminated exit sign above it. The door slammed shut behind him.

The doctor stepped forward toward the end of her bed. Their eyes met.

"So, how are you feeling? How's your shoulder?"

She was not in the mood for chitchat. "I'm fine," she repeated. Her voice was calm but assertive.

"Good to hear. You were lucky. Could have been a lot worse. Should heal quickly. I gave you a sedative so you could rest and start the healing process. Good to see you're awake. We're going to keep you here for—" Without warning, the large room turned dim. The electricity had gone out. Window coverings and the curtains surrounding the beds kept most of the natural light from filtering in. "Damn! Not again." He slammed his clipboard onto the foot of her bed and turned to attend to the more urgent matter.

Electricity on the island, like most Caribbean islands, could be sporadic and unpredictable at times, not just during storms. If the building had a generator, which she surmised it did, it would kick on within a couple minutes. Olivia saw this as her opportunity to make her exit. She would never be able to find her mother from where she was and certainly not from the local jail cell either.

She yanked the IV out of the back of her left hand, wincing for a moment, then pulled the curtain closed to envelope the bed. Looking for her personal effects, she spied a white plastic bag tucked into the shelf of her bedside table that appeared to have something soft inside. She grabbed it and peered into the top. To her horror, the t-shirt and shorts she'd had on earlier were soaked with blood. The flip-flops she had slipped on before heading outside to shoot her mother's friend were not spared either. Unfortunately she had no choice but to put it all back on and try to stay out of sight so as not to arouse suspicions.

Dressing quickly, she noticed her hand was bleeding where the IV needle had been. Pressing her right hand firmly onto the back of her left hand, she slipped out from behind the closed curtain and dashed toward the exit the detective had taken. There were voices behind her, but it sounded like they were more concerned with getting the lights back on than they were with keeping an eye on her.

Olivia pushed on the horizontal metal handle of the exit door with her right hip, slipped quickly through the small opening, and softly closed the door behind her. She found herself at the top of a set of stairs. The stairwell had an industrial feel to it. There were no steps leading upward so she was on the top floor of however many floors there were in the building. She bolted down the steps, going as fast as her two feet could carry her, one hand still pressing against the insertion location of the IV. Four stories later, she was at the bottom of the stairs, pushing open another door marked exit and stepping out onto a parking lot.

Hot, humid air hit her in the face, but the sun had already set. There was no bright sunlight to make her squint. Olivia was grateful she would soon have the cover of darkness in her favor. She had made her escape but needed to get away from the building as quickly as possible before they discovered she was missing. While she fought off dizziness filling her head, pain on the left side of her body exploded, and her knees threatened to buckle. She tried hard to push through and ignore it. Scanning the area quickly, she searched for something familiar. Panic rose inside her and she endeavored to vanquish it. A road on the far end of the lot became her target and she ran straight toward it.

Once on the sidewalk, she stopped just long enough to glance up and down the street, trying to get her bearings. Looking back at the front of the light pink building illuminated by lights along the ground, Olivia concluded it was a hospital but she hadn't seen it before. Straining to place its general location on the island, she wondered if there was more than one. The answer to that question didn't matter. She just needed to figure out where this one was located and whether or not she was going to be able to walk back to her mother's house.

A voice in Olivia's head urged her to get moving, something would look familiar. The street in front of the hospital led to a busier street. There were no street signs to give her a clue as to what either street was called. The waning light from the sun setting on her right would make it the western sky. Turning in that direction, she walked on the right side of the road facing oncoming traffic, feeling fairly confident she was walking west and taking a gamble her mother's house was even farther west.

CHAPTER FIFTEEN

B*eads of perspiration glistened on Olivia's forehead.* Even though the afternoon sun was gone, the hot evening air was thick with humidity. Her feet plodded along on the still warm pavement. They were feeling heavier with each step, sounding like sandpaper on a piece of lumber as they landed and slid across the loose grit and sand on the steamy tar. Her breathing became labored, each breath more deliberate.

Although she was seeing a different perspective on foot than in a car, Olivia had to believe she was moving in the right direction toward her mother's bungalow. It was more like slow motion but with every detail accentuated. A building here, a sign there looked familiar to her. As the road began to incline, she believed she had found the right way to head up the mountain. Her focus was on keeping her feet moving. There was a very real possibility they might come after her. After all, she was a wanted woman. Surely an APB, or whatever it was called on the island, had been issued for her. Unfortunately there were no alternate routes she could take to stay off the main road. All the side streets would take her in the wrong direction, away from the top of the mountain. She would just have to hustle and make her way up quickly. Retrieving the Jeep for transportation was essential for her to resume her search and have a chance of staying under the radar.

Pain suddenly shot from her shoulder down her left arm and into her chest. She groaned and her feet came to an abrupt halt as she glanced over to the bandage peeking out through the gaping hole in her shirt. What had happened . . . between her and the police? Keenly aware of the urgency to keep moving, she couldn't spare the time to acknowledge the pain. Taking a second glance, she could tell she was bleeding through the layers of gauze. A deep red wet stain glistened on her t-shirt. Olivia was struck by its irregular shape. She stared at it for a moment to see if she could tell if it was getting larger but then chided herself silently for losing focus. Time to push forward. She had to get to the top of the mountain.

She kept climbing, willing her body to move, ignoring the throbbing pain from her left shoulder. Cars approached, heading down the mountain, speeding past her, often too close for comfort, causing her to jump out of the way just in time to avoid being struck. At one point she ran into a mailbox on the edge of the street and the pain shot up her right arm. She moaned and grabbed her arm with her left hand, only to set off shooting pain in her injured shoulder. She paused to catch her breath. Her parched mouth ached for something to drink. It would have to wait. She pushed on. One foot in front of the other.

A siren in the distance stirred panic within her. She couldn't be seen, she couldn't afford to be caught. Quickly glancing around, she searched for someplace to hide in case the police were coming her way. As the sound of the siren got louder, Olivia lunged behind a large bush on the front lawn of someone's house. Crouching down low to avoid detection, she said a little prayer they would sail right on past. The siren got increasingly louder as it raced up the hill. As

Olivia remained motionless, she hoped she was well hidden behind her camouflage. She held her breath and closed her eyes. Just as the wailing sound reached near where she crouched, her curiosity got the best of her and she chanced a look.

To her relief, it was an ambulance. Not a squad car. As Olivia stood up from behind the bush, a rush of lightheadedness flooded over her. Her legs wobbled. She reached out to steady herself and pulled large leaves from the bush she had been hiding behind. Flailing to find a sturdier support, her hands latched onto a thicker branch. Finally her legs felt stronger and her dizziness dissipated. Returning to the hard surface of the main road, she resumed her trek up the mountain.

About two-thirds of the way up, she turned to look out over the harbor. There were no cruise ships docked at Havensight. If there had been any during the day, they were long gone now. The harbor was quiet. The lights downtown and across the water on Estate Bakkero were spectacular. Darkness had completely enrobed the island. It took on a whole different feel at night. Olivia loved it either way, day or night. One wasn't better, they were just different.

Olivia smiled and reminisced about how her mother had taught her the concept of being different. She used to tell little Ollie that just because people were different, whether they had different skin color or they were different in their beliefs or perhaps their size or shape, it didn't matter. One wasn't better than the other. They were simply different. End of discussion. End of story. There was nothing more to it.

Olivia loved her mother and many others did too. Liv Benning was a beautiful person. And that beauty was evident in her art. She easily identified the beauty around her and was able to capture it in her photography.

A familiar expression came to mind Olivia could easily paraphrase to describe her mother perfectly:

She had a heart full of love and forgiveness, eyes that looked for the good in people, and a soul that never lost faith.

A distant siren pulled Olivia back to reality and, after taking one more glance out to the harbor, she resumed her hike up the mountain.

After dodging a few more cars heading in her direction, Olivia finally reached the tricky intersection. Assuring herself she didn't have much farther to go, she made her way around the bend and headed down Skyline Drive. It was extremely dark and walking on the side of the road was even more treacherous than in daylight.

Olivia fought to stay focused. When her head started to spin, she halted her feet for a moment. Wincing at the pain in her shoulder as it pulsated throughout her body, she tried to keep her sights on getting back to her mother's house. It wasn't much farther. She pressed on.

Allowing her thoughts to drift away, she attempted to divert herself from the drudgery of walking and the discomfort in her shoulder. Visions of the calm, serene, deserted beaches on St. John filled her head. Salomon Bay and Caneel Bay were two of her favorites. Trunk Bay was also beautiful but usually more crowded, particularly during the high season. If only she could spend some time on St. John or anywhere on the islands with her mother again. She held onto a fading hope she would still be able to do that.

Finally she arrived at the top of the familiar driveway. Needing to rest for a moment, she dropped to her knees by the mailbox and the rest of her body followed along, hitting the ground with no gracefulness to speak of. Succumbing to her pain and exhaustion, she rolled over onto her side.

Anxious to retrieve her mother's car, she acknowledged she still had to trek down the hill to grab it. The Jeep meant a great deal to her. Not only independence but also the way to find her mother . . . or at least what had happened to her. For the moment she was going to try to forget what she had done to her mother's friend, push the horrific act aside.

Although her shoulder was throbbing, she gathered the strength to pull herself up and make her way down the steep driveway, willing her feet to go slowly. It took patience, but she worked hard to keep them from going too fast in her haste. Reaching the bottom and approaching the colorful little bungalow, she tried to latch onto positive memories but they were too hard to retrieve at the moment.

A quick trip into the house enabled her to change out of the bloodsoaked clothes. She also splashed water on her face and grabbed her wallet, phone, car key, and camera. Taking the time to apply a fresh bandage on her shoulder, she took a moment to examine her wound in the mirror. Curious at the sight of stitches, she wondered why they were necessary. A dull pain radiated down her arm.

The clock on the stove read 9:30. It had taken longer than she realized to hike up the mountain from the hospital. Not that it mattered. She had to switch gears and head back out. It was time to look for the location the elusive CK had indicated her mother should go check out. Unsure what she was looking for, Olivia had to believe somehow she would know it when she found it. The satellite images CK had mentioned in his fax didn't turn up when she and Sarah tidied up the mess after the house was ransacked. She was going to have to wing it.

There was a rumble in her abdomen, which she didn't have time to address, but she decided not to ignore it completely. After grabbing a quick bowl of cereal and a handful of ibuprofen, she left the solace of Serenity Villa behind her. Time to head toward the landfill.

CHAPTER SIXTEEN

Olivia *pointed the Jeep down the mountain* toward Charlotte Amalie with the windows rolled partway down and the salty sea air blowing in. Her route was going to bring her to the traffic light in front of the police station. The only way to avoid it was to take the road that ran along the north side of the island out to the east end and double back, adding at least a half an hour to the trip, time she didn't have. She would take her chances. As luck would have it, the light was red when she arrived. Waiting for the light to change, she felt excruciatingly uncomfortable sitting still. Imagining wanted posters with her photo on them next to the front door of the station, she prayed no one would walk by who could identify her. Movement to her left caused her body to stiffen, and she locked her eyes forward. Finally the light changed to green, and she gradually pressed the gas and calmly turned the corner onto Route 30 heading east.

At the top of the hill in Bakkero Estate, she turned left to stay on 30. She wound her way around tight corners, up and down hills, just as she had done on the way to the marina and Izzies a couple nights earlier, searching for Landfill Road as she drove. Of course there were no street markings of any kind that would help her. Pulling off the road to see if she could find a road map in the glove compartment, her hand only got as far as grabbing the handle. Then she realized she had already gone through it looking for the car key and there was no map in it at the time.

Fighting off feelings of discouragement, Olivia got back onto the pavement and drove more slowly, looking for the entrance. She had to believe she would see something that would give her a clue where to turn. She pressed on, staying to the left of the yellow line and glancing to the right, searching for Landfill Road. None of the side streets were well lit. Doubts that she would find it crept in. Then something caught her eye, and she slowed down to look more closely. It was a small wooden sign that appeared to read "Landfill." The lettering was worn, but she could just make out enough letters.

Olivia slowly turned the Jeep onto the hard-packed dirt and plowed into the darkness with trepidation, not sure what she would find. Fighting off the panic rising inside, she could only imagine what she might be driving into. The headlights carved a narrow path down the desolate stretch of road. There were no houses along the way to provide lights to guide her and the moon was not very bright. A shiver ran through her body, but she did her best to channel her mother's strength and kept going.

The road continued straight for a short while, jogged to the left, and then curved back to the original line. Creeping slowing along, Olivia kept her eyes in front of her but also glanced left and right to see if she could see anything out of the ordinary. Beyond the swath of her headlights and along the sides of the road, it was pitch black. She was losing faith she would be able to find anything. Yet the urgency to discover what her mother had been sent to photograph kept her moving forward.

Rolling down the windows the rest of the way, Olivia took a moment to listen to her surroundings, not detecting anything but the familiar "ko-kee" chirping sound of the Coqui tree frogs and a couple of dogs barking in the distance. Part of her was relieved at that observation. The rest pushed her to keep going. As she pressed the gas and moved farther into the black void, darkness filled in the space behind her. She tried not to focus on that part. Something lay ahead of her she had to find.

A light in the distance. Taking in a shallow breath, she touched the brake gently to stop her momentum and stared straight ahead. What could it mean? Just a night light of sorts to ward off potential break-ins? Or was it a light within a building someone was occupying? . . . Only one way to find out. She eased the Jeep farther down the road, crawling slowly toward the light. Finally she felt close enough and pulled the Jeep to the side, shut off the lights, and cut the engine. Grabbing the camera from the passenger seat, she scrambled out of the car, gently pressing the door closed until the interior light snuffed out but without closing it all the way. She slipped the wide leather strap around the back of her neck and set off down the deserted dirt road, her eyes adjusting to the darkness.

As she got closer she could see the light was shining on part of an outdoor area, next to a small building. A weathered shack of some sort. Rectangular in shape with dirty white sides and a dark roof. About the size of the container on a tractor trailer. She kept walking to get closer but got off the road to keep herself protected among greenery. With one hand on the camera, she pushed through the underbrush. Olivia couldn't see anyone around the building, but she kept up her guard just in case. Creeping slowly closer, she peered through the foliage and could see the windows on the building were covered. Was it to keep someone from looking in or to prevent someone on the inside from looking out? Outside, rudimentary benches loosely formed a large square in the clearing next to the building. The space looked ominous in its emptiness, as if something terrible transpired there and it was to be kept a secret.

This had to be the place her mother was supposed to see. Sensing she should start photographing, Olivia pulled her camera to her face. The clicking sounded loud in her ears as if the tree frogs would stop their chirping and listen to her instead.

Voices from behind. Gasping, she couldn't tell how many there were, but they were between her and the way back to her car. The voices all sounded male. Scanning the area quickly in the limited light, she ventured farther away from the road, into the bushes to avoid being seen, moving slowly so as not to make any noise. Once she settled in a spot where she felt safer, she turned to catch a glimpse of who was paying a visit.

The darkness prevented her from seeing faces, but she heard snippets of their conversation as they passed by.

"It's her. It's gotta be [unintelligible]."

"Yeah [unintelligible] the Jeep."

More garbled words.

". . . got to be here somewhere. Keep lookin'." Their accents revealed their island roots.

"If [unintelligible] her camera, don't let her leave with it. . . . Just don't let her leave." A sickening snicker followed the comment.

Mumbling continued between two of the men as they walked away from her toward the small building with the clearing on the side. A third got onto his cell.

She strained to keep an eye on the men as they unknowingly put distance between herself and them. Finally she could make out at least three, maybe four, silhouettes in the light shining from the shack. Their profiles blended together in one moving mass, sometimes revealing an individual body but usually just morphing in and out of a group of men on a mission. And she was part of it. They approached the small building and disappeared on the other side of it.

Terrified for her life, Olivia's instincts screamed at her to run. The men knew she was there and were intent on finding her. Listening closely, she could no longer hear them talking. Time to make a break for it. No more photos to be taken.

Carefully retracing her steps through the brush, she blazed her way with her hands back out to the access road. Branches with broad leaves smacked her square in the face and brushed up against her arms and legs leaving wet tracks behind. In her haste she rammed her left shoulder into a thick branch, causing stars to flash before her eyes and searing pain to shoot down her arm. She fought to ignore the assault on her body and find the road again. Once back on flat ground, she moved as quickly as she could. A half-moon had found its way out from behind the evening clouds, providing a little more light for her. The downside was the men who were after her could spot her more easily. She was terrified of where she was and who might be after her, but fortunately her feet took over. With one hand clutching the camera still hanging around her neck, she ran.

Her thin, muscular legs worked hard to move her quickly. Her thighs were burning when something caught her toe. A rock sticking out from the dirt road? A tree root? Mere clumsiness? No matter. The result was the same. It seemed like slow motion as Olivia plummeted toward the ground, landing hard on her chest before tumbling and landing, sprawled in an unladylike position. Lying stunned for a moment, she gasped to replace the air knocked out of her lungs. Shooting pain in her right foot deflected awareness of her shoulder pain. Stifling a blood-curdling scream, she bit her tongue to keep silent. Voices moved in her direction from behind her. She sprang to her feet, checking for the camera hanging from her neck, and resumed her sprint to the car with somewhat of a limp in her stride.

Olivia could just make out the shape of her vehicle with the moonlight reflecting off of it. Running for her life, she willed her legs to get her there. As she reached the Jeep, she shoved her hand into her pants pocket in search of her key. Her fingertips hit the bottom but only found a seam. Her eyes got wide. Panic ripped through her body. Where could it be? The voices behind her got louder. She needed to get out of there. *Where was the key?* In desperation, she pulled open the driver's side door and jumped in, closing it gently behind her. Alarmed the interior light stayed lit, she was afraid they would notice. "Damn!" Frantically scanning the inside of the car, she racked her brain to remember where she had left her key. The dome light she had just cursed stayed on long enough for her to see it was hanging from the ignition.

Quickly she grabbed it, cranked the engine to life and yanked the gearshift down to drive. She punched the gas, churning up dirt and gravel behind her as she made a U-turn and fled the scene, anxious to get back out onto the main road. She couldn't tell if the men behind her were still pursuing her on foot but, with the steering wheel in her hands, she felt less threatened and more in control. Pressing the gas pedal to the floor, she tried to put as much space between them as possible, her headlights piercing through the dark to show the way.

Before long she reached the end of the access road and came to an abrupt halt. She reviewed her options for a moment. Instead of turning left and heading toward Serenity Villa, she turned right, heading east, to try to elude her would-be captors. It crossed her mind too late, she probably didn't look either way before jumping out onto the main road. A quick glance into her rearview mirror assured her there was no one behind her. Breathing a little more easily, she knew she wouldn't feel better until she was safely back at her mother's place.

Following the sharp curves and changing elevations of the road as she took the long way back, she tried to remain calm as she progressed along the route, staying left of the center. The winding road brought her to Red Hook and around to the north side of the island. The throbbing in her shoulder forced her to drive with one hand, her left arm bent at the elbow and resting in her lap.

Lost in the close call she left behind, Olivia made the ride up the north side of the mountain purely by instinct and memory. She found herself at the tricky corner coming from the Magens Bay side but, at that hour, she was the only one there. Continuing through the intersection, she drove as quickly as she dared down the road toward her mother's house.

A strange light appeared in the distance. She kept driving, although she slowed her speed. It was a golden glow that grew brighter as she got closer. At first, she didn't connect with where it was coming from. Was someone having a party? Next door to her mother's bungalow?

Then she saw flashing lights. Red and blue emergency lights that were closer to her than the glow she had initially noticed.

Olivia could only drive a short distance before she was confronted by a uniformed officer. After crossing her fingers he wouldn't recognize her in the dark, she rolled down her window and he informed her the road was blocked off. She acknowledged his comment and quickly ditched her Jeep on the side of the road. Hopping out, leaving everything behind and pushing away frightening images, she quickly transitioned from brisk walking to running. An ambulance, with its siren blaring, screamed past her on its way from the scene. She glanced back toward it, curious who was inside. A firefighter? She sent up a prayer it wasn't.

As she got closer, she could feel the heat. It was like nothing she had experienced before. She coaxed her legs to move closer and found herself at the top of her mother's driveway again. Her face fell. Her heart sank. It was Serenity Villa. Completely engulfed in flames. Emergency personnel frantically worked to put out the fire. Their efforts seemed futile.

The scene was more than Olivia could handle. Her knees gave way for the second time that night by her mother's mailbox, and she went down hard. No one was close enough to witness it. Everyone else was focused on the fire. Her breathing deteriorated into wheezing as she grappled with the scene. As the world around her began to spin, she fought to stay conscious. The siren from another emergency vehicle arriving on the scene snapped her back to reality. Shooting pain ripped through her shoulder as she rolled onto her side and pulled herself into a sitting position, hugging her knees to her chest while watching helplessly as flames consumed her mother's home. The penetrating heat from the fire made the skin on her face feel like it was burning. Firefighters shouted above the roar of the fire while hustling to move the heavy hose from the water truck to a better position. They seemed to be losing the battle. There was nothing she could do. Her world was caving in.

Feeling an urgent need to run from the horrific scene, she used the mailbox post to pull herself upright. Making a dash for the Jeep, she fled the mayhem.

Throwing up gravel as she spun the Jeep around in a frantic U-turn, Olivia was desperate to leave it all behind. At the familiar corner above Magens Bay, instead of turning right to head down the mountain, she crossed over onto Skyline Drive heading east. Slowing down to search for the right driveway, she eventually found it though she'd only been there once before. Unfortunately, she had nowhere else to go.

CHAPTER SEVENTEEN

From the top of the driveway, she could tell lights were on inside the modest bungalow, and a car was parked in the driveway. Feeling fairly confident he was home, Olivia turned in, praying he was alone. Shutting off her headlights as she coasted down the driveway, she pulled the Jeep in next to his. As she exited the car, she glanced down the mountain to the twinkling lights of Charlotte Amalie. It was a similar view to what she had seen when she stopped during her trek up the hill on foot earlier in the evening.

Olivia shuffled to the front door but didn't knock right away. She stood still and listened with a tingling sensation in her stomach. There were no discernible sounds inside. Closing her eyes, she held her breath and knocked lightly on the door. Would he turn her away? At first she didn't hear anything. She rapped again a little harder, which stirred movement from within. A short bark and then footsteps. The inside door opened slowly and there stood Colton. His face brightened slightly as soon as he recognized her, but then he seemed to withdraw. Not the reaction she was hoping for but not entirely negative either. Just reserved, as if guarding his emotions. She certainly couldn't blame him.

Slowly, Colton opened the screen door and Jake ran straight to her, tail swinging back and forth, as if he knew her well and expected her to greet him. Olivia reached down and stroked his head before diverting her attention back to Colton. Gazing into his strong, suntanned face with laugh lines framing his eyes, she struggled not to be taken in. His light brown hair with sun-kissed blond highlights was unrestrained, falling loosely upon his shoulders. In spite of their brief, tumultuous history together, Olivia was tickled to see him. Reading his expression, she imagined he was trying not to react to her appearance, she was certain she looked like hell.

After an uncomfortable silence, Colton spoke first. "You're one of the last people I would have expected to be at my door this evening." His voice was flat and matter-of-fact. His eyes seemed to penetrate right through her. They looked cold and distant. Was he working hard to make them appear that way?

Her stomach tightened. Images from the evening she sent him away haunted her. His unanswered texts. Why had she ignored him?

She regretted her rash decision in a fit of anger. "Yeah, I'm sorry." Her throat tightened as it became obvious he was not going to welcome her as openly as his dog had. "Colton, I'm sorry . . . the way I treated you. It wasn't fair. I'm sorry."

The pair stood awkwardly at his front door. Silence hung in the air as they considered the situation.

"Are you okay?" He softened a bit.

"Yeah, I'm fine," she lied.

"Come in." Colton reached out and gently took hold of her upper arm, guiding her through the open door. Thankfully it wasn't her left arm. She didn't dare look into his eyes as she got closer to him. Her nose caught an interesting scent, and she wrestled conflicting emotions within her, fighting to stay in control. He allowed the screen door to swing shut on its own.

Olivia followed him into his home and managed a grin as she noticed he was wearing the same brown leather flip-flops he had worn every time she saw him. Seemed to be part of his everyday attire. They lingered when they reached the music room. She was relieved to see he was alone—at least no one else was in the general living area. Sheet music was scattered across the coffee table and a guitar rested on the sofa where it probably had been placed before he answered the door. It looked as though he had been in the middle of one of his creative sessions.

"Looks like I've interrupted—"

"No, it's okay." His face was not revealing any emotions he may have tucked deep inside.

"I'm sorry." She closed her eyes, trying to block out the horrific scene at her mother's house. "I had nowhere else to go."

He furrowed his brow. "What's going on?" He examined her face. "What's happened?" He reached out and took hold of her arm again, this time her left arm. Wincing, she pulled away from him. A subtle groan slipped through her lips.

"Olivia, you're hurt." His face looked pained as he searched her eyes for answers.

"My mother's place . . . it's gone." She was not going to acknowledge she was hurt. There was a much more pressing matter. "Someone must have set it on fire."

"*What?*" He looked stunned.

Grimacing from the horrific images in her mind, she nodded. "I was just there. It's totally engulfed in flames."

Colton's eyes widened, showing a sense of urgency she didn't feel. "There must be something we can do. We should get over there."

"I just came from there. I couldn't get very close to the house with my car. There were fire trucks and police cars on the street. I pulled off to the side of the road and ran up." A lump formed in her throat. "I walked partway down the driveway. The house was . . . it was . . . the flames were bright and the heat was awful." Olivia struggled to put into words what she had seen. "There was nothing I could do. So many people trying to put out the flames but there was . . . it was gone. My mother's . . ." Her voice trailed off as she attempted to wrap her head around what someone had done to their house. Then she stopped to consider if there was anything she had done that would have ignited a fire. The stove? The candle next to her bed? She was frantic to figure out if she was responsible.

Olivia felt his strong hands in hers. She fixated on the energy they generated together, yet she kept her eyes averted from his. He gently squeezed her hands, and she tightened her grip, wanting him to feel her response. She needed someone to hang on to. Her world spun wildly out of control. Aching to reach out and grab him, she pulled his hand closer, needing to feel he was there for her.

"Olivia, I'm sorry." He slipped his hands out of hers and moved them around her slender waist.

In response, she moved her hands to his waist. Stabbing pain shot from her shoulder as she shifted her body. She did her best to ignore it and tried to relax in his hands. A strange sensation shimmered throughout her body. They were entering uncharted territory.

Colton lifted her chin with his fingertips and he looked deep into her eyes as if examining her soul. His face remained rigid. There seemed to be a lingering question on his mind.

She wanted him to pull her closer. Harboring a naïve notion he could make it all better, she just wanted to get lost in his arms and forget about what was happening.

He maintained his distance from her, though.

How could she expect him to do anything else? She had screamed at him at her mother's house in an irrational fit of rage a couple nights earlier. A cold chill ripped through her body. A body looking for the warm touch of his hands but rejected. She had hurt him, and she couldn't blame him for protecting himself.

Dropping her eyes to the floor in painful remorse, Olivia pulled away from him. She had been wrong thinking she could show up on his doorstep. She was desperate, and he could see right through her. He wasn't fooled.

"I've made a mistake. I'll go. Look, I'm sorry I bothered you. I'm just . . . sorry." She turned and shuffled noiselessly toward the door.

Jake trotted with her and cried softly as if he was sad to see her go.

When she reached the door she turned back and gave Jake a firm stroke on his head. He looked up into her eyes as if searching for an explanation as to why she was leaving. His penetrating eyes tugged at her heart. There was a real connection between her and the sweet, furry canine she didn't understand. She had not experienced that with another dog, or any other animal for that matter.

Colton followed silently behind Jake but hadn't found his voice yet. His eyes locked on a random spot out the front window, blinking deliberately, appearing to be struggling with the situation.

Olivia's hand was on the door knob. She turned and looked into Colton's silent face. His piercing blue eyes were more than she could take. Her eyes closed as she became painfully aware of what he must be feeling.

"See ya." Her voice quivered and was almost imperceptible.

She turned away from him and pushed open the screen door, moving quickly through it. It closed with a soft click behind her.

CHAPTER EIGHTEEN

The sound of his front door shutting behind Olivia made her feel even more alone than she had felt when she knocked on it earlier. Colton had not prevented her from leaving. She had caused unimaginable damage to their new relationship when she dismissed him in her moment of utter rage. She shouldn't have been surprised he was hurt and not receptive to her arriving unannounced on his doorstep.

Walking slowly back to her mother's Jeep, she bit her lip to distract herself from the hurt she was feeling inside. Reaching out and taking hold of the door handle, she paused to think about where she should head next. The cold, cruel reality was she had nowhere to go. She was completely alone.

"Olivia."

She turned toward his voice and took in a quick breath, uncertain what his appearance meant.

He stood on the door step. Jake was at his side. Tail wagging.

"Yes?" Her voice was barely a whisper.

"Please come in."

She cocked her head and looked at him, trying to discern his intentions.

"Please come inside," he repeated, almost pleading with her. His voice was hushed but unwavering.

Olivia examined his face partially illuminated by the porch light, listening to what she was afraid were hollow words.

"I've already asked too much of you and I've hurt you. I'm sorry." She turned back toward the Jeep and opened the driver's side door.

Suddenly she heard footsteps descending his front entrance. Turning to watch him stride toward her, she released the handle and pushed the door closed, pressing her back against the side of the car.

In a heartbeat, he stood over her and his right arm slipped gently around her lower back. "Olivia, please come inside." His voice was low, raspy, and firm.

Not wanting to disobey his wishes, she stepped away from the Jeep and grabbed onto his hand. Jake was waiting with tail wagging on the front steps.

Once inside, Colton became a much more hospitable host, rummaging the refrigerator for refreshments.

Olivia slipped out onto the gallery with Jake at her heels, returning to the spot on the railing she had staked out the first night she arrived, looking out over the harbor. Only this time she wasn't seeing what she was looking at. Jake settled down not far from her and curled up with his back to the railing, keeping an eye on the situation.

Colton joined her with two drinks in hand. He didn't have to ask. He handed her a glass of white wine and he hung onto a bottle of beer.

"Well, how about that. You've got wine." She wore a wide grin, despite the solemnity of the circumstances that brought her to his doorstep.

He paused for a moment. "I bought some the other day . . . in case you came back."

His gesture spoke volumes to her. She suddenly felt worse that she had hurt him. It had been an irrational moment, one she wished she could take back. She prayed she had not caused irreparable damage.

"Colton, I am sorry—"

He held up his hand. "It's water under the bridge. Let's move on. You have more important matters to deal with right now."

"I know but—"

He reached out and placed a finger gently on her lips.

She couldn't help herself, she kissed it.

In response, he reached out with one arm and slipped it around her waist. Olivia allowed him to pull her closer to his body. Her wine sloshed above the rim of the glass, spilling down the side as she lurched forward, but he didn't seem to care. Her face was inches from his. Leaning closer to each other, their lips connected in a passionate kiss. She got lost in the pleasure.

A tingling sensation stirred throughout her body. Their kiss eased quite naturally into a hug. She didn't want to let go of him. Her nose was buried in his hair and she breathed in deeply. He smelled incredible. It was hard to discern exactly what it was, but it reminded her of a natural, woodsy scent. She hung onto him and he didn't pull away. His body was remarkably strong and sturdy, like he could go up against any foe and come out victorious.

He seemed to sense she needed the support. They held each other as the night sky twinkled above them and the sea breezes caressed their bodies.

Flames flickering against the night sky suddenly crashed through her mind. She tried to push them away, aching to be lost in his arms instead. Without realizing, she pulled away from him slightly.

He sensed her movement. "What's wrong?"

"Nothing. I'm fine. . . . Happy to be here."

"Look, why don't we go over to your mother's place. I'll go with you. Let's see what's going on."

"I can't. I'm sure there's nothing left to see." The unbearable images were forever burned into her memory. "I just . . . can't," she confessed, taking a sip of wine.

Colton seemed to understand and turned back to his beer. They silently let their eyes wander out to the blinking lights in the tranquil harbor.

As they watched a small boat traverse the water, he still appeared to be thinking about the fire. "All right, then why don't you try to get some rest? Maybe I'll take a ride over and see what I can find out."

"That's sweet of you. I'm sure there's not much to learn, but I appreciate the offer."

Colton drained the dregs of the beer from the bottom of the bottle. He took her glass and refilled it in the kitchen, returning with another beer for himself as well. They slipped an arm around each other's waist. Olivia hung on tight and sipped her wine, taking in the harbor in silence. Even with the tropical breezes off the water, she shivered. Colton pulled her closer and kissed the top of her head.

After finishing her second glass of wine, she felt drowsy. Her head became heavy and found a resting place on Colton's chest. He offered to let her sleep in his bed. He would take the couch.

Olivia didn't have a lot of options. He was being unexpectedly sweet despite how she had treated him. As her eyelids grew heavy, she allowed him to guide her away from the spectacular view from the gallery. Again, he vowed to take the couch.

Their hands intertwined as they walked to his bedroom. Jake trotted along with them but remained outside the door. Olivia drew on the warmth of his hand. She turned to face him. They embraced. Their lips connected again in a more passionate kiss. Olivia was completely drawn in by him. Their two bodies slipped easily onto the bed, t-shirts and shorts scattered across the floor.

Colton's eyes shifted to her bandage. He opened his mouth to ask and looked into her eyes. In response, she pressed a long slender finger onto his lips to silence him.

"It's nothing," she insisted.

He looked concerned as if he knew it was more than "nothing" but chose to honor her wishes to ignore it.

Two tanned, youthful bodies embraced again and became one. They explored each other's bodies in the excitement of being the first time they had touched intimately and then made love, slowly and passionately. They held each other tightly afterwards. Her grip was approaching desperation—his was more along the lines of cradling. He stroked her hair and whispered in her ear. "You're so beautiful." She fell asleep in the comfort of his arms wrapped around her from behind.

The sea breeze played with the light cotton curtains at the windows.

In the middle of the night, he slipped out from under the sheets into the cover of darkness.

CHAPTER NINETEEN

Olivia awoke to sunshine spilling into the small bedroom through east facing windows. Naked in a sea of sheets and a little groggy, she replayed the beautiful evening she and Colton had shared the night before. She rolled over, wincing from shooting pain in her shoulder while grabbing an armful of Egyptian cotton to snuggle with, hoping to go back to sleep. There was no one else sharing the bed she was in.

Her face fell. Was the night before just a dream? Or perhaps a mistake. The fiery scene from her mother's house came crashing back, and she wished it had just been a nightmare.

She called out, anxious to see if he was still in the bungalow. "Colton?"

His voice could be heard from the kitchen. Before long he showed up at the door to the bedroom wearing only boxers, with two mugs in his hands. His hair was tousled from sleeping the night. His broad shoulders seemed to just slip through the doorway.

Olivia was touched by his sweet gesture. As he approached, she could see wisps of steam escaping from the tops of the mugs. She guessed it was coffee. He sat down gently on the side of the bed she was on. Rolling over toward him, she gathered up the sheets to retain as much coverage as she could manage. They looked into each other's eyes. Then she realized she had just opened hers, and she might look even worse than she had the night before, if that was possible. Quickly rubbing sleep from her face and running her fingers through her hair, she decided that would have to do. It was all she had to work with.

"I couldn't remember how you take your coffee. I guess I was focusing on something else the other morning. There's some milk and a little sugar in it." He looked at her expectantly as he passed it to her. Too much time elapsed before she answered.

"Oh, you prefer tea, don't you?" His face fell.

"Oh! No . . . no, this is fine," she insisted, not wanting to diminish his thoughtfulness. Tightening her grip on the sheets next to her chest, she sat up. She didn't want to make a fuss. It didn't matter. Not in the big picture, anyway.

"Oh, no. I'm starting to figure you out." He leaned back and grinned as if getting a better perspective. "White wine usually means tea. If it's red wine, then it's coffee."

Olivia just looked into his eyes, with her eyebrows raised and her forehead furrowed, imagining all the women he'd had in his bed.

"Oh, really," she teased, nodding with a smirk, examining his face more closely.

Colton's guilty expression made her giggle, but she had no intention of making him feel any worse. Instead, she had other ideas. The night before had not been enough.

She thanked him and took the mug from him, taking a couple sips, trying hard not to shudder. He sipped his and beamed while gazing at her. When she couldn't stand it any longer she put her mug down on the bedside table and grabbed his free hand. He let her pull him toward her and just landed his mug on the table before sprawling on the bed.

186

He wiggled up next to her as she pulled the sheets aside to let him in. He encircled her body with his muscular arms. Breathing in his scent, she became drawn in. He quickly slipped off his boxers and then moved in closer. She exhaled and relaxed, allowing him to take control of her body. They embraced and kissed passionately. Again their legs and arms entwined in one another. It was beautiful, gentle lovemaking. She accepted him easily and willingly. He kissed her sweetly on her breasts and neck, brushing an errant strand of wavy blonde hair from her face. She closed her eyes and became one with his body. It lasted longer than the night before, as if neither wanted it to end. Afterwards she lay in his arms and watched the sea breeze pushing its way past the curtains.

Noticing his feet protruding from the end of the loose sheet, Olivia was tempted to ask about the missing toe on his left foot but decided against it. She wanted the moment to last forever, but before she was ready Colton whispered in her ear.

"I have to go."

Determined to prolong their time together, she rolled over and lay on top of him, gazing longingly into his eyes. The warmth of their bodies connected. She inhaled deeply to be able to remember his scent after he was gone.

Her finger found its way to his lips. "Shhhhh."

"I have to take the boat out today. I'm meeting a family that comes every year from Connecticut. They're very sweet." He grinned as if recollecting humorous details about them. "A little quirky, but nice. I'll be gone all day."

"Oh." Olivia's face fell. She was deeply disappointed.

"I would love to say I'll be back later, but my band has a gig tonight. The timing is usually pretty tight. I tend to go straight there from the boat." Then he added, "Stay as long as you'd like."

Her eyes glazed over and she stopped listening. She hadn't seen it coming.

He slipped out of bed and she watched as he dressed, admiring his physique and longing for his touch. He leaned over, brushed a thin blonde tendril from her face, and gently kissed her forehead. He slipped on his brown flip-flops and then left without another word.

Feeling as though she had been discarded, Olivia tried in vain to push aside the feeling it had all been a mistake . . . or they had different expectations of their relationship. She rolled back to her side of the bed. The coffee mugs were still sitting where they had hastily placed them. The steam was no longer rising.

CHAPTER TWENTY

Olivia *remained between the sheets* in Colton's bed, worries, doubts and fears swirling inside her head. Someone had torched her mother's house. She couldn't imagine who would commit such a vicious act or why. Her paltry possessions had been reduced to nothing more than the clothes on her back. Of course, at that moment, she didn't even have those on. And after her surveillance mission the previous night, she was no closer to finding out what had happened to her mother. She had no choice but to return that evening. The mere thought chilled her to the core, but she had to go.

In the meantime, she would have to come up with more clothes to wear. Perhaps she would head downtown and pick up a few things. Though uncomfortable with using her credit card, she didn't have much choice. She would have to shop wisely.

Alone in the quiet bungalow, sadness tugged at her heart, and she tried to fight it off. Self-doubt crept in. Was she ever going to find out what happened to her mother? Could she? Who was working against her? Who had set fire to the bungalow? What were they after? And why?

Olivia gasped. If they were after her, they could hurt Colton if they followed her to his house. Shuddering, she knew she couldn't stay—she was putting him in danger.

Slipping out of bed, contemplating the potential peril she had inadvertently dragged Colton into, Olivia gathered her clothes strewn across the floor and dressed quickly. When she got to the kitchen she realized Jake didn't seem to be there and called out, "Jake? . . . . Jake?"

No response. She looked around.

"Jake?". . . Silence. No pitter-patter of paws on the floor. Disappointed, a corner of her heart felt empty. Colton must have taken his furry companion with him. But did that make sense? He was going to be on the boat all day.

Grabbing the handle of the refrigerator she pulled but quickly became uneasy nosing into his things. Deciding she had no business helping herself to his food she closed the door and stepped away. It was time to head downtown and do some shopping for herself. Under the circumstances, her situation could be construed as an emergency. She would deal with the credit card bill when it arrived.

Olivia freshened up as much as she could and then gathered her few remaining belongings. Her wallet, phone, car key, and camera. A wave of dizziness washed over her, and she tried to brush it off but knew she needed something in her stomach. Reluctantly she returned to the kitchen and grabbed a sandwich roll from a package on the counter, vowing again to shop for her own food. Setting her sights for the Jeep in the driveway, she decided it was time to return to the ashes and face the truth.

CHAPTER TWENTY-ONE

O*livia steered the Jeep into the familiar driveway* but all familiarity ended once she passed the mailbox. Considering the risk of showing up where the police would expect her to frequent, she swore she wouldn't stay long. Slowly she guided the vehicle down the meandering asphalt path. The stench of ash and burned wood was thick in the air. Her eyes quickly scanned the scene, trying to take in the devastation laid out in daylight's stark reality. Yellow police tape cordoned off the area as if the damage could be confined within its boundaries.

The left side of the house was completely gone. Charred piles of timbers lay haphazardly where the walls had been. The scattered debris looked as though glowing embers lurked below the surface and would reignite with the stir of a stick. The outside wall on the kitchen side was partially intact and the attached gallery was also recognizable. Evidence pointed to the fire starting on the left side, where her mother's studio had been, moving toward the kitchen. Firefighters must have gotten there in time to try to fight it from the gallery side.

Then something struck her. There, in the middle of the charred remains, stood the refrigerator. At first she didn't see it because it was blackened from the fire and blended in, but she could make out its shape, standing tall in all of the blackened mess. A chuckle escaped her lips as she found frivolity amid the heartache.

In her peripheral vision, she noticed her mother's chair out in the side yard. It had been far enough away from the house to remain untouched during the fire. She turned and walked deliberately toward it, knowing her mother would be pleased the chair remained unscathed. Olivia stood for a moment and examined it up close, in case she would never see it again. She ran her hand along one armrest and then the other. They were unexpectedly smooth, as if worn from years of use. She turned around and sank down into it, gazing out to the bay and beyond. Whoever had committed the unthinkable act could never take away the incredible view. That was completely out of their control. Her thoughts returned to her mother and how much she loved her colorful bungalow and the view beyond.

"Mom, I'm sorry. I know how much you loved this place, and I really wanted to be able to keep it." She choked on her words. Both eyes welled and she clenched her teeth, trying to fight the tears. "God, I wish I could have made it happen." Anger rose inside of her. "There's nothing left!" Sitting forward on the edge of the seat she clasped her forehead with both hands. The idea of never coming back, never having a place to come back to on the island, was agonizing. A stabbing pain in her gut grabbed her attention. Hunger had passed. Her stomach was sick from the painful loss.

The smell of burned wood had been a pleasant scent for her. Fireplace fires during Boston winters. Roasting marshmallows over the coals. Not anymore. The aroma would now have a tainted smell.

Olivia was convinced someone had set fire to the house, and she endeavored to understand what her mother had been involved in that could have triggered such an act of destruction. What could her mother possibly have done to provoke someone to do something so horrific?

Olivia pushed away the reality only several yards away from her and let her eyes rest, instead, on the intense sunshine shimmering on the water. She allowed herself to be completely pulled in and she remained there. It was a safe place. In spite of it all, she didn't feel threatened. Time had no meaning there. The firm seat was becoming familiar to her, unexpectedly comfortable. This was her home. It was her mother's home, even if there was no longer a structure on the land.

A vibration in her pocket disrupted her serenity. She stood up to pull out the phone and her face fell. She didn't feel as though she had any other option than to answer it. There was no point in postponing the inevitable. She took a couple steps away from her mother's chair.

"Hi, Dad." Her voice was as even as she could manage.

"Hey, Ollie."

Silence for a moment.

Olivia clenched her teeth in anticipation of the impending conversation. She had no intention of telling her father about the tragedy at Serenity Villa. Not having any good news at all to share with him, she was regretting answering the phone. Her feet started shuffling back toward the house.

"Thought I would check back in. Are you wrapping things up?" His voice was matter-of-fact, as if he were talking to a subordinate.

She had known the call would come at some point, and she swallowed hard.

"Ol, you've been down there for a few days already. This is not about hitting the beach and going out at night like I know you like to do when you're there." His voice was stern. "You'd better be taking care of everything you're supposed to be." The volume escalated. "Get it done already!"

Olivia blinked a couple times, tilted her head and bit down hard. She struggled not to react, at least not verbally. Even her eyelashes remained remarkably still.

"I am." She left it at that. She was not about to get into any of the loathsome details with him.

He pushed further. "How much more time do you need?"

"I don't know . . ." As anger boiled up inside, her eyelashes fluttered in a blur.

Silence on the other end. He was clueless as to what was going on.

"Have you talked with a real estate agent about listing the property?"

His demanding tone grated on her.

"Yes." Her voice was firm. She started off on a loop around the charred rubble, just to keep moving and keep herself on her toes while talking to her father.

"All right, then. That's good." His condescending tone riled her.

Silently she willed him not to ask any more questions.

"Yes." Searching for a way to change the subject, she cleared her throat.

"What else do you need to do?"

Olivia needed to get him off the phone.

"It's complicated." She winced, wrinkling her nose. That wasn't going to fly. "There's still some paperwork."

"Oh, for God's sake, Olivia. Do I need to pick up the phone and make things happen? I didn't want to get involved with all of this."

". . . I'll handle it." She spoke deliberately, trying not to sound like she was pleading. He was treating her like a child. She felt like a child. She hated how he made her feel. Her feet kept plodding in a circle around the house.

"You keep saying that. It's not happening." His voice boomed. "Oh, I never should have let you go off and try to handle this yourself." He mumbled his lasts few words.

She closed her eyes. "You know how things work down here. Everyone is on island time." She hoped that would sound familiar to him and jog his memory.

"Not if I have anything to say about it!" His voice thundered in her ears.

"Dad, I'll take care of it. Please." Her voice quivered. The pleading had begun.

Silence on the other end. Not even any static. He was thinking.

"Olivia, let me ask you something."

Her eyes grew wide. She dreaded what was going to come out of his mouth next. "What?"

"Is there a . . . uh . . . a body?"

She rubbed her forehead with her free hand and clenched her jaw. Her response was barely audible. "No." How crass could he be?

Silence again.

"I see."

There was a tapping sound on the other end of the phone.

"I'll check back in with you again soon."

The click in her ear was a relief. She shoved the phone back into her pocket in exasperation. If only her father would stay out of it. She wished he would leave her be.

Olivia turned to head back to the familiarity of her mother's chair but the toe of her shoe caught on something. She looked down to see what was sticking out from under the blackened, splintered boards. It took her a moment to comprehend what she was looking at. The bare foot and partial leg were charred like the mess that covered them.

Taking a couple steps backward, Olivia's stomach turned at the sight. Who could it belong to? As nausea crept in, she wasn't sure she wanted to know the answer.

Olivia had seen enough. The grotesque leg protruding out from under the rubble forced unthinkable images of the rest of the body obscured by the charred debris. The discovery further changed the vibe of her mother's place, as if the fire hadn't done enough already. Striding toward the Jeep she gritted her teeth, trying to ignore her internal voice urging her to call the police. She knew she couldn't. She was a wanted woman. Besides, they would find the body eventually. And since he was already dead, there wasn't any urgency in the matter.

Glancing back to the blackened pile that stood in place of her mother's home, she almost expected to see a delicate wisp of smoke rising silently from the middle of the fallen structure. The refrigerator standing erect on the gallery side of the home put a smile on Olivia's face, though. There was something oddly amusing about it.

CHAPTER TWENTY-TWO

he shops downtown enticed shoppers inside by leaving their front doors wide open allowing air-conditioning to spill out onto the sidewalk, and sun-parched passersby got a refreshing blast on a hot and steamy tropical day. They catered mostly to the tourists, but Olivia stopped into a small boutique she had previously visited and located a sale rack near the back. Pleased to be able to pick up a couple of shirts, a pair of capris, and a couple pairs of shorts close enough to her taste, she located the checkout and stood behind two middle-aged women with a pile of clothing on the counter. One was excitedly chatting, not seeming to notice the other was preoccupied with her cell. They were both clutching the same tote bag, sporting the name of their cruise ship, as well as multiple shopping bags from other stores. Midway through their transaction, one of the ladies stopped the clerk and asked about the availability of an item in a different color. To Olivia's dismay, the clerk promptly rounded the counter and bounded toward a far flung corner of the store with the cruise ship ladies in tow.

Tilting her head, she let out a long sigh in frustration. Island time. Acknowledging she had no particular place to get to, she willed herself to dig deep and find patience. Waiting for the clerk to finish with the other customers, Olivia's thoughts crept back to the gruesome sight of the foot sticking out from under the rubble. Guilty pangs for leaving the unidentified body behind had her considering how she could inform the police without them knowing it was her. She wondered if the corpse would provide any clues to help them find who had set the fire.

From the opposite corner of the store, the clerk asked if she wanted to try on the garments in her arms. Olivia recognized the woman was trying to buy herself some time while she assisted the other customers, but Olivia declined the offer.

Glancing at the garments lying on the counter, she spied a cell left by one of the ladies infatuated by the number of colors a particular shirt came in. Without giving much consideration to possible outcomes, Olivia snatched the phone and tucked it under her arm. Calling across the small store she told the sales clerk she had changed her mind and was going to try on the clothes.

Once inside the dressing room, she quickly dialed the police, cupping a hand around her mouth and speaking into her pile of clothes to prevent the other three woman from hearing her. A female police officer answered with a thick island accent. Listening closely to see if it was Barnes, Olivia smiled as she pictured how infuriated she would be if it was her. She kept her call brief and to the point.

"Seems you missed something at the fire last night."

"Who is this and where are you calling from?" the policewoman snapped, sounding rattled.

"That doesn't really matter. The point is there's a body under the rubble."

"What rubble? Who is this?" she demanded with a tone of indignation.

Olivia grinned. It *was* Barnes. "Better tell the investigators to go have another look."

Click. She continued to enjoy the moment as she imagined the look on the officer's face at the sound of the click in her ear. Peeking out from the changing room, Olivia could see the three ladies turning to head back to the checkout. She hurried to get there first and slipped the phone under the clothes they had left on the counter. Sizing up Olivia with suspicious eyes, the two cruise ship ladies returned to their spot next to her while the clerk rounded the counter and resumed their transaction. Olivia glared back at them. Once they were finished, Olivia purchased her selections and quickly exited into the alleyway, practically bumping into the two ladies. Not having progressed very far, they were only at the next store window, chatting and pointing to paintings in the window. It was the gallery where Olivia's mother's work was on display.

By early afternoon, the heat and humidity were trying her patience. She made a quick stop to pick up a bite at a popular sandwich place tucked into another of the narrow alleyways. On the way back to her car, raindrops kissed her skin as a light shower passed quickly through. Slipping into the driver's seat, she remembered she still needed to pick up some groceries. Not her favorite kind of shopping, but necessary nonetheless.

Reaching the food store in a matter of minutes, Olivia parked the Jeep in one of the parking slots with the faded lines and crumbling asphalt. Walking deliberately toward the front door, stepping around potholes, she could sense people hanging around the entrance like they had nothing better to do, and she kept her eyes averted as she walked in. After grabbing one of the handheld baskets, she traipsed up and down a few aisles, gathering basics she would need over the next couple of days. Or would it be longer than that? Who knew?

Before stepping to the end of the shortest checkout line, she stopped to consider getting something for Colton as a sort of thank-you-for-letting-me-stay-at-your-place-even-though-I-treated-you-like-crap gift. She redirected her steps over to the alcohol section, taking a moment to peruse the wines and hard alcohol. Finally she chose a large bottle of coconut rum for him and a bottle of Chardonnay for her, amazed at how cheap the rum was since it didn't have to be imported.

After a relatively uneventful checkout, she returned to the parking lot. Just as she reached the Jeep, her pocket vibrated. "Oh, shit!" she bemoaned, figuring it was her father again.

She dropped the bags next to the car and retrieved her phone, fully expecting to just ignore the call, but it wasn't a number she recognized. The area code was 340. The U.S. Virgin Islands. She answered it.

"Hello?"

"Miss Benning?"

"Yes?"

"This is Lieutenant Woods of the United States Coast Guard."

She closed her eyes, afraid of what his next words were going to be.

CHAPTER TWENTY-THREE

A *painful jab shot though Olivia's stomach.* She pressed her free hand against her mouth for a moment to contain the subtle groan building inside of her. "Yes, Lieutenant."

"Ma'am, you need to come down to the station. We have a . . . uh . . . a . . . ma'am there is a . . . a body that has washed up on the eastern end of the island. We were called out to assist in the retrieval. It hadn't technically reached land, so we launched a rescue boat and retrieved it." He hesitated as if waiting to see if she would respond in some way to indicate she understood what he was relaying to her. "Can you stop by? Are you very far away? Do you need a ride?"

Olivia stood motionless in the hot summer sun, her phone pressed to the side of her face. His words echoed through her head. As she tried to make sense of them, an unintelligible sound emerged from her throat.

"Ma'am? Excuse me?"

Her mouth was dry. "I'll . . ." She swallowed hard. "I'll be right there."

Her peripheral vision became fuzzy. Numbness crept slowly through her body. Moving through the motions of loading the grocery bags in the backseat, she climbed into the driver's seat and fired up the engine. Distracted by the onerous news that awaited her, she drove to the Coast Guard station, just up the road on Waterfront Highway, not paying particular attention to the vehicles or pedestrians near her. Somehow she navigated successfully around them. As she pulled into the entrance the chain link gate slid to the right. Easily she found a parking spot in the small lot to tuck the Jeep into and walked toward the front door.

Upon entering the station, she barely noticed the cool air that brushed her face. Instead she focused on Lieutenant Woods, who strutted toward her with heels clicking on the linoleum floor. As he neared, it struck her that his call may have been merely a guise to draw her in so the island police could arrest her.

"Miss Benning, thanks for coming."

Thanks for coming? Quite cordial, even for the United States Coast Guard. Apparently there was no direct line of communication between them and the police department. She was temporarily off the hook but they would catch up to her at some point.

"I'm sorry to have to bring you in here, but I think you need to take a look."

Olivia's eyes got wide. Take a look? What was he expecting her to do?

"Excuse me?"

"The morgue is actually over at the hospital, but I can take you and you can identify—"

"Identify?"

"Yes. They will need you to make a positive identification."

Olivia took a deep breath. It was a lot to take in at once.

She looked into his eyes. "I don't know that I can." Her voice was low and raspy as if she was talking to herself. She took a step backward away from him and what he was asking her to do.

His face was solemn, yet stern.

She stared through a window across the room and shook her head in defiance.

"We need you to try," he urged her gently.

A sick feeling crept into her stomach. She couldn't believe it was all coming to this. Looked like her father would get his wish for her to wrap things up quickly.

Before she knew it, she was whisked into a government vehicle for the short ride to the hospital. It was a standard-issue black sport utility vehicle. Not a full-sized Suburban but probably something along the lines of a Yukon.

The light pink façade of the hospital was all too familiar. It was the last thing she saw before she made her escape. Following the lieutenant toward the same side entrance she had used as an exit, Olivia was relieved to see they were entering the building inconspicuously. The lieutenant retrieved a key from his pants pocket she surmised not too many people were privy to possess. After he swiftly opened the door and held it for her, he removed his aviator sunglasses and slipped them into his shirt pocket. Olivia walked next to him down a long hallway before reaching a series of doors on the first floor. Woods tapped four distinct times on the third door and took a step backward as it opened. They were greeted by a large black man in green scrubs, a white shower-cap-looking elastic rimmed cap on his head, and some sort of a microphone hanging from his right ear that curved around his jaw, the end of which was hovering near his mouth.

The two men exchanged a few words. The coroner glanced over the lieutenant's shoulder at Olivia while they conversed.

Her small frame shivered uncontrollably. She grabbed an errant strand of blonde wavy hair and tucked it behind one ear. Desperately trying to stand tall and be strong, she followed the lieutenant into the darkened room while the man in scrubs stood back and held the door open for them. The air was cool with a pungent odor of something sour mixed with some sort of antiseptic. She wrinkled her nose in response.

It was a relatively small room with a large metal posable light hanging over a single metal examining table in the middle. Olivia was grateful the table was empty. Rows of fluorescent lights in the ceiling had been dimmed, giving the room a strange glow. A grid of metal drawers ran along the wall opposite the door. The lieutenant took a position on the right side of the room as though he was trying to be unobtrusive. Olivia came to a stop next to the examining table, taking a second glance to confirm it was empty.

No one spoke as the coroner walked silently toward the large metal drawers. He took hold of a handle located in the middle of the wall and then froze. He turned to Olivia.

"Ma'am. You've probably never had to do this before. I have to warn you. This, uh . . ." He paused and cleared his throat as if he was struggling to find the right words.

Olivia searched his face.

"Uh, ma'am, you . . ."

Clearly the big burly ME was less comfortable dealing with the living than the dead.

"Doctor, I know what I am about to see will be none other than horrifying. I wish it didn't need to happen, but I think I'm the only person on the island right now who can ID her."

He raised his eyebrows, obviously taken aback by her directness.

"All right, then." He turned back toward the drawer and pulled on the handle. The sound of metal scraping on metal brought into view the outlines of a body shrouded in a white covering.

Olivia stepped tentatively closer. Her mouth felt dry and her breathing was shallow.

The coroner took hold of the top edge of the sheet nearest the wall and turned to her again.

"Ready?"

"Sure," she murmured, her legs twitching in anticipation.

Slowly he pulled the sheet down to reveal just the head of a woman with stringy blonde hair plastered to the sides of her head. Her skin was a sickening chalky white with pink blotches on her cheeks.

Olivia stared in horror but took a couple more steps closer to the body. Her wide eyes fixated on the pale, seemingly rigid body.

The two men looked to her for confirmation.

She blinked hard a couple times. Her jaws ached from clenching her teeth hard.

They gave her a moment to take in the grotesqueness of the body.

"It's not her." Her voice was barely audible. She closed her eyes in relief.

Olivia could understand why they might speculate the body was her mother, but obviously they didn't know her like she did. The only resemblance, and it was a stretch to make any kind of connection, was the color of her hair. She felt sorry for the unknown woman and her family and friends who had not yet received word of her fate.

The man in scrubs looked into Olivia's eyes and spoke gently. "The body has been in the water. That affects the way it looks. It's . . ." He seemed to be searching for the right words again. "Puffier than normal. And more . . . pale, too."

"How long was she in the water?"

"Taking into consideration the condition of her skin and the water temperature here among other factors . . . probably two to three days."

"How do you know?" She pressed further.

"I've seen more of these than I care to think about, but in the warmer water here in the Caribbean, a body will surface sooner after being submerged than it does in colder water up north. This one looks like two, maybe three days."

Olivia weighed his insight.

"It's not her." This time she was more assertive. Who was he to question her judgment? He didn't know her mother. Besides the timing was all wrong. Two or three days? That didn't add up. A wave of relief cascaded through her. Thank God.

The ME glanced to the lieutenant.

Woods spoke up. "Okay, Miss Benning. Sorry to put you through this. Thank you for taking the time. We appreciate it."

He started for the door and Olivia followed behind, but the coroner wasn't finished with her just yet.

"Just to be certain, could you leave a DNA sample with us? I'd like to run some tests to verify."

Annoyed, Olivia agreed but knew it would lead them nowhere. Before she reached the door she turned back. "How did she die?"

The coroner cleared his throat. "I, uh, don't know yet. I still need to perform an autopsy."

He hesitated and then shared what could only be seen under the sheet. "Looks like there may be ligature marks on her wrists and ankles . . . that's all I've made a note of so far."

Olivia nodded, acknowledging her understanding, and then turned and exited the cold room.

CHAPTER TWENTY-FOUR

Climbing behind the wheel of her mother's Jeep back at the Coast Guard station, Olivia was assaulted by a blast of heat from the tropical sun baking through the windshield. Leaving the door ajar and her leg hanging down, she reached for the ignition. With her hand suspended in mid-air, it hit her she had nowhere to go. She had left Colton's place that morning, resolving to leave it behind for good, but that novel vow wasn't going to hold up. Hating the idea of returning, especially when he wasn't there, she had no choice. Her back was against the wall. Reluctantly, she pointed the Jeep back up the mountain.

Her energy level waned as the events of the day plagued her. After storing her perishables in his refrigerator and stowing the rest in a cupboard, she left the coconut rum on the counter for Colton to find and looked for a corkscrew to open the bottle of wine.

With time to kill before heading back down to the landfill, Olivia counted on a glass of dry white on the gallery to help blur the scene at the morgue. The foul smell lingered inside her nose. Her heart broke for the woman she saw in the metal drawer. She hoped her family would find peace with such a tragedy, but she couldn't keep herself from rejoicing it wasn't her mother.

Olivia allowed herself to be drawn out onto the gallery, which was becoming a favorite space of hers. Rays emanating from the setting sun hovering over the horizon were captivating, yet fleeting. It wouldn't be long before it slipped out of sight. There was something almost magical about it, making her fantasize about what was behind it.

After the beautiful orange orb settled below the distant horizon, Olivia grabbed a bite to eat from what she had purchased and added a splash of wine to her glass. Alone in his quiet house, she paced from room to room, growing fearful of what the evening would bring. Again, she wondered where Jake was. It was little more than a passing thought, yet she yearned for his company.

As her eyelids grew heavy, she had a burning desire to rest. Settling onto the couch in the living area, her head found the armrest and she was soon sound asleep as the waning sunlight turned into evening darkness.

Olivia slept soundly until she was awaked by a strange dream. Disoriented, she squinted her eyes and looked around the room to ascertain where she was. As it all filtered back into her memory, she bolted to her feet, certain she had overslept.

The clock on his stove indicated it was time to head out.

CHAPTER TWENTY-FIVE

A s *Olivia approached, she noticed it looked different* than the night before. A primitive gate made out of metal tubing in the shape of two triangles closed off the entrance. A corner of each triangle overlapped in the center and were secured by a padlock. She had no choice but to ditch the Jeep along the side of the main road and hike in. Taking a moment to consider what she might run up against, she walked around to the back of the vehicle and opened the hatch. After rummaging through the emergency kit, she shoved a couple of flares into her back pockets. They might come in handy.

Fighting off tremendous trepidation, she started down the dirt access road. One foot in front of the other. Camera hanging from her neck.

The moon was not much larger than the previous evening. She hoped she would be able to see what she needed to see and capture it on film, while steering clear of anyone adverse to her photography pursuits.

The air was still, and the only sound was the familiar tree frogs serenading anyone who would listen. Ko-kee, ko-kee. Ordinarily Olivia would enjoy their cadence but not tonight.

The trek down the road was not arduous, it just took more time than she wanted to spend. She was anxious to get into place, under cover and ready to capture whatever was going to transpire down the deserted dirt road. Walking briskly, Olivia listened for vehicles from behind her and any activity in front of her, ready to dive into the bushes along the road to avoid being detected.

Several minutes passed as she made her way in the darkness. The air was still, even the tree frogs had fallen silent. . . . that was, until she got close to where she had staked out a vantage point the night before. There was some sort of activity going on. A completely different atmosphere. Sounded like shouting. Several people yelling. Anxious to get near enough to see what was happening, Olivia picked up her pace until she got as close as she dared and then darted into the brush to maintain her cover, one hand clutching the camera. She pushed her way through the thick bushes and came to a stop where she could see, yet remain hidden.

Olivia stared through the branches. There was a crowd of men. A lot of noise. Shouting. They were standing around in a loosely formed ring. She couldn't make out what was going on inside the circle. A dog barked in the distance. She pulled her camera toward her face and snapped photos. Sometimes the camera lens saw more than the naked eye, so she just kept going on faith. More dogs barked.

From time to time, she pulled back from the viewfinder to try to understand what was happening. Still, men shouting. Some jumping. Then the din of activity subsided and the ring of men settled back as if anticipating something else. There were a couple of high fives in the crowd. Olivia watched intently, trying to discern the situation.

Again, the shouting swelled. Something was going on in the center of the crowd, as if they were encircling some sort of activity, rooting on the participants. Was there betting going on? On what?

Olivia tried to work her way through the bushes to get a closer look. The crowd was now animated. She grew excruciatingly uncomfortable being as close as she was, but she needed to see.

She could hear dogs. Growling . . . snarling, some crying as if in pain.

It didn't make sense to her at first. She kept listening and observing the crowd. Then her face fell.

"Oh, God," she whispered. "No . . . please, God, no."

With eyes wide open, she tried to make out what was happening in the arena, through the crowd. The noise told the story. She winced, feeling sick to her stomach.

"Dear Lord, please make them stop." Olivia closed her eyes. She couldn't bear to see, yet she knew she had to take photos to capture what was going on for proof.

Olivia snapped photos in rapid succession. She was trying not to look, but she needed to capture the vicious act.

The crowd parted momentarily, allowing her a glimpse of the carnage. Dogs. Her mouth became parched and she tried to swallow. There were two black dogs in the center of the crowd. A ring of sorts. The two dogs were being encouraged to fight. Olivia couldn't make out the breed, mixed or otherwise. They darted quickly toward each other and seemed to be responding to the crowd's negative energy. Chants kept the two animals focused on attacking each other. Other dogs were restrained on the sidelines as if waiting for their turns.

Olivia took a step back, repulsed by the barbarity. Her head swirled. She had heard dog fighting was an issue in the islands, but she was sickened by seeing firsthand the extent to which heartless individuals would go to make money on such a gruesome activity. Unfortunately, gambling on dog fighting could be lucrative, not only for the onlookers who bet on the "game" but also for the "house," whoever took the risk to host the fights. Even though dog fighting was illegal, it was challenging for authorities to track down. As soon as there was a crackdown, the participants would pull up stakes and find a new location, usually as far off the beaten path as possible.

This was what her mother was intent on documenting and what Olivia needed to capture on her camera. She was stunned her mother had put herself in such extreme danger. And for what? Why was she gathering evidence? Who was she working with?

Olivia refocused on the center ring. The two dogs were viciously attacking each other. Repetitive bites along both of their necks had become bloody. Both exhibited symptoms they were reeling from their injuries.

Would the dogs have to fight to the death? Olivia was afraid she already knew the answer. She turned away as she heard multiple voices from the crowd encouraging them to continue. She couldn't bear to watch. The sounds emanating from the arena were more than she could stomach. The growling and snarling continued. An occasional yelp caused the crowd to cheer in its twisted sense of entertainment. The canine crying hit her in the gut. She leaned over and lost what little food was in her stomach. Her knees buckled and she landed hard on the ground, sharp pain emanating from her shoulder. Wiping her mouth, she searched for something to grab onto to pull herself up.

As she floundered, something nudged her hand and she yanked it back. At first, she couldn't tell what had touched her but soon made out a small animal in the dim moonlight. Sensing it wouldn't hurt her, she spoke to it and it crept slowly toward her. A puppy. It nudged her again. It was dark. Probably black. Olivia was drawn to its innocence, and she immediately felt the need to protect it. Would the precious little pup be forced into the ring to fight another, perhaps larger, dog? She gathered the strength to stand up. Her world spun for a moment, but she waited for it to straighten itself out before moving again.

She reached down to scoop up the puppy but strong hands pulled her away before she could reach it and she landed hard on the ground. There was movement in the bushes behind her. Animated voices grew louder. Her camera was snatched off her neck. A burning sensation was all that was left where the strap had hung. Someone pulled her arms behind her, yanking her upright. She groaned and tried to wriggle her hands out of their grasp, but their grip just tightened. Her shoulder exploded in pain.

"Get off me!" she screamed in desperation. "Get off!"

Olivia fought to get free. She knew her camera was gone but she had to escape. After witnessing their illegal activity and getting caught documenting it, her life depended on it.

The crowd in the distance continued to be wrapped up in the dog fighting and gambling at the expense of the innocent dogs.

Clearly a couple of thugs were going to make sure no one had any proof. They had flashlights. A bright light shown in her face. She winced and pulled away from the source. Their voices had the lyrical island accent. Without warning, there was a powerful arm around her neck, constricting her airways. She had trouble catching her breath. Her head was pushed down from behind. Her mind reeled. A silent prayer went up for help. Olivia vehemently wanted to walk out of there alive. With her face forced downward, she searched the ground to see what she could see in the limited and fleeting light.

Down at her feet, the beams from the flashlights danced. Several feet. More than just the two men she perceived were there. Others had joined the fray. Were they scuffling amongst themselves? A pair of brown leather flip-flops on light-colored feet came into view. Her eyes grew wide. She prayed it wasn't so. While she tussled with whoever restrained her, she wildly searched the ground to find the flip-flops again. Was the left pinkie toe shorter than usual? Too many feet moving at once to tell.

Again a brown leather flip-flop came back into view. A left foot in the scuffle with her captors. She strained to see if the toe was truncated. The feet danced in and out of the beams of light. She could see a small toe . . . that was cropped. But was it really? She couldn't be sure. The possibility hit her hard, as if someone had punched her in the stomach and kicked her behind the knees. Olivia struggled to remain on her feet. Her hands were held tightly behind her. She was outnumbered. Was he one of them? Islandese pervaded the frantic chatter.

Two shots rang out, momentarily halting the fray, and the hands holding her tightly abruptly loosened and fell away. Olivia landed awkwardly on the ground with one arm pinned underneath her. Fortunately it wasn't the one attached to her injured shoulder. In the pale moonlight she could see a couple male bodies lying on the ground not far from her. She scrambled to her feet and dashed through the bushes until she reached the deserted dirt road. There was no point in trying to stay undercover alongside the road. She broke into a run and bolted for her car. She ran for her life. From the bushes she had fled, another gunshot rang out in the night. Trembling, she could only imagine what was going on.

The commotion continued behind her. Loud voices. Did she hear footsteps out on the dirt road? Olivia kept her focus on getting to safety. She tore straight for the main road. Ignoring the ache in her legs and the burning in her lungs, she ran. It seemed as though the access road continued forever. She couldn't see the end. She kept running. No time to lose.

Finally, Olivia caught sight of the main road ahead of her. Her car wasn't much farther. She kept running, laboring to take in short puffs of air. Her heart beat rapidly, thumping wildly against the inside of her ribcage. Her feet reached the pavement of Route 30 and she turned right to head east. Her Jeep was just a few yards down.

Dumped impulsively off on the side of the road, it looked like she had been in too much of a hurry to park it properly. No matter.

Pulling the key out of her pocket, pressing the unlock button as she approached, she jumped into the driver's seat, leaving the door open and her left leg dangling as she melted into the seat and tried to gather herself. Her chest heaved. Figuring she was safe out on the main road, she took a precious moment to regroup. She had placed herself in grave danger and barely escaped. The brown flip-flops flashed through her mind. It didn't make any sense. How could he be involved in such a horrible activity? What a monster. Had she misjudged him completely? Hurt from betrayal seeped deep inside her heart.

The sound of the gunshots echoed in her head. Was he one of the ones to go down? She honestly didn't know if she cared.

Headlights approached from the east and the car passed on its way toward Charlotte Amalie. Olivia was glad to see another vehicle on the road. Lights in her rearview mirror announced another car approaching from the opposite direction. It also passed her, more closely than the first since it was on the left side of the road, on its way toward Red Hook.

Once she caught her breath, Olivia's sense of urgency returned. She was not out of danger yet. Unsure which way to turn, she figured anywhere was better than Landfill Road.

As she reached for the ignition key, something brushed up against her calf. Instinctively, she yelled and pulled her leg inside. Looking down to see what had touched her, she could just make out the pup from the bushes. Happy to see him, a flood of warmth spread throughout her body. His little legs had carried him away from the terror and trauma in the landfill, and he was searching her eyes to see if she would take him with her. Leaning over to scoop him up, she winced as pain shot through her shoulder. She pulled him in close to her chest and he whimpered softly, melting her heart. Undoubtedly he had been through a lot in his short life.

Another car approached in front of her. Olivia didn't pay much attention to it. She snuggled the puppy close to her face and stroked his back. The acrid smell of his fur made her nose curl up, but she knew it was temporary and the result of the conditions he'd had to endure. She hugged him anyway. Never wanting to let him go, she buried her face in his fur, yearning to bring him back to Boston with her. The side of her mouth turned up in amusement as she pictured how furious she would make her father.

The car passed the Jeep as the others had done, but when Olivia glanced into her rearview mirror, she noticed it was making a U-turn in the middle of the road behind her. She knew that couldn't be good. Gently placing the pup on the passenger seat beside her, she reached for the key and started up the engine. It looked as though things were going to get even more interesting.

Before she could put her car in drive, flashing lights appeared in her mirrors.

"Shit!" A patrol car pulled in behind her. She had a decision to make. Hang around to see how much more trouble she could get into or hit the gas and make a run for it. She shut the driver's side door while she took a split second to think.

Then she realized she didn't have much of a choice. Where was she going to run? She was on an island and it wasn't that big. And the roads weren't exactly conducive to a high-speed chase. She chose to stay put and see why the officer had stopped. She surmised it could just be routine. After all, her vehicle was pulled haphazardly off the side of the road. More likely, they had located a wanted woman and she wouldn't be going very far. Reluctantly, she turned the key to shut off the engine.

Olivia watched in her mirror as a uniformed officer exited his car and approached hers from behind. His broad shoulders swayed in the same cadence as the strides of his long legs, his flashlight swung in rhythm. Lights on top of his patrol car continued to pulse behind him. She blinked her eyes to get relief from the bright lights.

As the officer strutted toward her car, she rolled down her window. He leaned in, elbows resting on the window frame, shining the light in her face. He was a large man and took up most of the open window. Shielding her eyes, Olivia leaned away from his intimidating presence.

The little pup growled but only half-heartedly. Under different circumstances it would have been cute. She placed a gentle hand on his back and shushed him softly. She tried to reassure him even though she felt anything but assured.

"Ma'am, license and registration, please." He moved the light over to the passenger seat to see what growled.

"What seems to be the problem, officer?" She played the part of the innocent bystander.

"License and registration, please." Obviously he was not in a chatty mood.

Olivia opened the glove compartment and pulled out the requisite paperwork, handing it and her license to the officer. Movement in the rearview mirror caught her eye. The officer's partner was becoming interested in her situation. He exited the cruiser from the passenger side but stood between the two vehicles, talking into his shoulder mic.

As she squinted in the bright light of the flashlight, her body shivered at the prospect of where she would be heading from there. A local lock-up? A foul-smelling cinderblock holding area? Wondering if there would at least be a separate area for women, she shuddered at the mess she had gotten herself into. Like mother, like daughter. Her father would be proud.

"Miss Benning, I'm sure you're aware there is a warrant out for your arrest."

His words hung in the air. Her body stiffened and felt cemented to the car seat. A lump formed in her throat.

"You've been busy in the short time you've been on island. Might be a while until you see the light of day again, at least as a free woman."

They had her. She couldn't believe it was all going to end like this. Her stomach twisted in a painful knot.

The other cop popped in at the passenger side window. The pup sat up and growled again, directing his aggression toward the new arrival, but Olivia stroked his back and he settled down again. Her eyes welled at the thought she wouldn't be able to take care of him.

"Miss Benning?" He had his own flashlight that appeared even brighter than his partner's, if that was possible. New batteries?

"Yes?" Wincing from the lights in her face, she felt the full effect of being interrogated.

"What are you doing out here at night? On Landfill Road?"

She opened her mouth, contemplated possible answers, and decided to wing it. She wasn't technically on Landfill Road, and they would have no way of knowing if she actually had been there.

"I pulled my car over when I saw this little guy." She reached over and stroked his fur. "He seemed to be lost. No collar. Didn't seem to belong to anyone."

"Uh-huh." The cop with the brighter flashlight didn't seem all that interested in her story. Perhaps he had been expecting a different answer.

Unable to see the second face past his light, she just looked in his general direction, trying to hold her ground.

The officer at the driver's side window seemed to be feeling left out. Still holding her paperwork, he cleared his throat but remained silent.

Olivia slowly made out features on both of their faces. It looked as though the cop near the pup was an older man, perhaps a senior officer, who had gathered more information while he stayed behind in the cruiser.

"Miss Benning, I was surprised to see your car on the side of the road. Kind of late to be out and about. Don't you think?"

Unsure where the conversation was going, Olivia was feeling exceedingly uncomfortable having two cops as bookends. She looked from one to the other, carefully considering her response. "Not so much." She just threw it out there, as casual as she could make it sound, to see what would come back.

"Miss Benning, do you know what your situation is right now?"

She hung her head in shame. It was the end of the road for her.

The junior officer came alive. "We were just discussing there is a warrant out for Miss Benning's arrest." His voice was firm, insistent on bringing his partner up to date. "Possession of an unregistered firearm, unlawful discharge of a firearm, resisting arrest, escape while in custody, and the list goes on from there."

Olivia cringed. The words cut into her. She had not intended for any of it to happen. But somehow it did. Her father would be so disappointed. Her mother . . . would be devastated. The latter transgression tore into her soul more than anything else could.

The more senior officer took control. "Miss Benning, my partner and I need to have a moment. Excuse us." He gestured with his head to the younger man to meet him behind her car.

Olivia closed her eyes and leaned back against the seat, envisioning the gun in her hand on the gallery with Carson's bloody body and then revisiting the bungalow completely engulfed in flames. She then moved quickly on to the horror she witnessed earlier at the landfill. If Colton was alive, was he on her side or not? She had no idea.

A more immediate concern was her need to get out of there. If they took her into custody, she would no longer be able to search for her mother. And if she couldn't do it, who would?

She glanced into the side-view and rearview mirrors, trying to keep an eye on the officers.

A new set of flashing lights approached from behind. More company. Apparently capturing a fugitive wanted for murder was a priority for the police. They had found their most wanted woman. The squad car pulled in front of Olivia's car and backed up to close the space, sandwiching her between the two police cruisers. She was trapped. If escape had ever seriously entered her mind, it was no longer an option. She imagined she had the attention of at least half the officers on duty that evening.

The two arriving officers walked past her car and up to the first responding officers, still standing behind her car, and exchanged a few words. Three of the men turned and walked back toward their vehicles while one of the later arrivals took his place at her passenger side window.

Olivia sat still, holding her breath, waiting to hear him speak. He leaned in with his flashlight shining on his face, instead of hers. She recognized him as the officer who paid her a brief visit in the hospital. Detective Benson. The same hospital, of course, from where she had escaped. She closed her eyes and lamented the rash decisions that had led her to her current desperate situation.

"Miss Benning?"

"Yes." She could barely speak the word. She cleared her throat and tried again. "Yes."

He turned his flashlight toward her. "Ma'am, are you all right?"

Olivia was surprised by his apparent concern. "I'm fine." As fine as anyone could be who was wanted for murder and had just escaped from the wretched grasp of animal abusers. But otherwise, she was fine.

"You seem to be bleeding." He pointed toward the side of her face.

Olivia reached up and ran her hand down her cheek. There didn't seem to be anything wrong. She didn't feel anything unusual. Nothing hurt. But when she pulled her hand away, it felt wet. She turned the palm of her hand over and could see something red lit up by the flashlight. It didn't make sense. As she turned to her newfound friend, Detective Benson shifted his light with her glance. In horror, she could see a gash on the side of the small pup's body.

"No!" Olivia was devastated to see he had been injured, possibly at the hands of her intended captors. She was beyond words. But he was the lucky one who appeared to have gotten a second chance. Somehow he had found his way out of the grisly mayhem and followed her to her car.

"Poor little guy." The detective reached down and touched the top of his head gently. The pup was done growling. He leaned into the officer's hands. As the light shifted, he became lost in the darkness of the front seat and whimpered.

"Why don't I take him over to the animal shelter to get him some medical attention?" He reached down to pick him up.

Olivia lunged toward him, hand outstretched. "No! I'll take him." She didn't want to let him go. If the cop took him, she would never see him again . . . but then again since she was essentially in police custody, she probably would never see him again, anyway.

"We'll be heading back that way. It's not too far from the station." The officer's hands had stopped in midair. Olivia gasped as he scooped up the pup.

Her heart sank as the detective turned and handed the innocent little ball of fur to his partner, who had been lingering near the trunk of their cruiser. She swore she would find him and rescue him again.

Unexpectedly, the detective opened the passenger side door and slid in next to her, settling his oversized body into the seat. She winced as the overhead light illuminated the interior until he slammed the door shut. Suddenly the car felt smaller. An uncomfortably tight space. Confining. A strange smell permeated the vehicle. Stale cigar smoke? Appearing to be gathering himself, he directed his flashlight toward the floor. Finally he spoke.

"Miss Benning, unfortunately our last meeting was rather brief."

She shifted uncomfortably in her seat.

"You left before we could get some things straightened out."

Olivia listened intently, trying to remain calm.

"How is your shoulder doing, by the way?"

She was not in the mood to discuss her shoulder.

"It's fine, much better," she lied.

"Oh, good to hear."

Unable to endure the small talk any longer, she was through beating around the bush. "Look, what exactly are the charges against me? I didn't mean for any of this to happen." The anticipation of her mother's shame chilled her to the core.

"Well . . . initially we had some pretty hefty charges stacked up on you. It seemed like a tight case, especially with the gun found next to you and the gunshot residue on your hand. But then ballistics came back and changed everything."

"Ballistics?"

CHAPTER TWENTY-FIVE

"Yeah. Turns out you didn't shoot Carson."

"*What?*" She was stunned at the revelation. Could it be true?

"The caliber bullet pulled out of him did not match the gun you had used."

A flood of relief filled her. But it didn't change the fact he had been shot. Poor guy. Her mother would be heartbroken.

"There was only one shell casing from your gun where you had been standing, and we retrieved the bullet in the ground just a couple feet away."

"Then who—"

"We're working on the 'who,' but we located the casing from the bullet he or she used and whoever it was stood behind you, probably under cover of the brush. The bullet pierced your shoulder on its way to who we believe was its intended victim." He cleared his throat in a loud raspy way.

So that explained what happened to her shoulder.

"The officers who initially stopped you this evening weren't aware of this most recent information." He motioned toward the officers behind them with his head. "I just got the results."

Olivia was speechless for a moment, elated by the news.

"I suppose I could still hold you on escaping custody, but I don't think we had a chance to read you your rights before you checked yourself out of the hospital. Besides, I've got more important matters to worry about. Like who actually shot him and why."

His last comment brought her back to the bottom line. She wished there was something she could do to change the facts. Her heart broke for Carson . . . and her mother.

"Detective, I appreciate you letting me know—"

"Oh, and these are yours." He handed over her documents.

"Thanks."

His walkie-talkie squawked, abruptly pulling his attention away from her. He held up a hand as if that justified the interruption, slipped the two-way out of his belt loop and held it close to his ear.

Listening closely, she could make out something about Landfill Road. Report of shots fired. Working hard to maintain a face that looked disinterested, she reeled from the grotesque scene she had left behind that the officers would soon find.

Detective Benson pulled his handheld radio to his mouth and indicated he was nearby and would respond. More squawking with other officers checking in and the dispatcher acknowledging. Finally he turned to her.

"Ma'am, you're free to go. I need to respond to this call." He patted his two-way. "But I would like to talk further about the incident at your mother's house. In the meantime, if you think of anything I should know, you give me a call." He fished his card out of the left pocket of his standard-issue blue short-sleeved collared shirt. "I mean that. You call me. All right?" He took a swat at her shoulder in a clumsy attempt to connect in a friendly and supportive way.

Olivia frowned at his awkward motions in the dimly lit car. "Okay, thanks. I will," she blurted out to appease him.

The detective grabbed the handle and opened the door, which illuminated the dome light briefly, causing her to squint again. He quickly exited her car, slamming the door behind him, and jogged to the squad car parked in front of her. He had a job to do.

The cruiser spun out of the dirt alongside the road in order to change directions and head back toward the landfill. The squad car behind her replicated the movement.

Kicking herself, she realized she should have asked the detective what Carson's last name was. Could he be the CK who was sending cryptic faxes to her mother? Damn, she had missed her chance.

Thinking back to the day she had met Carson, she realized she had lost the opportunity to ask him directly. She chastised herself for both blunders.

Olivia sat alone in the car. No flashing lights. No cute puppy in the passenger seat.

CHAPTER TWENTY-SIX

O*livia drove slowly back up the mountain,* visions of the events on Landfill Road haunting her thoughts. Realizing she had been foolish to go back into the lion's den for a second night, she conceded she had risked her life and had nothing to show for it.

With nowhere else to go, she decided with nervous trepidation to return to Colton's place.

Reaching the top of his driveway, she could just make out a car parked at the end of it. Keeping her eye on the vehicle, she descended the drive. At the bottom she was astonished to see it was Colton's Jeep. *She had been mistaken!* It wasn't him she had seen earlier. She couldn't park her car and get out of it fast enough.

She ran to the door and burst through it without knocking.

"Colton!" she squealed, anxious to see him.

There was no immediate answer.

"Colton?" A little louder.

She ran into the living area to find a man sitting on the far end of the couch, leaning back with one leg propped casually across his knee, one arm across the back of the couch and the other resting on the armrest she had slept on earlier. He held a can of beer in the hand on the arm rest.

The man on the couch wasn't Colton.

Olivia stared at him, not sure what his presence meant.

"Hello, David." Her voice was uneven and a bit hoarse.

"Olivia." His face was solemn, clearly not there for a social visit.

"Where's Colton?" She choked on her words as a lump formed in her throat.

"I thought you were him."

"Why is his car here?" Already suspecting she knew the answer, she desperately wanted a different explanation.

"Because I drove it here."

Puzzled, Olivia looked at him. "I don't understand."

"We were in his car heading back from our gig out in Red Hook, and he pulled over on Route 30 and got out. Told me to bring his car back here."

Images from the landfill flooded her mind again.

"Oh, God."

"What the hell happened?" he demanded, his voice rising as he scooted toward the edge of the couch.

Olivia was seeing a different side of David from the meek and mild, reluctant chauffeur she met the day she had arrived on the island.

"I'm not exactly sure." Her voice wobbled with her confession.

"Tell me what you do know." His voice boomed more loudly than would seem possible for such a small-framed man.

She relayed what she could piece together. There wasn't much to tell. Just a lot of unanswered questions.

"I've got to go see if I can find him." He smashed his beer can on the coffee table so hard the sides crumbled, reducing it to a fraction of its original size. Remnants of his beer sloshed out. Heading toward the door, his strides were long and deliberate. He stopped just short of being able to grab the knob and turned back toward her, his eyes ablaze with fury.

Olivia was startled by his affront and took a step back even though he was already across the room.

Pausing to point a grease-stained finger at her, he drew in an audible breath. "You have no idea what you have stirred up around here. . . . *No idea.*" In what appeared to be a threatening gesture or just added emphasis, he shook his finger at her. Turning back toward the front door and grabbing the knob, he mumbled, "I never should have made that phone call. Just trying to do the right thing. This is what happens." He charged out, slamming the door behind him.

She listened to the sound of Colton's Jeep churning up gravel as it backed up and then sped up the driveway.

What had she done? Was it Colton on Landfill Road? Was he participating in the unthinkable activity she would never comprehend or had he seen her car and tried to come to her rescue? Had she left him behind to take on the vicious men who had grabbed her? Not that she could have done much to help. God, she hoped it wasn't him. If it was . . . she prayed he was all right.

CHAPTER TWENTY-SEVEN

S leep did not come easily for her. She lay on the couch waiting and listening, hoping to hear the Jeep return to its spot at the end of the driveway. The sound never came. She paced the house trying to make sense of it all.

Olivia finally fell asleep in the middle of the night but jolted awake in the morning to an odd sound out on the gallery. Blinking sleep out of her eyes, she stumbled toward the sliding glass doors. The sound continued. It was a kind of squawking. A large sea gull was perched on the railing, probably looking for food, perhaps a regular visitor on Colton's gallery. Sliding the screen door open, Olivia laughed as the gull flapped its wings at the sound but didn't fly away. He seemed surprisingly comfortable with her presence. She was tempted to retrieve food from the kitchen to feed him but then realized she might be encouraging an unwanted behavior.

But then again, did it matter?

Olivia let it go. She needed to get out of his house. Grabbing a roll and a bottle of water to take with her, she left Colton's bungalow behind. The morning was already unusually hot and humid.

Feeling drawn to her mother's place, she tried in vain to push aside the horrible images piling up inside her head on the way there. She coasted down the driveway, guarding against unrealistic hopes of seeing something different at the bottom. As expected the view was the same as the day before. A black, burned-out shell of her mother's former bungalow. Piles of charred ashes. Hopefully no more bodies sticking out from under it.

Making her way over to her mother's empty chair, she settled down into it. Fortunately the view out to Magens Bay hadn't changed. She breathed it in, needing it to be a part of her. Permanently. She got lost in the view. The bright morning sun danced on the sparkling turquoise water of the bay. The sea breeze played with her hair but she barely noticed.

Olivia allowed herself to replay the evening she'd had with Colton. She had felt special in his arms. He had made love to her so gently, she hadn't wanted it to end. She got lost in the memory. Praying he was okay, she punched his number into her cell to try to reach him. It rang endlessly until eventually his voicemail kicked in. His voice on the greeting sounded odd to her.

As the strong summer sun rose in the sky, she folded her legs underneath her and leaned back in her mother's chair. Her eyelids grew heavy and she succumbed to her fatigue. Gentle breezes blew as she napped in the sunshine like her cat.

A voice from behind aroused her.

"Olivia!"

She spun around to see a familiar face.

"Sarah." With a flood of relief at the sight of her friend, Olivia untucked her feet and walked over to greet her, faltering momentarily as her legs recovered from their slumber.

"What the hell happened?" Sarah's eyes grew wide as she surveyed the property. "I hadn't heard."

Abhorred by the atrocity, Olivia turned away and opened her mouth to speak, but the words got caught in her throat. Her gaze darted randomly around the edges of the yard before coming to rest on the burned-out shell of the bungalow, and she fought to push away her anger and pain.

Sarah watched her struggling. She stepped closer and placed a caring hand on her shoulder.

Olivia appreciated the gesture. She reached up and found Sarah's hand, taking it in hers.

They stood at the edge of the destruction, taking in the senselessness of it, appreciating each other's company.

Finally Olivia broke away.

"Pretty shitty, isn't it?" Olivia took a few steps away from the remains of the house, needing to distance herself to be able to talk about it.

"Yeah, I can only imagine how you feel right now. I'm sorry."

"This was my mother's world. She was unbelievably happy here. She dreamed of being here forever. I had planned to come down and join her at some point. We could have been an amazing team. . . ." She turned and glanced out to the bay. "God she loved it here."

"I'm sure she did. What's not to love?"

Even though Olivia interpreted it as a rhetorical question, she felt compelled to respond. "Yeah, right?" Inching closer to the view, she lamented, "I just wish it didn't have to end this way."

"Do they know how it happened?"

Olivia displayed the palm of her hand and turned away, not wanting to discuss it.

Sarah remained silent, seemingly unsure of what to say to make her feel any better. Finally she found her voice. "Hey, listen. Why don't we go grab a bite to eat? I'm starving, and I haven't been to Izzies since I met you there the other night. Let me buy you lunch . . . brunch. Whatever time it is. As long as it involves a Bloody Mary."

Olivia smiled at the suggestion.

"Sounds great. I'd like that. Thanks." She could use a break from hanging out next to the ruins. "I'll take my car and meet you."

"Okay. I'll see you there."

The two split off, but Olivia paused momentarily at her driver's side door to glance back at the remains of the bungalow and then beyond to the view to the north. As her gaze returned to the island, her eyes landed on the refrigerator in the midst of the debris. She had never taken the time to clean it out. A perverse curiosity of what it looked like inside drew her to it. As she heard Sarah's car head up the driveway, she backtracked toward what used to be the kitchen. Ducking under the yellow tape, climbing gingerly over the charred rubble, she reached out for the handle of the blackened refrigerator. Almost expecting it to still be hot, she touched it quickly to test the waters. It proved to be cool, so she grabbed the handle firmly with her whole hand and pulled. To her surprise the door swung open easily, and she peered inside for the first time. Not sure what she expected to see besides moldy food, Olivia surveyed the contents. At first, nothing seemed out of the ordinary until she opened the bottom drawers.

The vegetable drawer was not a surprise. Some withering carrots, a mushy mango, a couple brown bananas and a few onions starting to sprout. The meat drawer, however, proved to be much more interesting. Olivia hadn't known her mother to be much of a meat eater. To find meat in the drawer would have been surprising. What she found, however, was even more unusual.

CHAPTER TWENTY-EIGHT

O livia caught up to Sarah standing next to her car in Izzies parking lot, and they walked in together. For Olivia, it felt oddly strange. She almost expected Colton's band to be setting up in the corner of the outdoor bar and grill. Instead, a man played island rhythms on shiny steel drums, accompanied by his partner on guitar. Usually Olivia enjoyed the sound of steel pan music. Not that day.

It all came flooding back. The brawl. Getting knocked down. Her throbbing cheek. Ice on her face on the ride back. She was perplexed as to why Sarah had suggested the place.

Since there were only a handful of patrons, they easily found a place at the bar, not too far from where they had sat a few nights earlier. The bartender was a handsome man with a medium-brown complexion, wearing a black Izzies logo t-shirt. His name tag said "Red" and hung cock-eyed below his left shoulder. He offered some friendly banter and was quick to take their order and return with their drinks. Sarah's was a Bloody Mary and Olivia's, a mimosa.

The two women sipped their cocktails with minimal conversing. As the steel pan duo took a break, the soothing sound of the ocean lapping against the beach behind them became the music. The feel of Izzies in the daytime was dramatically different than at night. It was as if the bar had two different personalities. Both inviting. One was calm and relaxing. The other seductive and alluring. A bit flirtatious. Olivia liked them both but, at the moment, she needed the calm she derived from listening to the sound of the ocean waves.

She glanced up to see a familiar face come into view at the end of the bar. A sinking feeling dropped into the bottom of her stomach as she squinted to discern who was sauntering toward her. There was no mistaking the tall, attractive man with a medium build and the pronounced angular features of his face.

Surveying the bar, his face lit up when he spied her. There was an arrogance about him as he crossed the floor toward her as if he needed to put on an air for anyone watching.

Olivia searched his face as he drew near. She furrowed her brow and clenched her teeth in response to his unexpected arrival.

"What are you doing here?"

He chuckled.

She was not amused, holding her glare steady.

Seated between the two, Sarah turned back and forth to search both of their faces.

"I thought you might need my help."

"Look, I've got it under control." Olivia's voice was firm, her lips pursed in anger. She couldn't fathom trying to explain to her father what she had gotten wrapped up in.

"I'm sure you do, but I knew you would appreciate a hand and maybe wrap this up more quickly." He patted her on the back of her shoulder with a chuckle as he turned to see who was sitting next to her.

Olivia jumped in to try to stay in control of the conversation. "Sarah, this is my father, James Benning."

Sarah turned toward him and graciously extended her hand. "Pleased to meet you."

"This is . . . Sarah." There was no point getting into any more details. The fewer, the better.

Her father acknowledged her real estate agent briefly but made it obvious he was not interested in idle chitchat.

Sarah politely excused herself and sauntered confidently to a table at the other end of the bar with her drink in hand. Clearly she knew a number of ladies in a group that had just arrived, and they greeted her exuberantly.

Olivia longed to join them but turned to her father and took a moment to look him over. A handsome man in his forties, he had prominent cheek bones, and smooth, oddly pale skin. The breeze off the water tossed his light brown wavy hair about his head. A couple strands drooped uncharacteristically onto his forehead. He was relatively tall but not terribly wide and had a strong torso that was proportionate to the rest of his body.

His attire almost embarrassed her. He looked like he had walked out of his last business meeting and just took his suit jacket off and left it in the car. He had on a long-sleeved, white pinpoint shirt with narrow blue pinstripes and gray flannel trousers. The rolled-up sleeves were the only indication he was unwinding from his flight. She imagined he had boarded the first plane to the island at his last airport changeover. Glancing down, she smirked. He still had on his wingtip shoes. Sand had found its way into the crevices along the edges on his walk from the parking lot.

"How did you know I would be here?"

"I didn't." His voice was matter-of-fact.

Olivia examined his face more closely. "So why did you come?"

"Doesn't everyone make Izzies their first stop after arriving on the island?" His voice was louder than she would have liked. He appeared far too happy with his hands raised above his head as if trying to lighten the mood.

She wasn't going to bother to address his rhetorical question. It just didn't make sense he would get off the plane and go straight for Izzies.

"That and the fact I know it's too early for hotel rooms to be ready to check in. I came to hang out with a younger crowd while I waited. The bars in the larger hotels tend to be older couples. Not as much fun." His wink made her squirm at the implication.

While Olivia acknowledged he was single, recently eligible, and good-looking, she shuddered at the prospect of him trying to pick up someone closer to her age than his own.

"Look, I can handle things here." Her voice was even more assertive, trying to deliver a clear message to him.

"I just thought . . ." He stepped closer to her and rested a hand on the back of the bar stool Sarah had vacated.

Olivia could smell alcohol on his breath. Must have been a long flight. She wasn't aware of where his travels had led him over the past few days, but she didn't care either. She continued to push back.

"I don't need your help!" The volume of her voice escalated. "Why do you think you can just show up here and take over?"

"Olivia." He dropped his gaze to the ground as if silently assessing what he had walked into.

Furious he had arrived unannounced on the island, her mother's island, anger seethed throughout her body.

"Why are you here?" she demanded. "You don't care about any of this. You never have!"

His face grew solemn as he examined her eyes. Slowly he climbed onto what had been Sarah's bar stool.

"Yeah, I do. . . . I always have." His voice quieted.

Olivia's eyes widened. Her eyebrows raised. Was he serious?

"What?" Her voice was raspy as if she was talking to herself, barely believing what she was hearing.

Red approached and asked her father what he wanted. He ordered a Glenmorangie Scotch Whiskey.

Olivia interjected, "You know, you *are* in the islands. Rum is the way to go here. A lot cheaper, too." Of course, none of that mattered to him. He was going to get what he usually ordered. Such a creature of habit. Or just plain stubborn. Either way, same result.

Without hesitation, he changed his drink order to a double and then resumed their discussion.

"Olivia, I have *always* loved your mother." He sounded indignant, speaking slowly and deliberately. "And I believe she loved me too. We just had different objectives. Her passion was being here, on the islands. She couldn't . . . or wouldn't go back. My life was in Boston. I had a career I had worked hard to be successful at. We took different paths. Unfortunately you got stuck in the middle, and I insisted you needed to get a good education so you stayed with me."

Feeling a bit shell-shocked, Olivia could only stare at her father, listening to what spilled out of his mouth. His words sounded odd to her. Searching his face, she wondered if she should believe him. He had never stopped loving her mother? Should she have tried to get them back together? Why hadn't she? A huge burden of guilt landed squarely on her narrow, young shoulders. Olivia suffered a nasty jab in her stomach as she realized there may never be another chance.

Her father's eyes dropped to the floor as if reflecting on what could have been. Finally he found his voice.

"Look, I know this has been hard on you. . . . Probably, somewhat unfair, too."

Grunting in response, Olivia stared into his eyes as her anger mounted. Was he kidding? Of course it was unfair to her. She didn't have a say in any of it. Living in Boston with him was nothing less than miserable. She hated the fact he was never there, always traveling on business. When he was home, he was usually on the phone. He worked long hours and was busy in the evenings with meetings and dinners out. Olivia was incredibly lonely and longed to be with her mother on the beautiful island of St. Thomas where the weather and the soothing turquoise water were consistently temperate, year round. She hated him for keeping them apart.

"Your mother and I both made choices and . . ." He groaned as if a lifetime of guilt plagued him. "We also made some mistakes along the way. We're human. Nowhere near perfect. I'm sorry if that hurt you in the process, but we certainly didn't intend for that. We made the best decisions we could at the time."

Red returned with her father's drink. Olivia watched as he snatched it up eagerly.

Sipping her mimosa, she felt herself soften as she thought about her father baring his soul. The choices they made were difficult ones, although certainly misguided. She shook her head, still not agreeing with the decisions and wishing it could have been different. Her heart ached at the realization her parents cared for each other even though they chose to live apart. Who did that? Who did that to their daughter? Life for the three of them could have turned out differently. She struggled to quell her wrath.

The cruel reality of it all was nothing could be done to change her parents' past. Regrettably her only option was to return to the present and the arduous task at hand. Yet, anger directed at both of her parents and bitter disappointment still churned inside.

She needed to distance herself from her father. He was not welcome in her island world. He was making her angry at her mother, and she resented his presence. The son-of-a-bitch had no business being there. He had a long history of showing up and taking over. Olivia knew this was not going to be an exception.

She flashed back to the time she and her friend, Laurie, launched a babysitting business when they were in junior high. Her father barged into the middle of it, insisting the parents of the kids under their care had to sign a contract and agree to certain terms and conditions. Their business fizzled before it ever got off the ground. Her father told her she would thank him one day when she understood the liability headache he had saved her from enduring.

If Olivia recalled correctly, he also destroyed her lemonade stand business the summer between third and fourth grade by charging her for the table and chair she used. At the time she didn't understand what the term "rent" meant. He probably told her she was learning about the cost of running a business.

More recently, her father got too involved in a more personal matter. Weeks before the junior prom, she had garnered the courage to ask a guy she had been admiring from the next seat over in algebra class. Every time he leaned in her direction to double check a homework answer, butterflies fluttered in her stomach. Olivia was so elated he had said "yes" she made the mistake of sharing her excitement with her father. The young man had a sudden change of heart after receiving a phone call from James Benning outlining the restrictions and rules that would be in place that evening. Then, as it all played out, her father had an unexpected business trip that came up at the last minute and Olivia sat home alone the night of the prom while her friends took selfies and posted them on every social media outlet available. To say she was devastated would have been an understatement. She hated her father for it.

Olivia drained the rest of her mimosa and set the glass down on the bar. She pulled some cash out of her pocket and threw it down next to her glass.

"I'm out of here," she announced.

Her father gave her a side glance but returned his attention to his drink.

She wasn't interested in hanging around to see how the conversation was going to deteriorate after he had thrown down a few more. Walking away without looking back, Olivia left him with his drink to join Sarah where she still sat with the group of ladies. They spoke for a moment and Sarah nodded.

Rummaging through her purse resting on the floor by her chair, Sarah pulled out a wad of keys that barely fit inside her fist and handed them off. Olivia slipped them into her pocket and then turned and strode back toward the exit.

Walking past her father, who had become wrapped up in a conversation on his cell while hovering over his double Scotch, Olivia headed out to the parking lot. This time there were no footsteps behind her. No one called out her name. She walked alone.

"Good luck finding a place to stay," she mumbled, predicting the more upscale hotels would be completely booked. Chortling to herself, she pictured his face as he came upon the tragic remains that no longer could be called Serenity Villa. Of course, he never called it that. He never saw anything about it that exuded serenity. To him, it was just an "oddly painted house on a God-awful, hot island." He was a New Englander through and through. Not only did he not mind the long cold winters, it was as if he thrived on the challenge of them. He was like many of the particularly sturdy Yankees who laughed in the face of winter storms. Olivia could take them or leave them but given the choice, she would choose to be right where she was. There was something about the Caribbean that spoke to her. The mild year-round weather, the hospitality of the people, stunning sunsets, cooling sea breezes, turquoise waters, snorkeling with sea turtles, and views that went on forever from any vantage point on the island. It was a slower, simpler way of life. Not that people didn't work hard, but it wasn't the frenetic, fast-paced kind of work like it was back in the States, particularly in New England. Yankees set the standard for the term "rat race."

As Olivia approached her car, her phone vibrated against her leg. She slipped it out of her pants pocket and noticed the first three digits were 340. She pressed the talk button and answered the call.

"Hello?"

"Miss Benning?"

"Yes?"

"This is Lieutenant Woods."

She held her breath, terrified to hear the next few words out of his mouth.

"Yes?" Her voice quivered.

"Ma'am, I need you to come down to the Coast Guard station again. . . . There's another body."

CHAPTER TWENTY-NINE

O*livia's heart sank.* Indiscernible words tumbled almost imperceptibly across her lips.

"Ma'am?"

Grappling to make sense of what he was saying, she cleared her throat.

"Okay. I'll . . . I'll be right there."

"Thank you, I appreciate it."

"Lieutenant?"

"Yes, ma'am."

"Could I just meet you at the hospital?"

"Yes, that would be fine. I'll meet you at the side entrance where we went in last time."

"Okay. I'll see you there. I'm about fifteen minutes away."

"That's fine. Take your time."

Olivia slipped her phone back into her pocket and slumped with her back against the driver's side door. Could it be her mother this time? She prayed it wasn't. Her plan was to find her alive. "Please . . . no."

Leaving behind her father and his glass of Scotch at the bar, she steered the car back toward Charlotte Amalie. Back to the scene where she had escaped custody. She arrived at the pink four-story building and pulled her car around to the side. The lieutenant's vehicle was parked in a slot directly in front of the side entrance and he waited patiently near the door, standing erect in his bright white uniform, hands on his hips, gold aviator glasses sitting prominently on his tanned face.

Olivia pulled into the slot next to his vehicle and shut down the engine. She heaved a heavy exhale full of the burden she carried and closed her eyes. She dreaded what he was asking her to do. It was all becoming decidedly overwhelming. When she opened her eyes he was approaching the car, wasting no time in tackling the task at hand.

"For God's sake, give me a minute," she snapped as she reached for the door handle. He was certainly in more of a hurry than she was.

"Miss Benning. Thank you for coming. I know this is hard for you. Believe me, I do."

She barely had her door open, but he was already rambling on much further than was necessary, not that rambling was ever necessary.

Holding up her hand as if stopping a line of traffic, she trudged toward him. "It's fine. I'm fine. Let's just get this over with." She sounded more nonchalant than she felt.

Following the lieutenant to the small, nondescript, windowless side door, she waited while he unlocked it. Side-by-side they made their way down the all-too-familiar hall, arriving at the same unmarked door as before. Woods rapped gently on it and soon the same dark-skinned linebacker dressed in green scrubs let them inside the cold smelly room with metal drawers on the far wall.

Olivia shivered as she recalled her previous visit. This was the last place she wanted to be on the island. Dozens of beautiful white sandy beaches dotted the perimeter, all with sparkling turquoise water. She would have given anything to be on any one of them instead of inside the local morgue.

The medical examiner must have assumed she was now completely indoctrinated into the world of autopsy because he didn't hesitate before opening the drawer to show her the most recent arrival in his examining room. It was the drawer to the left of the one he had pulled out during her last visit.

She took a step back as the sheet-covered body came into view.

The lieutenant took the lead this time. "Miss Benning, this body is actually a male. But we were hoping you might know him and be able to shed some light as to who he is."

Although comforted by the revelation, she shot him a glare for not sharing the corpse's gender earlier as he found a spot on the far wall to lean against. What a huge relief, though. It wasn't her mother. She took comfort in the fact she was still out there somewhere.

"Okay, I see." Of course, she didn't believe she could be of any assistance, but she was already there. She would take a look.

The ME pulled back the sheet for her to see. The fabric fell away to reveal not only his head, but a good portion of the torso.

Olivia's heart stopped when she saw the broad shoulders on the white male. Her legs seized up and her feet felt like they were stuck in cement blocks. Her body refused to step any closer. She squinted her eyes.

The cadaver had stringy, shoulder-length dark blond hair plastered to his head and neck. His skin, however, looked nothing like the chalky white skin of the female Jane Doe she had seen before. Instead it was healthy-looking, smooth and tan. He looked like he would open his eyes at any moment and wonder why they were all staring at him.

Olivia stared at the corpse, standing so still every muscle in her body stiffened.

"Doctor, can you tell how long he's been in the water?" She wanted to hear it had been a while.

The coroner looked surprised at her question. "We don't know exactly but in relation to the female you saw, this one spent much less time submerged . . . if at all. We still need to get clarification as to where this body was found."

"I see." Since his answer didn't give her much to go on, she needed to ask the question a different way. "Do you know how long he's been dead?"

"No, not yet. I haven't performed the autopsy yet."

Olivia finally got her feet to move and slowly inched closer to the body. The silence that hung in the room was almost distracting.

The two men looked to her to reveal who it was. Their expectations were palpable.

Olivia stared at his face, longing to see what the eyes looked like behind the closed lids, what his hair looked like when it was clean after a shower. Another question reached her lips. "Would it be possible to see his feet . . . his left foot?"

The ME and the lieutenant both raised their eyebrows and looked at each other. The ME spoke first.

"Ma'am, ordinarily it wouldn't be an issue, but there are no toes on his left foot."

Her eyes grew wide. She looked to him for clarification.

"Apparently they were . . . removed."

"Removed?" She was struggling to understand.

"Yes, cut off." He looked uncomfortable. "In some sort of an accident or by . . . someone. It's not a pleasant sight."

Like the rest of the body was? Olivia shuddered and closed her eyes, trying to push the picture of the corpse's toeless foot out of her mind's eye.

So she would never know. That was the only identifying feature she knew of on his body. She hadn't gotten to know him well enough. The air in the small morgue became noticeably stuffier.

CHAPTER TWENTY-NINE

"I'm afraid I don't know who this is. I don't recognize him."

"You sure?" The ME urged her to think harder, "You don't have any thoughts?"

She had asked too many questions, sounded too interested. They could tell she had at least an inkling about who he might be. But she wasn't going to cave in.

"Not really." She held her voice steady.

"'Cause we have a second corpse that came in at the same time as this one. A black male. I can't show you that one because his face was messed up. There's not much to recognize. We'll have to try to use DNA, but I was hoping if we could identify the white male then that might help us ID the second one . . . if there is a connection between the two."

"I'm sorry, I can't help." She had already detached herself, ready to walk out the door.

The ME held his gaze for a moment, as if expecting her to reconsider. After an awkward silence, he shook his head with disappointment clearly written across his face and replaced the sheet on the corpse's head. He put all his weight behind the end of the drawer and shoved it back into the wall as Olivia wondered, was it him? A painful twinge in her stomach made her grimace.

The lieutenant shifted his stance and re-engaged. "Thank you once again, Miss Benning. We appreciate you taking a look." He sounded as if he uttered those words several times a day and said them without thinking about them or feeling their meaning. Retreating back out through the morgue toward the door, he stepped to the side to let Olivia go ahead of him.

The two marched side by side back down the dimly lit hall and out the side door into the bright sunshine. As soon as the door clicked shut, the lieutenant moved uncomfortably close to her, his face in hers.

"Look, Miss Benning, we're not playing here. If you know something or have an idea whose body that is, you need to speak up. *Now*." He kept his voice low but firm. He reached out with one hand as if he was going to grab her upper arm but seemed to think better of it and pulled back. His face was still inches from hers. His warm breath brushed her skin and it smelled sour.

"What are you holding back?" His voice grew louder.

"Nothing!" she cried, taking a step back. His confrontation scared her, so she looked around the parking lot and beyond, praying she wasn't alone with him.

The lieutenant held his gaze then stepped away from her. Snatching his aviator sunglasses out of his shirt pocket, he slipped them on and then abruptly turned on his heel and stomped off to his vehicle. He quickly climbed in and slammed the door shut. After starting the engine, he pulled out of the parking slot and squealed his tires as he exited the lot.

Olivia stood in his wake, reeling from their encounter. Was there anyone left on the island she knew . . . who was on her side?

Returning to her Jeep, she tried Colton's cell again, hoping beyond hope he would pick up. Disappointed he didn't answer, she took a moment, instead, to check in with her friend, Laurie.

Olivia listened as the phone on the other end rang several times. Finally she heard a click and her friend's sweet voice. Just the sound of it perked up her spirits.

"Hey, girlfriend! How's it going down there?"

"Not bad. Things are progressing."

"Are they? That's good."

"Yeah, it is. I—"

"Anything I can help you with? Because you know I would do anything for you."

Olivia beamed. Her dear friend meant the world to her. Always positive and encouraging. They had gotten each other through their share of bumps in the road. She could count on Laurie. She was sure Laurie felt the same about her.

"Yes, of course I do. And I appreciate it. Thanks."

"Anything at all. You just name it."

"Awesome. Thank you. As a matter of fact, I was just wondering if you would take another look at the mail."

"Sure! Absolutely. I'll be going over later today. Is that soon enough?"

"Oh yeah, that should be fine."

"I'll give you a call when I get there, but is there anything in particular I am looking for?"

"Yes, actually. That package you called about a couple days ago. The one addressed to my father?"

"Yes, I know the one you mean."

"Okay, good. I'd like you to open it."

"Open it?"

"Yes, open it. I know I said you shouldn't, but I've changed my mind. It might be important."

Silence hung on the other end, suggesting Olivia might have to persuade her. Had she had second thoughts since her initial offer?

"Livvie?"

"Yes."

"I was just at your place this morning and it wasn't on the counter where I had left it."

Olivia's eyes grew wide.

"I had left it on top of the stack of mail, but this morning it was gone. I assumed your father returned home last night and picked it up. Was he supposed to fly in yesterday?"

Olivia carefully considered her response, not wanting to reveal her surprise and concern over the missing package.

"He must have. I don't know the specifics of his schedule, but that must be what happened."

"So you don't need me to stop in and feed Chloe anymore?"

"Yeah, I think you still should. That is, if you don't mind."

"Of course I don't mind. I usually just go on my way to work."

"It would be great if you could. My father's schedule is so erratic, and I don't think he would even think about taking care of Chloe if he was there."

Olivia thanked her profusely and assured her she would be wrapping up soon and heading home. They would head out on the town when she did.

Her friend was pleased to make tentative plans, and Olivia hung up looking forward to their night out.

Olivia fired up the engine of the Jeep and exited the hospital parking lot heading to the east end of the island.

CHAPTER THIRTY

*J*ames' *eyes concentrated on the ice* in the bottom of his glass as if he were inspecting a rare archeological specimen. He was elsewhere, lost in time and location. Glancing at his phone, he couldn't understand why his buddy hadn't replied to the text he sent after he landed. James had specifically suggested Izzies knowing his friend was fond of the place and undoubtedly would be willing to meet him there. He figured after a few drinks his friend might have some insight on tracking down Liv, so he could get off the godforsaken island that felt like a blast furnace. Sweat trickled down his back inside his shirt. Rolling his sleeves farther up his arms and tugging at his shirt to unstick it from his torso, he was unable to fathom how anyone could live in the tropics year round.

Exuberant laughter from the table of women rattled him out of his disparaging thoughts of the island. He jiggled the glass causing the cubes to clatter and clink inside, deliberately intending to hail the bartender.

Delivering piña coladas to a couple of twenty-somethings at the other end of the bar, the sound of the empty glass caught Red's attention. His head turned and he quickly made his way over, scooping up the glass with long, slender, dark-skinned fingers.

"Yes, sir. What can I get for you? Another Scotch? A double?" His island accent was thick and rhythmic. One crooked finger pointed lazily at his patron as he backed up toward the wall of hard liquor behind him, anticipating his response.

James nodded his head once, giving his consent to the bartender. As he turned to survey the patrons at the other end of the bar, he asked himself if he was drinking to forget or to get numb. It didn't really matter, but he decided it was a little of both. Desperate to forget what might have been with his beautiful first love, Liv, and anxious to let go of the pain of losing her forever. He counted on the Scotch to help him forget, get numb, and move on.

Red went straight to work emptying his glass, refilling the ice, and pouring two more shots. Before he could return with it, however, James hopped off his seat and sauntered down the bar toward the two ladies with the piña coladas. He caught Red's eye and tilted his head toward his target to say he would take his drink down there.

"Hello, ladies." His voice was silky smooth and the girls were taken aback by his unexpected arrival. He slid onto the empty stool next to the brunette with a strapless white top, light-blue-and-white-striped cropped linen pants. Her friend had wispy blonde hair and was dressed in a black halter top and a short white skirt. They giggled in response.

Red delivered his drink to the new location without raising an eyebrow and quickly retreated to attend to the ever-present task of washing out dirty glasses accumulated in the sink. Turning his back on the bar, he became immersed in the sound of running water and clinking glasses.

James carried on idle chitchat with the young women for a few minutes until a couple of young men, closer to their age, entered and sat down on the far side of them. The bartender approached the two quickly as if he knew them and spoke directly to the man with his arm in a sling. They all laughed and engaged in banter back and forth as the injured man glossed over the details of his injury.

After the girls made it clear they were more interested in the new arrivals than him, James turned away, trying to sit more erect and look confident. He scanned the tables, surveying the rest of the patrons with lonely eyes. Silently he slipped off the barstool and made his way toward the exit after dropping a couple twenties on the bar for Red.

CHAPTER THIRTY-ONE

Figuring *he had allowed enough time* for Olivia to recover from his unannounced arrival on the island, James Benning pulled his small white rental car out onto Route 30 heading west toward Charlotte Amalie. It was time to catch up with her and get the situation under control. Enough was enough. With much more important matters to worry about, he resented having to take time out of his hectic schedule to be in the steamy tropics, particularly in August. It was one of the most undesirable places to be. He'd rather spend time skiing in Colorado than sitting on a beach in the Caribbean.

After wiping perspiration from his forehead with the back of his hand, he reached for the air-conditioning controls. Both the fan and temperature were already at their highest settings. He groaned. Arriving unannounced at the car rental booth, he'd had few choices.

Nearing downtown, James' progress slowed as he encountered traffic congestion. The number of cars on the road, especially taxis, was in direct proportion to the number of cruise ships in town. On this day, two large ships towered over the dock at Havensight. A third was docked at Crown Bay.

James inched through the section of road near the docks and into downtown until finally he was able to turn right at the police station and make his way up the mountain toward Serenity Villa, slowing at the sharp curves and swearing at the oncoming cars. Driving on the left side of the curving mountainous roads was not enjoyable for him. Far from it. He did not embrace the challenge.

Near the top of the mountain his four-cylinder rental struggled to make the climb, coughing and sputtering, threatening to stall. James smacked the steering wheel and yelled at it as if it would respond to his sense of urgency.

"Foreign shit box!" he shrieked as his face turned red and the veins on the side of his neck protruded grotesquely.

Hitting the brakes, he gave it a moment to collect itself, and considered pulling off the road. But there was no room for error much less a breakdown lane along the edge. In one last ditch effort, he floored the gas pedal again. The little white sedan chugged the rest of the way to the top, knocking and pinging as if it were on its last cylinder.

Relieved the car had not stalled, James rounded the bend with his eyes darting in all directions, not knowing where to look for oncoming cars.

Before long he was heading down Crown Mountain Road, and he slowed to look for the right driveway. It had been a long while since he'd been there. He was hoping he would recognize it. Perhaps he would be able to see Liv's Jeep that undoubtedly Ollie would be using to get around the island. Of course, the car would need to be sold, too.

As a familiar beat-up rusty white mailbox came into view, he slowed the rental to a crawl. Turning into the drive and heading down the curving path, he glanced down the hill, looking for the colorful cottage with the Jeep parked in front. His glimpses through the trees didn't catch anything familiar. He had the sinking feeling he had chosen the wrong driveway, but he would have to get to the bottom to turn around anyway so he continued. An odd structure slowly emerged from the camouflage of trees as he got closer.

Ignoring an uncomfortable spasm in his gut, he brought the vehicle to a stop in front of black, charred ruins cordoned off by yellow tape. No Jeep. It couldn't be. He had the wrong driveway, but was still curious, like a rubbernecker at an accident scene. After shoving the car into park and cutting the engine, he slowly excited the vehicle, leaving the driver's door ajar.

Taking a couple small steps toward the police tape, he scanned the scene, trying to make sense of it. His eyes came to rest on the east side of the house that was still standing and his face fell, recognizing the colorful wall and part of the gallery that were relatively untouched. It was Serenity Villa. Struggling to comprehend what he was seeing, his mouth moved almost imperceptibly but no words came out.

Finally he found his voice, quiet at first. "Oh my God, Liv. What the hell happened?" he implored, certain she was to blame.

"*Damn it!*" He turned and lunged toward the car, slamming his palm on the hood so hard, he left a small dent. "*Damn it!*"

Quickly sliding his phone out of his pants pocket, he pressed a couple buttons and could hear it ringing in his ear, but she wasn't answering. After four rings rolled over to her voicemail, he hung up and smacked the hood again. Turning and glaring at the charred debris, he clenched his teeth in anger. His daughter had made herself scarce, undoubtedly fearful of his wrath, acknowledging he had let his temper get the best of him on occasion, particularly when a situation turned abruptly out of his control. This would certainly fit into that category.

James looked around the property, and his eyes came to rest on the chair in the side yard. An empty chair. Mindlessly he wiped sweat from his brow with the back of his hand, cursing the oppressive heat and then started across the yard. After only a few steps, his foot kicked something hard. He stopped to examine a rectangular piece of wood. Soiled with ashes from the fire, it didn't look like much of anything to him, but he flipped it over.

Serenity Villa

There was surprisingly little damage on it. He re-clenched his teeth and scowled. Taking the stance of a baseball pitcher, he hurled the sign, aiming it deep into the center of the burned timbers, condemning it to a burial amid the ashes, essentially erasing the last piece of evidence of the bungalow's existence.

He continued his walk over to the chair and sat on the edge of the seat. Looking out to the bay, he had to admit there was a certain appeal to the view from that chair. The sunlight shimmering on the calm waters of Magens Bay was almost inviting.

His gaze wandered out to the horizon. He didn't notice the Bananaquits chirping in the trees behind him as he was preoccupied with determining his next move. A prudent man would probably go directly to the police. However, a man whose past had crossed paths a few times with the police, albeit when he was much younger, knew he should go a different route. His temper tended to rise up at the worst of times and get him into trouble, particularly with authority figures.

CHAPTER THIRTY-TWO

T he sound of a vehicle coming down the driveway caught his ear. Assuming it was Olivia, he turned toward the sound but didn't recognize the car. His face fell in disappointment. Getting up from the wooden chair, he took a couple steps toward the driveway, squinting to determine who was arriving.

It was a large vehicle. Black, maybe navy blue, SUV. Looked like some sort of government car. Arching his back, his guard went up as the driver pulled the car next to his and cut the engine.

The door opened and a young man in a white uniform stepped out. Looked like Coast Guard. James was impressed with how white and neatly pressed his uniform was, an impeccable presentation from his hat down to his highly polished shoes. He certainly looked like the real thing.

As the guardsman approached, he removed his hat and tucked it under one arm. He came to a stop a few feet from James, removed his aviator sunglasses, folded them, and slipped them into the pocket on the front of his shirt.

The two men stood there with their eyes locked. Neither spoke at first, as if trying to discern why the other was there.

Finally the Coast Guard officer spoke. "Afternoon, sir. I'm Lieutenant Woods." He extended his hand.

Olivia's father extended his in return. "Afternoon, Lieutenant. James Benning."

After the introductions were completed, they looked at each other as if expecting the other to say something significant.

Woods found his voice first. "I was hoping to find Miss Benning here. Olivia Benning."

"Yeah, that's my daughter." He narrowed his eyes and examined the lieutenant closely as if trying to understand his motive.

"I see. She's not answering her phone. I had no idea where else I might find her."

James laughed a short, cynical snicker and nodded his head. "Yeah, I tried, too." Then he grew serious. "What's this all about?"

The lieutenant mirrored his sobriety. "I can't really say. This is a private matter." He straightened his back and stood taller.

James closed his eyes and exhaled, flaring his nostrils and clenching teeth into a forced grin. "I'm her father. I think you can share with me what you were going to share with her." His voice got louder with each word.

The man in white didn't appear swayed by his confrontational style. He just looked calmly at him for a moment.

His non-response infuriated James. "For God's sake, tell me what the hell is going on!"

The guardsman cleared his throat and looked directly into James' eyes. "I'm sorry . . . but I can't. This is between Miss Benning and The United States Coast Guard."

His statement hung in midair, agitating James further.

"What are you talking about? I'm her father! I think you should be able to talk with me about what is going on with her mother."

"I'm sorry, sir. Miss Benning is over eighteen. Whatever agreement she has with us is entirely confidential. I've probably said too much as it is."

"That's ridiculous!" His frustration was escalating.

The lieutenant couldn't let it go at that. "And aren't you and your wife divorced?"

Olivia's father's nostrils flared again. "What's that got to do with anything—" His right hand lunged and grabbed the neatly pressed white shirt with a sweaty fist.

Taken by surprise, the lieutenant took a step back. James' fingers slipped from the wad of fabric he had grabbed. He took one look at Woods' flaring eyes and thought better of going after him again.

Visibly anxious to diffuse the confrontation and make his exit, Woods pulled a business card out of his shirt pocket and offered it to James. "If you hear from Miss Benning, please let her know I have some information for her . . . that she would definitely be interested in."

James glared in response and finally reached out and snatched the card out of his hand.

"Okay. Thank you. I hope to hear from her soon." Woods turned and walked back toward his government-issue vehicle with a determined stride. He scrambled quickly inside as if he was expecting someone to pursue him, turned the car around, and drove back up the winding driveway.

Olivia's father tossed the business card aside and then saluted the exiting vehicle but not out of deference to the uniform.

He sauntered back to the empty chair, faltered for a moment and grabbed the back of it until he recovered his balance, and then sat back down on the edge. His thoughts turned to a recent visit to his doctor stateside. A cloud passed in front of the sun, obliterating the bright, optimistic light.

CHAPTER THIRTY-THREE

James Benning was furious. His ex-wife's bungalow that he had planned to put on the market had been reduced to a heap of charcoal, and he was sure she didn't have any insurance on the property. His daughter was nowhere to be found. Where was she staying? His wife . . . ex-wife . . . had passed away in a boating accident. But there was no body. How did anyone know it was a boating accident? Who knew the circumstances to be able to make that kind of conclusion? Many unanswered questions.

He had to check into a hotel somewhere. That would be a good place to start. It would need to be down near the waterfront to avoid having to traverse the treacherous mountain. Air-conditioning was a prerequisite. It didn't have to have a view or be on the water. It would all be lost on him. However, since he expected and needed a certain level of service, he chose to head over to The Reef in Bakkero Estate to see if there was a room available. He didn't see any reason why he shouldn't be comfortable if he was going to have to endure a few days in the sweltering heat while he straightened out the situation Olivia was unable to take care of. Deeply disappointed, he despised incompetence. He had taught her better than that. . . . Well, even if he hadn't taught her directly, he certainly showed her by example. She should have been paying attention.

James stood up from the chair that looked out over the bay and instantly became lightheaded. He grabbed onto the edge until his dizzy spell passed. Slowly he made his way back over to his car, staggering with each step. One hand grabbed the door handle and held it for a moment while the other gripped the edge of the roof. Gathering himself, he shook his head. His situation was worsening.

Once he gained his composure, he took one last look around in disgust and climbed into his disappointing island rental, tossing his phone on the seat next to him. After rolling down the windows and grumbling while turning the car around in the tight driveway, he set his sights on finding a hotel downtown.

On the way back down the mountain, his cell rattled to life with a loud, clangorous ring that sounded like an old-fashioned telephone. Trying to focus on the sharp curves and oncoming cars, he stole a glance and recognized the number. He knew he needed to pick it up, yet he let it ring a few times more before he finally pushed the button for speakerphone.

"Yeah. What's up?"

"James, it's Dr. Vincent."

No shit. Just the person he didn't want to hear from.

"Yeah, Doc. What's going on?" It was difficult to hear over the breeze through the open windows and the noise from passing cars. He pressed the buttons to close the windows and poked at the air-conditioning controls, desperate to get some cooler air moving, even though they were already cranked up to the highest settings.

Part of him didn't want to know why the doctor was calling.

"James, I got the lab results back. Listen, could we sit down and talk about this face-to-face? I would like to go over them in person. Are you in town? Could you stop into my office? I'm really swamped but I will certainly make time for you."

He exhaled a long, extended breath. His doctor probably had the results spread out on the desk in front of him.

"Listen, Doc, I'm out of town at the moment. Not sure exactly when I'll be back. Why don't you just give it to me straight?"

Silence on the other end of the phone.

"James, I . . . uh . . . I would like to speak with you in person. Face-to-face."

"Of course you would. That's the way you do things." He chuckled out loud. "But I have no idea when I'll be back in the States. This could take a while. Just give it to me straight. I have to hear it at some point. I'd rather it came from you. We've known each other for years. Tell me what you know."

More silence on the other end.

"James, really. I think we should meet to discuss this."

"Look, I appreciate your attempt to sugarcoat this, but I am two plane rides away from you in the godforsaken sweltering heat of the Caribbean. Believe me, I do *not* want to be here. This is not a vacation, and I don't know how long it will take. Just level with me. I need to know. I'll handle it. I know I've done it to myself."

More silence.

"*Mike!* Just tell me!" He was halfway down the mountain but becoming more and more agitated by the call, desperate to know.

"All right, if you insist. Are you sitting down? Are you some place safe?"

"For God's sake, you are killing me! Spit it out already."

The doctor condensed the lab results in a couple of concise sentences. Silence on the other end of the line indicated he was waiting for his long-time patient and friend to respond.

James listened with no expression on his face. He blinked a couple times trying to take it all in. His eyes glazed over and he didn't make the next curve.

Screeching tires, shattering glass, and the unmistakable sound of metal against metal were the last sounds before he lost consciousness.

CHAPTER THIRTY-FOUR

O*livia was startled awake by a strange sound* in unfamiliar surroundings. She tried to make out shapes in the shadows of the room. As her grogginess cleared, she realized it was her cell and she was at Sarah's house. Since it was still dark outside, she surmised it was the middle of the night. Fumbling hands finally located the phone on the bedside table next to her "meat drawer find" from her mother's refrigerator. At first glance she didn't recognize the number, but the Virgin Islands area code compelled her to answer it. A nagging feeling reminded her calls in the middle of the night were never good news. She blinked a couple times and then pushed the talk button.

"Hello?" she whispered hesitantly.

"Miss Benning?"

"Yes?" Her voice croaked as she tried to shake off her sleepiness.

"This is Detective Benson of the Virgin Islands Police Department." He let that sink in for a moment. "We've met a couple of—"

"Yes, Detective, of course. I remember you. Why—" She rubbed her eyes in an attempt to wipe away the slumber she had been completely immersed in. "What's going on? Why are you calling?" She stifled a yawn in his ear.

"Miss Benning, your father has been in a serious automobile accident."

Her eyes flew open wide. She tried to make sense of what the detective was saying. "An accident? How? . . . How could this be? He just got here yesterday. Oh no. . . ." Olivia struggled to take it all in. She reached over and turned on the light on the small table next to the bed. Her eyes flinched at the sudden brightness. "What happened? When?"

"We're not exactly sure when it happened. Probably sometime yesterday afternoon. There were no eyewitnesses. He, uh . . . he went over the edge coming down Crown Mountain."

"Oh God." She listened to his words, trying to comprehend their meaning.

"I'm sorry, Miss Benning, but you need to come to the hospital."

"Of course." Her voice was tentative and hoarse. "Okay."

"Take your time. I'll meet you at the front door."

"The front door," she repeated.

"Yes, ma'am. I'll see you when you get here. No rush."

"All right. I will . . . I'll get there as soon as I can." She was trying to grasp his instructions. "Thank you . . . thank you for . . . for calling. I will be there." She pressed the button to end the call and stared off in the distance out the window. No sign of the sun yet.

Glancing up, Olivia noticed Sarah had slipped into the guest room she had so graciously offered. Hovering just inside the door, she seemed to understand from the one-sided conversation it was a grim situation.

"I'll drive you to the hospital. Get some clothes on and then we'll go."

Olivia looked down and realized she was scantily clad in a cami and short shorts for sleeping. After she took a few minutes to put on something more appropriate, they piled into Sarah's car and started out toward Charlotte Amalie. Few words were spoken on the twenty-five minute ride. Sarah inquired about, and Olivia repeated the side of the conversation Sarah had not been privy to.

In the silence, Olivia tried to process her father's fate. She dreaded going into the morgue for a third time. Of course, this time, she would actually be able to recognize the body on the cold examining table or inside the metal drawer. Shivering in anticipation, a lump formed in her throat and her heart grew heavy. She tried to shake off how alone she felt. Had it really come to this? Orphaned at twenty-three. She knew his drinking would do him in.

Sarah turned into the main entrance and pulled her car into a visitor's slot. The clock in the car read 4:12. It seemed odd to Olivia to be arriving at the hospital in the middle of the night. The sky was still dark but clear with stars twinkling above. As the two ladies exited the car, Sarah extended her arm in a maternal gesture around Olivia's shoulders. The night air was cool and refreshing, not giving away any hints of the heat soon to arrive with the daylight.

As promised, the detective was waiting for them just inside the main entrance. He was hunched over, engrossed in a conversation on his cell. Who else was he waking up? As soon as he saw them walking through the front entrance, he ended the call and straightened his posture.

After Olivia and the detective exchanged pleasantries and she introduced Sarah, the three padded toward the elevators. There was an odd, astringent smell hanging in the air, though not nearly as bad as the pungent odor of the morgue. As they waited for the elevator to arrive, she realized the morgue was on the first floor, yet they were waiting for the elevator that traveled to the floors above.

She opened her mouth to question their destination but the sound of the doors opening caught her before she could utter a sound. The three entered and Olivia watched Benson push the button for the third floor.

"Where are we going?"

"Room 333. They just got him stabilized down in emergency and were able to move him up to a room."

Relief flooded through Olivia's body. "How is he? Was the accident bad? Was it his fault?" Oh, she prayed it wasn't. How much had he had to drink after she left Izzies? "Was there anyone else involved? Is everyone else okay?" She was anxious for answers.

"Looks like it was a single vehicle accident. He's pretty banged up. Probably was unconscious for a while. I think it took some time for anyone to notice he was there, and once they did, it took a while to reach him and . . . extricate him."

Olivia blinked her eyes a few times, trying to picture what her father had endured. She wasn't sure what to ask.

"So . . . is he going to be okay?"

Benson paused. "I'll let you talk with the doctor."

Olivia did her best to control a flinch. The detective didn't sound very positive. A tear caught her by surprise and she brushed it away.

The elevator doors opened and they entered the third floor directly across from the nurses' station and turned left to head down the hall. It was relatively quiet except for a couple of nurses who were conversing and referring to a clipboard one of them was holding. They looked up and paused their discussion as the threesome passed.

Anxious to get to her father's room, Olivia walked next to the detective but scanned the room numbers as they went. Sarah followed along respectfully, a few feet behind them.

When they reached Room 333, Sarah clearly understood the delicateness of the situation and excused herself, heading to the floor lounge to grab a cup of coffee. Detective Benson opened the door and moved to the side to let Olivia go in first. Barely breathing, she stepped into her father's room. Her feet came to an abrupt halt.

Dressed in a loose white-with-navy blue-print hospital gown, her father lay motionless in the bed with the top half of the mattress raised halfway up. Olivia barely recognized him. He looked thin and pale. His head was wrapped in white gauze bandages and a bag with clear liquid hung from an IV stand next to his bed with a line connecting it to the back of his left hand. Bloody scratches and cuts etched his face and arms. His right hand was also wrapped in the same white gauze bandages and rested alongside his still body.

There was another bed in the room, closer to the window, but it was empty. Olivia let her eyes wander away from her father for a moment. She observed how neatly the empty bed was made up, ready for the next patient, and was struck by how completely flat it was with the sheets and blanket tucked in tightly. A pillow rested at the head. Both beds had a small bedside table next to them and fluorescent lighting above. A narrow rollaway table in the shape of a large squared "C" loosely framed three sides of the empty bed. Her father's rolling table had been pushed up against the wall parallel to his bed. He didn't need his at the moment.

Olivia stood a few feet away, longing for him to say something. The stillness in the room was deafening. She couldn't tell if he was conscious or not. *Please be okay. Wake up. Be happy to see me.* Taking a few steps closer, she could feel the detective inching into the room behind her. Her feet froze. It was hard to see her father in his condition. Weak. Defenseless. Dependent. They were entering unfamiliar territory. He had always been incredibly strong. Powerful. Resilient. In-your-face obnoxious at times. She questioned if it was really him.

The silence was broken by a voice behind her.

"Miss Benning."

Olivia swung around to come face-to-face with the same doctor whom she had met during her brief stay at the same hospital a few days before. Under different circumstances, she would have been amused, but she just didn't have it in her.

"Yes, Doctor?"

There was a flicker of recognition in his eyes as he hesitated and examined her face but then let it go, moving on to the matter at hand.

Olivia appreciated his professionalism.

"Thank you for coming in."

"Of course. How is he? Is he going to be okay?" Olivia was getting impatient. She needed to know his prognosis.

"Your father suffered a fairly significant concussion in the collision. Contusions and abrasions over a good portion of his body. He got quite a beating inside the vehicle going over the side. Fortunately underbrush and trees stopped him from going any farther than he did. Poor guy was so far off the road and in such treacherous terrain it was difficult for the fire department to reach him. Took a while. By the time they got to him, he was pretty dehydrated and suffering from heatstroke. He'd been baking in his car in the afternoon sun. The windows were all rolled up. He probably had the air-conditioning on but, of course, once the car crashed and the engine cut out, there was no A/C." The doctor paused, gauging Olivia's reaction. "It took us a while to get his body temperature down to a normal range."

"Good Lord," she murmured. She knew how much her father hated the heat on the islands anyway. It must have been torturous for him.

A loud but shaky voice rang out behind them.

"Oh, I hope you're not believing all of this. Don't let him paint such a nasty picture for you."

They all turned toward the pale figure lying on the bed. He sounded somewhat like her father but barely resembled him even though he was awake.

"Dad!" Relieved he was conscious, Olivia hurried to his side. "Are you all right?"

"I'll be fine. Just need to get out of here and I'll be a lot better." His voice sounded strained and gravelly as he brushed aside the severity of his condition.

Sitting gingerly on the edge of the bed, Olivia leaned closer to him, looking deeply into his face. His eyes held the proof he had suffered a trauma. They were bloodshot and the lids were red around the edges. Never having seen him look so physically injured before, she needed to feel the warmth of his hand but didn't dare touch him, afraid of hurting him. Feeling uncomfortable being close to his fragile body, she slid off the bed and resumed her position next to the doctor.

The doctor stepped closer and continued. "We're going to keep him here for the next few days. I've ordered some tests. We'll see what those results are."

"Doc, I told you, I'm fine. I don't need to be here." In one rapid motion he tossed the bedspread aside with his left hand and swung his feet around to meet the floor, pulling the IV line taut. The plastic bag with clear liquid sloshing inside swung precariously from its hook.

Both Olivia and the attending physician lunged toward the bed with outstretched arms to keep him from advancing toward the door.

"Dad!"

"Mr. Benning, please stay put. You need your rest."

"Oh, really. In this place? If you can bring a wonderful glass of Scotch, then I'll be able to rest. I don't suppose you have anything like that around here, do you?" He chuckled to himself.

The doctor cleared his throat. "Of course not. Just stay put. You are seriously hurt and we need to keep an eye on you for a while. You're not going anywhere for the time being."

Cringing at the doctor's last statement, Olivia knew how much her father hated to be told what he should do. Fearing their encounter was not going to have a positive outcome, she watched as her father stared into the doctor's eyes, held his gaze for a moment and then, unexpectedly, seemed to give in. He leaned back onto the raised portion of the bed. Taking a few steps closer, Olivia gently pulled the covers over him as he pulled his legs up onto the bed. It was clear he was not happy but at least he was acknowledging a level of uncertainty. Perhaps he already had an inkling.

Standing in the background, the detective broke his silence. "Miss Benning, we should let your father get some rest."

Olivia was relieved she had an out. "Absolutely." She turned to her father. "You take care. Get some sleep. I'll be back later." She leaned close to him and kissed him gently. The bristle on his cheek brushed roughly against her delicate, young skin causing her to wrinkle her nose and close her eyes in response. She tried to clear her reaction from her face as she raised up and backed away from him.

He had a characteristic twinkle in his eyes, which worried her. Fighting the urge to admonish him, she whispered so only the two of them could hear.

"You stay put. You hear me?" She held onto a stern look to make it clear her message was unequivocal.

"Yeah . . . of course." His words were barely audible.

She glared at him and then stepped away. He was a grown man. He was going to have to make his own decisions. She shuffled toward the door and then turned back.

"Good night, Dad. Or . . . good morning?"

"Good night, Ollie."

Olivia and Detective Benson re-entered the hallway, and he closed the door behind them, leaving James with his doctor.

Turning to the detective with an expectant look on her face, she needed to have a word with him.

"Benson, what the hell is going on? Did someone do this to him?" She glared at him intently, demanding an honest answer.

He looked like he was unsure how to respond.

"We can't be sure. My men are still investigating. It's too soon to tell."

"Not for me. Those thugs that have been after me had something to do with it. I just know they did. Although I don't know how they could have figured out this quickly he is connected to me."

"I don't know yet. It could be. I have to consider all the possibilities. And given the type of people your mother, and now you, have gotten mixed up with, anything's possible."

She shook her head. "Who are these people?"

"Olivia, they're not anyone you should be wrangling with. They're dangerous." His tone turned stern. "They have no respect for life. They're running a very lucrative operation and anyone who stands between them and their profit . . . let's just say they won't hesitate to get rid of anyone who does. But then again, you saw firsthand what these people are like, didn't you?"

Clearly he had made the connection as to why she had been parked near Landfill Road the evening of the dog fight. Olivia bristled at what her mother had taken upon herself and now she was tangled up in.

"I know," she reluctantly admitted.

"I'm serious, Olivia. Don't think you can take on these people. They're ruthless." His words were firm. His eyes were stern. "I'm going to post a uniformed officer outside your father's door to be on the safe side."

Olivia inferred the sentry would be as much to protect her father as to keep him from leaving.

"Detective, look, I know showing up at the landfill wasn't the brightest idea. I'm just trying to find my mother. I need your help. I know she's out there somewhere. I think she's still alive. I can feel it. She and I are close. We have a connection. I know she's still out there."

"I understand your desire to find her. Believe me, I do. And I can assure you we are doing all we can. Please let us do our job. Stop putting yourself in danger."

"It's just not happening fast enough. Her life could depend on how quickly we get to her." She felt the volume of her voice rising and tried to bring it under control.

"I understand. Listen, Olivia, tell me this. Is there anything, any information your mother may have mentioned to you or left behind at her place that would give us a better idea of who these people are or where we might find them, which would help us to find her?"

Struggling to maintain a poker face, she was afraid her expression revealed she was holding back. She remained pensive, trying to decide if she should mention the disc before she had a chance to take a look at it. Finally she concluded she should see it first. Convinced her mother had left it for her to find, Olivia would need to find a computer she could use.

"Nothing comes to mind, Detective." She looked defiantly at him, then tried to appeal to his softer side. "You've got to find my mother. I miss her so much."

Detective Benson looked deeply into her eyes, as if searching for the right response.

"We'll do our best." He reached out with a gentle hand on her shoulder. "You should think about staying here tonight. I can't guarantee your safety if you don't."

"Yeah, I think I'll pass on your invitation. Thanks all the same. I'm not real keen on hospitals."

They both looked up as Sarah approached them from down the hall, sipping steaming hot coffee from a paper cup in her right hand. She looked from Olivia to the detective and back again.

"Hey, guys. How's it going?" Her tone was upbeat, almost lyrical.

"We're good." She gave Sarah a glance to show her how ready she was to get out of there.

After bidding farewell to the detective, Sarah reached out, extending her arm around Olivia and escorted her toward the elevator.

Olivia traipsed alongside Sarah willingly. Her body ached from her concern for her father on top of everything else. Too much to think about. Hoping she had made the right move by not giving the detective the disc from her mother's refrigerator, she needed to take a look first. She patted her back pocket to make sure it was still there, only to remember she had left it sitting on the bedside table at Sarah's house so she wouldn't lose it or damage it in some way.

Sarah and Olivia practically skipped on their way to the elevator, leaving Benson behind. The detective called down the hall to them, asking Olivia to reconsider staying at the hospital that evening. When she waved him off, he pleaded with her to at least be careful and stay out of sight.

Olivia had a passing thought of Colton. Where he was. If he was okay. Whose side he was on. She couldn't stop thinking about him.

Sarah pressed the down button and tossed her cup into the garbage can between the two elevators, distorting her face in disgust. "That tasted awful," she grumbled. "Someone should be smacked for trying to pass that off as a cup of coffee." As she pressed her eyes closed and shuddered, the doors on the left opened.

Relieved to leave the hospital, Olivia couldn't get onto the elevator fast enough, bumping into Sarah on the way in. Thankfully it was empty. As the doors closed behind them, she began to process her father's wretched fate. The short ride down to the first floor was mercifully quiet, yet filled with the inherent tension of being in a hospital.

The doors opened on the first floor. Olivia looked up into the hazel eyes of a dead man.

CHAPTER THIRTY-FIVE

"Olivia!" *His dark-skinned face appeared shocked* to see her as she froze in the doorway to the elevator. He held his right arm close to his body, supported by a sling.

Olivia's entire body jolted at the sight of him. Her mind raced, trying to make sense of what she was seeing.

"Carson?" She was incredulous. How could it be? She had been grateful to receive the news *she* hadn't shot him, but he had, nevertheless, been shot by an unknown assailant.

"Yeah, it's me. Last time I saw you, you were pointing a gun in my direction." His chuckle at her disbelief sounded forced.

"I'm glad you're okay. I thought you were—"

As the elevator doors started to close both she and Carson extended an arm to block them. Sarah stood unobtrusively in the back.

Olivia stepped forward and their faces became quite close. She reached out and hugged him. His body turned rigid inside her arms.

"Ow! Easy there!" He stepped back, out of her hug.

"Oh, I've hurt you! I'm sorry. I didn't mean to." She hung onto his arm but stared at him in disbelief. "I'm glad you're okay." Before the elevator doors could close again, Sarah slipped out behind Olivia, forcing her to remember her manners. "Carson, this is Sarah."

"Pleased to meet you." He extended his left hand since his right dangled lifelessly in the sling.

Sarah spoke and the two clumsily shook hands.

Olivia continued. "Carson is a friend of my mother's."

Sarah nodded once in acknowledgment.

The three stood awkwardly in the lobby of the hospital like teenagers at a school dance until Carson found his voice.

"Is everything all right? Were you visiting someone upstairs?"

"Yes, everything is fine." She chose to ignore his second question. "How are you? Are you healing okay?"

"Yeah, sure. I'm on the mend. It wasn't too serious."

Olivia recalled that fateful day on her mother's gallery. "It looked awful. *You* looked awful. God, there was blood everywhere."

Carson chuckled again. "Yeah, I'm sure it was pretty bad. I'm sorry you ended up in the middle of whatever is going on. These people seem pretty dangerous. I'm glad you're okay."

Olivia was curious about his involvement. "Carson, what did you say you do . . . for a living?"

"I run a water sports shop on the east end." Appearing anxious to take his leave, he reached over and pushed the button for the elevator and then turned back toward her. The same elevator doors she and Sarah had just walked through opened up and he promptly stepped on.

While holding the door open with his free hand, he leaned over and pressed a button for one of the floors with the hand hanging out of the sling. "See you 'round."

Olivia stepped closer to him as he let go of the door. Their eyes connected. As the elevator doors started to close, Olivia noticed a bulge in the shape of sunglasses in his shirt pocket monogramed with the name Caribbean Blue Security.

Olivia shoved her hand between the doors just as they reached the middle. They sandwiched her hand momentarily but then rebounded to the sides again. With a puzzled expression, he looked to her for an explanation.

"Carson, can I ask you something?" This time she held the door open. She was in control.

"Of course." He calmly held his expectant gaze, looking almost defiant.

She stepped closer to him. "Were you the . . . did you communicate with my mother by fax?"

He squinted his eyes and examined her face. "By fax?" He restated her question and paused for a moment. "No . . . we never communicated by fax."

Olivia looked long and hard into his hazel eyes, looking for a flicker or a hint he wasn't being entirely truthful with her. Just as the silence grew uncomfortable, an elderly couple approached from behind Olivia and stepped onto the elevator. Reluctantly she loosened her grip on the door, and they both closed. She couldn't help wonder what he was hiding, if anything.

Sarah looked at Olivia and it was understood it was time to head out. They burst through the front doors on their way to the parking lot.

Outside, Olivia scrunched up her face as she considered why Carson might be at the hospital. Her curiosity was piqued.

Across the parking lot, a couple of men walked away with their backs to them. The taller one reminded her of Colton. The color of his hair. His body frame. The way he moved. She inhaled as she took a closer look, and deciding it wasn't him, chided herself for letting her imagination wander.

The morning sky was becoming brighter and there were more cars in the parking lot than when they had arrived. Quickly they found Sarah's car and hopped in, exiting the parking lot and leaving the hospital behind.

It was a quiet ride back to Red Hook. They chatted briefly about Olivia's father's condition, but the rest of the time was spent in reflection.

Arriving at Sarah's place, they pulled in next to Olivia's Jeep. Slowly they trudged up the steps to her front door, and Sarah froze in her tracks. Nearly running into her from behind, Olivia stepped around Sarah to see what she was looking at.

The front door was ajar.

CHAPTER THIRTY-SIX

The frame next to the knob was in splinters. An odd-shaped hole took the place of the lock.

As Sarah stepped backward, Olivia moved with her, down a few steps. Their eyes were fixed on the open door. They turned and looked at each other and then back again. Neither wanted to be the first to say anything. Finally Sarah put her concern into words.

"Maybe we should call the police. Detective Benson."

Olivia turned and looked her in the eye. "Are you kidding? It will take them forever to get here. Besides, whoever broke in is long gone. Let's go take a look." She brushed past Sarah and ran back up the steps, but then offered, "Call the cops if you want. We'll probably have it all figured out by the time they get here."

Moving slowly and looking somewhat reticent, Sarah followed behind Olivia and entered the front door. Her place was ransacked. Drawers emptied, lamps overturned, shelves cleared off onto the floor. It seemed as though nothing was left untouched. Neither spoke. Their footsteps were silent as they surveyed the damage. Olivia nearly burst with guilt.

"Sarah, I am sorry."

Clearly struggling to take it all in, Sarah stood still, staring at the mess.

Olivia turned and looked toward her friend. "Do you think they took anything?" As soon as the words left her mouth, she realized the question was premature.

"I have no idea. It will take me a while to figure that out."

They split up and entered their respective bedrooms. Olivia was the first to yell out.

"Oh shit!"

"What's wrong?" Sarah appeared at the bedroom door.

Olivia flopped onto the bed and slammed her fist into the pillow. "My disc is gone! I left it on the bedside table figuring I wouldn't be needing it at the hospital. Now they've taken it. Damn it!" She smacked her thigh in frustration.

"What was on the disc? Who would have wanted it?"

"Oh, Sarah, I'm not exactly sure." She considered how to fill her in. "It seems as though my mother was trying to document some illegal activity and the slugs caught on to her. She was able to put together a CD she left behind at her house, but I didn't have a chance to look at it yet."

"So how does this involve you?" Sarah's eyes narrowed as she started to put the pieces together. "Does this have to do with the fire at your mother's house?"

Again Olivia hesitated, trying to determine the best way to explain to her new friend she had gone into the lions' den on a whim, following in her mother's footsteps. At the time it seemed perfectly logical, but as she explained it to Sarah, it came out sounding entirely absurd. Unquestionably foolish. Downright dangerous.

"I tried to pick up where my mother left off, but it seems they have caught on to me, too."

"What? Olivia, are you serious—"

Olivia's eye grew wide and her mouth dropped. "Oh no!"

"What?"

"Somehow they knew to look here. Sarah, you're in danger. Just by me staying here I have put you in great danger. I'm sorry. I need to get out of here. I can't have you risking your life for me. We don't even know who these people are or what they look like."

Sarah held up her hand like a crossing guard on a school morning, exhibiting remarkable calm. "I have a better idea. Before you leave, let's switch cars."

Olivia examined her closely. She sounded serious.

"I can't do that," she spoke firmly.

"Of course you can. Think about it. If you're driving my car, they will never suspect it's you."

"But if you're driving mine, they will think it's me and you could get hurt."

"Don't be silly. They'll see who's driving and will lose interest."

"Oh, Sarah, I don't know. I don't like it."

"Nonsense. That's our plan. I have a couple showings on the north side this morning and then your car will just sit in the parking lot at the office for the afternoon. It will be fine. If nothing else, it will confuse them for a while."

They exchanged keys and Olivia reluctantly took the Explorer, anxious to separate herself from Sarah and get her out of danger. Not much was going to stop these savages. Who knew how many people had already lost their lives in the name of their profits. They were making their point quite clear. She needed to put as much distance between herself and them as she could and find a safe spot to regroup. A serene neighboring island like St. John would do.

CHAPTER THIRTY-SEVEN

t was still relatively early in the morning, especially for island time. Looking around at the crowd, Olivia noticed there weren't many tourists to speak of. She shared the ferry ride with islanders who were commuting to St. John for work. It was an interesting array of people, all sitting patiently for the short trip to Cruz Bay. She found a seat at the stern with views of what she had left behind.

The ride was fairly noisy from the sound of the engine but thankfully brief and the view of the ocean was spectacular. Olivia recalled one return trip on the St. John ferry several years earlier when she just made it onto the boat. She had no sooner stepped on board than the crew cast off. Scouring the crowded ferry for a place to sit, she caught the eye of several people as she searched the main deck. It was mostly men, which made her less than comfortable. Quickly figuring out the only available seats were down below in the bowels of the boat, she cautiously descended the steep, narrow metal steps and nervously surveyed the cramped quarters. Not much to see there. No windows. No way to look out. It wouldn't have mattered if it was day or night. The view was the same. Four white walls and the deafening thunderous reverberation from the engine. The tight space was crammed with islanders, all men, who were returning home after work. It didn't seem to make a difference to them where they were seated. It was a means to an end. Getting home after a hard day. She found a spot at the end of one bench seat after a couple guys appeared to take pity on her and make room.

Usually Olivia enjoyed the passage between St. Thomas and St. John but on that trip, she couldn't wait for it to be over. She fought off horrific images of what might happen if the boat had an unexpected emergency. Water gushing into the compartment she swore wasn't meant for anything other than cargo. Certainly not people. Only one way out. Up the metal stairway she envisioned would be crowded with men scrambling to escape from certain death. She would be left behind to fight for her own life.

Pushing away the terrifying worst-case scenario from the past, she refocused on the present. The breeze off the water and the slowing of the engine helped. The ferry pulled into Cruz Bay. Two nimble crew members jumped onto the dock as it approached and tied up the boat with large ropes. Once it was secure, the passengers were given the "all ashore" clearance.

Olivia held back and waited for the crowd to disembark. She was certainly in no hurry. Having no particular place to go, she had plenty of time to get there.

She lazily got up and shuffled along behind the last few passengers heading off the boat. There was a long line in front of her. Olivia blinked in surprise as the profile of a man passing along the outside of the boat caught her attention. Light brown hair with blond highlights. Pulled back into a ponytail. It looked like Colton. Her heart raced. Could it be him? Oh, why had she fallen behind? She needed to catch up, see if it was actually him. God, she hoped so. An excited twinge rippled through her stomach and her heart beat faster.

"Damn!" she yelled at no one in particular, regretting letting so many people go in front of her.

As her situation had changed, she rudely pushed past those passengers she had politely let pass moments earlier, desperate to catch up to the man. She had to find out if it was Colton and prayed it was.

Spotting him nearing the end of the dock, she could see he was dressed in a light blue tee and long board shorts. He appeared to have sneakers on his feet, which didn't seem to fit Colton's style. He was walking next to an older man with predominantly gray hair blended with some black and white. Jostling and bumping past elbows, pushing her way through the crowd, moving like Sunday parishioners leaving a church service, she tried to keep an eye on the man of interest. As soon as she made it past two or three people, she was pushed back by just as many. At times it felt like she was standing still. It was a losing battle. She lost sight of him. Still keeping an eye out, she scanned the end of the dock where taxis waited to whisk arriving passengers to far flung places on the island.

Olivia kept pushing, yet her feet moved much more slowly through the crowd than she would have liked. Finally she reached the end of the dock, and stopping dead in her tracks, searched the immediate area. Nothing. No dirty blond ponytail in sight. She couldn't believe her luck. Turning around, she looked back toward the ferry and spied the guy with the light blue tee hovering near his acquaintance who was bent over tying his shoe. He was looking straight at her.

Her heart skipped a beat as she was caught in a distant sea of blue, but she was sailing on the wrong sea. It wasn't him. The guy's face brightened as he seemed intrigued to connect with her, but that was as far as she was going to let it go.

Abruptly turning, she shook off her disappointment and started the trek over to the park, looking forward to taking a walk on the trail to one of the magnificent beaches along it. On her way, she punched in Colton's number again in the hopes she could reach him, but her call skipped to voicemail. She didn't wait to hear his outgoing message.

As she passed through town toward the park visitors' center, she encountered several taxi drivers who wanted to give her a ride. Trunk Bay? Cinnamon Bay? Annaberg Ruins? They would take her! She politely declined, "No, thank you." Where she was going, she could walk.

Olivia didn't need to get anywhere fast. She just needed to get away . . . away from the danger on St. Thomas where she had left her father under the watchful eye of the local police. She had to count on them to protect him.

Somehow just setting foot on St. John made her feel safer. There was something about being on the island. It had a much different vibe from St. Thomas. Much more low-key. Peaceful, serene, and predominantly undeveloped. At night, it took on a stillness unlike anything she had ever experienced, particularly in the city.

Olivia hiked up the steep hill behind the visitors' center to gain access to Lind Point Trail that wound its way along the shore and provided beautiful views of Cruz Bay. She stopped long enough to glance across to where the ferry had docked earlier. It was now heading back for its return trip to St. Thomas.

Traversing Lind Point Trail posed an element of peril. Exposed roots crisscrossed the dirt path and loose rocks lay in wait to move under unsteady feet. Along the way she admired huge aloe plants growing naturally in the arid environment. Picturing the scrawny aloe plant she was trying to keep alive on a windowsill back in Boston, she chortled out loud. It didn't look like it belonged to the same plant family as its Caribbean cousins.

The trail meandered through the woods, narrowing at times, twisting and turning and eventually descending through a tight section before spilling out onto the breathtaking beach at Salomon Bay. At times it became necessary to grab onto overhanging branches to keep from slipping or descending too quickly. Olivia reminded herself to be patient and not rush in her quest to reach the bay. Once her feet touched the soft, bright white sand, she stopped in her tracks. No one ever seemed to be on the beautiful beach when she was there. No matter what time of year she came, she had it to herself undoubtedly because it was accessible only by boat or hiking the Lind Point Trail. Even though Salomon Bay was the first stop on the trail, Olivia was happy to make it her last stop. She figured she couldn't get much better than a private beach.

Walking over to the water's edge, Olivia slipped off her sandals and tossed them behind her. Slowly she entered the tepid turquoise water, breathing in deeply as the bottom of her feet felt the wet sand ooze up around her toes. The water remained clear no matter how far she advanced into it. Scanning her surroundings, she was relieved she was completely detached from civilization. Only a catamaran passed lazily across in front of her, close enough to tell there were a dozen or so people on board but far enough away she couldn't make out their chatter.

Voices in the woods startled her. Turning toward the sound, she listened intently and searched for movement. At first it was hard to tell the gender of the voices. Her sense of potential danger heightened. She couldn't make out how many people there were, but they seemed to be heading down the trail toward the beach. Getting closer. Her heart beat faster, but she tried to convince herself they were harmless. If they meant her harm, they wouldn't announce their arrival by talking on the way there. By the time a young couple emerged from the trail, she was considering her options to run.

Lost in their conversation, they didn't notice her at first, but then stopped in their tracks when they did. Obviously disappointed to find someone else on the beach, they exchanged hellos and continued across the sand toward the path back to the trail.

Olivia let out a cleansing breath, relieved she wasn't in danger after all. Settling onto the sand with her toes in the water, she let her eyes wander across the turquoise bay, back toward St. Thomas. The blazing sun nearing its apex in the sky baked her skin while the gentle breeze off the water caressed it. Taking in the beauty of her surroundings, she attempted to sort through her thoughts, replaying the events as they had transpired since the call in Boston.

Although she set out determined in her quest to find answers, the reality of her pursuit had become too overwhelming. Worse, she had put herself and Sarah in grave danger. Perhaps her father, too. And Colton? She wondered who he really was and what his involvement was. And who was she to think she could take on these people? Whoever they were. She'd been foolish. Selfish in her attempt to find her mother. But, as she recalled, she hadn't received a lot of help when she first arrived. She had no other option but to do it herself—of course now she was in way over her head. The disc she insisted on looking at first, before she handed it over to the police, may have held vital information the detective could have used to stop these horrible people . . . perhaps find her mother. Of course, now it was in their hands. Probably destroyed. She had nothing. Not even any photos that could be used as evidence, much less a camera.

A rustling in the woods reminded her how vulnerable she was. Feeling threatened, she jumped up and spun around to face the direction the sound had come from. With her back to the water, she scanned the woods along the beach, searching for whatever had made the sound. It came again but she couldn't detect any movement. There were no voices this time. Her eyes widened, and she foolishly took a couple steps backward toward the water as if that was going improve her situation. She chanced a glance up the beach and down the other way to see if she could see anyone who might be able to come to her aid. Even the young couple that had passed by earlier was nowhere to be seen. For once, she wished she wasn't alone on the beach. She tried talking herself into thinking it was simply a mongoose making its way through the underbrush, but she wasn't very convincing.

Again the sound came. Her back stiffened and the tips of her fingers tingled. Her respiration became shallow and she could feel her heart beating rapidly inside her ribcage. She swallowed hard, surveying the beach again, trying to decide her best escape route. The sound became louder and movement caught her eye. Something dark. Gray? A couple shapes. Moving through the woods. Toward her. She wanted to run but her feet wouldn't move. She just stood still. Staring at the movement.

To her relief, a donkey slowly emerged from the mangroves along the edge of the beach. A second plodded behind. Two of the many harmless donkeys that were wild on St. John and roamed freely. Olivia enjoyed seeing them. Locals weren't always as enamored with the furry critters, but there was something quite adorable about them. Perhaps it was the way they could look you in the eye, if you could get close enough, and give you the impression they thought humans took life far too seriously.

Admonishing herself for letting her imagination get the best of her, she watched the two long-eared beasts saunter down the beach and onto the dirt path leading back to the trail until they were out of sight. Turning her face up toward the sun, she sat back down, pressing her feet into the wet sand. Gentle waves tickled her toes each time they reached the shore.

It didn't occur to her the donkeys may have been frightened out of the woods by something . . . or someone.

CHAPTER THIRTY-EIGHT

D etective *Benson stood with his shoulders uncharacteristically slumped* at the end of the hall on the third floor of the hospital. Gazing out the windows, his eyes were directed toward a flowering Flamboyant tree with bright orange-red blossoms. The gentle breeze jiggled the branches full of deep green leaves. A Bananaquit bird with its bright yellow breast hopped from branch to branch, but the detective wasn't seeing any of it. Lost in his work, he shook his head in disbelief he hadn't solved the case yet. He ran the tips of his fingers across the deep lines on his forehead, carved from years on the force worrying about keeping the public safe.

His makeshift office set up near the nurses' station allowed him to monitor the situation that had taken on a life of its own over the last few days. So many bodies had been delivered to the morgue he figured he might as well hang out close by. He should be one of the first to know of any new additions.

His frustration was mounting, though. He had expected to have the case wrapped up already. This was one of the tougher ones he had been assigned to in all of his years on the force. He couldn't let it slip away from him. There were unidentified bodies on the first floor and dangerous perpetrators loose somewhere on the island. Chances were they wouldn't return to the landfill for another night, yet he had to try to anticipate what their next move would be. What went on sickened the stomach of even a seasoned cop like himself.

His phone jangled noisily inside his pants pocket. He grabbed it and answered in a gruff, impatient voice.

"Yeah, Benson here." He listened intently and then his face fell.

"Oh, God . . . no," he implored with a raspy voice, exhibiting signs of a lack of sleep. Closing his eyes, he used his free hand to try to rub the tension from the side of his head.

"Are you sure?" He leaned up against the cold rough concrete wall, needing the support. Opening his eyes again, he found a branch swaying in the breeze outside the window to focus on.

"Good God. Please tell me you're wrong." Listening to the harbinger on the other end of the line, he blinked firmly several times, fighting back his emotions and then hung up.

Slowly he gathered himself and started to close the distance between himself and James' room, pausing for a moment halfway down to consider the difficult task ahead of him and then continued down the hallway.

Nodding to the uniformed officer seated outside the room, he tapped lightly on the door and then pushed it open to see Olivia's father pulling on a dress shirt. Since James was on the phone with his back to him, Benson maintained his position at the door and took the opportunity to outline the impending conversation in his head.

Still buttoning his shirt and shoving the tail into his pants, the phone cradled in the crook of his neck, James turned his head as if to acknowledge the detective's intrusion. He cut his conversation short, assuring the person at the other end of the line he would call back.

"So glad there's at least a shred of privacy in the hospital." His obvious grumpiness was tempered only slightly by his sarcasm.

James flopped down on the edge of the bed, folded his hands—resting them on his legs—and looked up expectantly. His body language implied he was at the officer's mercy, ready to be submissive, but Benson knew otherwise. And what he was about to tell him would certainly push him into action.

"Mr. Benning, I'm afraid I have some rather . . ." He was trying to decide how best to break it to him. "It's Olivia."

James' eyes grew wide and he sat up straight, grabbing the edge of the mattress with both hands. "What's happened? Where is she?" Clearly the detective couldn't answer his questions fast enough.

Benson paused, wishing he didn't have to utter his next few words.

"She's been in a car accident. Her car was discovered off of Hull Bay Road."

James stood up quickly as if to take leave of the room and head out after her.

"Is she all right? Where is she?"

Benson hung his head. "I'm afraid she didn't make it. I'm sorry."

"How could this be?" His face grew ashen as he listened.

The detective chose to provide a few more details to allow her father to understand the gravity and inevitability of the situation.

"Sir, the vehicle went over the side of the road and down the embankment earlier this morning and burst into flames on impact. . . . They could only identify it by the license plate."

"No." James' voice was barely audible. Turning away from the detective, he walked to the window that looked out over the front parking lot. He poked a couple fingers between the slats in the horizontal blinds as though trying to get a clearer view outside. He appeared to be expecting someone to arrive.

The detective waited patiently for Olivia's father to process the news.

James turned from the window with fire in his eyes.

Benson had seen that look before. Usually it was on a suspect they were trying to arrest who felt like a caged animal and was willing to try anything to get away because he had nothing to lose. He instinctively took a step backward, even though James was across the room. The detective watched his nostrils flare and the color of his skin flush as anger ripped through his body.

"*You* are responsible! How could you let this happen? You had the information you needed. I gave you the CD." His voice rose as he spoke. "Oh, you will pay for this. First my wife and now my precious daughter. You will pay for your ineptitude. You'll wish it was you and not them."

James turned back toward the window, gazing out to some distant point as if searching for a place where his heart could stop hurting.

"I'm sorry" was all Benson could think of to say. He turned and unceremoniously walked out, leaving Olivia's father alone to grieve in private. Under his breath he lamented, "Why didn't she listen? She just couldn't stay out of it and let us do our job. Damn it!" He smacked his palm on the frame of the door as he exited.

Outside the room, he leaned over and grabbed the shoulder of the officer on babysitting duty, forcing the rookie officer to look up.

"Looks like he's going to make a run for it."

CHAPTER THIRTY-NINE

W*rinkling her nose as she zigzagged* through the set of double doors into the hospital foyer, Olivia noticed the sour aseptic smell seemed much stronger than usual. Pressing the elevator button, her body shivered uncontrollably. Too many memories in the short time since her first visit. She had never been fond of hospitals on the mainland, and the number of trips thus far to this island hospital was getting out of hand.

Feeling safer moving about the island under a cloak of darkness, Olivia had delayed her return until evening. The sun had long since set. She proceeded to the third floor and exited the elevator where the floor was relatively quiet. In the still of the night, she almost felt the need to tiptoe down the hall toward her father's room. An older woman seated at the nurses' station glanced up as she passed. Farther down the hall an orderly collected dinner trays, disrupting the calm with each noisy addition to a tall rolling cart that already was overloaded.

As she approached his room, she was disappointed to see there was no officer posted outside. Concerned her father's safety had been ignored, she reached the door for Room 333 and pushed it open. She stood in the doorway and her mouth dropped open. It was pitch black.

She reached for the light switch next to the door and hated to wake him up but flipped it on.

There was no one in the room. Both beds were unoccupied and made up neatly in anticipation of the next two patients' arrivals. Olivia glanced from one bed to the other. She couldn't understand what it meant.

Retreating from the empty room, she walked back to the nurses' station. There had to be an explanation.

The elderly nurse with gray hair pulled back in a bun looked up as she approached the desk. "Can I help you with something?"

"Yes, please. My father, James Benning, was in Room 333 but now it's empty. Can you tell me where he is?"

"And you are?"

Olivia hesitated, staring at her blankly, knowing she had already given her the information she needed. "Olivia Benning. His daughter." She spoke slowly, trying not to sound condescending.

"Let me take a look." She pulled out a clipboard and flipped through the first couple of pages, running her finger from the top to the bottom of each page. After the third page, she flipped back to the first page and repeated her motions.

Olivia grew impatient. How difficult could it be to keep track of patients in such a small hospital?

"Anything?" she asked, trying not to offend.

"I don't see any record he was ever in that room. You said 330?"

"No! 333." She spoke firmly, trying to stay calm but feeling herself losing patience.

"Oh, okay. Let me look again." She repeated her actions with the clipboard but still shook her head. "I'm sorry, I don't see a James Benning in any room."

Olivia's head fell forward in exasperation.

In a calm but firm voice she asked, "Who can I speak to, to find out where he is?" She wasn't backing down. She wanted some answers. He couldn't just disappear without a trace. Or could he?

The nurse opened her mouth to speak when the elevator doors opened and a man stepped off and walked toward them. He stopped short of reaching the desk.

"Olivia?" His voice had a definitive tone of disbelief.

Turning to look into the eyes of Detective Benson, she was relieved to see a familiar face, but he appeared shocked to see her. She was afraid to hear what might have happened to her father.

"Detective, where is my father? He's not in his room."

Benson glanced over at the nurse and then placed the palm of his hand gently on Olivia's lower back. "Why don't you come with me? I can fill you in." Leaving the nurse behind they boarded the same elevator he had just stepped out of. As soon as the door closed, the detective turned to her with a shocked look on his face and grabbed one of her shoulders.

"You're okay! We had received word you . . . you were hurt . . . in an accident. But you're fine. Good to see." His expression was a blend of bewilderment and relief.

"What happened to my father?" She wanted answers. Was he all right? Did he check himself out? A wave of guilt for leaving him in the care of the Virgin Islands Police Department washed over her.

"We had to move him."

She was relieved he was still in the hospital. He hadn't escaped. Or worse.

"So where is he?"

"We moved him one floor down. For security reasons. To keep him safe. A moving target is harder to hit."

Olivia didn't like the sound of that, but she appreciated their efforts to keep him safe.

The elevator doors opened again, and they were on the second floor, which was set up identically to the third.

"What room number?"

"Two nineteen."

They took a right off the elevator this time, and she followed along next to the detective as they made their way to her father's room.

As expected, there was a uniformed officer outside. He was standing next to his chair, which made him seem much more official and certainly more intimidating.

Olivia took the lead and pushed the door open. She was pleased to see her father was in the far bed located closest to the window. He seemed to be resting. His eyes were closed but, oddly, he was curled up in a near fetal position facing the door. Never having seen him looking as vulnerable, she felt sad for him. Something had changed since she had seen him last.

Feeling helpless, she stood there looking at her father, unaware the detective had followed her into the room. His voice from behind rattled her.

"You should wake him. He'll be pleased to see you."

"Oh, no. He needs his rest," she whispered so as not to disturb him. "I'll just tiptoe out. I can stop back in again in the morning."

As she brushed past Benson, she heard a rustling sound behind her.

"Olivia?" His voice was shaky, his expression approaching shock.

"Yes, Dad." She felt uncomfortable she had intruded. "I'm sorry, I didn't mean to wake you." She walked slowly over to his bed.

"Are you kidding? I'm happy to see you. Come over here! I knew they were wrong. It just couldn't be." He fumbled clumsily to sit up and throw his legs over the side of the bed. She stepped closer to him and leaned over so he was able to reach out and hold her in his arms. They hugged tightly, like they had never embraced before.

Olivia was surprised by his enthusiasm. Probably a side effect of his pain meds. She looked closely at his face and noticed how pale he looked. He appeared to be getting worse instead of better. It concerned her deeply.

Her father's face fell as if he was reading her thoughts. He looked as though he had something to say, but Detective Benson came to life behind her before he could open his mouth.

"Miss Benning, there is a matter we need to discuss."

Olivia stepped away from her father's embrace and turned to Benson. "There is?"

"Yes. Olivia, this morning there was a terrible accident on the North side."

"I'm sorry to hear that." She searched his face, hoping for more information.

"A vehicle went off the road . . . Hull Bay Road . . . and down the embankment and burst into flames."

Olivia's eyes grew large. "Oh, how awful."

The detective looked directly at her. "I think it was someone you know. It was a Jeep. Your Jeep."

Her eyes grew wider and she gasped. "Sarah!"

"You two switched cars, didn't you?"

Olivia sat down on the edge of her father's bed and covered her mouth with both hands. "Oh, no . . . that was supposed to be me," she blurted through splayed fingers.

"We're going to have what's left of the car checked out, but I would guess the brake lines were cut. There were no tire marks where it left the road." His voice was even and his expression stern. "I'm sorry."

The detective turned and exited the room.

Her body aching from the shock of the news, Olivia's eyes brimmed with tears she didn't attempt to quell, reaching the corners of her eyes and trickling down her cheek. Brushing them away without caring where they fell, she felt her father's hand on her forearm, patting gently to let her know he was there for her. She didn't feel worthy of his touch. Desperate to pull her arm away, she struggled to remain motionless in the awkwardness of the moment, not willing to hurt his feelings. Silence filled the small room.

An unknown female voice paged a doctor to a room on the first floor. She had a fleeting inclination it might be the morgue.

Olivia remained next to her father until he fell asleep. Images of Sarah and her idea to switch cars haunted her. Why hadn't she insisted on taking her own car? She would never forgive herself. The floodgates of grief opened. Her body shook as she sobbed uncontrollably, on the edge of the bed, while her father snored loudly. After wiping her well-sodden cheeks with the back of her hand the best she could, she slipped back out to the hallway. Her stomach felt sick with guilt.

Detective Benson was waiting for her just down the hall. Olivia couldn't stand it any longer. Knowing she had selfishly waited too long, she needed to tell him about the CD she had found in her mother's fridge. It was embarrassing to admit she had hung onto it and then let it slip out of her hands. It could have been useful. Shouldering the consequences of her actions felt unwieldy, and she needed to come clean. Not that she would be able to sleep any better, but it was the right thing to do.

He looked up expectantly as she approached.

"There is something you should know."

Detective Benson's eyes lit up.

"There's a CD."

Olivia shoved her hands into her back pants pocket, struggling with the guilt associated with her confession.

"I found it in the refrigerator at my mother's house after the fire. It looked like something she wanted to make sure got documented, no matter what happened. It seemed to have survived unscathed. I didn't have a chance to take a look at it but I have an idea what's on it was important enough to preserve even beyond her . . . death."

The detective's eyes widened.

"But . . . someone took it."

Detective Benson's expression turned ugly, obviously contemplating the impact of the information. He clenched his teeth.

"What the hell happened?" His patience was clearly growing thin.

Olivia felt painfully ashamed. Could the information on it have prevented Sarah's death? She didn't know the answer, but she'd have to live with the possibility.

She filled in the details for him about leaving the disc at Sarah's house and the break-in while they were at the hospital visiting her father.

"Great timing, Olivia. How long did you have this?" He sounded like a parent reprimanding his child. His bushy graying eyebrows furrowed over tired, bloodshot eyes.

"I'm sorry. I wasn't sure what was on it. It could have been nothing."

"Thank God your father got a CD and turned it in to us."

Olivia inhaled quickly. "What?"

"Yeah, I bet your mother sent him a copy, too. She's a bright lady, isn't she?"

"Yes, she is." Olivia was pleased to be speaking of her mother in the present tense.

"My men are evaluating the photos on it to see if anything is useful to us."

She was enormously relieved.

"Oh, and Olivia, your father's rental car checked out okay. It wasn't tampered with from what my guys could tell. Probably a matter of distracted driving."

The conversation turned to her safety, and again he insisted she stay the night at the hospital. He couldn't protect her anywhere else, except perhaps the jail. Resisting initially, she finally agreed to flop onto one of the couches in the lounge. First, however, she needed a breath of fresh air. As she approached the elevator doors, they opened. A man with a familiar face stepped off.

"David!"

"Hello, Olivia." His tone was not welcoming and he brushed past her.

Curious who he was there to visit, she tagged along, fingers crossed it was Colton. Tickled at the possibility, she sprang lightly on her feet as she stepped behind him.

He stopped abruptly and turned around to face her. "Olivia, leave well enough alone. You've caused enough damage."

"Are you here to see Colton? Is he okay?"

David looked deeply into her eyes, like he was considering his response. "I haven't seen him."

A strange pause hung in the air. He seemed uncomfortable uttering the words, as if they were forced. She struggled with images from Landfill Road . . . and the morgue.

"I have more important things to worry about right now," David murmured as he strode off down the hall.

Olivia couldn't help but wonder if "I haven't seen him" meant "I haven't seen him yet" and he was on his way. A twinge in her stomach sent shivers up her spine. Anticipating the possibility, she followed behind David, catching up to him easily.

Outside of Room 207, David placed a hand on the door and turned back to look at Olivia.

"What are you doing?" Clearly he was annoyed by her presence.

"Who are you seeing, David?" she implored, ignoring his question.

A peculiar smirk slowly crept onto his face. "Someone I think you've met."

Olivia's excitement surged inside of her. Unable to contain herself any longer, she pushed David against the door, and the two spilled into the room.

Her excited anticipation quickly turned to bewilderment. The patient was not who she was expecting to see, who she was desperately hoping it would be. She stood transfixed. The patient was a woman with shoulder length brown hair. Her face was cut and bruised and both hands were wrapped in white bandages. She looked like she was asleep. Olivia suddenly recognized who she was looking at. Opening her mouth to speak, she closed it again as she gazed upon the patient. Finally she found her voice.

"Sarah, it's you. Please be all right," she whispered so as not to wake her. Relief flooded through her. She took a step closer. "Oh my God, what happened . . . ?" Her voice trailed off, not talking to anyone in particular.

David wasn't going to let the one-sided conversation go any further. He stepped in front of Olivia, his hand extended to block her from advancing any farther.

"Okay, look. You need to—"

"How do you—" She looked from Sarah to David and back again. "How do you know each other?"

"She's my mother."

Olivia's eyebrows raised. "Oh, I see." She was thrilled to learn of their connection.

"But she's not yours. It's time for you to leave. You've done enough." His voice was firm. Grabbing her by the upper arm, he spun her around and led her to the door.

"Is she going to be okay?" Wincing from his powerful grip, Olivia wiggled to get free, determined to turn and get another look at Sarah.

Clearly intent on getting her out of the room, David didn't address her question.

Olivia tried again to squirm out of his grasp, but he was stronger than he looked. She gave in and let him shove her through the doorway.

The automatic door closed on its hinges with a dull thud behind her.

Sarah had survived the crash. Given how the detective had described the scene, it was a miracle. Olivia prayed she would recover fully. As much as that was a relief, it wasn't Colton. Her thoughts returned to the male body on the table in the morgue.

The door reopened behind her with a squeak.

David stood with one hand holding it open and the other on his hip. The latter quickly shot forward to point to Olivia. With nostrils flared, fury burned in his eyes.

"You have brought all of this on us. Back off already." His voice was hushed but firm. "These people you've pissed off have no regard for life. They've proven they're murderers. My mother could have been one of their victims." Anguish was chiseled onto his face.

"I'm sorry it wasn't me in that car. It should have been. David, I'm so sorry." Olivia cringed at the painful images of Sarah getting ensnared in the dangerous mess she had inherited from her mother. She continued to pray Sarah would recover from her injuries.

A dull pain shot through her chest, causing her to draw in a quick breath and tuck her left arm close to her body. Her body ached with guilt. If this was her payback, she certainly deserved it.

A feeble voice inside the room caught their ears.

"Mom!" David turned and lunged toward her bedside.

Olivia caught the door before it closed completely and pushed it open so she could slip through.

"Sarah," she whispered, stopping halfway to the bed to give David and his mother some space. Carefully he embraced her as if she were a delicate china doll.

Sarah turned and forced a weak smile when she saw Olivia. She slowly lifted her arm and reached out to her.

Closing the gap between herself and the bed, Olivia gently grasped Sarah's outstretched hand.

"So glad you're alive. I'm sorry, so sorry. What happened?"

While Olivia inspected her friend's bruised and scratched face, Sarah managed another smile.

"Let's just say it's a good thing I used to do gymnastics."

David sat on the edge of her bed as they listened to his mother recount her story.

Sarah explained how she jumped out of the Jeep partway down Hull Bay Road once it became obvious there were no brakes. Fortunately she was driving on the left so the bushes along the edge broke the momentum of her body hurtling through the air. Since she lost consciousness, she never saw where the Jeep ended up, but she hoped no one else got hurt.

Picking up where his mother left off, David's tone was nothing short of a reproval of Olivia. "The police said the car kept going for a while before hurtling off into the ravine on the right side of the road. It burst into flames. You ended up nowhere near the Jeep so, at first glance, they assumed whoever was driving had died inside." He turned and glared at Olivia. "Of course, they thought someone else was driving." He turned back to his mother. "You were brought into the hospital by a couple guys who live near where you landed."

Olivia's body started to quiver, deeply shaken for putting Sarah in such grave danger. Feeling David's continued disdain for her, she expressed her relief Sarah had survived and then excused herself so mother and son could have some private time together.

As Olivia grabbed the handle of the door, Sarah called her name.

"Guess my plan to switch cars wasn't so hot, was it?"

Olivia turned and recoiled, releasing the door handle. Although it was sweet for Sarah to acknowledge it was her idea to switch cars, Olivia shouldered the responsibility entirely. "Sarah, I never should have let you drive the Jeep. I should have thought it through and realized how dangerous it could be for you. I am sorry to have put you in harm's way. So sorry you got badly hurt." She closed her eyes. As she opened them again, a tear escaped and traced its way down the side of her cheek. "I'm . . . sorry."

Turning back toward the door, she quickly made her exit.

In response to Lieutenant Benson's previous urging and the fact she had nowhere else to crash, Olivia found her way to the lounge at the end of the floor and chose a pseudo leather, modern couch to flop down on for the night. It didn't look or feel all that comfortable but she figured it was never meant to be slept on. However since she was exhausted, fatigue washed over her and she drifted off quickly.

Olivia never noticed the men who slipped in during the middle of the night or the hand that covered her nose and mouth with a wet cloth.

CHAPTER FORTY

*I*t *was dark when Olivia opened her eyes.* So dark she couldn't make out where she was. Her head felt fuzzy. She remembered lying down in the hospital lounge, but blinking her eyes didn't help to discern her surroundings. They weren't adjusting. It didn't make sense.

Desperate to get off the couch and find the light switch, she rolled over to her left side, but her arm hit something hard. It was cold and smooth. Running her hand along it, she concluded it must be the wall. Rolling to the right she bumped into the same type of hard surface. It wasn't making any sense. Wasn't she on the couch? One side should be open. She tried to sit up but hit her head so hard a white light flashed in her eyes.

"Ow!" She rubbed her forehead with the tips of her fingers and dropped back down.

Olivia then moved her hand up toward what she had bumped into. Running her fingers along it, she could tell it was a flat metal surface.

Then it hit her. The smell. A sour, acidic odor that reminded her of visits to the morgue. Panic exploded inside of her. She was in one of the drawers. Screaming filled the inside of the box as she pounded her fists on the sides and ceiling. Someone had to be around. Someone had to hear her. Her breathing quickened. Her heart thumped loudly. How much oxygen was in the confined space? She kept screaming and pounding her fists. There was little room to move.

Please, God, don't leave me to die in here. Please, no.

She paused, venturing to take a deep breath, and listened to see if she could hear anyone. Nothing. She panicked. More screaming escaped her lips. Her voice grew hoarse. More pounding. Her fists were getting sore. Her chest heaved. Fearing the limited air would run out soon, she fought with herself to slow down her respiration.

Then she remembered her phone. If she could just slide it out of her pocket, she would be able to call for help. She felt a glimmer of hope until she reached down to pat the front pocket of her pants. Nothing was there. It was gone. Whoever had put her into the morgue drawer wanted to make sure she didn't get out.

The air in the drawer was getting thin. Desperate to attract someone's attention, she pounded again, knowing she might use up what little air she had left. She prayed someone would hear her.

Unexpectedly, a strange calm came over her. Had she resigned herself to death? No one was going to hear her. Olivia felt herself losing consciousness, but she endeavored to stay lucid. If these were her last few minutes, perhaps she should have a chat with God. Seemed appropriate. It had been such a short life. She was sad to think it would end this way. Not that she had contemplated much about the end. Twenty-three-year-olds were supposed to have plenty of time to worry about that. At least she had tried to find her mother.

Suddenly there was a muffled sound. Was it the door to the morgue? She yelled out and pounded her fists again. Gasping as she felt herself being pulled backward, she realized the drawer was moving. Bright light flashed in her eyes. She winced as it took a moment for them to adjust from the pitch black.

"Olivia!" It was the detective's voice. Movement behind him told her he had brought reinforcements with him.

Struggling to get out of the drawer, she tried to turn on her side and take in full breaths. The sour odor of the morgue hit her in the face. She grabbed the metal side with both hands. It was cold and hard and dug into the palm of her hands.

Two strong hands lifted her out. Gasping for air, she instinctively grabbed onto the detective's shirt and hung on tight. Her feet wobbled when they hit the floor.

"It's okay. . . . You're okay." Benson reassured her and held her tightly.

As the rapid heaving of her chest slowed, Benson looked around the room and guided her gently to a sturdy leather chair over in the corner pulled up close to a metal desk. Grabbing onto the arms, she flopped into the seat, plunking her feet down firmly on the floor. It was good to be in a space larger than a coffin.

Shoving his pudgy fingers into his shirt pocket, the detective pulled out a phone and handed it to her. "This must be yours. Found it on the couch you were sleeping on last night."

Relieved to have it back, Olivia watched as Benson walked back over to the open drawer. Something caught his eye as he glanced down. Reaching in, he picked up a pair of gold aviators.

Someone must be wondering where they had misplaced their sunglasses.

CHAPTER FORTY-ONE

Olivia burst out of the morgue and ran to the elevator. Needing to get to her father quickly, she pushed the up button several times and impatiently shuffled her feet in place. Finally the doors on the right side opened and thankfully the car was empty. She slid in, pressing the button for the second floor and the button to close the doors. It wasn't working fast enough for her liking. Stepping out of the elevator before the doors completely opened onto the second floor, she turned right and fast-walked with a deliberate gait to his room. When she got there, he was fully dressed in his street clothes and zipping the side of his carry-on bag. He turned toward her as she charged through the door.

"What are you doing?" she demanded, walking closer and examining his face, noticing how pale his skin was.

"Ollie, it's time to go home—"

"No! . . . No! We need to find Mom."

Her father's head dropped and his gaze fell to the floor.

"Look, we—"

"You go, if you want to. I'm not giving up." She stood up straighter and her back stiffened.

James sat on the edge of the bed and motioned for her to join him. Reluctantly, she complied with his request.

"There's something you need to know . . . and I don't really know how to . . ." He kept his head turned away from her. "Ollie, I need to get back home to see my own doctor."

"What?" Her voice was barely audible, her eyes searching her father's.

"I'm not doing well, Ollie. I don't know how much time I have."

Her eyes widened. Growing concerned for him, she reached over and took his hand. His head hung as if in shame.

"What's going on?" Her voice quivered.

He raised his head and connected with her, hesitating, but then finally admitted, "I've got cirrhosis of the liver." He looked into her eyes, clearly with a heavy heart. "I've only myself to blame."

Letting his hand drop, she got up and walked away, trying to put as much distance between herself and her father's pathetic circumstances as possible, circling around the foot of the bed and stopping at the window. She glanced outside without noticing the bright rays of sunshine streaming in, broken up by the fronds of a grand palm tree undulating in the gentle breeze.

"How much time?" Her voice was even, with no emotion.

"I don't know. I don't think they know for sure. I just got the news."

Olivia stood at the window gazing out with her arms folded tightly against her chest, lips pursed, shaking her head from time to time as she processed. Her father remained silent, perhaps allowing her the time she needed.

Finally she turned back toward him, glaring intently, teeth clenched. ". . . I'm sorry to hear your unfortunate news. But, like you said, you did it to yourself. I'm not leaving here until I find out where Mom is."

Olivia stormed out of the room. Her father let her go without calling after her.

Detective Benson entered James' room as an aide was removing his breakfast tray. He took one look at him fully dressed and surmised his plans. He understood. And he would be relieved to have both of them off island.

"James, have you seen Olivia? I haven't seen her since her scare earlier."

"Her scare?" Puzzled, James looked at the officer.

"Yeah, I'm sure she'll tell you about it." He didn't want to get into it with her father. "Any idea where she is now?"

"Not really. She left here earlier in a huff. I tried talking to her about leaving the island, and she wouldn't even consider it."

Their eyes met as each acknowledged where she had gone. James grabbed his bag and the two men hurried out to find the detective's car.

CHAPTER FORTY-TWO

B eads of perspiration formed on Olivia's forehead during the walk from the taxi stop. If her father refused to look for her mother, that was his burden to carry. She vowed to stay as long as it took.

Olivia felt drawn to Serenity Villa. Perhaps it was the memories. Certainly the view was a big part of it. Perhaps it was the possibility of finding something. She felt closest to her mother when she was there. But the charred remains of the once brightly painted bungalow stood as a painful reminder of what had been taken.

The chair. The empty chair still faced out toward the stunning view. Walking toward it, she studied the lines and curves, stopping halfway to stare. Confidently she resumed her gait and then reached out to place a hand on the top of it, running it down the slats on the back of the chair and across one arm. It was smooth and hard and heated by the sun. She squatted and leaned over to peak under the seat. Her eyes widened.

Reaching underneath, she pulled out a small plastic storage container that had been secured to the underside with duct tape. Her heart skipped a beat. Peeling open the lid, her eyes bulged. Wads of money were rolled up and secured by rubber bands. She could see twenties, fifties, and hundreds on the outsides of the rolls. There was an envelope on top. Olivia's name was scrawled on it in her mother's handwriting. She gasped and then quickly picked it up. After gently setting the container on the ground, she slid slowly into the chair and opened the envelope. Pulling out a handwritten note, Olivia let out a long cleansing breath before unfolding the paper, almost afraid to see what it said.

Olivia, my dear, sweet daughter, I love you very much. If you are reading this, something terrible must have happened and I'm sorry. I'll admit, I may have been a bit foolish trying to track down the horrible people C.K. sent me to document. I may have overstepped boundaries and gone beyond what was expected of me but you know how I feel about anyone who abuses animals. It cannot be tolerated. These people are barbaric. They can't be human. Horrible creatures. If I have lost my life in pursuit of trying to stop them and protect the animals from further abuse, I'm okay with that. I don't know that you are at the moment but I think you will be with time. I know you. And I know what an incredible person you have become. You have a beautiful soul. And you are a very smart young lady with a good head on your shoulders. (How else would you have found this?! I knew you would!) Be strong. Stay strong. Follow your heart. As Thoreau said, "Go confidently in the direction of your dreams! Live the life you've imagined." You go girl. Go after what you want out of life.

I had hoped it would be you and me here on the island but apparently that wasn't God's plan. (Maybe it was his plan but then I got involved and sent everything awry. I have a tendency to do that!) Serenity Villa is yours. I hope you will be able to keep it. I know how much you love the place. The money in this box should help you maintain it. (The bad guys don't need it anyway.) There's no mortgage. Just some basic upkeep for a killer view!

Olivia, my lovely child, I wish I could hug you one last time. Know that, wherever I am right now, I'm not far away. I will stay close to you and watch over you like I couldn't do here on earth. You were always in my heart, though. I am so proud of you. I know your father is, too. And even though our relationship didn't work out well, we both love you very much. The two of us were probably a bit too stubborn to give in to what was important to the other. You can pin that on both of us. Unfortunately you got stuck in the middle. I am truly sorry for that.

So Olivia, keep an eye on your father for me, if you can, but follow your heart and go after your dreams. Don't hang onto your sadness. Let it go. Find a way to be happy. I may be gone but I'll always be in your heart.

Love you always, Livvie,
—Mom

Olivia refolded the note and slid it back into the envelope. Her eyes were full and both of her cheeks glistened with tear tracks.

So that was it. Her mother was really gone? She was not ready to accept it. She had simply found the box prematurely.

Gravel and broken asphalt crunched under the tires of a vehicle descending the driveway. She turned in the chair to look but stayed seated, slipping the box back underneath and re-securing it. The dark four-door sedan stopped at the end of the driveway near the remains of the villa. Two men got out and she recognized them both.

Her father spoke first as they crossed the grass over to her. "I knew we'd find you here."

Casting a blank stare, she chose not to engage him.

The detective apparently felt the need to chime in, too. "Olivia, it's not safe for you to be here or anywhere alone."

"I'm not leaving until I find her." She turned away from them, back toward the view, remaining resolute.

"Ollie, they found your mother."

Her head spun around to look at her father again, but she could tell by the tone of his voice and the look on his face it wasn't good news he was delivering. Her face fell. Her whole body stiffened.

James took a couple steps closer to her. "They had her all along." He paused, seeming to let that sink in. "You saw her in the morgue."

"*No!*" Olivia refused to believe it. A dull pain radiated through her chest causing her to lean back in the chair.

"I'm afraid so."

He reached over and placed a gentle hand on her shoulder. She pulled away from his touch.

"You didn't want to believe it was her. And she didn't look anything like your beautiful mother when she was alive." He paused again. "I saw her, too. It was agonizing. But they confirmed it was her with the DNA sample you gave them."

Olivia felt like someone had just kicked her in the gut. She was hearing her father's words and they stung the very depths of her soul.

"It can't be . . ." Her voice trailed off. She was devastated.

"Sorry, Ol. I'm sorry it turned out this way." He stood silently to her side, his eyes lowered as if in prayer.

Olivia sat motionless, holding her gaze out to the bay. Finally she swallowed hard and got to her feet. Turning toward her father, she fell into his embrace, sobbing like she had never done before. He wrapped his arms tightly around her thin, trembling frame. They were lost in the moment, lost in time.

CHAPTER FORTY-THREE

O*n the short drive to the airport* in the Virgin Islands squad car, Detective Benson tried to fill in the blanks for Olivia. "Eyewitnesses spotted three suspicious looking men leaving the morgue and alerted hospital security. Probably the same animals that grabbed you from the lounge and locked you in the drawer. Hospital security detained them just long enough for my men to get there and follow two of them back to where they were holed up. Unfortunately the third went in a different direction and got away. It was the break we needed, though. Sorry it was at your expense, Olivia. Hopefully you're not too worse for the wear from being in the morgue."

She snorted a short laugh and then turned toward the side window to watch the oncoming cars go by. "I'll be in therapy for a while." She was half serious. The scars of the trip were deep. Glancing toward her father in the front seat, she knew her pain was far from over. He turned toward her as if he could sense her eyes on him.

"Did you know your mother took her maiden name back after we separated?" Sounding indignant her mother would do such a thing, he unknowingly diverted Olivia away from his dismal situation.

She glared at him, furrowing her brow. It was the first she had heard of it but failed to see why he looked hurt. Did it matter? Especially now? They were divorced. Her mother had every right to take back her maiden name at any point. Olivia speculated if she ever got married and, heaven forbid, it ended in divorce, she would certainly take back her name. How much more arrogant could he be?

"Apparently she didn't waste any time after she got here. That explains why the police were running into dead ends in the beginning of the investigation. We had given them the wrong last name. Borgstrom is what they should have been looking for."

Olivia silently considered the revelation. It certainly made sense she would take her name back. Her mother was staunchly independent. And Olivia admired her for that. Obviously she kept Benning as her professional name since she had already built her career with it.

There were still more questions.

"So, Detective, what was my mother doing? How did she get mixed up with these horrible people?"

"Your mother was freelancing as a photographer for the local paper. When this investigative story came her way, she took it to heart and was trying to get enough information to catch the criminals and enough evidence to convict them."

"So that's what was on the CD."

"Yes, exactly. Your mother did a great job documenting their activity. Because of her we have been able to capture quite a few of the perps and put them behind bars, and they will stand trial for all of the horrible things they have done. And, for the record, they are not from the fair island of St. Thomas or any of the U.S. Virgin Islands, but, unfortunately, they've put a dark blemish on the territory. They are transients who dealt in untraceable cash, traveling by small boats and moving from island to island probably at night without going through the regular channels for entering the islands."

The box of cash under her mother's chair came to mind.

"They took advantage of the fact we have strays as many of the islands do. The good people of the humane society work hard to rescue the ones they can. They do a great job caring for the animals and placing them in permanent homes here and in the States. The thugs must have had someone here, though, a local who knows the island and knows his way around, has connections . . . someone to help them find places to hold the gambling events. We're still working on that piece of the puzzle."

Olivia found it odd he called them "gambling events." Perhaps he couldn't bring himself to call them what they actually were.

Watching the cars crossing the intersection in front of them, she found the back and forth movement hypnotizing. She was ready to get off the island and head back to Boston. A night out with Laurie would be a great diversion. There was nothing more for her to do on the island. Yet there were still gaps in her understanding of the tragic events that had transpired.

"So who called us to let us know my mother had been in a boating accident?"

"We traced the number your father gave us from caller ID on your home phone and discovered it belongs to an auto repair shop here on the island. Uh, David's Garage. We talked to everyone who worked there, but no one had any idea what we were talking about, of course."

David? So that was the phone call he was referring to at Colton's place. He took a huge risk returning her mother's car to her, and he undoubtedly tried not to get any more involved than he had to. David was a good guy deep down, he had wanted to do what was right. But how did he know?

"It's a small island. Word gets around even if no one wants to talk to the police about it. I bet they tried to unload your mother's car there to make a few bucks."

"And the night of the fire I saw an ambulance leaving the scene. Please tell me it wasn't a firefighter who got hurt fighting the blaze."

The detective nodded his head. "Unfortunately, it was one of the first responders. Fortunately his injuries were not life threatening. He suffered burns over a portion of his body, but the doctors expect him to make a full recovery."

Olivia listened politely to Benson's explanation but was anxious to continue with her questions.

"What about the . . ." Olivia stopped to realize she had called in anonymously to report the leg sticking out from under the charred remains. "I heard something about a body being found under the rubble of my mother's house." Shuddering at the image in her mind, she closed her eyes. "What was that all about?"

"That was the poor sap who started the blaze. He lit himself on fire."

Her eyes widened. "How do you know?"

"People watch too many TV crime shows. He thought he could douse the place with an accelerant, leaving a trail leading up to it. When he lit the match to drop at the end of it, he ignited himself because he was surrounded by gas vapors. Poof! He got his. We're running DNA tests to see if we can ID him."

Olivia wrinkled her nose and then pictured the other bodies in the morgue. The males. Disappointed she didn't know Colton well enough to know his last name, she figured there was no point in asking. Feeling she knew the answer to her question, Olivia returned to her mother's circumstances. "The medical examiner said her body had been in water for two to three days. That just doesn't make sense. We got the call several days before I came down here."

The detective looked up into the mirror at her, a strained look on his face, appearing to contemplate the next words out of his mouth.

Her mouth opened slightly and she gasped. "She was alive when I got here!" The realization hit her firmly in the gut.

He hesitated. "It looks that way."

Recoiling from Benson's bombshell, Olivia replayed the events since she arrived on the island, running through scenarios, trying to figure out if there was anything she should have done differently to have found her mother in time. It was impossible to know.

As the light turned green, wailing sirens from behind them caused the detective to glance up into the rearview mirror and keep his car in its place. As the sirens got louder it became obvious there was more than one emergency vehicle approaching. Two police cars screeched to a stop on either side of the detective's car and a third pulled up behind it, lights flashing, sirens silenced as if on command. Benson looked from one side to the other, as surprised as his passengers. A uniformed officer opened the detective's door, motioning for him to get out. They exchanged words, animated in their gestures.

Olivia was bewildered. What was happening? The two officers flailed their arms as they spoke to Benson. Then she had a sickening thought.

The local connection for the animal abusers?

She glanced to her father, who didn't seem all that concerned. Olivia looked from one side of the car to the other and out the back window to see what was happening. Her father was on his phone as if nothing out of the ordinary was going on.

Without warning, an officer opened the front passenger door and grabbed her father by the arm, pulling him out of the cruiser. In the scuffle that ensued, his cell was knocked loose and landed on the pavement.

Olivia was horrified at the scene unfolding in front of her. "Dad!" She slid to the other side of the car to plead with the officers taking her father into custody. "What are you doing?" she shouted to them through the open door.

They pulled his arms behind his back and slapped on handcuffs. He didn't seem to be putting up much of a fight.

Olivia grabbed the rear door handle and pulled but it wouldn't budge. Since the car was designed for transporting criminals, she was trapped in the backseat and desperate to get to her father. They were making a mistake dragging him off and cuffing him.

Olivia spied the small rectangular opening between the front and back seats, similar to the pass-thru in a yellow cab. It wasn't huge but she believed she could get through it. She had to.

Diving head first through the narrow slot, she shimmied the rest of her body through, scraping her legs on the way but barely noticing the pain. Her body tumbled into the front seat and she scrambled out the passenger door in time to see an officer guiding her father into the backseat of a squad car with the lights still flashing.

Several people had gathered on both sides of the street to take in the spectacle, but rushing toward her father, Olivia ignored them. "Dad! What's going on?" Turning to the nearest officer, she implored, "Why are you taking him?"

"Ollie, it's all a mistake. Don't worry about me. You go ahead home." Her father tried to reassure her.

"But I can't, I'll stay with you."

"No, Ollie, listen to me. You need to get on the plane. . . . " He seemed to be struggling, choking on his words. "You need to take your mother home. She's probably already on the plane. You need to escort her home."

Olivia's head drooped. She felt torn, not wanting to leave her father, yet her responsibility to her mother was undeniable.

"Ollie, I'll be all right. I'll straighten out the misunderstanding and be home soon. You go. I love you."

Olivia reached through the open door and grabbed onto his shoulder, looking into his eyes, searching for strength.

An officer stepped between her and her father. Pulling her arm out of the squad car, he slammed the door shut. Reluctantly she stepped back, hands in the air. "Okay."

Turning toward the detective's car, Olivia looked to him for an explanation. There he stood with his hands on his hips, shaking his head, with a pained expression on his face that told her the situation had taken a turn he hadn't seen coming. Reluctantly, she climbed back into his car, this time in the front seat, and they continued the trip to Cyril E. King, her heart aching and her shoulders sagging.

Detective Benson pulled up to the sidewalk in front of the tiny bustling airport, barely squeezing in between two other cars. Taxis were double parked, dropping off riders and their luggage.

Even with her father's belongings, Olivia was traveling lightly. No longer in possession of the tattered rollaway she arrived with, she had packed her few remaining pieces of clothing into her father's bag.

The detective gave his assurances her father would be dealt with fairly, and he apologized for the way it turned out. If there was a misunderstanding like her father insisted, he would be released as soon as it was cleared up.

Leaving the detective behind at the curb, Olivia carried her heavy heart toward the airline ticket counters, pulling her father's rolling suitcase behind her. Trying to shrug off the buzz around her, Olivia scanned the crowd until her eyes came to rest on a familiar face. She stopped dead in her tracks.

Leaning up against one of the round cement pillars along the sidewalk, a man held a small black puppy in one arm. His other arm was in a sling. A larger dog sat obediently at his feet. The man was smiling at her.

As a rush of conflicting emotions overwhelmed her, she did her best to sort through them and consider her next words.

"Where the *hell* have you been?" Anger won out over the rest of her feelings.

He closed his eyes as if wincing in pain.

Glancing at his sling, she crept a few steps closer. She felt herself soften but vowed not to give in entirely until she got an explanation.

Watching him slowly open his eyes, she detected a look of remorse, as if he were pleading with her to forgive him.

"So, what happened?" She wasn't going to ask why he hadn't called. That sounded entirely desperate, and she certainly wasn't going to let herself slip into that category.

"I'm glad I caught up to you before you took off." He ignored her question, laughing somewhat nervously.

Olivia didn't share his amusement.

"It was like you fell off the grid." Extending her arm, she finished her sentence with a flourish.

"Yeah, it's been ridiculously frustrating being without a phone."

Biting her lip, it took everything she had not to react. Was he really going to pull the "my phone died" excuse? Trying to stay calm, she pushed further.

"What happened?" she demanded more firmly, not wanting to drag the story out of him. "I imagined the worst when I didn't hear from you."

Lifting his injured arm, he raised his eyebrows as if to ask why she hadn't put the pieces together yet. "I lost my phone the other night, along with all my contacts in it, the same time I got this." He paused and his expression turned stern. "You never came back to my place. I stopped by your mother's a few times but, of course, you weren't . . ." His voice trailed off.

"It *was* you that night." Terrifying images crashed through her mind from the landfill. "I'm sorry you got hurt. . . . It was because of me, wasn't it? You came after me, didn't you?" The blame lay firmly on her. "I should never have gone in there. Oh, what was I thinking? I'm so sorry, Colton."

Relieved he was okay, she felt herself falling for his sparkling blue eyes all over again.

"Yeah, I was shocked to see your car at the end of Landfill Road." He reached out and pulled her toward him. She hugged him gingerly, trying to avoid his injured arm and the tiny puppy, remaining close with her hands on his hips after their embrace. They kissed passionately, stirring feelings inside her again.

"I know it was foolish, but I wanted to find out what my mother had gotten involved in."

"You put yourself in incredible danger, Olivia."

"I know. And you as well. I'm sorry."

Standing together in the warmth of the Caribbean sunshine, they reflected on how lucky they both were to have survived, relatively unscathed. Colton brought it back to the present.

"And from what I understand, this little guy belongs to you." He handed her the squirming furry pup who promptly washed her cheek with his rough, wet tongue.

She recognized him from the fateful night. He had a small white bandage on his side she imagined was keeping stiches clean. "How did you know?"

"I know some people down at the shelter. We got it all figured out."

The twinkle in his eyes suggested it was more complicated than he was revealing.

"That's where I got Jake." Colton reached down and stroked his loyal dog's head.

Olivia pulled the puppy in close. His tiny pink tongue darted in an out wildly until it found her nose. Burying her face in his soft warm fur, she was relieved he smelled noticeably better than the first time they had met. The humane society had taken good care of the pup.

"I'm thrilled to see him again." Her heart swelled with puppy love. "Thanks for bringing the little guy."

"You can take him with you. I brought a dog carrier you can use for the trip. It's regulation size for the airlines. They shouldn't have a problem with it. They're used to dogs being rescued off the island all the time. There's one condition if I loan it to you, though."

She furrowed her brow and looked at him expectantly. "And that is . . ."

"You have to bring it back." He smiled coyly.

She returned his smile, loving the idea.

Leaving Colton at his position on the pillar, Olivia checked in with the airline. Before she entered the double doors to get into line for Customs, Olivia bolted back toward the sidewalk to Colton with the puppy tucked under her arm.

"Did they give you any problems with the pup?"

"Oh, they pushed back a little and told me I should have made arrangements ahead of time, but I wasn't going to take no for an answer. I just waited patiently until the ladies behind the counter had their say. If you keep your mouth shut and let them talk long enough, they talk themselves into it." She giggled softly.

He chuckled in response to her somewhat limited, yet effective, street savvy.

She grabbed him around the waist with her free arm and kissed him passionately again, hanging on longer than the previous encounter. It had to last her all the way back to Boston. They separated and looked deep into each other's eyes.

"I *will* be back . . . soon." She placed one more kiss on his lips and then turned and walked away to face the unenviable task of accompanying her mother back to the States one last time. Reluctantly closing the distance between her and the door to Customs, Olivia turned back to wave one more time and silently mouthed, "Good-bye." Feeling heartbroken with her eyes brimming, she swiftly brushed away a tear before it could spill over onto her cheek. Colton's eyes seemed to reach out to her in her sorrow.

Raising his hand to wave in return, Colton watched as the doors closed behind her. The tips of his fingers curled and his arm drooped as if from an imperceptible weight, but then smoothly transitioned toward his loyal companion. Reaching down he stroked the coarse fur on Jake's back, a wistful feeling churning in his abdomen. He and Jake slowly headed back to his Jeep, plodding along. There was nowhere they needed to be any time soon.

CHAPTER FORTY-FOUR

Olivia took one look at the long line, predominantly made up of tourists who snaked their way up and back within the black ribbon line dividers, and her eyelashes fluttered in aggravation. It was going to be a long, sweltering wait. Taking a second glance around, she had to admit it was an interesting crowd.

Next to her in line was a family that could easily have been the same dysfunctional foursome from Izzies. In front of them was a young couple leaning into each other with interlaced hands, who looked to be heading home from their honeymoon. On the other side of her was a middle-aged guy with dark skin, dreadlocks, and a guitar at his feet whose head bobbed to inaudible music. There were no visible headphones.

Amused by the characters surrounding her, she hid her smirking face in the soft fur of her little pup. Euphoric to be reunited with the little guy, it occurred to her he would need a name, but she wanted to take the time to give that some thought. It was important to get to know him first, so that task was pushed to a back burner.

A boisterous voice from behind her came from an elderly woman.

"Isn't he the lucky one to get rescued!" she gushed, her voice uncomfortably louder than it needed to be.

Olivia turned toward her, and the woman gasped as she took in the full view of the sweet pup.

She was a short, heavyset woman, dressed in a short-sleeved white polyester pantsuit and matching white high-heeled sandals that made her look like she was teetering on the brink of falling. She sported short, bleach blonde hair that stuck out on the sides and round tortoise shell glasses too large for her face. Thick lenses magnified her large brown bloodshot eyes framed with heavy mascara-coated lashes. Her lips were puffy and accentuated by bright orange-red lip color. Beads of moisture randomly punctuated her forehead. Her meek and mild husband looked like a "yes dear" kind of spouse and stood behind his wife, dressed in shades of beige.

"Oh! He is just precious! Look at those sweet brown eyes." Her voice escalated with each sentence as she reached out to pet his fur.

The elderly woman's unexpected advance caused Olivia to flinch away from her. The pup shivered in response, nuzzling his head into her neck.

"He's a little shy," Olivia explained, shielding her little furry friend.

The older woman retrieved her hand slowly, narrowing her eyes to examine Olivia's face. Her demeanor soured from Olivia's rejection. It spurred her on but in a different vein.

"Of course, if I could live on this beautiful island, I don't know if I'd want to leave it."

At first Olivia was struck by her insensitivity, but the woman had no way of knowing the circumstances the little dog had been rescued from. Nonetheless, her words still hung in the air.

As the line started to move, Olivia turned around and inched forward to keep up with the person in front of her, pushing the empty dog carrier with her foot, hoping her turned back would signal she was through chatting. But the woman behind her was not finished.

"But I mean really! Maybe these dogs don't want to leave." She went on to expound on why people shouldn't be allowed to take them.

Olivia had stopped listening. She was stuck on the woman's initial declaration that she wouldn't want to leave if it were her home. Suddenly her eyes grew wide. Snatching up the dog carrier, she turned abruptly toward the elderly couple behind her, pushing her way back toward the end of the line, clutching the small pup and excusing herself as she went. Before long she reached the glass sliding doors and exited back out to where the airline ticket counters were located. She walked straight to the counter she had just checked in to, ignoring the line of people behind the ropes waiting to be called next.

The young woman on the other side of the counter looked up in surprise, recognizing her from before.

"You have to get my mother off the plane," Olivia demanded, leaning forward for effect. She didn't have to mention anything about a casket. The ticket agent knew what she meant.

"What? There's no time. I couldn't possibly—"

"Yes, you can. The plane doesn't take off for over an hour." She stared deep into the woman's eyes until she blinked. Olivia wasn't backing down.

"I'll have to see . . ." Appearing helpless, she looked around, searching for someone to assist her.

Olivia maintained her stance at the counter, trying to look as tall and confident as she could muster.

Not readily locating anyone, the ticket agent became less certain she could make it happen. "I really don't think I can do that." A look of despair filled her eyes as she continued to search the area.

"Of course you can. There is plenty of time. I would bet she hasn't been loaded into the cargo hold yet." She sensed the woman was either new to her job or had never dealt with the situation of transporting a coffin.

"Security would have to get involved. There would be more inspections. Certainly more questions. I don't know if the appropriate staff are available. This is an entirely unusual request."

Olivia stood firm, held her body rigid, and looked into the woman's eyes with a puzzled look on her face. The message was clear. The woman was not making any sense, and Olivia was going to stand there until she did.

The agent's navy-and-red-striped scarf, tucked under the collar of her blue cotton shirt and tied in a loose knot at the base of her neck, flapped wildly in the breeze off the water. Nothing else between them moved. It had turned into a standoff. Olivia folded her arms across her chest on top of the puppy to convey her intentions not to budge.

Finally an older woman, who Olivia prayed was a supervisor, approached the counter. After Olivia explained what she was requesting, the rookie fell silent and let the other agent take over. She picked up the phone and made a discreet call to locate Olivia's mother's casket. It quickly became clear the precious cargo had been loaded, but they would be able to unload it before the plane departed.

After confirming the airline had her cell number, Olivia dashed out to the sidewalk in front of the tiny airport. She surveyed the line of cars inching past the drop-off area, glancing left and right, searching for a familiar car. Her hand flew up, waving frantically, and her face lit up.

Spying Colton a few cars back, she ran toward him, cutting across the slow-moving line. As she approached, his mouth fell open and his eyes grew wide. Putting the Jeep in park, he shooed Jake into the back seat and then leaned over and grabbed the handle to open the passenger door for her. She slid in with the small brown pup still tucked under her arm, tossing the dog carrier into the back seat. It ricocheted off the inside of the car and tumbled onto the seat, knocking up against the Australian shepard. His back legs twitched in response.

"Sorry, Jake," Olivia offered but he didn't seem to be bothered by it. Colton's face was awash in disbelief and sheer joy.

"So good to see you." He leaned over and gently took hold of her left upper arm, planting a gentle kiss on her lips. Their eyes locked and time was suspended for a moment until honking from the cars behind them brought them back to the present.

Colton shoved the Jeep back into drive and smoothly eased it forward to close the gap between his front bumper and that of the safari taxi in front of them, then came to a stop again. Olivia turned and gently placed the small pup on the backseat next to Jake.

"Poor thing is unbearably hot from me holding him."

Colton looked at her expectantly, appearing anxious to hear an update but refrained from pressing her.

Gazing forward, beyond the cars in front of them, she shook her head almost imperceptibly. "I suddenly realized I was making a huge mistake. I got caught up in the arrangements made without my input." She turned to look directly at Colton. "My mother wouldn't have wanted to be buried back in the States. She never would have wanted to leave the island. What was I thinking? What were *they* thinking? I'm going to see to it *this* is her final resting place. She would have wanted it that way."

Colton seemed pleased with her conclusions. He reached over and gently massaged her shoulder, moving his hand along to the back of her neck.

A tingling sensation ran down her back.

They cleared the booth at the airport exit and accelerated down the airport access road to the light at the intersection. Olivia glanced to the backseat then whispered to Colton, "Oh, look at those two."

He looked up into the rearview mirror and grinned broadly. Jake was on his side, stretched across the entire length of the backseat, looking contented. The little pup was snuggled in close to the elder dog's chest with one forepaw resting across his own eyes.

"Looks like someone else has gotten attached to the little guy."

A warm sensation she hadn't felt in a long time swelled inside her.

CHAPTER FORTY-FIVE

Several days passed before Olivia found herself at the former site of Serenity Villa, one last time. She found comfort in the sea breeze caressing her face, the familiar squawking parrots in the treetops above her, and the magnificent, unwavering view of the sun glistening off the water below. Gazing out to the bay and beyond, she tried to commit it all to memory, make it part of her soul. The uncertain future of the property lay in fate's hands.

For Olivia, her loss was still agonizingly painful but she had no more tears left. The irony of spreading her mother's ashes near the ashes of Serenity Villa struck her. It all felt horribly wrong. There could never be anything right about it. It was never meant to end that way. The cute bungalow her mother loved, on the island she adored, reduced to ashes. Her mother's life snuffed out far too early.

Images of unfulfilled dreams crashed through Olivia's mind as she struggled to come to grips with the reality of the tragic events. Sadly, her mother would never find love again, never be able to help her daughter pick out a wedding dress, never know what it felt like to have grandchildren tug at her sleeve or climb into her lap. Too many "nevers."

Closing her eyes, she prayed more earnestly than she had ever prayed before that her mother was safe in God's hands and could find happiness again. "Take good care of her. We'll miss her. . . ." She swallowed hard, choking back the pain. "I love you, Mom. Miss you." Olivia held her gaze out across the bay, allowing herself to get lost and become mesmerized by the sun sparkling on the water.

Sensing Colton behind her, she turned toward him. He had remained out of sight after returning from a walk down to the end of her mother's road, out of respect for her privacy as she spent her final moments saying good-bye.

Clearing his throat, he looked as though he hated to speak the words. "I'm afraid it's time." His voice was rough and his eyes were forlorn.

Olivia's face fell as he interrupted her solitude. She knew the time would come too soon. Her stomach wrenched into a knot.

"Okay, I guess I'm ready," she acquiesced, fighting back the swell of emotions spilling from her heart.

Colton took her hand and led her to his car.

"I will rebuild," she affirmed while climbing in. "I will. She would have wanted me to."

He listened sympathetically and glanced toward her as he fired up the Jeep.

"I hope they found all those horrible people. . . ." Her voice trailed off as she glanced out the window to the pile of blackened rubble, all that was left of her mother's bungalow. She turned away to try to leave it all behind and commit to memory how it had been, not so long ago.

As they descended the south side of the mountain in silence, neither wanted to focus on her impending departure. They both knew she would be getting on the plane this time. Even the dogs seemed somber, lying together on the backseat. In spite of the heat, Jake was stretched out on his side across the entire length, and the small pup was lost in the fur of his underside.

As Olivia's phone vibrated in her pocket, she slipped it out, pressing the icon to answer the call, switching it to speakerphone and dropping it into her lap.

"Hello."

"Olivia, it's Detective Benson."

"Hey, Detective."

"I thought I would bring you up to date on what we've got."

Glancing over to Colton, she wasn't sure she wanted to hear what he had to say.

"Okay . . . go ahead."

"We're glad you pulled your mother's casket off the plane. That caused an unexpected stir in the illegal ops we've been trying to track. Because of the change in plans, the casket had to be re-examined by TSA before it could be released back to the funeral home. Turns out there had been thousands of dollars of cash stashed inside they were trying to smuggle off the island. There was even a large bag of heroin thrown in for good measure. It had been made to look like a pillow and was tucked under your mother's head."

"Heroin? Good God."

"Yeah, smugglers have been testing the waters, so to speak, here in the Caribbean, trying to find alternate routes for moving drugs into the States. Apparently these people had an insider at the funeral home who had access to the casket before it was sent to the airport, and we were able to track him down and apprehend him."

He let that information sink in for a moment.

"Anything else?"

"Yeah, this guy Carson who keeps popping up. My gut tells me he was the local guy we've been trying to nab. My gut feelings haven't steered me wrong yet with this sort of character over the years. I think Carson was the third guy at the hospital who got away. Fortunately we had already picked him up on a minor charge so we've got him in custody. We're also counting on a break with the sunglasses from the morgue drawer. We had them tested for DNA and we're waiting for the results to come back. Someone wore them on their head at some point because there was a strand of dark hair caught in one of the hinges.

"Oh, and the rookie cop we sent over to your place to take prints from your mother's Jeep did a great job. He remembered to check for prints on the rearview mirror. It's the most common place to find prints because the first thing the perps do when they get into a strange car is to adjust the mirror. But they don't usually think to wipe it down afterwards. They usually get the door handles, the steering wheel and stick shift but that's about it. Turns out it was Carson's prints on the rearview mirror of your mother's car."

Olivia listened intently, anxious to hear if her father had any involvement.

"He's an interesting character," Benson continued his background story on Carson. "Very smooth operator. A con man in many ways. Slick with the ladies."

Her mother came to mind and she raised her eyebrows in response. She found it hard to believe Carson was actually involved with her.

"Apparently he dumped her car off at the local garage where your phone call came from, but he never returned for it. . . . Has a rather sordid background. Grew up here. His father was a patrolman for many years on the island until he was shot and killed in the line of duty. Happened when Carson was just a kid. Devastated the family. When he was old enough, he sat for the test to become a police officer but didn't pass. After that he disappeared off the radar for a while, that is until now. He had been working for a security company fairly recently but was fired from that job. He was probably down on his luck, flat broke, and looking for an opportunity when someone approached him to be the local guy to help them out. He knows the island, can get around without standing out."

Olivia grew curious. "If Carson was their local contact, why would someone have tried to shoot him?"

While her question was met by silence, Olivia's eyes grew wide. "That bullet was meant for me, wasn't it?"

"I'm afraid so. Fortunately for you, he or she wasn't a very good shot."

Shaking off her brush with death, she continued her line of questioning. "So was he the CK who was trying to communicate with my mother by fax?"

"No, Carson is actually his last name. It's what he's always gone by. Not sure if anyone knows his first name." Benson chuckled to himself.

"So who is CK?"

"He's an investigative journalist at the local paper who your mother was working with to catch these thugs. Charles . . . uh, Charles Knightstone. Actually owns the paper."

"And what did he have to say about all this?"

"Unfortunately, we haven't been able to get in touch with him yet. But we will keep at it." He cleared his throat. "Messages left at his work and home numbers have gone unanswered."

Olivia sat in silence, processing his update, but a more pressing matter pushed its way forward. "What about my father? Is he involved in all of this?" Under her breath she declared, "I swear to God if he is, I will . . ." She didn't feel the need to finish her sentence as she pictured the possibilities.

"Honestly, at this point, we are still trying to get it all straightened out. His name is on the deed for the last property these people used to hold their . . . uh, gambling events. He's not the only name listed as an owner—actually he's sitting right here. Would you like to have a word with him?"

Olivia could feel anger rising inside of her as she overheard the detective telling her father who he was on the phone with.

"Olivia! It's going to be okay." Her father sounded anxious for her to believe him. "It's not what you think. Please hear what I'm saying. It's just a misunderstanding."

"You own the property where they had the dog fights? How could you?" She was incredulous.

"No! No, Olivia, listen to me. Yes, my name is listed as one of the owners of the property. I went in on it many years ago with my buddy, Rod. Remember him?"

Olivia shivered. Of course she remembered him. Her father didn't have a lot of friends, but Rodney was a childhood pal of his and her least favorite. On the surface he appeared to be an outgoing, all-around fun guy who was the life of the party. If he was in the room, it was his voice she heard above everyone else's. And it was always all about him, no matter what "it" was. He needed attention to feed his ego. He hid behind his loud personality.

At one party at their home, he made an advance at Olivia, touching her inappropriately, which was so shocking she didn't know how to react, much less how to tell him to back off and keep his hands off her. After all, she was just a kid, and he was one of her father's best friends. It took her a few years to understand he actually had low self-esteem and needed constant affirmation. Her father must have provided that. It wasn't often they got together but, when they did, Olivia worried James drank more than usual. On top of it all, they acted as though they were still sixteen, and Rod could talk him into anything. She wasn't surprised he had talked her father into buying a place on St. Thomas as an investment, probably sight unseen.

"Sure, how could I forget?" Olivia didn't try to hide her sarcasm.

"He must have let the property fall into such disrepair, it looked abandoned. Probably didn't want to spend the m—"

"I don't give a *damn* about all of that. About Rodney or some lame investment you got involved with because of him. Especially if it has anything to do with my mother getting murdered."

Silence on the other end of the line.

"Hey, I'm pissed at him for getting me involved in all of this, too. I don't need this right now either. Oh, and he was the one who was supposed to pick you up at the airport when you first got here but couldn't because he had already been arrested on some other charges. Look, I need you to know I was not directly involved, and I will get it straightened out and be able to come home soon."

"Great." Her tone was flat, without emotion. After the revelations of the past couple days, it didn't matter to her when he was able to get back home.

The detective came back on the line and assured her he would keep her up to date on the investigation and see if they could get her father home before too long. He left words unspoken, yet clearly understood, about her father's deteriorating condition.

Olivia had one more question for the detective. "So, how did my mother die, exactly? What did the medical examiner find during the autopsy?"

Colton shifted in his seat but kept his eyes on the road.

After an agonizingly long hesitation, the dead air became painful to her ears.

Undoubtedly, Benson was choosing his words carefully. His tone was even and matter-of-fact. "Olivia . . . do you really want to know?"

Olivia paused to search within her for an answer. The air was heavy and silent again. "No . . . no, not really."

"Look, take solace in this. Because of your mother, we have shut down this illegal operation and rounded up quite a few of the shit heads who were involved in it. They are all facing charges relating to animal cruelty and you can count on them getting prison time. Of course, there's drug trafficking and money laundering as well. We're confident we have been able to apprehend most, if not all, of them."

Olivia tried to embrace the positive spin Detective Benson put on the tragic events. She ended the call but tension still hung in the air. It wasn't broken until her phone rang again. She glanced down and noticed it was Laurie.

"Hey, girlfriend! What's up with you?" She tried hard to sound upbeat.

"Liv, I just wanted to check in. It's been a while since I've heard from you. Wanted to make sure you're okay. What's going on? Is everything okay? I hope so. When are you coming home?"

Olivia considered letting her carry on with all of her questions but chose, instead, to cut her off.

"Everything's fine." She knew that was a complete lie and Laurie would be able to detect her transparent tone, but she was going to run with it anyway. "I'm heading to the airport now. I'll be home—" She caught herself. "I'll, uh, I'll be back by tonight." In spite of everything that had transpired there, St. Thomas was feeling much more like her home than Boston.

"I'm glad! Can't wait to see you. Missed you. Listen, Olivia, I took the liberty of opening a letter hand addressed to you from Abigail Adams Studios." She let that hang in the air for a moment.

"Okay . . ." Olivia frowned at her admission she had opened her personal mail without asking first.

"Do you want me to read it?"

Seriously? "Uh, hopefully it's good news." She had to believe Laurie wouldn't bring it up if it wasn't good news.

"Okay, here I go." Her friend read the letter announcing Olivia had been selected to do a six-month apprenticeship with Abigail Adams Studio and went on to expound on how much Abigail Adams was looking forward to working with Olivia to develop her talents further.

Stunned, Olivia sat back against the seat of Colton's car. She had applied on a whim, never actually expecting to be selected. The tingling sensation in her stomach made her nose crinkle. She was thrilled at the prospect. Abigail Adams was an amazing talent and to study under her was an incredible opportunity. Olivia aspired to be able to pick up where she left off with what she had learned from her mother.

Laurie posed a few more questions in rapid-fire fashion, but Olivia told her she would catch up with her when she got back. Uncertain when she would see Colton again, she wanted to spend the last few moments she had on the island with him. After ending the call, Olivia turned her focus back to Colton and the nagging fact they would be saying good-bye shortly.

After a resounding "congrats!" from Colton and the slap of a high five over the news, the celebration quickly fizzled as the conversation stalled. The two were keenly aware of the silence inside the car as they neared the airport access road, contemplating what lay ahead of them.

Soon, however, the silence was again broken by Olivia's phone. This time it was a text, and she cocked her head as she read the caller ID.

"Hmmm. It's from the airline. Says my flight is delayed an hour."

Colton turned toward her, his face beaming. "Great! That just bought us more time. Let's go grab a bite."

Olivia certainly wasn't going to argue. Colton made a U-turn and they headed back toward Frenchtown, stopping at Alice's, a small eatery on the water frequented by locals and known for great food with authentic

Caribbean flavor. The owner and her family had lived and cooked on the island for several generations. Even though it was a comfortably casual place, dogs were not welcome. They left Jake and the pup in the Jeep with the windows rolled down, shaded by an old coconut palm.

Olivia followed behind Colton as they walked around to the back of the restaurant, out onto the deck overlooking the channel separating St. Thomas from Hassel Island. Olivia's heart nearly stopped for a moment as she took in the stunning view out to the water. Scanning the lunch crowd on the deck, she noticed an attractive older man at the far end who stood out from the rest because he seemed overdressed for the establishment.

Navy-blue-and-white checked tablecloths fluttered in the breeze on small round tables. They found an empty one close by the entrance to the deck along the railing. Olivia pulled out the metal chair and the sudden sound of it dragging across the deck floor startled her like the grating sound of fingernails on a chalkboard. She shuddered. Patrons at the next table turned toward the interruption for a fleeting moment. Ignoring them, Olivia sat down with her back to the rest of the deck, turning to sneak another glimpse at the oddly dressed gentleman.

Since the indoor restaurant was open to the outdoor deck, Colton walked inside to place their order at the bar, leaving Olivia alone at the table. Even though she was in the middle of the raucous lunch crowd, loneliness crept slowly under her skin. The weight of recent events had taken its toll. She concentrated on slowly inhaling deeply and letting out a cleansing breath.

The uncomfortable feeling someone's eyes were on her broke her efforts to re-center herself. Glancing around furtively, not noticing anyone in particular looking her way, she tried to brush it off and blame it on fatigue until she felt a hand on her shoulder and a voice from behind.

"Excuse me, Love." He had a delightful British accent.

Olivia turned to look into the eyes of an attractive man who looked to be in his late forties, early fifties, with wavy light brown hair that was neatly trimmed. She pulled back from him to get a better perspective. Her eyes widened as she realized he was the gentleman who had been sitting at the far end of the deck. He was dressed in a light blue button-down oxford shirt and gray summer wool pants.

"So sorry to bother you, dear. I couldn't help notice you when you walked in. I have to admit, the sight of you shook me for a moment. You must be Olivia."

Her eyes grew wide. How did he know?

"And you are . . .?" She quickly glanced over toward Colton who had become engaged with a couple at the bar. Laughter and animated conversation suggested he knew them.

"Oh! Sorry, Love. Forgive my terrible manners. I was flustered when I saw you. I knew it was you. You look just like her."

Olivia continued to examine his face closely. There was a sadness in his eyes he seemed to be trying to push beyond. His skin was unusually pale considering he was in the Caribbean. Probably worked too much and didn't get outside enough, similar to her father.

"Who?"

"Oh, your mum!"

"And tell me again who you are?" She grew impatient.

He chuckled, Olivia presumed at the fact she had to ask a second time, and then slipped into the chair across the table from her, not making the annoying sound that she had.

"I'm Charles." He interlaced his fingers and placed his hands in front of him on the edge of the table. "Olivia, I would have known it was you in the dark. I'm glad to have bumped into you. It's fate, I tell you." His eyes took on a warmth as he spoke.

"Nice to meet you, Charles." She guessed he was a rather formal guy since he didn't tell her she could call him something other than his proper first name.

"And you're here under such dreadful circumstances. I am sorry about what happened to your mum."

Puzzled, she tilted her head, considering how he could have known.

"I'm sorry, how do you know my mother? I'm not exactly clear on that." She examined his face more closely.

"Olivia, your mum and I worked together."

Suddenly it came to her. Her face lit up in recognition. "Charles Knightstone."

"Exactly. She spoke of me?"

"Not exactly. I heard your name from Detective Benson."

"Oh, I see." Disappointment settled in. His face grew serious. His gaze fell far beyond Olivia's shoulder.

She waited for him to gather himself and continue. Finally she pressed him. "So she was working for you when she died?" Olivia knew she had dropped a bomb in his lap, but she didn't care. She wanted to see what he had to say for himself.

"Your mother was an admirable woman." He was dodging her question. "So strong. Determined. Always willing to look out for those who could not look out for themselves. That's one of the many reasons I loved her."

Loved her? In what way? What were they talking about here? She felt compelled to ask. "You loved her?"

"Oh, yes. We loved *each other*. We were quite close. I had an awful feeling something terrible happened when it had been so long since I heard from her. And Olivia, I'm sorry. I blame myself. Not her. I should have pulled her off the story when it got too risky. Although I don't know if she would have listened to me. . . . This was a cause near and dear to her heart. You know how she is." His eyes took on a sad hollowness.

"Why didn't you at least try?" Olivia pleaded, her anger welling up within her.

"Olivia, I can't tell you how sorry I am." His voice quivered. "We had such plans together."

She was listening.

"We talked about getting married in the fall. She wanted us to meet first. She wouldn't make any specific plans until she was able to introduce you to me. Your approval meant the world to her."

Stunned by the words spilling naturally out of his mouth, Olivia blinked her eyes quite deliberately as she tried to picture the two of them together. She hadn't seen any of it coming.

"I see." She spoke slowly, trying to convince herself as she uttered the words.

"Now that will never happen. So much will never happen." His face was etched with a sorrowful expression. "Olivia, I am grateful to have finally met you. I am truly sorry for the events that took your mother from you. If I could go back in time and change them, I certainly would." He stood up. "I hope someday you will find it in your heart to forgive me, but I won't blame you if you don't. I know I never will. Hold your mother's love close to your heart. She loved you dearly."

With that, he turned away from her and slipped noiselessly off the deck, disappearing around the side of the restaurant.

Olivia sat in silence with a lump in her throat, contemplating his comments. Part of her felt sorry for him, but if he had intended to make her feel better, he had failed miserably. And the idea her mother had planned to marry again surprised her. She admonished herself for it. Why shouldn't she? Her mother deserved to be happy. Olivia just didn't like finding out about it from a stranger. Although, he wasn't a stranger to her mother.

Colton returned with their sandwiches accompanied by a glass of Pinot Gris for her and an IPA for himself.

Olivia looked into his eyes, hesitating for a moment, and then asked the question dangling on the edge of her lips. "Did you see the man I was talking to while you were at the bar?"

He looked at her with a puzzled expression and her face fell.

"A man? No, I didn't see you talking with anyone."

In spite of the jovial din of the busy outdoor eatery, they ate in silence with little chatting between them. Colton attempted to stir up a conversation, but she didn't engage. He seemed to understand she had plenty on her mind and didn't push it.

On their way off the deck, after finishing their lunch, Olivia noticed a local newspaper lying on one of the unoccupied tables, folded in half with the front page on top. A photo caught her eye. She stopped abruptly in her tracks and picked it up.

There was a file photo of the British man she had just been talking with. Eagerly she read the headline:

Virgin Islands Times Owner Found Dead. Police Investigating.

Olivia's eyes grew wide and darted through the body of the article, searching for details.

"No evidence of forced entry . . . robbery unlikely . . . no cause of death released . . . an associate, who asked to remain anonymous, would not deny the possibility of suicide."

The world stood still momentarily and no air entered her lungs. Words would not form on her lips.

The ripple effect of evil doings . . .

CHAPTER FORTY-SIX

Consumed by a wistful air of sadness, they pulled up to the passenger drop-off area in front of the airport. Colton got out and pulled her suitcase out of the back as she walked around from the other side of the car to join him on the sidewalk.

"Are you sure you don't want to take the little guy? To keep you company?"

"No, I appreciate you rescuing him for me, but I can't even think about trying to provide any stability for him when I don't know what lies ahead for me. I know you'll take good care of him until I can get back here." She glanced into the back seat and beamed. "Besides, it looks like Jake has already adopted him."

Colton chuckled. "Yeah, we'll be sure to look out for him." He reached over and pulled her close, burying his face in her hair. "You take care of yourself." His words were almost pleading.

Olivia got lost in his arms as they hugged each other tightly. She swallowed to clear her throat as she tried to find the right way to describe what she was feeling.

"So glad we met. . . . I'm going to miss you. I'll get back as soon as I can." She choked on her words, having no idea when she could return. Whenever it was, it wouldn't be soon enough.

"I'm sorry for everything you've been through. But I'm here for you . . . always will be." His voice was low as he spoke into her ear.

"Thanks for everything. See you . . . see you when I can get back here."

They pulled apart to look directly at each other.

"I'll have a chilled bottle of white waiting for you." Colton had a twinkle in his eyes.

Olivia grinned, tickled at the thought.

Another kiss and then she pulled away, lowering her head as she plodded along reluctantly to the ticket counter. After checking in and leaving her bag, she blew one final kiss to Colton and passed through the sliding glass doors to get into the line for Customs.

Colton turned around and climbed back into his car. As he pulled slowly away from the curb to merge into the airport traffic, sunlight hit him in the eyes. He grabbed the visor and slapped it down. The imprint of aviators was evident on the underside of the visor.

It was a quiet ride back to Riptide.

ABOUT THE AUTHOR

Penny Goetjen is the author of murder mysteries where the milieu play as prominent a role as the engaging characters. Her love of travel inspires her writing as evidenced by her current titles. Although Connecticut has been her home longer than anywhere else, she also has a deep-rooted fondness for the Caribbean; Charleston, South Carolina; and the tumultuous coast of Maine (especially in the warmer months). A self-proclaimed eccentric, she loves writing by candlelight, particularly on dark, gray days or in the late hours of the night. Fascinated with the paranormal, she often weaves a subtle, unexpected twist into her stories. When her husband is asked how he feels about his wife writing murder mysteries, he answers with a wink, "I sleep with one eye open."

CPSIA information can be obtained
at www.ICGtesting.com
Printed in the USA
BVOW11s1850131016

464971BV00005B/7/P